The Kandinsky Conundrum

Also by Alessandra Comini from Sunstone Press

The Kandinsky Conundrum

A Megan Crespi Mystery Series Novel

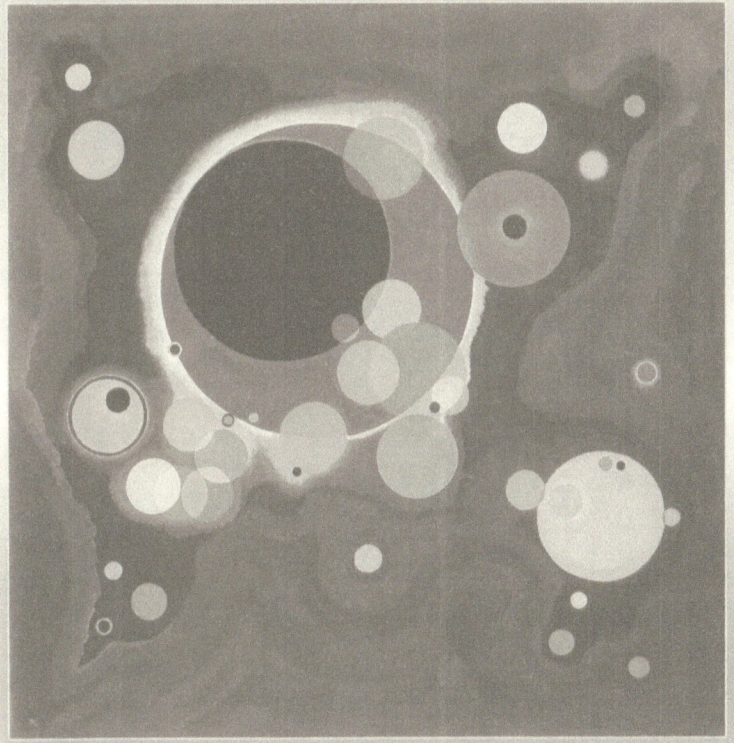

Alessandra Comini

SUNSTONE
PRESS

SANTA FE

This book is a work of fiction. Names, characters, places, and incidents are either the product of the author's imagination or used fictionally. Any resemblance to actual events or locales or persons, living or dead, is entirely coincidental.

Sunstone books may be purchased for educational, business, or sales promotional use. For information please write: Special Markets Department, Sunstone Press, P.O. Box 2321, Santa Fe, New Mexico 87504-2321.

Book and cover design › Vicki Ahl
Body typeface › Minion Pro
Printed on acid-free paper
∞
eBook 978-1-61139-542-6

Library of Congress Cataloging-in-Publication Data

Names: Comini, Alessandra, author.
Title: The Kandinsky conundrum : a Megan Crespi mystery series novel / by Alessandra Comini.
Description: Santa Fe : Sunstone Press, [2018]
Identifiers: LCCN 2018002668 (print) | LCCN 2018006039 (ebook) | ISBN 9781611395426 | ISBN 9781632932136 (softcover : alk. paper)
Subjects: LCSH: Women art historians--Fiction. | Art thefts--Investigation--Fiction. | Mystery fiction. gsafd
Classification: LCC PS3603.O477 (ebook) | LCC PS3603.O477 K36 2018 (print) | DDC 813/.6--dc23
LC record available at https://lccn.loc.gov/2018002668

WWW.SUNSTONEPRESS.COM

SUNSTONE PRESS / POST OFFICE BOX 2321 / SANTA FE, NM 87504-2321 /USA
(505) 988-4418 / ORDERS ONLY (800) 243-5644 / FAX (505) 988-1025

To Ralph Broadwater,
the boy who wanted to write art history,
the man who became a physician

The Propylaea (left) in the Königsplatz and the Lenbach House Museum (right) in Munich

List of Characters

Megan Crespi: retired professor of art history and expert on early twentieth-century European art, specializes in solving art crimes.

Rick Bodewell, MD: Megan's student of four decades earlier, now a distinguished surgical oncologist at Sloan Kettering.

Iris Togarassy: co-owner of Munich's successful new gallery The Blue Rider and wife of Laszlo Togarassy.

Laszlo Togarassy: co-owner of The Blue Rider and husband of Iris Togarassy.

Igor Rasputin: billionaire Kandinsky collector from Odessa.

Yabeda Tupinsky: president of Russia, former ally of Rasputin.

Boris Zima: tycoon art collector from Moscow and bitter rivals with Rasputin.

Katrina Keller: conservator and associate director of the Lenbach House Museum in Munich.

Herbert Keller: five-year-old son of Katrina Keller.

Marigold Lamb: amanuensis to ballet dancer Alexandra Danilova.

Baron Heinrich von Frauenberg: free-spending young owner of "Paleo" in Munich.

Max Mürrisch: new, disliked director of the Lenbach House.

Dzhim Kabalovitschy: the "hermit of Amiinyi" island near Odessa and a computer wizard.

Tigr Chastnyy: photographer genius who develops a 3D method for replicating objects, lives with Dzhim Kabalovitschy at Amiinyi.

Raisa Sokolova: Boris Zima's private secretary and agent in Munich; later goes by the pseudonym Svetlana Chernykh.

Diliana: Slovakian nanny to Katrina Keller's son Herbert.

Alyksandr (Alyk) Miesel: Munich civil engineer and woodworker.

Walter Krankenhauer: neo-Nazi leader in Munich.

Ottkar Hasstmann: neo-Nazi leader in Berlin.

Niki Wächter: night guard at the Lenbach House.

Pavel Meninkov: Rasputin's Odessa agent.

Dieter Löser: chief detective with the Munich police.

Ivan Ivanov: Boris Zima's Moscow agent.

Natasha Ivanova: wife of Ivan Ivanov.

Dimitri and Anatoly: Ivanov's two van drivers.

Heinrich Wölfflin: technician at the Lenbach House.

Reinhold: Lenbach House guard.

Paul Ritter: associate conservator at the Lenbach House.

Stanislav Volkov: conservator at the Tretyakov Gallery in Moscow.

Officer Besorgt: Munich police officer.

Greta Bachert: secretary at the Lenbach House.

ON SEPTEMBER 2, 1980 the widow of Wassily Kandinsky, known for her ostentatious taste in diamonds, was found strangled to death in her remote Swiss chalet. All her jewelry was gone. None of her famous husband's paintings had been removed, it would seem. The case was never solved.

1

THEY SAW IT HAPPEN. The aggressive motorcyclist came out of nowhere and forced the car in front of them to veer into a steep ditch off the German highway. The careless cyclist sped on and never looked back.

"Megan! Are you all right?"

"I think so," a shaken Megan Crespi assured her former student, Rick Bodewell, who was at the wheel. He had had to brake hard and suddenly.

They came to a stop in front of the stranded vehicle. A woman's voice was screaming for help. Megan and Rick ran to the crimson Mercedes Benz convertible of the struggling occupant. No one else was in the car.

"*Still bleiben*! Stay still! We'll get you out," Megan commanded. Rick began to tug at the now deflated airbag. The moaning woman's long gray hair was entangled in the limp airbag.

"Here, use this," whispered Megan, handing Rick her Swiss Army pocket knife, its scissors already extended. They proved to be the perfect tool and within minutes the woman, who looked to be in her seventies, was released.

"Thank you, thank you," she said in English. "My god, that motorcyclist from hell appeared out of nowhere crossing in front of me."

"Yes, we saw it," Megan soothed.

"But it could have been much worse," Rick said, looking at the convertible's crumpled front fender.

"I am Iris. Iris Togarassy. And you?"

"This is Professor Megan Crespi, and I am Rick Bodewell."

Suddenly the Togarassy woman gave a scream of pain. She had extended her right arm to shake hands and the resultant pain was exquisite. Exquisite and immediate. Tears ran down her cheeks and her eyes opened wide in surprise.

"Don't worry. You're in good hands," said Megan. "My friend is a physician."

"Oh, thank god for that."

"You most likely have a dislocated shoulder," Rick said. "I could try to reset it here. But it would be best to take you to an ER. Do you know how far the nearest hospital is from here?"

"Füssen. There's one in Füssen. But it's about forty kilometers south of here," Iris Togarassy moaned. "But my home, our house is just there." She nodded in the direction from which she had come. "Oh, couldn't you please take me there?"

"All right. It would be best to get you onto a straight-back chair if I'm to reset your shoulder."

"Does that thing have water in it?" Rick continued, pointing to Megan's Spider Man thermos docked in their blue Opel station wagon.

"Yes, yes. Although it has Dasani drops in it for sweetening..."

"Never mind that. Please get it and my med kit." Megan ran to their car and back with the items he had requested.

Rick took the thermos and placed it in Iris's right hand. Reaching into his medical travel kit he produced a pain killer. Iris swallowed it immediately.

With infinite care Rick lifted the woman from behind her convertible's steering wheel and carried her around to the passenger side of the station wagon, placing her gently on the back seat.

"Now just give us directions to your house," he said, getting back into the driver's seat. From the front passenger seat, Megan solicitously twisted around to the injured woman. In a weak voice Iris gave directions.

"Continue south from here, just a few kilometers. There will be a turnoff to your right just before Nesselwang. Our house sits a bit beyond it on a small lake. It's just about fifteen minutes from here."

As they drove in silence, Megan found herself wondering if this accident was an indication of things to come for her and her travel companion. Four decades earlier, Rick Bodewell had been Megan's student at Southern Methodist University in Dallas. A science major intrigued by Megan's approach to art history courses—"the cultural content of artistic form"—he had kept in regular contact with her even after finishing medical school and joining Sloan Kettering Hospital in New York as a surgical oncologist. Now, just a few months after the sudden death of his wife, Rick had accepted his former professor's invitation to travel with her around Bavaria to visit all of "mad" King Ludwig's castles. It was something he had always wanted to do after learning in one of her classes about the castles' erratic young owner and his frenetic friendship and lifelong obsession with Richard Wagner. Megan in turn had hoped that by doing something so completely foreign to her friend's daily routine, Rick's mourning might be partly ameliorated, even if just briefly. And so, she made the unusual offer to her devastated friend and he spontaneously accepted.

The two travelers presented an interesting contrast. Petite Megan, a teaching career of forty-one years at Columbia University and Southern Methodist University behind her, was a perpetual brunette with sparkling brown eyes. Dedicated to keeping physically fit despite a proclivity to what she termed stomach stoutness, she was now, at the age of "eightyish," active in solving crimes in her field of nineteenth-and-twentieth-century European art. Rick, renowned in his chosen field of surgical oncology, was tall, dignified, with graying hair, and black-rimmed glasses. His eyes were very blue and he possessed an infectiously genial and calming manner.

After arriving in Frankfurt one fine morning in late August, they had picked up their rental car—a blue Opel station wagon—and driven first across country to Bayreuth. There they immersed themselves in three marvelous evenings of early Wagner operas: *The Flying Dutchman*, *Tannhäuser*, and *Lohengrin*. They also spent the better part of one day in and around Wagner's famous villa, Wahnfried, graced by the bust of a young King Ludwig beaming benevolence opposite the front façade.

Having imbibed their fill of Wagnerian ambrosia, the two friends had begun a leisurely journey down to southern Bavaria to see Ludwig's royal residences by Füssen at the foot of the Bavarian Alps. Then they planned to visit Schloss Berg on the Starnbergersee, where Ludwig and his psychiatrist guardian, Dr. Bernhard von Gudden, both mysteriously drowned in 1886. That suicide/murder had never been fully explained. Megan and Rick were both of the opinion that Ludwig, a strong swimmer, had murdered and drowned his keeper, then committed suicide in the shallow water where both bodies were found.

The duo's ultimate destination in Bavaria was Munich, where Megan had been invited to speak on the painter Wassily Kandinsky by her good friend and colleague Katrina Keller of the Lenbach House Museum. The lecture would be repeated at Schloss Berg two days later for the Bavarian Kandinsky Society and the Munich Wagner Society. It was expected that, as co-author of the oeuvre catalogue of Wassily Kandinsky's late Paris works, she would be speaking on that subject, since the museum owned eleven examples. And yet the lecture title she had given Keller was enigmatic: "Double Kandinsky." While in Munich, the travelers would be able to admire in depth two of their favorite Blue Rider artists: the Russian Kandinsky for Megan, and the German Gabriele Münter, for Rick. The painters' lives had intertwined for well over a dozen years and they had both been founding members of the German Expressionist movement, The Blue Rider.

***

Fifteen minutes passed quickly and they pulled up to a rustic house overlooking a lake which was indeed minuscule. The home was a cozy half-timbered structure containing a second floor and an attic. Hearing the car drive up, an inquisitive maid opened the front door, knowing the Togarassys rarely had visitors. She gasped at what she saw. Her employer was being lifted out from an unfamiliar car by an unknown man. What had happened?

Rick carried Iris inside and gently seated her on a hard-backed chair in what was obviously the living room. Megan followed close behind, carrying Rick's medical kit, her eyes fixed on her friend and his unexpected patient. In her mind, she visualized an ancient Egyptian scene she had once seen showing a physician setting a fallen man's dislocated shoulder by merely pulling hard on the affected arm. She hoped Rick was not about to do that.

"Now I must ask you to sit up very straight," Rick enjoined his patient. "Do not slouch. You are suffering muscular spasms and they are pulling in the humeral head. Keep your arm next to your side and pull it down toward your feet as far as you can." Iris did as she was directed, trying to control her instinct to sob.

"That's right. Now raise your elbow ninety degrees with your fingers pointing upward. Good. This is relaxing the biceps tendon. Right now, the top of your humerus is sitting in front of its socket." Iris nodded her understanding.

"Now I'm going to massage gradually down your arm starting with your bicep. Try to relax as best you can. The pain killer should be starting to take effect."

Slowly and deliberately, Rick rotated the humerus to release the superior glenohumeral ligament and present the favorable side of the humeral head to the glenoid fossa. Then little by little, he massaged his patient's arm down to the elbow. All of a sudden there was a clunking sound. The shoulder was restored and had resumed its rounded contour. And Iris's pain was gone.

"Oh, how marvelous!" Thank you, thank you. I was so afraid I'd have to go to the hospital."

While Rick talked with Iris, cautioning her to sit still for a while, Megan looked around the wood-paneled room, taking in the comfortable leather furniture and the images on the walls. They were small wooden Russian icons.

Megan's gaze came to a stop in front of a much larger image across the room. It was a framed oil on canvas. Entering from the left side of the picture a helmeted knight in body armor held an upright spear. He was mounted on a white horse whose neck and chest were also protected by armor. In the center of the picture two men held the horse by the bit. The background was made up of rolling hills and trees on the left and a fortress-like building with towers on the right. The image rang a bell in Megan's mind. She was very familiar with it and yet she did not recognize the painting. Then she realized why she knew the work. It looked exactly like Kandinsky's *Mounted Warrior* of 1903, but that particular painting had been left unfinished by the artist. The early work was on permanent exhibit at Munich's Lenbach House Museum.

How could Iris Togarassy own a verbatim version of Kandinsky's unfinished, famous work? One that was *completed*? Indeed, a conundrum.

2

A FURIOUS IGOR RASPUTIN sat in his Odessa office overlooking the Potemkin Stairs, made famous by Sergei Eisenstein's celebrated 1925 motion picture *The Battleship Potemkin*. But it was not the historic 192 steps the fifty-eight-year-old, steely-eyed Odessa billionaire saw. It was the image of Russia's bellicose president, Yabeda Tupinsky. The wretched little man had just reneged on his oath to help fund Rasputin's noble cause. Personal acquaintances, both men were long-time members of SRRV—*Sdelat' Rossiyu Rossiya Vnov'*—*Make Russia Russia Again*. It was the movement that had propelled Tupinsky to power, netting him a record-breaking three terms as president. It had been SRRV sentiments that had enabled Russia's stealth invasion of Ukraine's rugged peninsula Crimea. Jutting into the Black Sea, Crimea's two historic ports, Yalta and Sevastopol, were now again under Russian control. Russian once more, so many decades after Nikita Khrushchev's 1954 jaw-dropping "gift" of the Crimea to Ukraine. And now Crimea's natural gas fields in the Black Sea were once again Russian. Soon, if Tupinsky held to SRRV's outline, Odessa would also be rightfully returned to Russia, along with the rest of Ukraine.

Until his telephone call just now, Tupinsky had been solidly behind Rasputin's grand idea of a Patriots Museum. It was an idea for which Russian funds had already been promised. Funds which would now never arrive. And yet construction of the bold museum building was well underway, the initial costs borne by Rasputin himself.

But citing more "urgent" matters, his former ally had abruptly severed himself from the ideals and efforts of Rasputin's life goal: *Rossii svoyu sobstvennuyu—To Russia Its Own*. As an extra precaution, he and Tupinsky had always referred to the secret plan by its English translation initials: TRIO.

There was only one man in Russia more fickle than Tupinsky. That fanatic Kandinsky collector in Moscow, Boris Zima. He had at one point offered to donate one of his major works to Rasputin's project, but the offer was laced with requirements. Rasputin had reluctantly agreed to them, but then, suddenly, the promised gift was withdrawn without explanation. Zima refused to answer or return his calls. Rasputin now nursed a simmering hatred of the treacherous man whose surname literally meant "cold."

The baldheaded, square-shouldered Odessa billionaire who, as a youth, had with black humor changed his surname from Romanov to Rasputin—the hypnotic, self-proclaimed holy man who exerted enormous influence over Czar Nicholas II and his family—closed his eyes and thought of what was always his consolation, the ballet. Classical ballet, as in the days of Czarist Russia. Not this post-modern nervous nonsense. Then Rasputin's eyes opened wide and a smile came to his lips. What must be done was clear. It was time to initiate The Plan.

3

IT HAD BEEN A PROLONGED, frustrating, and expensive legal battle. But in the end Katrina Keller had won her suit against the Bavarian State for possession of the country house in Murnau. The house, and everything in it, had been returned to private hands. Justice was served. Katrina's grandmother Emmy would have been proud, were she still living.

Emmy, who had always lived in the shadow of her renowned sister Ella. She, who had loaned half her inheritance for Ella's "urgent" need to purchase the Yellow House in 1909. Fräulein Celebrity had never paid her back. But the loan document of so long ago was crystal clear and incontestable. The house now legally belonged to Emmy's granddaughter, not to the State.

Katrina's profession at the Lenbach House would keep her in Munich, of course, but from now on she would be making regular visits to the little market town on the Staffelsee. Her five-year-old son Herbert would love the country setting, and Kandinsky's old harmonium would give his extraordinary musical talent full play.

4

"AH, MY SHOULDER IS ROUNDED AGAIN," Iris Togarassy said in relief as she looked at herself in the mirror over the living room fireplace.

"And the pain is gone," she added in astonishment.

"Yes, all this is good and normal. You are returned to yourself," Rick said.

"I cannot thank you enough, Doctor Bodewell, and you too, Professor Crespi. How lucky I was—if we had to meet on the highway—to have, shall I say, 'run into you'?"

They all smiled, although Megan's joints were aching from the sudden braking and it had been a painful effort for her to limp to the couch and sit down. The maid, Hanna, had placed a pot of chamomile tea and teacups on the table near the fireplace and they were enjoying the warm and soothing drink.

"Ah, I see you are looking at our Kandinsky," Iris said, smiling at Megan.

"Indeed I am. It's unusual to see Kandinsky in a private home. And such a wonderful, early Kandinsky."

Megan was not going to let Iris know that she was aware of only one picture by Kandinsky that looked like this and that it hung in the Lenbach House. And it was *unfinished*.

"Might I ask how you came to own it?"

"Oh, my husband Laszlo gave it to me for our fiftieth wedding anniversary. We have recently opened an art gallery in Munich after years of assembling a trove of early twentieth-century works at auctions and from people who wanted to sell works they had inherited."

"How exciting that must be for you both," volunteered Rick.

"Yes, it is. In fact, I was on my way to Munich and the gallery when we, um, when we had our 'encounter' on the road."

"What is the name of your gallery?" Rick followed up.

"*Der Blaue Reiter*—The Blue Rider."

"How fantastic. I learned about the Blue Rider group in my classes with Professor Crespi," Rick said, smiling and turning to his former teacher.

"I remember the name came about because Marc loved horses and Kandinsky loved riders, and they both loved the color blue," he continued.

For some reason Megan was not smiling. Rick looked back at their hostess and continued happily.

"Oh, yes, I love them all. Wassily Kandinsky, Franz Marc, August Macke, Alexej von Jawlensky, and his Russian lover Marianne von Werefkin. But the one I really adore is Kandinsky's partner, Gabriele Münter. Their relationship really affected their art."

Megan allowed a brief smile to flit across her face. She joined the conversation.

"Yes, Dr. Bodewell fell head over heels in love with Münter's work in my class. In fact, he wanted to go to Munich and research her for his senior paper. But I realized he was born to be a physician, not an art historian, and so did not encourage him." Megan looked affectionately at her former student.

"Oh, I know what you mean about falling in love with Münter's art," Iris said. "Her work is so compelling, so colorful. Will you two be going on to Munich? It would be wonderful if you could visit our gallery."

"Definitely," Megan said with genuine emphasis. She could hardly wait to get to the Togarassy's new gallery. Should prove to be quite interesting. Or perhaps comical? Odd that she had not heard about a new gallery handling Blue Rider works from Katrina Keller at the Lenbach House. Discreetly, Megan aimed the Google Glass she was wearing at the "completed" Kandinsky and took a photo from across the room.

"Where is it? What's the address?" Rick asked, eager to visit the gallery.

"It's in Schwabing, of course!" Iris laughed triumphantly. "The bohemian part of the city where Kandinsky and Münter lived before they moved to Murnau. In fact, it's quite close to the church of Saint Ursula, which he painted."

"Oh, yes, the beautiful picture dating from nineteen-eight," Megan broke in.

"Rick, you remember the picture. It depicts the newly built domed church with its single tower in the upper right background and revels in a marvelous park in the foreground. Takes up more than half the picture. A park of many different color daubs—yellow, green, red, white, blue—and indications of a group of picnicking people on the lower left."

Megan delighted in describing the picture that resided at the Lenbach and which she knew well. She found herself half wondering if Iris was about to say *that* painting was in her husband's gallery.

"Well, the address is Hohenzollerngasse thirty-six. You can't miss it. And we're about to open a new show: *Hommage à Kandinsky*. Oh, I'm so pleased. I must call Laszlo and tell him you will be visiting. When will you be arriving in Munich?"

"We don't know for certain yet," answered Megan. "It depends on how long we decide to stay in Füssen visiting the two Ludwig castles. And then we're going on to Murnau for Rick's sake. Well, I love the village too and I've been there twice. Have taken dozens of photographs of Münter's house there and of her grave up by the church."

Megan looked happily at Rick, pleased at the thought that he would soon be in the little German hamlet by a lake he had so wanted to visit when in college.

"Oh, but haven't you heard?" Iris said. "The Münter House can no longer be visited. It's in private hands now and visitors are turned away."

"*What*?" Megan was shocked. Why hadn't her Munich colleague informed her of this astonishing news? Now she had a challenging new goal: to show Rick the *interior*, not just the exterior, of the Münter house.

She knew the Yellow House quite well because as a young art history student she had paid a visit of homage to Ella, as she was called, just one year before the eighty-five-year-old painter's death in May of 1962. Megan had been surprised that Münter's English bore the trace of an American accent. This was due to the fact that at the age of twenty-one in 1898, after receiving substantial inheritances upon the death of their American dentist father, she and her older sister Emma had spent two years in the United States. They visited their extended family in Missouri, Arkansas, and Texas.

And Megan had had something of interest to show Münter as the artist sat in her big "thinking" armchair facing her young visitor. Photographs Megan had taken of the railroad station in Marshall, Texas where the budding artist had once descended from a train to visit relatives. Situated in the primeval woodland lakes district of the state near the Louisiana border, the town was an important stop on that "gateway to the West," via the Texas and Pacific trans-continental railroad. Münter was tickled to hear some interesting facts Megan told her about Marshall. Oscar Wilde had passed through the unavoidable junction to lecture in nearby Jefferson in 1882 and in the same decade the actor Maurice Barrymore was shot and one of his troupe killed in front of Marshall's railway station. It truly was the Wild West, the artist marveled.

Megan also showed Münter photographs she had taken of the historic Ginocchio Hotel and Restaurant, opposite the train station and built just two years before the artist arrived. On the second floor, she had spotted and photo-graphed some small reverse-glass paintings—*Hinterglasmalerei*—because the technique reminded her of that used by Münter and Kandinsky in imitation of Bavarian folk paintings. The artist agreed.

"But *they* depicted saints and *yours* are landscape views," she pointed out.

The painter was enchanted by the Marshall images Megan showed her, and was prompted to recall the photographs she herself had taken in Texas with what she referred to as a "Bull's Eye." This was an Eastman Kodak Box No. 2 and Münter said she still had the "*Kodak-Rollfilmkamera*" somewhere around the house. Probably in the basement, Megan thought, where during World War II the artist had hidden, behind a false wall, paintings, watercolors, and drawings by Kandinsky, herself, and other members of the Blue Rider group who had been pronounced "degenerate" by Hitler.

The elderly artist had plied her visitor from Texas with questions about other places she had visited in the state over a half century ago and she beamed in recognition at Megan's mention of various locales and customs. At one point, she took an old picture album from a shelf and showed Megan a photograph of herself on a mule. They had quite a laugh about having to ride sidesaddle in her practical country frock. Another shot, this one taken by Münter, inadvertently included the photographer's own top-knotted, tightly corseted lithe shadow.

"Ah, I was so slender in those days," the artist sighed.

But now, coming back to the present, some instinct prompted Megan not to mention to Iris that she had met Kandinsky's partner in person. Who knows? Perhaps there would be some reverse-glass paintings in their gallery. New ones passing as old ones. Then Megan chided herself for taking such a dim and distrustful view of the Togarassys. But coming across the completed rendition of a well-known *unfinished* Kandinsky painting in the home of an art dealer, and one just opening an exhibition of Kandinsky works, set off alarm bells in Megan's head.

5

WHEN ALEXANDRA DANILOVA became the prima ballerina of the Ballet Russe de Monte Carlo in 1938, an eighteen-year-old British fan, Marigold Lamb, introduced herself backstage to the thirty-five-year-old Russian artist by announcing firmly, "You need a secretary to handle your affairs, and I am that secretary." Touched and impressed, Danilova—"Choura," as she was called by intimates—hired her on the spot and during the next fifty-nine years Marigold Lamb was a loyal amanuensis and close friend to the ballet star, traveling the world with her.

In 1997, when Danilova died at the age of ninety-three in her Manhattan home, Marigold handled the estate. She did so scrupulously, carrying out her employer's every wish, even the peculiar bequest that a painting entitled *Swan Lake*, given to her personally by an admiring compatriot Wassily Kandinsky in Paris, be sent to one Igor Rasputin in Odessa for an organization called *To Russia Its Own*.

New York friends of Danilova were not surprised. World War II had forced the Ballet Russe to a new home in America and the ballerina was reluctant to return to Russia in the hectic aftermath. But she did finally visit Saint Petersburg a few years before her death. At the Kirov School, the former Imperial Ballet School where she had studied as a child, she was enthusiastically feted as one of the institution's most distinguished former students. This had touched her heart and it was there that a young ballet aficionado from

Odessa reached out to her and impressed upon her the idea of nativism and the mandate "to Russia its own." He pointed out that her success was due to the initial nurturing Russian environment which had molded her life and career. A stellar career she had shared and shaped with fellow Russians—choreographers George Balanchine and Léonide Massine, and ballet impresario Sergei Diaghilev. He addressed the fact that another great, Wassily Kandinsky, had spent his childhood in Odessa and graduated from the Grekov Odessa Art School. And so it was that Danilova's thankful bequest came to pass.

Marigold, then seventy-seven, had accompanied the large Kandinsky canvas—former centerpiece of the ballerina's home—to Odessa. It was an unusual painting in that it incorporated colorful features from the artist's early Blue Rider years in Munich with the geometrical hallmarks distinguishing his later Bauhaus years of non-objective art. Against a totally black background spanning the upper half of the canvas, a series of different sized color spheres of pink, yellow, light blue, green, and white swirled in their spheres within infinite space. The lower half of the 1914 artwork was dominated by background blues and yellows, with a few long parallel streaks of black shooting into the picture space from the lower left. What looked vaguely like a horse and rider commanded the center, along with a small blue lake complete and a white swan. On the right was a brace of black, threatening cannons.

"You and I, we live *between* two worlds," Kandinsky had commented when he gave the work to Danilova in Paris. She had always meaningfully repeated those words to friends admiring the artwork enshrined over the dinner table in her New York home.

Marigold had re-uttered those enigmatic words to a receptive young Igor Rasputin, who eyed the woman with interest. She looked to be in her mid-seventies. What a trove of information concerning her illustrious mistress she must have in that old head of hers. And he remembered the cameo role Danilova had played as a ballet coach in an old American film from the 1970s, *The Turning Point*.

He promised Marigold that Danilova's extraordinary Kandinsky painting of "two coexisting worlds" would form the nexus for a museum of historic Russian art he was planning to found in his native city on the Black Sea.

And now, twenty years later, and despite the sudden cancellation of matching funds from President Tupinsky, that Patriots Museum was becoming a reality.

6

THE NEO-CLASSICAL BUILDING at Richard-Wagner-Strasse 33, facing the backside of a glaring new copper tube-sheathed addition to Munich's celebrated Lenbach Haus, had not changed since its construction in 1899. Neither had its ownership.

Attractive young bachelor Heinrich von Frauenberg, last scion of one of Bavaria's most ancient noble families, had inherited the handsome edifice, but little else. Prone to partying, expensive cars, and travel abroad, his Monaco gambling debts had taken their toll. Bankruptcy was just around the corner. He was going to have to sell Paleo—the name emblazoned on his family building façade because it shared the street with Munich's famed Paleontology Museum. He himself was rarely at gloomy Paleo. He preferred living on his super yacht in Monaco's Port Hercule—his gateway to the world. But soon, unless he had a lucky streak gambling, he would have to sell even the three-story yacht.

This was when he was approached by a Russian man from Odessa who offered him an immediate way out of his debts without losing his yacht or Paleo. The offer of one million euros came with an unusual condition: that the payer have full and exclusive access to the Paleo edifice—all floors, including attic and basement—for one month. But it was imperative that no one, not even he, Baron von Frauenberg, would have access to what would be an empty Paleo.

It took only ten seconds for Frauenberg to make his decision. A briefcase with bundles of crisp high denomination euros had been opened in front of him. The remaining sum would be wired to his Monaco bank that very day.

And thus, shortly after construction of a spectacular new two-story wing for the Lenbach House Museum was completed, structural activity at Paleo commenced.

The two blueprints, however, were poles apart.

7

IN HER ROLE AS CHIEF CONSERVATOR at the Städtische Galerie im Lenbach-Haus, better known as the Lenbach Museum, the poised, serious, red-haired woman in her mid-forties occupied a unique place. Respected by her fellow workers and esteemed by other restorers throughout the city and abroad, Katrina Keller was in constant demand for advice and consultation. In addition, she had served as interim director of the museum when the director died suddenly of a heart attack. Her hopes that the position might become permanent, due to lack of action by the city, were dashed when, after two years, a new director was named. It was an extremely odd choice and one that did not sit well with the museum staff. Nor did it favor the nineteenth and early twentieth century beginnings of the venerable institution. The fact that Katrina was named associate director with a sizeable uptick in her salary did little to assuage her disappointment, although she could certainly use the money.

Dr. Max Mürrisch, a tall, wiry, energetic man with thick clipped blond hair, was an adherent of modern German art and actually wanted to rearrange the Lenbach collections to favor his primary interests. Even though Munich already had fine museums of contemporary art like the Museum Brandhorst and the Pinakothek der Moderne.

Additionally, Mürrisch expressed irritation that the Blue Rider collection of artists took up almost the entire top floor with multiple exhibition rooms to itself. The collection was the largest of any museum in the world, thanks to Gabriele Münter's bequest. The fact that one of the rooms was totally dedicated simply to works of art reproduced in the *Blue Rider Almanac*, published by Kandinsky and Marc in 1912, seemed totally unnecessary to him. Another expendable room, in his opinion, was at present devoted to the *woman* artist Gabriele Münter's paintings and to what Mürrisch called knickknacks—Münter and Kandinsky's folk art collection. He also disapproved of playing throughout the rooms background music by composers of the same period as the Blue Rider: Alexander Scriabin, Arnold Schönberg, Alban Berg, and Anton Webern. "Art is silence," he mandated in total contradiction of Kandinsky's famous synesthetic experience of music and colors.

There was one thing he was able to accomplish upon arriving at the Lenbach. All eleven of the Russian painter's large works from his late Paris period on the museum's third floor were immediately relocated to the new basement gallery. This effectively thwarted Katrina Keller's request to scrutinize and evaluate the condition of each of the artworks using the museum's newly acquired digital X-ray equipment. She was concerned that the paintings had not been closely examined since the museum's acquisition of them decades ago, and even that inspection was only superficial in scope.

As if that were not enough, the first thing Mürrisch did upon taking up the directorship was to suspend from the new entry atrium's ceiling a blinding cone of 450 colored glass panes and polished steel by the modern artist Olafur Eliasson. And the artist was not German. He was Danish.

For Katrina Keller, this was the last straw. Her indignation knew no bounds. And so she was ripe for the picking when a visitor from Ukrainian Odessa asked for a private dinner consultation with her.

8

"WHEW! It's good to be back on the road," Megan sighed. She and Rick had made their farewells to Iris Togarassy and resumed their journey south to the town of Füssen, known as the "romantic soul" of Bavaria.

As Rick drove, Megan examined the single Google Glass shot she had been able to get of the so-called Kandinsky on the Togarassy wall. Too bad it was from across the room. A close-up could have recorded whether or not there was a signature. A Kandinsky signature. Even that would be suspect.

"Tell me something," said Rick, interrupting Megan's thoughts.

"What?"

"Why do we see Kandinsky's first name spelled both 'Wassily' and 'Vassily'?"

"Good question. It is rather confusing. His Russian given name was 'Vassily,' but when he came to Germany the spelling was changed to 'Wassily,' because Germans pronounce 'W' like our 'V.' And also because in German 'V' is often pronounced like an 'F' and Kandinsky clearly wanted to hear his name pronounced with the original 'V' sound and not 'Fassily.'"

"Well, that's complicated but clear. I think."

In spite of the unplanned detour, they reached Füssen by four-thirty in the afternoon and drove directly to the hotel Megan had chosen for them, Hotel Fantasia on Ottostrasse.

She had reserved two adjoining rooms and upon examining them they discovered that both rooms had lavender walls and immense double beds mounted on purple box stands. The unusual color theme was carried out in the reception room as well, even at the check-in counter where an enormous black-and-white photograph of the two Ludwig castles in the area took up the entire adjacent wall. The older, smaller castle, square, with four rounded towers at each end, was the neo-gothic Hohenschwangau—"high swan district"—where the future king spent much of his boyhood. Overlooking it from a higher, rugged hill, was the fantasy castle which Ludwig built, Neuschwanstein—"new swan stone"—paid for out of his personal fortune.

"So many *schvans*," murmured Rick happily.

"Do you remember the painting I showed in class that depicts a five-year-old Ludwig with his baby brother Otto feeding two swans under the supervision of their mother, Queen Marie?"

"I do. And I remember you told us that Ludwig did not care much for his mother, who favored Otto. In fact, you showed a revealing photograph of them at a table outdoors, the boys in their teens. I remember that Ludwig's tightly pressed legs were twisting away from his mother and the table."

"Yup, that's body language everyone can understand."

"And poor Otto went insane at quite a young age, if I recall correctly."

"Quite right. He had to be locked up under supervision. For Ludwig, already in the thrall of eccentric, unpredictable behavior, it was very alarming, not because he so loved his brother, but because he feared the same could happen to him. That was when he began his retirement from the world, preferring the seclusion of his castles."

"I also remember that Ludwig was very handsome, at least as a young man."

Megan immediately produced her iPhone and pulled up the famous coronation portrait of an eighteen-year-old Ludwig in his royal garb. He was quite tall, very slender, with intense brown eyes, and very curly black hair.

"So different from the way he looked later when he became corpulent and grew a full beard," Megan commented, beaming up a second image of the ill-fated monarch.

The two friends took a ramble around Füssen's old town and down to the Lech River where they sat for a while on a bench watching other tourists.

"Rick? I'm going to ask you a medical question," Megan said seriously.

"Fire away."

"Are you feeling any hunger pangs?"

" Ha! That's funny, I was just about to ask you the same question."

"Good. When I was here my one and only time before, I chanced upon a really good restaurant. It's called Hirsch. Shall we find it?"

"Lead the way."

They located the restaurant, which was part of an eponymous hotel and heartily enjoyed a cream of asparagus soup before indulging in filet mignons that came with forest mushrooms, cauliflower, and potato tartlets. Megan left her mushrooms uneaten as she had a primordial fear of them. Amused, Rick reached over and devoured them in a single bite. He and Megan were both too full for dessert but enjoyed sitting in the restaurant garden over coffee. The temperature was amazingly warm for August, but even so, Megan wound a scarf around her neck, ever fearful of coming down with a cold—a worry that had plagued her all her teaching and lecturing years.

She took out her iPhone, did a bit of searching, and opened up an article she had written about King Ludwig and Wagner titled "The Visual Wagner: Environments, Icons, and Images." After a bit of scrolling down she found what she was looking for.

"Rick, I just want to give you a sense of the amazing relationship Ludwig and Wagner had in the first years of their friendship. For the teenage king, it was utter adoration; for Wagner, just about to be fifty-one, it was manipulative. The young king had had to initiate a search for the debt-fleeing Wagner, whose trail led from Vienna to Switzerland to Stuttgart. There Ludwig's representative presented the flabbergasted composer with a ring, the king's photograph, and the command to come to Munich. Furthermore, the king would provide Wagner all he needed financially and promised that his *Ring* cycle would be produced there. Now listen to Wagner's slobbering letter of thanks:

Beloved, gracious King,

I send you these tears
of most heavenly emotion,
to tell you that now
the marvels of poetry have come
as a divine reality into my poor, loveless life. That life, its ultimate poetry,
its finest music, belong henceforth
to you, my gracious young king;
dispose of it as your own.
In utmost rapture, faithful and true,

Your subject,
Richard Wagner

"I see what you mean. The god had found his prince, or rather his king."

"You put it nicely, Rick, in fact just as Wagner did when he wrote a friend: 'If I am Wotan, then he is my Siegfried.'"

"Ouch! So what happened next?"

"Well, in order to be near Wagner, Ludwig took up residence at Schloss Berg on the Starnbergersee, about twenty miles south of Munich, and he rented a nearby house, the Villa Pellet, for Wagner. Sent his carriage for him every morning and they spent working sessions, planning productions of his operas in Munich. And sometimes an opera was performed before an audience of one, Ludwig. It was at this happy 'engagement' time that Wagner wrote a friend 'I fly to him as to a lover.'"

"So tell me, Megan. What's your thinking on whether or not there was a gay aspect to the affair?"

"I don't think so on Wagner's part. But he certainly encouraged the king's hero worship. And although there were definite homosexual aspects to Ludwig's later life, the boy was not in love with the man; he was infatuated by the artist."

"Complicated."

"Yes, but understandable in the light of how Ludwig the child grew up reading the German legends of Parsifal and Lohengrin. Legends which were depicted on the walls of his parents' Hohenschwangau castle. You'll see. And, of course, the same at Neuschwanstein as well. And factor into the mix that Ludwig saw his first performance of *Lohengrin* at the impressionable age of fifteen, and ten months later he saw *Tannhäuser.*"

Megan could hardly wait to show Rick the two castles he had yearned to see for so long.

That night both friends fell asleep immediately on their purple box beds, the car scare of the morning already only a distant memory.

9

THE FIRST PART of Rasputin's Plan necessitated a return visit to what locals called "the hermit of Zmiinyi." A habitual recluse, the extraordinarily gifted computer wizard lived and worked by choice on the insignificant little island of Zmiinyi off the western shore of the Black Sea near Odessa. Its total population numbered under one hundred souls, and Dzhim Kabalovitschy's household contained only one other member, his younger, protective lover and amanuensis of many years. He was Tigr Chastnyy, previously a much-sought-after medical and science photographer in Odessa.

It was on Tigr's earnings, in fact, that they had moved to the secluded island in order to concentrate without interruption on what had become their mutual work. Years of labor that, after countless tries, had merged. Dzhim, using linear and discrete mathematics, had developed a three-dimensional scanning application using Tigr's technique of two camera photography with fringe projection. The result was a three-dimensional color visualization of a painting that could be communicated to a large format 3D printer. The process was capable of capturing forty million 3D color points per shot, presenting in microscopic detail the painting's Chroma topography and texture, exposing an artist's particular tactual method, stylistic approach, and gestural brushstrokes in microscopic detail if desired.

In the right hands, such a method could significantly advance fine art restoration, but in other hands, the ability to clone works could, with the input of a competent conservationist, lead to texturized replication so exact that it would be impossible to tell the copy from the original.

It was for the latter reason that Igor Rasputin was at this very moment sitting in the hermit of Zmiinyi's modest living room.

10

"IF I KNOW YOU, Megan, I know you're going to recommend we visit Ludwig's parents' castle first. Right?"

Rick and Megan were having a buffet breakfast in the cheerful dining room of their hotel. They both felt ready to take on the day after a good night of sleep and early morning exercise.

"Well, I do think it makes sense taking on things chronologically and visiting Hohenschwangau first. After all, that's where Ludwig and Otto grew up. And once you see the extravagant wall panels you'll understand why young Ludwig responded to Wagner's musical embracement of the legends so passionately."

At the reception desk before breakfast Megan had confirmed what time and from where the next shuttle bus to the two castles would be leaving. They boarded it with plenty of time to spare, commandeering the front seats on the left—one of Megan's standard operations when deciding to tour by bus.

Hohenschwangau was the first stop and they joined the group of noisy tourists from the bus since walking around independently was not allowed. The square castle was the official hunting and summer residence of King Maximilian—son of Ludwig I and father of Ludwig II—and his Prussian wife, Queen Marie. They lived in the main building, the tour guide explained in English, while the two princelings stayed in the annex. "Just as well," Megan whispered into Rick's ear, "since Ludwig so disliked his 'prosaic' mother."

The tour group was led up a grand staircase and the guide stopped briefly on the landing, pointing to a marble statue that greeted them. It was of the young Ludwig, standing with his right hand on his hip.

"Here we have an imposing, life-size effigy of the king done soon after he came to the throne."

Megan waited for the guide to identify the sculptor but instead he turned and started to climb the second staircase.

"Wait a minute," she heard herself crying out. "Aren't you going to tell us the statue is by the sculptor Elisabet Ney?"

"Well, if you like. A sculptress from Münster, Germany carved this likeness."

"I think it is most important that you inform people in your tour that a *woman* sculptor made the statue. Especially for your American visitors because they see statues by her everyday on television."

"How can that be?" The rattled guide asked in disbelief. And he was not the only one to do so.

Megan turned from him to the tour group and, unconsciously assuming her professorial stance, explained what she meant to fascinated listeners.

"Elisabet Ney was born in eighteen-thirty-three and she spent the first half of her illustrious career in Europe, sculpting not only Ludwig—she did a bust of him too—but other important figures like the King of Hanover, philosopher Arthur Schopenhauer, Jacob Grimm of the Grimm brothers' fairy tales, Chancellor Otto von Bismarck, and the violinist Josef Joachim. She even sailed to the island of Caprera off Sardinia to sculpt Giuseppe Garibaldi."

One of the women in the tour group had pulled out a notebook and was busy writing down what she heard. Megan continued, warming to her subject.

"Now here's where the American TV exposure comes in. At the age of thirty-nine, Ney migrated to America and ultimately settled, with her handsome Scottish physician husband, in Austin, Texas. It was there she was commissioned to sculpt the politicians Sam Houston and Stephen F. Austin. Both life-size statues are displayed in the semicircular Statuary Hall in the United States Capitol and a favorite spot for television interviews is in front of a bronze statue that stands between Ney's two marble ones. So, every day millions of people in the United States see her statues without knowing who created them."

Appreciative smiles awarded Megan's mini-lecture and gave her the courage to add a verbal footnote. She glanced sweetly at the tour leader as she spoke.

"And by the way, it is now proper, thanks to feminism, to refer to a woman sculptor as exactly that, 'sculptor,' and not the old-fashioned gender-defining 'sculptress.'" With that Megan handed the invisible mike back to the guide.

He hurried the group up the well-lit stairs, explaining that total electrification of the castle took place in 1905. The extensive illumination allowed the group to study in detail some of the more than ninety murals devoted to medieval German romances. The tour guide pointed to scenes showing Lohengrin, the swan knight legend upon which Wagner's *Lohengrin* of 1848 was based. It was the first opera sixteen-year-old Ludwig heard by the composer.

As they looked at the various scenes from the Lohengrin legend, Rick mischievously sang the opera's famous Bridal Chorus in Megan's ear, only he sang the parody—"Here comes the bride, big, fat, and wide; here comes the groom, thin as a broom." Megan giggled and batted Rick away as other tourists in the group stared at them disapprovingly.

After being immersed in the Parsifal and Lohengrin sagas for some forty minutes, they were only too ready for the second castle of the day, reclusive Ludwig's fantasy-turned-reality, Neuschwanstein, built as an homage to Wagner and a resplendent retreat for himself. The five-story extended building complex had been left unfinished after seventeen years of construction because of Ludwig's early death in 1886 at the age of forty. Now it looked down imperiously upon them from atop the nearby rugged Alpine ridge of the Pöllat gorge. As the bus wound its way upward, the turrets and pointed towers seemed to beckon invitingly to them.

"You know who else adored Wagner on a dramatic level almost equal with Ludwig, Rick?"

"No idea. Who?"

"Alma Mahler. I've been reading her early diaries, from eighteen-ninety-eight to nineteen-two, and she wrote that *Tristan and Isolde* was 'the work of God.' Pretty high praise, huh?"

"Certainly is. By the way," Rick asked, "just out of curiosity, did Kandinsky like Wagner?"

"Ha! It was at a performance of *Lohengrin* at the Bolshoi Theater in Moscow where he had the life-changing synesthetic response of seeing colors while hearing music. That was when he abandoned his law career and went to Munich to study painting. For him music and color were indivisibly linked. He associated each note of the scale with an exact color."

"Ah, yes, I've heard of that. In the medical field, we consider their ability to hear colors or see sounds as an interesting neurological condition. A number of famous people have had it. For instance, the physicist Richard Feynman, who saw letters of the alphabet in colors, and Eugen Bleuler, the Swiss psychiatrist who coined the term 'schizophrenia.'"

"Um, *love* learning that. I know a number of composers and musicians who were synesthetic. Franz Liszt, for example, Jean Sibelius, Olivier Messiaen, Rimsky-Korsakov, Leonard Bernstein, Amy Beach, Itzhak Perlman, and even Duke Ellington."

"That's quite a range. And who was Amy Beach?"

"Ha! I was hoping you'd ask. She was a very fine turn-of-the-last century American composer and concert pianist who is only now being rediscovered. Her *Gaelic Symphony* is her best-known work. We sang some of her choral music when I was at Barnard and in the St. Paul Chapel choir, where we referred to her as 'Mrs. Ha Ha Beach,' since her professional name took not only her husband's surname but also his preceding initials: H. H. A. Beach."

"Interesting. And wasn't van Gogh also a synesthesiac as far as sounds were concerned, suggesting colors to him?"

"Yes. To use your medical terminology, his manifested as timbre synesthesia."

"Well, I suppose I'll just have to accept the fact that I do not have any synesthesia," Rick said, pretending to be disappointed.

After a winding ascent, the bus deposited Megan and Rick and their fellow tourists right in front of the castle's ornate gateway where they listened as the guide told them the building history of what was intended to be a medieval knight's castle devoted to the German legends taken up in Wagner's operas. The great irony was that Wagner never set foot in the castle.

Once inside the lower walled courtyard, the tour guide declared and emphasized that taking photographs was not allowed inside. Megan immediately put her iPhone back in her multi-pocket black sling purse and discreetly switched from her Prima Classe sunglasses to her Google Glass. Usually she resorted to the camera spectacles only when studying artworks on paper or canvas. This would be a first for her, photographing entire rooms. But she remembered from her previous visit decades ago, when climbing great sets of marble stairs was less of a strain, that the king's suite of fourteen completed rooms included painted borders with scenes from Wagner operas, and this time she planned to add them to her photographic trove for PowerPoint presentations. So taking a refresher course in the form of visiting Ludwig sites with Wagnerian motifs was most welcome.

The group was taken directly to the two most important rooms of the castle. The first was the Minstrels' Hall with its gallery for musicians and its murals depicting scenes from *Parsifal* and the legend of the Grail. The second enclosure was the Throne Room. It extended through two floors at one end and had arcaded walls on two levels.

Blue, gold, and reddish purple were the predominant colors. On the floor was a mosaic of plants and animals, while the ceiling was a blue sky studded with stars. An enormous candelabra hung over the center of the room and at one end white marble steps led to an apse where Ludwig's throne was to stand—a furnishing never carried out. And hardly crucial, as the king only rarely gave audiences.

Of greater interest to Megan and Rick were the king's bedroom and study, the bedroom with its ultra-dark wooden panels and ubiquitous saga images on mock-tapestries, and the study in which paintings illustrated the Tannhäuser legend, its erotic elements clearly presented. Megan's Google Glass got good shots of all the images and, opening out from the king's study, the artificial grotto with its moon and cascading water. Beyond the grotto was the king's winter garden, bereft at the moment of any plants.

"Whew! I think I have a pretty good impression of Ludwig's extravagant taste now," Rick opined as they returned to the tour bus.

"You're going to like his Schachen hunting lodge then. It's quite a contrast. From the *outside* that is," Megan laughed.

"Inside it's a lavish Turkish room that Ludwig bought and imported from a world's fair in Paris."

"I think then that maybe I can skip it. Not if we still have Linderhof and the Herrenchiemsee palace to see."

"I'm in total agreement. And also, I'm hungry and wouldn't mind a brief nap after we eat something. What about you?"

"Well, being twenty-one years younger than you, my dear Frau Professor Doktor, I do share your hunger but not your wish for a nap. If you don't mind, I'll just explore Füssen a bit more while you lie down."

"Perfect. And if it's still there, I know a pearl of a pizzeria near our hotel. It's actually called La Perla."

The two friends laughed and then fell silent, each enjoying the superb, ever-changing views of the green forests, blue lakes, and snow-topped foothills of the Bavarian Alps.

11

NEW DIRECTOR MAX MÜRRISCH had really done it now.

He had managed to antagonize associate director Katrina Keller and the entire museum staff, as well as baffle the museum world at large with his inaugural exhibition announcement. It was to be an homage to Franz von Lenbach, the academic painter who had built the 1891 Tuscan-style yellow villa that formed the architectural heart of the eponymous museum.

The only problem was that the once popular nineteenth-century realist painter, aside from a few kitschy country scenes of lounging shepherds and a plethora of carefully executed copies of masterpieces in Italy and Spain, was primarily a portrait painter, and of the same man, over and over again. His subject was Germany's first prime minister, Otto von Bismarck, unifier of the German states in 1871. Lenbach painted more than seventy images of the Iron Chancellor, a number challenged only by his portraits of Bismarck's counterpart in Britain, Prime Minister William Gladstone, whom his longtime opponent Benjamin Disraeli once described as "God's Only Mistake." Somewhat dull stuff for museum goers.

The exhibition was to be balanced by a small-scale repetition of Joseph Beuys' massive and ultimately successful *7,000 Oaks* project in Kassel. In Munich's case, seventy young oaks would be planted in clusters around the museum. Surrounding cement and pavestones would simply have to be removed. Enchanted by the newly appointed director, the Munich city council had already given permission for this. Now, for even more trees, Mürrisch was attempting to cajole the council to remove, from the adjacent Königsplatz, with its great Propylaea and gleaming Glyptothek, the paving laid down in Hitler times as a Nazi parade-ground.

Well, good luck with that, Katrina snorted sarcastically when she heard what Mürrisch was up to. She had much more important things on her mind now.

She was sitting in Schwabing's exclusive restaurant, Tantris, at a corner table reserved for her and the important visitor from abroad she had agreed to meet. He hailed from Odessa and during their short telephone conversation he had stressed the confidentiality of their meeting while praising her conservation work, mentioning in particular her restoration of Franz Marc's *Blue Horse* at the Lenbach. An overly enchanted child had gone right up to the picture and kissed the horse, setting off alarms and damaging the surface paint.

What did the visitor have in mind, Katrina wondered? She had located Igor Rasputin online, but ascertained very little about him other than that, as inheritor of a far-flung cargo shipping company, he was considered one of Ukraine's wealthiest men. And as a resident of the second largest country in Europe, his reach extended from the Sea of Azov to the Black Sea and, via the Bosporus and Hellispontos, into the Mediterranean.

Fiddling with the heavy cloth napkin in her lap, Katrina's thoughts were interrupted by hearing her name spoken softly.

"Frau Doktor Keller?"

She looked up to see a tall, bald-headed, clean-shaven man smiling down at her inquisitively. He was dressed in a stylish brown suit with light brown striped shirt, and dark brown tie.

Nodding affirmation, she waved him to the chair opposite her. After an exchange of a few pleasantries, the visitor came right to the point. His German was excellent and he spoke in a low, moderated tone of voice Katrina found appealing.

"I have been watching the antics of your new director and have reason to believe you are not happy with the situation. Am I correct?"

Instinctively, Katrina found herself trusting Herr Rasputin enough to affirm his statement with a simple nod. Rasputin cleared his throat.

"It is obvious to me, Frau Doktor, that the two single most important artists in the Lenbach collection are going to be sidelined in favor of modern trivia."

"And whom do you identify as the museum's two most important artists?"

"Why Kandinsky and Münter, of course. The relocation of the abstract Kandinskys from the third floor to your basement gallery is an outrage I have witnessed with my own eyes."

Katrina was pleasantly surprised. Of course, Kandinsky was universally considered the most important artist in the Lenbach collection, but to hear someone speak of Münter in the same breath, and identify her by surname only was most unusual. Most people, when talking about women artists, referred to them by given name and surname.

"I am going to tell you something I usually do not share with people in the art world, Frau Doktor."

"Yes? What might that be?" Katrina's curiosity and favorable impression of the mild-mannered man opposite her were increasing.

"In the early nineteen-eighties my father, an avid collector of Russian artists Jawlensky, Werefkin, and Kandinsky, came across some small reverse-glass paintings by the German Münter and, being interested in other Blue Rider artists, he acquired them. I grew up with those glowing paintings and their radiance remains with me today."

Rasputin could not have said anything more pleasing to his listener's ears.

"I must say that I am astonished by your putting Münter on the same level as Kandinsky."

"Ah, but for me she is. A very different kind of genius, but definitely a genius."

"I should dearly love to see photographs of your Münter works someday. Are they similar folk art themes such as we have here in the Lenbach?"

"Yes, indeed. Very like. Purposefully 'naïve' images of saints or peasants, for the most part."

"That sounds right."

"Now let me tell you why I have asked that you have dinner with me. This may take a bit of time, however, so shall we order drinks and food first?"

Katrina did not know which was nagging more, her appetite or her curiosity.

After they had placed their orders—salmon on a bed of couscous, flavored with a creamy tarragon sauce, asparagus tips, and a fine pinot grigio—Rasputin took up his artful narrative again.

"You may know that Russian president Yabeda Tupinsky fervently backs the SRRV—the *Make Russia Russia Again* movement. And that many Ukrainians, including myself, are supporters of this movement. Like Tupinsky—a personal friend, incidentally—like Tupinsky, I am a believer in old Russia as it was in imperial days, and the need to return to our previous geographical boundaries. For many decades, in my own way, I have worked to preserve our artistic heritage." Rasputin paused, then asked in a low voice.

"I wonder if I can count on your total confidence?"

Fascinated by the man, Katrina quickly nodded in assent.

"As a proud Odessan Russian, I have for many years believed that culture created or nourished in Russia should be highlighted *in* Russia." He paused dramatically, not mentioning that the organization's specific aim also included locating Russian art abroad and *relocating* it to Russia. Rasputin looked intently at Katrina who, nodding her head in comprehension, steadfastly returned his gaze.

"I have named my own personal goal 'TRIO—To Russia Its Own' in English. And in the fervent hope and belief that soon Odessa will be returned to Russia I have done what I could to assemble beforehand, data and objects that represent Russian genius. To that purpose I am in the process of building a new museum in my native Odessa, where so much Russian culture was nourished. Just look at Danilova! Look at Kandinsky!"

Katrina nodded her head in recognition of the two artists' formative years in Odessa.

"My TRIO Museum will be a Russian cultural showcase. And President Tupinsky supports my plan." Rasputin did not mention that the wretched man had just reneged on his promise of financial support.

"How very gratifying for you, Herr Rasputin. Certainly not everything that reflects Russian genius is beholden to Moscow."

"I see you understand my aim, Frau Doktor." Rasputin beamed at her.

Their dinner having been served, a brief silence ensued as they ate the delicious fare. Then over coffee and crème brûlée, Rasputin spoke again.

"Now I want to show you what is at the heart of my museum of Russian art." He took a photograph out of his breast pocket and reverently handed it to Katrina.

She gasped. It was a Kandinsky, but a Kandinsky of two worlds. Or rather *between* two worlds.

12

IT WAS NOT THE FIRST TIME the Amiinyi Island couple had been to Munich. In fact, they had met each other years ago in the Schwabing studio of German civil engineer-turned-woodworker, Alyksandr Miesel. It was an anniversary they celebrated together in Munich every year. And now a balding, overweight Miesel, long in the employ of Igor Rasputin, was looking forward to showing the two men into their spacious downstairs studio and second-floor apartment overlooking narrow Richard-Wagner-Strasse 33.

Of Ukrainian descent on his mother's side, Miesel was the great grandson of one of the seventeen woodcarvers who had worked four-and-a-half years on the sculpted *boiseries* of Ludwig's Neuschwanstein study paneling. It was from this legacy that Miesel had inherited his love of woodcarving. His own apartment was on the other side of the city and so he was temporarily ensconced next to his friends' ground floor studio in the even roomier quarters his tasks required.

Some of these tasks had included specific "tourist" photography, discreet measurement calculation with laser and crystal prism, and the inconspicuous planting of range and calibration sensors. Additionally, Miesel had combed through Munich's antique stores selecting certain objects and storing them in his workroom. And lastly, he was in the final stage of completing the construction of an ongoing addition to the building.

Both Paleo apartments and work spaces had been provided by a mutual Ukrainian acquaintance. And both apartments looked directly out onto the unpretentious back of the glittery new Lenbach House addition.

13

IN MOSCOW, vodka baron Boris Zima picked up his landline phone on the first ring, a frown spreading over his wrinkled face. If it was who he thought it was—Raisa Sokolova—the woman was in for a scolding.

"Boris. It is I. Sorry not to have called you earlier, but it's only one hour later there, so you should not complain." The caller's voice was deep pitched and calm. She was speaking very quietly.

"All right, all right, Raisa. Just tell me what is going on. Any action yet?" Seventy-eight-year-old, white-haired Boris Zima, wealthy Moscow collector of Kandinsky, and rival of Ukrainian Igor Rasputin, could never remain angry with his beguiling, fifty-year-old personal secretary and special agent for very long. There was something sadly mysterious about her that charmed him. And in person she was commanding and self-possessed—tall, slim, with black hair, dramatic arching eyebrows, and piercing green eyes.

"Yes. Rasputin is having dinner at this very moment with the associate director of the Lenbach House. I'm about to send you a photo of them together so look at your cellphone. She's quite glamorous, with red hair. They seem to be deep in conversation. Very serious. No laughter or smiles."

"Never mind what color her *hair* is! How were you able to identify her?"

"You are impatient, Boris. It was *by* the color of her hair that I confirmed identification. The museum has a folder with floor layouts and images of the top personnel, and she is pictured there. One Katrina Keller. I've followed her at quitting time back to her home in Schwabing several times now. But tonight, was a winner. I trailed her after she left work and now I'm in the same restaurant as she and Rasputin are, only on the other side of the room. I have a clear view of them."

"Why would he be conferring with the associate director of the Lenbach? Does the wretch think he can get them to cough up a Kandinsky for his stupid museum?"

"I doubt it. The Lenbach would hardly deacquisition a work by one of their star artists."

"But he has enough money to *buy* one outright, if he could persuade the museum personnel."

"Do not worry, Boris. Remember, the Lenbach is owned by the municipality of Munich. There would have to be a lot of red tape to go through, and I doubt that the city fathers would agree to selling any painting from the Münter bequest."

"But I *am* worried. After all, when she turned eighty, Münter *gave* them literally hundreds of his works. I can just see those officials lusting over funds to enhance the museum. What should we do?" Zima's voice began to rise hysterically. Raisa could just picture the sniveling man dabbing his huge nose with an expensive handkerchief.

"Leave it to me, Boris. My man here gained entry into Keller's apartment while all the inhabitants were out and now I have it bugged."

"Yes, that's good, that's good. But even if you do find out that she's willing to part with a Kandinsky what the hell can we *do* about it?" His voice was now a high shriek.

"Do not worry. I have the means to dissuade her if it comes to that."

"How?"

"*She has a young son.*"

14

DINNER THAT EVENING was at the same excellent restaurant where they had dined the previous evening. Rick had ordered a bottle of two-year-old Masseto merlot and they were going over the day's events as they cut into their steaks. Megan began speculating out loud between bites.

"You know, it's only twenty-eight miles from here to Ludwig's Linderhof Palace, and if we left at a reasonable hour tomorrow morning we might have time to visit a certain famous composer's house that's not too far away."

"Another composer? Who might that be. I thought only Wagner reigned over these parts."

"Well, the man—ah, I wish I could *just once say* 'woman'—the man I'm thinking of was also a German opera composer, very famous, and much performed."

"Hmm Can you at least give me an idea of the time period?"

"He lived until nineteen-forty-nine."

"Oh. Thanks. Big help."

"Okay, I'll name some of his operas. *Salome, Elektra, Der Rosen...*"

"...*kavalier*," Rick supplied with excited recognition. "Wow, that's exciting. You mean Richard Strauss lived near here?"

"Yes. What he once built as a summer residence in Garmisch soon became his principal residence. It was built in nineteen-eight. I've been to the villa, and it really is worth visiting. And it was built with the money he made from the success of *Salome*—which his unmusical, busybody employer, Kaiser Wilhelm II, complained had 'ruined' his reputation. And now at Garmisch there is a Strauss festival every year and opera fans attend from all over the world."

"I've heard of Garmisch but in conjunction with the word Partenkirchen."

"That's right. They're villages right next to each other and they share the same Alpine valley at the foot of Germany's tallest mountain, the Zugspitze. Fun?"

"Fun. Let's do it."

Megan pulled out her iPhone and within seconds located a road map of the area. She spotted something and waved the screen at Rick, pointing to a town name.

"And just look! If, on our way up to Murnau tomorrow evening, we made just the shortest of side trips, we could also visit Oberammergau."

"*Und was ist* Oberammergau?"

"Oh, sure, you know what Oberammergau is, Rick. That's where the whole village—about two thousand people—participates in a Passion Play every ten years. It begins with Jesus's entrance to Jerusalem, shows his crucifixion, and ends with his resurrection. Tourists flock to see it from countries all around the world."

"Are they performing it this year?"

"No, only in years that end in the digit zero."

"Do you know why the villagers started doing this?"

"Yes, as a matter of fact, I do. The story is that back in the seventeenth century the bubonic plague was sweeping the area and the residents of Oberammergau vowed that if they were spared they would perform a passion play every ten years. After taking that vow, not a single other inhabitant of the village died from the plague. How about that?"

42

"Ah, those early so-called miracles. As a physician, I find it hard to believe that right after a vow was made there were no more plague victims. But it makes a lovely story."

They divided a chocolate mousse dessert and partook of an after-dinner drink as well: anise for Megan, a brandy for Rick.

Slightly tipsy, Megan recited a German tongue-twister poem she suddenly remembered, prefacing it with the information that not only was there an upper—*ober*—Ammergau, but also a lower—*unter*—Ammergau. And that one gets to both by going over—*über*. Then she recited:

> *"Heut' kommt der Hans zu mir,*
> *freut sich die Lies.*
> *Ob er aber über Oberammergau,*
> *oder aber über Unterammergau,*
> *oder aber überhaupt nicht kommt,*
> *ist nicht gewiß!"*

Then she translated:

> "Today Hans is coming to me,
> rejoices Lies.
> But if he comes over Oberammergau
> or over Unterammergau,
> or comes not at all,
> that's not certain!"

"Wanna try it?" Megan asked triumphantly.

Rick was roaring with laughter. They became a bit more serious as they discussed which hotel in Murnau they should reserve for the next night after their side trip to Oberammergau.

This time it was Rick who took out his cellphone—a Blackberry, larger and thicker than Megan's iPhone. He pulled up several picturesque hotels then zeroed in on one called Klausenhof am Park that claimed to be "just two minutes away from the Schlossmuseum and Münter's Yellow House." They read a few approving reviews and were convinced it was the right hotel.

"But it looks as though we'd each have to reserve a suite," Megan said, ever practical about prices.

"Not if we were to reserve only one suite that has two beds. Shall we do that?"

"Um, I guess so. And we'd take turns getting dressed in the bathroom. Oh, but I'd be doing my exercise routine in the morning and I certainly wouldn't want you to see me doing that."

"Well, you know from our stays in Bayreuth and Füssen, my morning exercise is outdoors, jogging."

"So, you would stay away while I do mine?"

"I'd give you thirty minutes. Do you think that would be enough?"

"Make it forty-five so I can wash up and get dressed for the day. I'll meet you down at breakfast. Good?"

"Deal."

They decided Rick should call the hotel to make sure at least one of its several suites had two beds and upon receiving a positive answer, Rick made the reservation. Then he turned and looked at his former professor inquisitively.

"Just what is it you *do* for your exercises?"

Enormously pleased by the question, Megan summarized her routine.

"Well, to myself I call the series FSAB: that stands for flexibility, strength, acerbic, and balance."

"*Acerbic*?"

"Oh, I always get that word mixed up. I mean aerobic."

"That's better. I was frightened for you, Megan. Go on." Rick was grinning broadly.

"You mean you really want to know?"

"I really, really want to know."

"Okay, then. For flexibility, I do bed exercises in sets of twelve: upper body/arm twists, head and eye twists, then twelve bend-overs to touch the bed beyond my toes.

Suddenly feeling self-conscious under Rick's engaged scrutiny, Megan stopped.

"Are you sure you want to hear this?"

"Go on."

"Well, then I lie on my back and concentrate on all sorts of rotary leg exercises, all in sets of twelve, ending with twelve Yoga boards and planks, still in agonizing sets of twelve. After that I rest a bit, breathing deeply in and out, humming so that my throat vibrates, and doing Kegel exercises."

Megan stopped her narration and looked at Rick accusingly.

"You can't *possibly* be interested in all this. It's becoming embarrassing."

"Ah, but I can. And Kegel exercises are good for males as well, so don't be embarrassed. He was in fact quite interested in Megan's routine as she was unusually agile for her age.

"After that I stand up and do five different limbering exercises. I don't have to count. I just do them to the spiritual 'Swing Low, Sweet Chariot.'"

"I see. And your strength exercises?"

"For those at home I lift four-pound weights in many directions. On trips like this I use full water bottles."

"Ah ha. Very good. We still have the 'acerbic' exercises as you say."

"For *aerobic* I do six minutes of steady trotting throughout the ground floor of my house. Remember Mowgli in *The Jungle Book*? How he could run for hours at a steady trotting gait? Well, I pretend to be Mowgli. Because of ballet lessons as a child my arches have fallen, so the trotting begins to hurt after a while."

"I didn't know you studied ballet."

"Oh, yes, for five years, at the 'Edith James School of the Dance' in Dallas. And one summer Alexandra Danilova came to teach us—what an inspiration! Her commands were all in French: *demi-plié*, *grand plié*, and something that sounded like '*sudicudiplié*.'"

"So, you must be very good at your final exercise, balance?"

"Only so-so. For balance, I stand in front of my bathroom sink mirror on one leg with the other one bent in at the knee. When I've achieved balance, I circle my hands twelve times. Then same thing on the other leg. Sometimes I have to cheat and touch the sink to steady myself. But at least I can *do* it. So that's my daily FSAB schedule."

"No wonder you want forty-five minutes! Now just one last question."

"Yes," Megan said, a little disappointed that her physician friend did not compliment or express approval of her exhausting exercise routine.

"Why do you do almost everything in twelves?"

"Oh, that's easy. Three is my favorite number and so this way, with twelve, I get lots of threes."

"So why not do a baker's dozen and get thirteen in?"

"Because one and three add up to four and I hate the number four."

"You *hate* the number four?"

"Yes, ever since childhood the number has spooked me."

"Hmm You are a strange one, Megan. I bet you also count stairs."

"That's true, I do. But I'm in good company with that one. Anton Bruckner was obsessed with numbers; he counted everything, steps, stairs, you name it. But he managed to write eleven great symphonies."

"Isn't he the composer whose music a critic said was 'polyphony gone mad?'"

"That's what the critic said. But now we're just grateful for polyphony *in* symphonies."

"Well, anyhow, I congratulate you, Megan, on the tenacity with which you do your daily exercise. You are in amazing condition at your age."

Megan beamed.

"However, as far as your counting things is concerned, your compulsive counting may be an indication of OCD."

"What's OCD again? I've forgotten what that stands for."

"Obsessive Compulsive Disorder."

"Oh, come on now, Rick. I don't have that."

"No, I don't think you do either, but it is interesting that many people who do have it believe the number four has significance and they will do things in sequences of four."

"But I do things in sets of *three*." Megan was beginning to feel defensive.

"Ah, *three* is all right then. Not to worry." Rick was having fun pulling Megan's leg.

Time had passed quickly. Realizing they had better go to bed if they were to get their early morning activities in, the two friends walked briskly back to their hotel and bade each other goodnight.

Tomorrow Ludwig's Linderhof Palace and Strauss's Garmisch villa! Rick's spirits had definitely been lifted.

15

KATRINA KELLER continued to stare at the photograph Igor Rasputin had handed her. The Kandinsky painting was unlike any other she had ever seen by the artist. The lower half of the work was executed with the broad brushstrokes and intense colors of red, orange, yellow, green, blue, indigo, and violet associated with the Blue Rider years of 1911 to 1914. The subject matter was a recognizable theme: a stick-figure horse and rider floating on the left, and on the right, pertinent to the year 1914, a group of black cannons facing the horse and rider. The unusual center had a theme never before seen by Katrina: a great white swan in a miniscule, blue lake.

But while the bottom half of the painting was pure Blue Rider, the upper half completely bespoke the later Bauhaus School years during which, in a thousand variations, Kandinsky explored a cosmos inhabited by geometrics and color spheres. The infinite space in this painting was black, echoing the threatening black of the cannons below. A philosophical picture if ever there was one.

"But I have never seen this Kandinsky," Katrina finally said. "Where, where did it come from? It certainly isn't in any catalogue raisonné of his works."

"Frau Doktor, that I cannot disclose. I can only say that the source was impeccable. Now, if you have the interest, I should like to show you photographs of other Kandinskys that will be part of our Odessa museum. They range from his earliest works to his very final works. See here, this first one: signed right there on the lower right, it was painted in eighteen-ninety-eight and shows Odessa harbor with two schooners at anchor. See how the ripples of the water attract the dabbling attention of his brush."

Katrina had seen similar works, but certainly this was the best of the lot. Before she could say so, Rasputin handed her two more photos. Both were vibrant street scenes painted in Murnau, probably before 1910. Again, Katrina knew similar works, but had never seen these. They certainly looked genuine. But again, before she could speak, her dinner companion handed over more images. And so it continued until he had placed some eleven pictures in her hands. All of them from the early years of Kandinsky's career. Only the "swan" painting gave any hint of the abstract—or non-objective, as Kandinsky always referred to it—work to come.

"I am honored that you have shown me the wealth of your museum, Herr Rasputin. But tell me. May I speak of these extraordinary works to others? Or is this what you have requested I hold in confidence?"

"I would prefer that for now you speak to no one of this."

"Of course. Certainly. As you wish."

"Now, Frau Doktor, the question I wait for you to ask me is why. Why do I show you these works?"

"I have been wanting to ask you the whole time we have been looking at them. Yes, indeed, why have you shown these precious images to me?"

"Because I have an unusual request and, if granted, an extraordinary thank you."

"Yes?"

"Let me tell you what the thank you would be first. I propose sending, at my expense, all these unknown Kandinskys to you, to the Lenbach House Museum, for an exhibition. It would be an exhibition that would attract hundreds of thousands of visitors. And..." Rasputin's voice lowered conspiratorially, "...it would reinstall Kandinsky to the prominence and physical place he deserves in the museum. Put crassly, it would restore the museum's reputation after the disaster your new director is bringing upon it."

Speechless, Katrina stared at the man across the table from her. She could not believe her ears. He was voicing her private thoughts concerning the museum's new direction. Nor could she believe how instantly attractive his proposal was to her personally.

"And your 'unusual' request, Herr Rasputin?" Katrina was filled with curiosity.

"First let me say that I completely understand the Lenbach could not reciprocate with an exchange loan of its own Kandinskys to Odessa. Especially as the paintings have been on the road at other museum showings during the two-year construction of your new addition."

"Yes, that is quite true. It will be a long time before any of our Kandinskys are lent out again."

"Here is what I am asking. In order to show the whole range of our great artist's work at my Odessa museum, I should like your permission to use the latest state-of-the-art photographic techniques developed in my homeland to create high-quality images of your museum's abstract, non-objective Kandinskys to have on the walls of my museum. They would provide the needed balance and give visitors a fine idea of Kandinsky's three great periods—Munich/Murnau, Weimar/Dessau/ and Paris. What do you say?"

Katrina was silent for quite some time as she pondered multiple aspects of the question. Try as she might, she could see no negative consequences to the request. A small favor, considering the prospect of a blockbuster show at the museum. She thought of one aspect, however, and her reply spoke to it.

"You would develop and display such photographs in a size different from the original paintings, would you not?"

"Of course. That goes without saying. Never could a visitor mistake one of the photographs as an original work. That would be made clear on the labels." Rasputin laughed out loud at the preposterous idea.

Her one reservation satisfied, Katrina turned to the practical matters such a task would involve.

"We can't have your photographers working during museum visitor hours."

"Certainly not. With your permission, we would work during one evening without stop. It should take no longer than one session to set up our equipment and do the photography. I understand that all the abstract Kandinskys painted in Paris are now in the basement."

"Yes. That is where they have been banished," Katrina heard herself saying.

"And of course, you would be present during the session, if it is convenient."

This presumption on the part of Herr Rasputin erased any further reservations Katrina might have had.

"When would you like to initiate the session?"

"Would Friday be too soon?"

16

RICK HAD GIVEN MEGAN plenty of time to get through her exercises, shower, and dress before he returned from his forty-five-minute jog along the

Lech riverbank. He found her in the hotel breakfast room, cheerfully downing what she called her "senior pills." It was eight-thirty and they had more than enough time to load the car and arrive at Ludwig's beloved Linderhof Palace by opening time. Relatively small in size, it was large in ornate content, Megan had told him.

Rick offered to do the driving again and Megan accepted, but hoped he did not think she was too old to be driving. After all, she had driven all over Europe the past few years solving cases of forged and stolen artworks. She voiced her thought.

"I'm happy for you to drive, Rick, but remember I can take over anytime you feel tired."

"Of course, Megan. That's a given."

The Alpine scenery stretched out beautifully to their right as they drove through the Ettal valley and toward their first destination of the day.

"Megan? Why is Linderhof called a 'Schloss' but is a palace, while the castles Hohenschwangau and Neuschwanstein are also 'Schloss' designations?"

"I see your confusion, but in German the term 'Schloss' can designate any building that looks like a castle *or* palace, or, for that matter, manor house, or château. After the Middle Ages kings' residences were no longer built as defense fortresses. A real fortress would be a 'Burg,' as in Martin Luther's hymn 'A Mighty Fortress is our God—*Ein Feste Burg ist unser Gott.*'"

"I love that hymn." Rick began humming and Megan joined in.

Megan broke off suddenly when she spotted a sign indicating the turnoff for Linderhof, pointing it out for Rick. They wound their way through the forested, mountainous terrain leading to what had previously been the site of Ludwig's father's royal hunting lodge. After parking and mounting two flights of stairs, they looked out across the water parterre that fronted the white palace beyond. Broad white walks ran on either side of the long, shallow basin. A gold fountain ensemble of Flora and three frolicking putti held forth in the middle. At full throttle, the fountain's jet shot up to almost a hundred feet. All around the white palace were adjacent hedged gardens laid out in French style and smaller pools with gold putti flexing their bows and arrows. There were even live swans to feed—homage to the two pet swans kept there by Ludwig the "Swan King."

They decided to visit the palace interior first, saving the famous Venus grotto for last. While the white exterior was restrained, the interior greeted them with a rococo riot of flashing mirrors, rich tapestries, populated paintings, lush velvet, and gold glitter. Allowed to wander on their own, they visited the dazzling mirror room, which lived up to its name, and then entered the King's enormous bedroom with its blue-and-gold bed and matching high canopy. A magnificent candle-studded cut-glass candelabra hung suspended in front of it and was topped by a busy ceiling fresco.

"But it's so chilly," Rick said. "I would never want to sleep here."

"Yes, it's a pretty lonely place. But Ludwig was notoriously shy. For example, as you'll see when we get to the oval dining room, he had his meals served in a manner that didn't require any servants. Instead his dinner table could be lowered through the floor, a meal set upon it, and then sent back up to him."

"There have certainly been times when I wished I could eat that way at the hospital for a few minutes' peace," Rick laughed.

Exiting a very French-looking Rose Room, they entered the palace's Gobelins room and marveled at two giant Sèvres porcelain peacocks.

"And if I remember correctly there are three more of these big birdies in the Moorish kiosk Ludwig had created outside," said Megan.

"Okay, I think I'm really ready for the outside," Rick announced after they had seen the remaining public rooms, all lavishly decorated in gold rococo style.

Once outdoors, they took a look inside the Moorish kiosk with its peacock throne.

"See? I was correct," Megan congratulated herself.

"Sure were. But the throne looks more like a bed with a satin headboard than a place to sit."

"Well, perhaps that's where Ludwig actually slept. Who knows? As he got older he established a routine of sleeping through the day and roaming the countryside at night. Roaming either in his ornate coach drawn by six white horses or, more humbly, by sleigh with only four white horses. Often with a young man of his choice with him."

"But why the drastic change in his lifestyle?"

"Partly because he had *lost* Wagner, at least his physical presence. The court and councilors around him were alarmed at the hold the composer had over him and they feared Wagner would interfere with politics—which eventually he did try to do. So they forced Ludwig, in December of eighteen-sixty-five, to 'disinvite' Wagner from remaining in Munich."

As they were walking slowly up a hillside toward the Venus Grotto, Megan stopped for a moment to catch her breath.

"I'm thinking of something Wagnerian Ludwig had built for himself nearby but which we can't see because it was burned down at the end of World War II."

"What was that?"

"It was a simple—for Ludwig—log cabin called Hunding's Hut. The interior was derived from a set for the premiere of *Die Walküre*. A huge live ash tree was smack in the center of the room and the cabin was outfitted with bear-skins and weapons."

"That would have been really fun to see," admitted Rick.

A few minutes later they reached the Venus Grotto and Megan pushed the well-marked button on a large boulder facing them. A door to the artificial cave slid open and revealed a narrow corridor leading to the main chamber. It contained a miniature lake fed by a waterfall, as well as a small stage. A drop-scene above portrayed the first act of *Tannhäuser* featuring the thirteenth-century minnesinger, who, after a year of enjoying the love of Venus in her enchanted underground realm, begs her to allow him to return to the world. In the center of the miniature lake floated the cockle shell boat in which Ludwig would sit for long periods as he gazed upon the mural. In his final years, having found a new idol to adore in the brilliant Hungarian actor Josef Kainz, the king would have him recite for hours from the grotto's small stage.

"There's a photo of the two men I used to show classes. Do you remember it, Rick?"

"I do, actually. A bearded, older Ludwig, in ordinary dress, is standing to the left, looking tall and aristocratic, and next to him on a chair the young actor is *sitting* in the presence of his monarch. Kainz doesn't look too happy about it all, if I recall correctly."

"Right. Too many private performances in that claustrophobic grotto!"

The friends imbibed the atmosphere and once outdoors again, they talked at length about the strange, tortured personality responsible for the cave. It was based on the blue grotto of Capri. Special lights installed by Ludwig could change the grotto from Capri blue to Venus red. It was, Rick and Megan agreed, a unique homage to Wagner.

17

AFTER A JOLLY DINNER at the Ella Restaurant on nearby Luisenstrasse and return to the Paleo house, Alyk, as his Dzhin and Tigr called him, took his "island boys" to see their workroom space. Proudly, he showed them the studio in which they would be setting up their camera equipment and 3D printer. He had already installed the requested camera tripod and large easel. He had placed full spectrum soft box lighting with polarized sheets on either side of the tripod and set them at angles of forty-five degrees to the easel opposite. He had also supplied the outsize vat, four hairdryers, and rolls of bubble wrap his friends required. Unlike their apartment on the second floor, their studio was on the ground floor right next to Miesel's framing room. There he had already assembled a trove of large twentieth-century canvasses ranging from the 1930s to the 1940s. Culled from various antique stores around town, it was their size and their frames that mattered, not their anonymous creators or indifferent subject matter.

Alyk was gratified at the island boys' reaction and lingered, making conversation as the two convivial men unpacked their equipment and meticulously set it up. He was justly gratified when they expressed their thanks and hearty approval of the equipment he had assembled.

Then he led his friends down past the building's impressive wine cellar and into the cavernous subbasement which, except for a narrow walkway, was packed with compressed clay soil from floor to ceiling. There, to their admiration, he showed off his own work to them.

They talked about the largesse of their mutual patron and his devotion to task. His utopian ideas were infectious and all three men were longtime converts to his patriotic cause.

"When do we obtain the artworks?" Dzhim asked, eager to go to work.

"Friday evening."

18

MUNICH'S NEWEST ART GALLERY, The Blue Rider at Hohenzollerngasse 36, was very near the church of Saint Ursula.

Right in the *heart* of Schwabing, Laszlo Togarassy congratulated himself for the 100th time. A tall, gray-haired, and impetuous man in his mid-seventies, he knew it had been a question of being at the right place at the right time. He had been discussing potential rentals with his real estate agent when notice of the available new property came in. The space was never advertised. Togarassy instantly snapped it up, even though the monthly rent was high. It was worth it to be in the center of Schwabing, where bohemians and the wealthy inter-mingled and the arts were of primary interest. It was a real coup, Laszlo told himself.

And now there was a new element. His wife Iris had described to him how she had suddenly been forced off the road and into a ditch by a motorcyclist and her subsequent acquaintance with an American art history professor who seemed to be extremely knowledgeable about the Blue Rider, and Kandinsky in particular. She had urged the woman and her travel companion—a kindly physician who successfully reset the dislocated shoulder she had suffered in the mishap—to visit the gallery.

Laszlo was concerned. How would the professor react to his exhibition? Would she understand the motive, the rationale for it? He now had a few more paintings he could add and a number he should, perhaps, subtract.

Laszlo walked out onto the street, stood in front of his elegant gallery, and looked appraisingly at the eye-catching window display with its sign: *Hommage à Kandinsky*. Yes, if an expert were to visit his show, it might be wise to continue keeping the possibly offensive ones in the backroom gallery. By closing just one door it could be easily shut off from the main exhibition space. Yes, that would be best. No point in courting trouble.

19

"THIS IS THE BEST IRISH PUB in Schwabing," the obese man in a hoodie and blue jeans said over his shoulder as he held open the door of the noisy Nikolaistrasse establishment for his companion, who was of slighter build and also wearing jeans and a hoodie. He had taken the hour's flight from Berlin to Munich earlier that morning. Now, clothes wet from the unexpected shower, the two men looked eagerly around the crowded room.

"Hey, grab the empty corner table back there and I'll get the drinks," Walter Krankenhauer commanded his guest after assessing things.

Ottkar Hasstmann grunted assent and strode quickly to the unoccupied table and sat down, his back to the wall. He looked around the room. It was noisy and filled with mostly university students. It was certainly quieter at the corner table Walter had spotted and they would be able to converse without others overhearing. A group of screeching girls was holding forth at the bar.

"Here we are," Walter said, placing two bottles of cold red ale on the table. He sat facing his visitor from Berlin.

"So. What's going on with the Neue Nationalgalerie's Kandinskys, Ottkar?"

"The news is not good, I'm afraid. We have identified all of them, even those in storage, but now they are being lent out to other museums because of such lengthy restoration going on at the Nationalgalerie. We have found one large, pretentious one on display at the Bauhaus-Archiv Museum, however, so we are ready to participate on K Day, whenever that is, albeit at a less dramatic level."

"*Ja*, that's why I asked you to come to Munich, Ottkar. Ever since we discovered the computers at our party headquarters have been hacked, I've had to be extra careful with sensitive information. Same goes for our phones. We think they are being tapped."

"That's uncanny. We too have been attacked. Malware. Our phones as well. We know for sure they are being tapped. Think it might be the government?"

"Who else?"

"*Ach*! Ever since they closed down our rally in Frankfurt last month we've been under scrutiny."

"Our liberal government still hatefully calls us neo-Nazis, even though we no longer call ourselves that."

Walter bent over toward his Berlin comrade and began the tirade he had been directing at his Munich followers so successfully.

"*Germany for Germans* is something every right-thinking German ought to care about. Not allowing foreigners and refugees to overtake our cities, our customs, our language, our art!"

"I hear you, Walter, I hear you."

"And that means clearing our language of foreign terms, especially English words. Our beautiful language has, as they say, become *Denglisch*—Deutsch-English."

"Yes. Like *das Baby* instead of *Säugling* and *das Basement* in place of *Untergeschoss*."

"Or combining German and English like *der Zoom* of a camera lens, or *abgefuckt*. Why even Chancellor Agata Merle uses the word *Shitsuck*! She seems to have no idea what the English really means."

"It gets even more serious when you consider that the new sick joke is: 'why speak German well if you can speak English poorly?'"

"We have got to purify our language the same way we must cleanse our art of foreign works, new or old."

"Yes, art, especially art. We have too many non-German artists taking up precious space in our major museums. You look at Frankfurt, Cologne, Hamburg, Hannover, Darmstadt, Stuttgart, Düsseldorf, Leipzig, Dresden, even Nuremberg." Ottkar stopped, out of breath and incensed. Walter took over.

"That's why I think our simultaneous protest against Kandinsky holdings in museums all across the country will be so successful. Everybody knows who that snooty Russian was. We are ready. And, Ottkar, next we'll target his Russian friend Jawlensky and that Russian broad of his, Marianne von Werefkin."

The two men took refreshing swigs from their ale bottles and were silent for a while, nodding their heads and smiling at each other in mutual understanding and satisfaction.

"So, obviously, if you invited me to fly down from Berlin, you can now, in confidence, tell me the K Day date?"

Walter glanced around him, then leaned toward Ottkar.

"Friday, late afternoon, just as museums are closing."

"Excellent! To our success." Ottkar raised his bottle.

"To our success. To *Germany for Germans.*" Walter clinked his bottle against Ottkar's.

20

STOPPING IN GARMISCH for lunch before tackling the Strauss villa, Megan and Rick had found by chance a garden restaurant that featured waffles. It was called Hoffmanns Bistro & Wafflehouse. They had thought they were not all that hungry, but one look at the menu changed how they felt. From a long list of appetizing sounding waffles, they settled on dividing three: a spinach one with feta cheese, a Caprese with homemade pesto, and for dessert, a waffle heaped with sliced strawberries. A feast indeed.

"I always heard that Strauss was a Nazi collaborator," Rick said between gluttonous bites.

"Well, that reputation stuck for many decades after World War II, even though he was cleared of collusion. Toscanini summed up how people felt about him when he said something like: 'To the composer I take off my hat; to the man, I put my hat back on.'"

"Oh, that's wonderful. But *was* he a collaborator?"

"Let me put it this way. His life was his music and to ensure its performance he was open to compromise. For example, in early Nazi days, because of his international fame, Strauss accepted appointment as president of the State Music Bureau—one from which he was soon fired, by the way. And as a conductor, he still conducted Mendelssohn and Mahler—Jewish composers banned by the Nazis. And then too his own daughter-in-law Alice was Jewish and when she was placed under house arrest at the Garmisch villa, he used his connections and influence to ensure her safety and that of her two sons—his grandchildren. Just think. The grandsons were called 'dirty Jews' and stoned on their way to school!"

"Was he able to protect them all through the war?"

"Yes. But not Alice's extended family members. Some thirty of them died in the Theresienstadt concentration camp. I think one grandchild still lives at the villa. We might see him there today if that's so. And when I visited the villa umpteen decades ago, I was ushered in by the daughter-in-law herself."

"That must have been thrilling."

"Actually not. I had no idea who she was at the time. Only found out later. But she was very kind to me and let me photograph Strauss's desk and piano and a painting of him conducting."

"Who did the painting?"

"I'm trying to think. Can't remember at the moment. It will come if I don't try. That's the way it is when you get older."

"Heck, I have to do that now, too," confessed Rick, finishing his espresso.

They paid the bill and returned to their station wagon. Some minutes later, with the help of an online map, and after passing Alpine villas built by other wealthy Munich residents, they pulled up in front of the Strauss villa. Far back from the road, it was a large, white, three-story affair with a round turret on one side and a red roof. Majestic trees, a long green lawn, and the mountainous Alpine backdrop framed the house.

Things were not as Megan remembered from those many decades ago when she had simply gone up to the door and knocked. Now there was a discreet sign giving the times of the next opening for visitors. They were in luck. They had only fiteen minutes to wait.

"I wonder what happened to the villa when the Americans arrived at the end of the war?" Rick asked.

"Well, now, that's a most interesting story. American troops arrived at the house to seize it on the very day Hitler committed suicide. An eighty-year-old Strauss faced them calmly and announced he was Richard Strauss, composer of *Der Rosenkavalier* and *Salome*. Amazingly, the soldier in charge knew classical music and was very fond of Strauss operas!"

"You're kidding."

"No. After that everyone wanted his autograph and they walked around the inside of the villa admiring things. From then on Strauss had visits from American soldiers. One of them, a certain John de Lancie was an oboe player and knew Strauss's orchestral writing for oboe extremely well. So he asked Strauss if he had ever considered writing a concerto for oboe. Strauss's answer was a simple 'No.' But the American's question stuck in the composer's mind and six months later he actually wrote one!"

"Did the oboist soldier know?"

"Yes. Strauss made sure that the American rights went to de Lancie who was then with the Philadelphia Symphony Orchestra. One thing I remember though is so many of the American soldiers asked Strauss who the Beethoven bust he had in his living room was, that he whispered to a friend: 'if anybody else asks me who that is, I'm going to say it's Hitler's father!'"

"Ha! Did Strauss compose any new music after the Hitler years?"

"Definitely. The year the war ended he wrote a string elegy, a lament for what the Nazis had destroyed—German culture. He called it *Metamorphosen*."

"Honestly, Megan, one would think you were a musicologist rather than an art historian."

"Ha! Would that I could have been. Music has always been my first love. You know that I play flute and guitar. And piano by ear, but I am truly only an amateur. I don't have the brain for music theory. I absolutely love reading *biographies* of composers, more, frankly, than even those about artists, but as for analyzing a musical score in detail, it all seems like math for me."

"Aren't mathematicians frequently good at music? I've heard so at least."

"I think that theory has been somewhat debunked, although you can't deny that many mathematicians are good pianists. And Albert Einstein played the violin. Did you know that?"

Before Rick could answer, the front door to the villa was opened and a smiling woman dressed in a dirndl greeted the small group of visitors that had formed around Rick and Megan.

They were led around the ground floor with pauses by Strauss's desk, his grand piano, a double profile portrait of him behind his teacher Alexander Ritter. On another wall hung a large oil painting of the composer in later life, seated in the orchestra pit of an opera house with baton raised, conducting. What Megan had forgotten was the number of small antique paintings of religious subjects that graced the walls. On display in a standing all-glass cabinet was Strauss's travel jacket, gloves, and hat, along with his small kit of necessities. One wall displayed a musical manuscript sheet written in the composer's own hand and in front of another wall was a beautifully rendered maquette of a white and gold set for *Der Rosenkavalier*.

"What an enchanting mockup," said Rick, studying the detailed scale model appreciatively.

On another wall was the dramatic contemporary poster by Lovis Corinth for Strauss's early opera *Elektra*.

"I don't remember seeing all these neat things last time," Megan whispered as she recorded images on her Google Glass, since photography was not allowed.

The tour group was taken to see the second floor of the villa with its many bedrooms for Strauss's extended family. On one of the bed tables was a fascinating photograph of a still youngish Strauss with his wife, Pauline, and their teenage son Franz. Megan, always alert to body language, directed Rick's attention to the fact that Richard, on the left, had his hand half hidden in his jacket pocket and was leaning back ever so slightly, while on the right, young Franz, a wan expression on his face, was leaning backward against a table. It was as though both were trying to avoid not only the enormous hat Pauline, in the center, was wearing, but also one of her famous tirades. The professional soprano ruled the nest at home, switching in a second from constant gabbing to petulant outbursts of temper. She had her left hand on her hip in the photograph and the gesture spoke volumes. Megan recalled a Pauline story.

"There's a famous story Alma Mahler tells about being in a theater box in Vienna with Pauline while one of Strauss's early operas, *Feuersnot*, was being premiered in Vienna. She began critiquing it loudly, saying it didn't have an original note in it, and afterward, when Richard elatedly joined them in the box, she shouted at him that he was a thief and that he disgusted her."

"*And they stayed married?*" Rick was horrified.

"Yes. In spite of everything she was a tremendous inspiration to him in his music. He even wrote a *Symphonia Domestica* which was autobiographical."

After the tour Megan and Rick roamed around to the back of the villa admiring the well-kept grounds.

"I've never seen a Strauss opera or heard one of his tone poems, but now I certainly have that on my list of things to do," Rick said as they returned to the car.

"I'm willing to bet you already know one of his tone poems."

"How so?"

"You ever seen *2001: A Space Odyssey*?"

"Of course. Why?"

"Remember the dramatic music that opens with a trumpet fanfare?" Megan dramatically hummed the five perfect intervals she meant—three up, two down.

"Yes."

"Well Stanley Kubrick used the opening of Strauss's tone poem *Thus Spake Zarathustra* for that film."

"That means there are two Strausses in the film because I remember for sure that Johann Strauss's *Blue Danube* waltz is played also, you know, during the space station docking scene."

"You're so right. I'd forgotten about that. And, I don't mean to sound professorial, but you do know, don't you, that the two Strausses—Johann and Richard—are not related?"

"Yes, my dear professoressa. I do know that much." Rick did sound a bit offended and Megan hastened to mollify him by switching the subject to Nietzsche's historical novel of the same name as Strauss's inspiration, commenting on the full title, *Thus Spake Zarathustra: A Book for All and None.*

They had returned to the car and stood for a minute, taking a last look at the villa in which Strauss had lived for forty years until his death at eighty-five in 1949.

"So, what do we do now?" Megan asked her friend who was looking unusually thoughtful.

"Hmm?"

"I asked what you would like to do now."

"Oh, I'm sorry. I was just thinking about how much Annette would have loved seeing this villa."

He was talking about his wife. Megan gave him some time, then made a suggestion she thought might take his mind off what could not be changed.

"Listen, we could visit another Ludwig site if you like before we leave. It's just about six miles south of here."

"Oh? What's that? We haven't talked about a Ludwig castle being here."

"Well, it's the least known of his buildings. Thought I'd surprise you, now that we're near it."

"What's it called?"

"It's known as the King's House on Schachen."

"Oh?"

"Yes, and it has a superb view of the Zugspitze."

"Have you been there?"

"No. Just read about it."

"What's it look like?"

"It's a rather simple timber-framed hunting lodge type structure with a balcony. The ground floor and exterior are supposed to be unpretentious, but the second floor is all extravagant decoration in a Turkish style and it's furnished with divans and a central fountain. I read that Ludwig rarely used it except to celebrate birthdays and on his name day."

"Sounds intriguing. Let's go."

"Okay. I'm game if you are. Oh, one thing I should tell you. It's a three-and-a-half-hour hike from the road."

Rick burst into laughter. His sad mood was dissipated and Megan was grinning with pleasures.

21

AFTER THE CONCLUSION of his prolonged, productive dinner with the associate director of the Lenbach House, Igor Rasputin acted on an impulse. Instead of returning to his Mandarin Oriental Hotel suite, with its corner window view of Munich's twin-towered Frauenkirche, he would walk over to Paleo, greet his agents Dzhim and Tigr, and see how the two hermits were taking to the big city. His Munich-based agent Miesel had probably shown them their studio space and second floor suite by now. And all their requested equipment was in place, thanks to Miesel.

Rasputin turned into Richard-Wagner-Strasse, glanced at the back of the Lenbach House, and entered the front door of Paleo unobserved. He could hear cheerful voices and walked toward the sound.

"May I?" he said as he walked into the studio he had allotted the hermits.

"Igor Igorevich Rasputin!" they cried almost in unison, excited to see the man who was paying them such a handsome wage for three nights' work. In Dzhim and Tigr's case the extra money was more than welcome, as their own funds were being drastically depleted due to some unexpected medical expenses Dzhim had incurred.

Alyksandr waved his hand toward the boys.

"You see, Sir, our islanders have made themselves quite at home here. The cameras are ready to go."

"And our apartment upstairs is *luxurious*," added Tigr happily. "We hope to stay through the week if convenient with you. So much to see and do in Munich." He had never completely adjusted to life on Dzhim's Amiinyi island.

"Of course, you may stay on. As long as you like until the end of the month. I will have no more use for this place after our business is done. Excellent. Excellent. Now look here. I have scheduled a moving van to arrive at precisely five on Saturday morning. Does that give you enough time?"

"If the artworks are here by nine o'clock Friday evening, yes," answered Dzhim.

Rasputin looked at Alyksandr who nodded vigorously in affirmation.

"Explain to me this enormous vat here." Rasputin looked commandingly at Dzhim.

"This is where we develop the gossamer overlay sheets that we then immediately transfer to the old canvasses Alyk has been working on in his studio. Heat is then briefly used to bind and blend."

"And all the canvasses have now been partially scraped, primed, and prepared for transfer. I need just one more day for final sizing of the frames," Alyksandr added confidently.

"With all the old paintings I bought for this job, I now have an abundance of both canvases and frames."

"Then all is well and I will bid you gentlemen good night. Until Friday evening."

"Until Friday evening," the men echoed merrily, watching the bald man with the brusque manner disappear down the hall.

22

KATRINA KELLER, justifiably excited, was pondering her extraordinary dinner discussion with the persuasive man from Odessa and their Kandinsky agreement. On the one hand, she suddenly had the unique possibility of staging a blockbuster exhibition featuring unknown works by one of the stars of her museum's collection. For the public and scholars to see Kandinsky works unknown to the West represented an amazing opportunity. On the other hand, she could not help but feel the "trade" arrangement was not quite fair. The man did not even ask for an exchange show in Odessa of the Lenbach House Kandinskys in return. Intuitively, he had understood the difficulties such a request could make. He desired only permission to photograph her museum's rich trove of the painter's work, using the latest scientific techniques. And then exhibit them, clearly marked as photographs of Kandinsky works in the Lenbach collection, in his museum when it opened. Such a modest request.

She must remember to tell her American colleague Megan Crespi about the exciting prospect when she arrives in Munich on Friday.

23

APART FROM SAILING to distant ports on his luxury yacht, gambling was impulsive young Heinrich von Frauenberg's greatest passion. Recently, there had been one million euros in his bank account, thanks to the bizarre agreement concerning his home, Paleo. The building was to be exclusively accessible to that eccentric Russian, or whatever he was, businessman. Now Heinrich had been able to indulge in his gambling passion and all that came with it—women, alcohol, and drugs. He was literally on a high and had cracked lips to show for it.

The young Baron's favorite gambling site was on the French Riviera in the small sovereign state of Monaco and its Monte Carlo casino La Rascasse. Like a dream come true, the casino was conveniently located at the very foot of the dock where his yacht was moored at the far end. But right now, after a week of betting and winning, things were not going well at all for Heinrich. After four grueling hours, he had lost a fabulous ace-high four-of-a-kind hand when, after two 20,000-euro raises, he confidently called what astoundingly turned out to be a royal flush—the highest hand in five-card poker. Heinrich had been so certain in thinking his opponent was following Sun Tzu's dictum:

"All warfare is based on deception." But he was wrong and now he had a 40,000-euro debt.

Yes, he could cover the debt and the casino would float him for thirty days without interest, but it was going to take a huge bite out of his funds. And the fortune from the Russian that seemed so vast a week ago had already dwindled appreciatively without the addition of a 40,000-euro debt. To say nothing of the money he had dropped around town the past few days wooing various young women to be his nighttime companions. Also docking charges had risen unexpectedly and he had had to let one of his employees go, bringing his yacht service staff down to just two.

What to do?

The answer came to him easily. He would return to Munich and hunt down the man who had "leased" Paleo from him. Tell him he had underpaid and demand more. A lot more. He lit up his short crack pipe and inhaled. Yes, he would fly to Munich that very Friday.

24

OBERAMMERGAU HAD NOT BEEN a disappointment although the two friends did quite different things. Rick was eager to test his hiking stamina and after agreeing to meet in two hours at the top of Mount Laber—Megan by cable car, he by the steep mountain trail over the Schartenkopf—they went their separate ways.

First studying online what to see in Oberammergau, Megan was surprised to learn that there was an "Eisenhower Museum." Apparently during and just after World War II, the owner of the house where some Eisenhower papers and paraphernalia were, had managed the US Army's recreation center.

The Eisenhower cache captured Megan's attention because as a student at Barnard College eons ago, she once had a personal encounter with the then soon-to-be America's thirty-fourth president. The fall of her freshman year he was serving as president of Columbia University and when Christmas loomed, a group of classmates joined her and her accordion in serenading Eisenhower in front of his residence, which was on the far side of the Barnard/Columbia campus. Their singing was heard inside the house and after a few minutes Eisenhower and his wife opened the front door and stood smiling and listening to the carols while Megan accompanied them on her accordion. Soon the press arrived asking questions while photographers circled round taking shots.

"Please sing 'Rudolph the Red-Nosed Reindeer,'" Mamie Eisenhower requested. Embarrassed, Megan had to admit she did not know the song. The next day in her Barnard mailbox there was a large envelope containing the sheet music to the song and a note from the publisher saying simply: "The next time you are asked to play 'Rudolph,' you'll have the music." There was also a surprising moment of fame. A photo of Megan and her accordion appeared the following day in Milan's *Corriere della Sera* where her Italian grandparents spotted it with the caption: "A girl of Italian descent, Megan Crespi, serenades the president-elect of the United States."

I really must remember to tell Rick my Eisenhower story, Megan thought as she drove to the unpretentious Ettalerstrasse house containing the general's items. She was a bit disappointed by the small exhibit, but it had sparked an amusing memory.

After the Eisenhower intermezzo, she located the Oberammergau Museum. It was a three-floor affair with intricate Bavarian wood carvings, ranging from large to miniature, right down to an eighth of an inch. Megan took the opportunity to sit down for some twenty minutes during an interesting video showing the Passion Play from beginning to end.

Inspired by the recorded spectacle, Megan exited the museum and walked past a row of frescoed building facades interspersed with balconies and colorful shutters. She took a look inside the actual theater where the play was held, but the large, efficient auditorium did not inspire any lingering.

Her final goal was the birthplace of the early twentieth-century author who had written such genial descriptions of Bavarian life, Ludwig Thoma. She remembered one book in particular, *A Municher in Heaven*. The three-story house had a colorful façade decorated with a fresco showing people in various groups and activities, including a woodcarver working on a large Madonna-and-child sculpture. The great wooden roof overhang protected a large wooden balcony, and the entire building exuded the cheerful homeliness of Thoma's writing. A good goal with which to end Megan's tour of the small town, a modest endeavor that had nevertheless taken up almost two hours.

Returning to the car, she drove along a stream to the Laber cable car station, parked, and waited in a noisy line for the next lift. It was a spectacular ride up to the top where she drank in the 360-degree view that included the distant silhouette of Munich and a near vista of Ludwig's Schachen House and the Zugspitze. Certainly, it was considerably cooler at the top, but Megan, always prepared for temperature emergencies, pulled out her black wool beret with brim and a matching scarf for her throat.

She did not see any sign of Rick on the viewing platform or at the steps leading up to it from the hiker's trail so she went inside the small, cozy restaurant and looked searchingly around. There at a table for two next to one of the great panorama windows sat Rick, his cheeks bright red from his exertions. He had taken his jacket off and hung it on the back of his chair. Megan waved, caught his attention, and in another second plopped down on the chair opposite him. Exchanging stories and sipping draft beer, they ordered from a mouth-watering menu that featured Bavarian specialties.

They began with potato soup, then ordered pretzels, Rick's with *Weisswurst* sausages, Megan's with seasoned beef patties—*Frikadellen.* For dessert, they both had plum cake and Megan recounted to Rick how the guards at the Albertina Museum in Vienna where she first studied the drawings of Egon Schiele, had all laughed at her attempts to say the German for plum cake—*Zwetschgenkuchen.*

The next cable car back down to town would be leaving in fifteen minutes, so the two mountaineers drank up their espressos and joined the jolly line forming for return to ground level.

"How long do you think it will take us to get to Murnau," Rick asked.

"It's so close, really. I figure about twenty-five minutes or so."

"Great," Rick breathed in relief. "I'm really ready to check into our hotel that's just 'two minutes' away from Münter's house. And guess what? This time *I'm* the one who can't wait to go to sleep!"

25

RAISA SOKOLOVA HAD HEARD this sort of tirade before. Her employer's pathological jealousy of Igor Rasputin's success in acquiring Kandinskys for his so-called Patriots Museum. After all, Boris Zima had only recently refocused his sights on Kandinsky. He had directed his previous efforts to building up a superb collection of Jawlensky and Werefkin, Macke and Marc. The result, factoring in the three unusual Kandinsky paintings he had bought on the black market some forty-plus years ago from a shady Swiss source, was second only to the Lenbach House Museum in Munich. What made his Kandinsky works so rare was that they were portraits; hardly a major motif associated with the artist. And they were all three colorful, glowing portraits of the same person: the artist's young wife Nina. Images unknown to the world of art. Only one portrait of Nina by Kandinsky was known: a 1917 portrayal of the seventeen-year-old girl executed the year of their marriage. It showed her from the waist up, head slightly tilted, with brown hair, large, dreamy eyes, long, slender nose, and full lips. From the neck down there was very little detail. Instead a commotion of brightly colored brushstrokes took over articulation of the body.

And now, to appease Boris, Raisa reminded her ranting employer of the splendid Blue Rider collection he had already built up in Moscow—certainly superior to Rasputin's Odessa collection and certainly more accessible on the whole. Every year Boris loaned on a rotating schedule three major Blue Rider works—but no Kandinskys—to the city's world-famous Tretyakov Gallery. And after all, how many foreign tourists visited that Ukrainian outpost as compared with the hundreds of thousands who visited Moscow, the "heart" of Russia, every year?

Somewhat mollified, Boris asked her if there was anything new to report on Rasputin's movements and meetings in Munich. To this, Raisa had a positive answer.

"Indeed I have things to tell you. After his dinner with the Lenbach's associate director, I followed him and, surprisingly, instead of returning to his hotel, he walked in the direction of the museum but went one block *beyond* it, to the Richard-Wagner-Strasse. Then he entered the front door of one of the buildings on the other side of the street from the back of the museum. Now here's the strange thing: he did not ring for admittance; he opened the front door *with his own key.*"

"With his own key?"

"Yes, with his own key. That would mean either he has a friend who lives there and who has given him a spare key, or, possibly, he maintains an apartment there himself. But in that case, why is he staying at one of Munich's most expensive hotels, the Mandarin Oriental? That's where I'd tracked him the night before last and confirmed that he was a hotel guest."

"That *is* bizarre."

"And furthermore, he left the Richard-Wagner-Strasse building after some twenty minutes—I was prepared for a long wait—and returned to the Mandarin Oriental."

"Well, you are dogged, I certainly give you that."

"Of course. Thank you. I am going to continue surveying the Lenbach House because if anything concerning Kandinsky happens, if, say, a transport van pulls up to the museum's loading dock on Richard-Wagner-Strasse, we'll know something of interest is going on."

"So, you do think it's possible that Rasputin may have made an arrangement with this—what did you say the museum woman's name is?"

"Katrina Keller. I can only tell you that after a very serious and prolonged dinner, when they stood up, they shook hands as though confirming something important."

"All right, Raisa. I am absolutely sure Rasputin is up to something, so by all means continue your surveillance. On him *and* on her."

"As I told you, I've had Keller's apartment bugged, so I have her under surveillance in case she deviates from her daily routine."

"What about weekends?"

"That's when I'm out there in Schwabing myself, doing a visual as well as an audio. Keller has a ground-floor apartment at Osterwaldstrasse eighty-nine near the Englischer Garten. She goes out in the afternoon with her boy Herbert who's probably five or so. They walk to that enormous park, do a different small circuit each time, then return to the apartment. She doesn't do any grocery shopping. A nanny—a woman from Slovakia, or somewhere, named Diliana—tends the boy during the week and she does the shopping."

"So, you've established a steady routine for the woman, the nanny, and the boy. That's good."

"Yes. What I haven't ascertained yet is if the boy actually attends school or not."

"Why is that important to know?"

"In case we have to apply pressure down the line."

"Good. Raisa, I think you do have all bases covered."

"Yes, I do. Um. There is one thing about the boy, though."

"Oh?"

"There's something a little odd about his mannerisms when he's out walking. Occasionally he starts jerking his arms around. Or he kicks his legs for a few minutes. Other times he seems to be just staring ahead without focusing on anything."

"Do you think the kid is epileptic or something?"

"Might be. If he needs to be taken, that could put additional pressure on Keller to cooperate with us."

"Excellent. Long live epilepsy then."

26

FOR MUNICH NEO-NAZI PARTY BOSS Walter Krankenhauer, K Day could not come fast enough. His forty-six members were energized and ready. Only one more day to go. The plan was to initiate their protest at exactly 5:30 pm in the Königsplatz so as to attract the most attention. The huge square was always filled with tourists at this time and a protest concerning so well-known an artist as Kandinsky would certainly attract curiosity. All the slogan banners had been printed and Walter thought they were quite effective. Against a red background, large black letters spelled out the name "Kandinsky" with a broad, large red X blotting out some of the letters. Below, also in black letters, was the slogan: "Only German Art in German Museums." A second set of twenty-four posters replicated one of the Russian artist's most incomprehensible paintings—stupid circles of all sizes and colors against an ugly, meaningless black. Any child could have done it. These replicas would be set on fire after the protesters marched slowly over to the Lenbachplatz and fanned out in front of the Lenbach House Museum. The press would be covering the demonstration by then and photographs of the poster burnings would be circulated in international as well as local newspapers. Television coverage would hit the evening news broadcasts. The police would actually be protecting the protestors as they stood with their burning posters in the front of the Lenbach. Walter could already imagine how the new addition's polished copper façade would reflect the flickering flames.

It should be quite a spectacle.

27

THEIR BREAKFAST at the Klausenhof am Park Hotel in the old market town of Murnau took place at the time Rick and Megan had agreed. Exactly forty-five minutes after they had awakened and gone their separate ways—Rick to his outdoor jogging, Megan to her bed and floor exercises.

The single suite they had reserved with two beds possessed a very large bathroom and plenty of privacy. After retiring to their beds, their pillow talk had just begun when Rick, true to his declaration of being ready to go to sleep, did so. Megan stayed up a half hour longer, checking and sending out e-mails. She also looked in via her iPhone's Amcrest App at the shenanigans of her beloved Maltese dog back in Dallas. Button was staying at her sister's house and when Megan checked out the scene she was able to watch her little darling at play with Tina's four Japanese Spaniels. Such a welcome spectacle. Button, who had been blind for the past couple of years, was nevertheless quite self-sufficient and when he accompanied his human on a recent trip to Scandinavia concerning the theft of several Edvard Munch paintings, he had actually pointed the way to an amazing discovery regarding the perplexing case.

The Klausenhof am Park's online claim had proven to be true. It really was only two minutes from the hotel to Münter's Yellow House on the Kottmüllerallee. But since Megan's visit to the elderly painter so many decades ago, the barnlike building that stood on a sloping hillside with a circular garden in front, had changed. Changed for the better. From the red shingled roof and freshly painted yellow-and-white wooden exterior with its light blue shutters, it was obvious that the country house had been substantially renovated. The casement windows were scaled down, giving the house a sense of height with what looked like, from the front, three stories. Because of the house's placement on a steep incline with its yellow basement dug deep into the slope, the cellar constituted another floor with window and door opening onto the garden area in front as one approached the house from town. This was the *Millionenkeller*—Cellar of Millions—where Münter had successfully hidden her priceless trove of Blue Rider paintings from the Nazis.

"You can't see it from here, Rick, but there are train tracks in the valley below the garden. The Munich-Garmisch line. That's where Kandinsky painted his wonderful picture of a black train with its rippling black shadow streaking across the bottom of the picture past the green landscape and two heavily laden telegraph/telephone poles."

"I remember that dramatic picture with its puffs of white smoke very distinctly. Above, in the distance, you can see a few houses on the other side of town, and on the lower left there's a small woman dressed in red. She has blonde hair and is waving a white scarf at the train."

"Really? I don't remember a woman's figure being in that painting," Megan looked at Rick with admiration. Then she pointed to the hill opposite them.

"If you look straight across from here you can spot not only the white Schloss on the left, but, on the right, the old town church as well—see its onion bulb tower? When we drive over to visit Münter's grave, you'll see that, right at the spot where she is buried, you can look across and see the Yellow House here quite clearly. It's an exciting photo to take. And I like thinking that she is somehow looking back at the home she lived in for so long."

They turned back and looked again at the Yellow House, so familiar to them from Münter's loving images of it. Viewed from the east, as they were looking at it now, there did indeed seem to be an extra level—the lowest one painted yellow. But that really was just the cellar, set in the embankment, Megan told Rick again, and when they looked at the house from the side or the rear, he would immediately see it was a deep cellar sunk in the gradient with just a band of its yellow showing. Rick remained dubious.

As they continued to gaze at the house, there was one element Megan did not remember or recognize. And that was a wooden picket fence, about four feet high, surrounding the house and its grounds. Megan was absolutely sure the fence had not been there before.

When they walked up the slope to the back of the house, where she had entered on her previous visit some fifty years earlier, the fence rose some two feet higher. In the middle of the fence, a padlocked solid wooden door faced them. On it was a large metal plaque that read forbiddingly:

PRIVATE PROPERTY. No trespassing.
For artist Gabriele Münter,
visit the Schlossmuseum

"My god, so it's true what Iris Togarassy told us. The Münter house can no longer be visited. This is outrageous!" Megan was furious.

"Do you think all her paintings and personal things have been moved to the Schlossmuseum then?" Rick was hopeful.

"Hm. I know that a number of paintings held back from her colossal gift to the Lenbach went to the local museum here. I'm not sure about her personal things though." Megan looked at the Yellow House again.

"You know, Rick, still and all I'd like to at least peek through a window of the house."

"Oh, oh. Come on now, Megan. The sign definitely says no trespassing."

"I know, but I want to see if any of her things might possibly be still inside."

"And how are you going to do that?"

"Let's see what the grounds look like on the far side of the house," Megan said, immediately heading off in that direction. Rather unwillingly, Rick followed slowly behind her.

"Aha! Looky here!" Megan pointed to an expanse of wire fencing affixed to wooden posts spaced some six feet apart. At one of the posts near them the wiring was severely sagging, almost unattached. On the other side of the sloping hill several beautiful brown horses were grazing. Before Rick could say anything, Megan had hoisted her right leg over the drooping wire, then her left, and was headed straight for the house.

"I'll be right back," she sang out reassuringly.

The front of the house was not as she remembered either. A blue lattice encompassed a blue wooden balcony on the second floor which was set under a hipped roof. But the narrow entry door below was still in place on the left and next to it, a tall triple-paned window. It took just a moment for Megan to press her face to the middle pane of glass. What she saw was encouraging. The winding wooden stairway leading up to the next floor was still there. And it was in very good shape. Megan knew that the stairway panel facing the steps had Kandinsky's stenciled fantasy frieze of miniature mounted riders on it. On the floor by the staircase she spotted part of a child's toy train set and train track. And on the far wall she could see just enough of the bottom of a framed painting to realize it had to be a self-portrait by Münter, one she knew very well from her first visit to the house.

That was all she needed. After taking one Google Glass and one iPhone close-up shot each, she raced back to the wire fencing where Rick was anxiously awaiting her. She was triumphant.

"The interior looks refurbished. The Kandinsky staircase is still in place. But more importantly, I saw part of a *Münter self-portrait* on the wall! Now all we have to do is discover the new owner of what was formerly a state museum."

"Possibly you could find that out over at the Schlossmuseum." Rick was eager to get his athletic companion back across the fence wires. He reached out a hand to help her and was gratified when she took it.

"Good thing I always wear slacks," she commented.

"That's right. You were always in slacks when you taught us."

"You know when women began wearing slacks at SMU?" Megan asked.

"I hadn't thought about it."

"Well, you remember my mother founded the Italian Department there, don't you?"

"I do."

"She began the fad locally after slipping and breaking her arm on campus. Getting into a dress was difficult for her, so she began wearing slacks and never looked back. Soon other women faculty members began doing the same, and by the time I joined the university almost all the female faculty members were wearing slacks."

"And the pace has not *slackened*," punned Rick.

"That was nicely horrible," Megan grinned. "But I can also tell you that

I remember the days, while I was still teaching in New York, when the Frick Library had a sign at the door forbidding entry to women in slacks."

"Tsk, tsk, now that's real discrimination," Rick pretended to be shocked.

They took a number of photographs of the house, especially the garden area where Münter and Kandinsky had posed for photographs of themselves gardening in country dress—she in a dirndl, he in lederhosen. Then they strolled back down the hill and walked along the Burggraben till they got to the white Schlossmuseum. This Schloss definitely looked more like a multistory house than a castle or a palace, Rick commented in disappointment as they entered.

Before looking at the collection, Megan politely asked the entrance guard if she could talk to someone from the director's office. She slipped one of her business cards into the guard's hands. The woman went over to a house phone, spoke into it for a minute while reading from the card, then returned smiling.

"Herr Doktor Friedel will be with you shortly." A few minutes later a young man approached them as they waited by the small book shop. He was smiling broadly.

"Professor Doktor Crespi! How nice to have you visit us. I know of your excellent work on Kandinsky and the other Blue Rider painters."

"Thank you, Herr Doktor Friedel. Before we came here we, of course, went to the Yellow House, but we were stunned to see it is no longer a museum. Is there any way it might be visited?"

"I am sorry, but no one is allowed to visit the house now. And the party to whom the Bavarian State turned over the premises insists on anonymity."

"But surely you at the Schlossmuseum know who it is. Right?"

"I'm sorry, but I cannot say one way or the other." Friedel shifted his weight uneasily from one leg to the other.

"Well, may I ask you this, Herr Doktor? Did some or all of the artworks from the Yellow House pass into the Schlossmuseum's already large Münter collection after state ownership of the house was transferred to a private individual?"

"Not to my knowledge, no." Friedel answered immediately and definitively. After a few pleasantries, the young man left and Megan and Rick moved toward the exhibition rooms.

"So the big question now is, if the paintings that were in the Yellow House didn't go here or to the Lenbach, then where the heck are they?" Megan whispered to Rick, who rolled his eyes upward and shrugged his shoulders in shared frustration.

"I can't believe I didn't think to check the Münter House online before we left," Megan chastised herself.

Inside the galleries a pleasant surprise awaited them. A large and permanent exhibit of Münter's art was handsomely installed in both the south and west wings on the second and third floors of the museum. And an entry placard stated that there were over eighty of her paintings, drawings, and graphics in the collection. The works dated from 1902 to the year of her death, 1962, thus covering all periods of her work. Another placard stressed that the Yellow House was not purchased by Kandinsky but by Münter in 1909, one year after it had been built. Fortifying why it was referred to as the "Russian House" by the villagers and in most literature, was the fact that not only Kandinsky but also his two Russian compatriots Jawlensky and Werefkin often visited there, discussing art in the evenings, strolling the streets and painting in the countryside around Murnau during the daytime.

"I'm really glad they explain that," Megan said triumphantly. "I once illustrated an article on the Blue Rider with one of the postcards sent to Münter addressed to her simply: 'Care of the Russian House, Murnau.' As though the house belonged to Kandinsky."

"Ha! That's a good one. Of course, in those days home ownership was uniformly presumed to be by the male inhabitant," Rick commented quickly, seeing that Megan's feminist hackles were rising as she recalled the, to her mind, sexist postcard.

"Look over there," he said. "That's a variation on Münter's portrait of Kandinsky at his harmonium in the Murnau house."

"So it is. What fun. It seems to be a reworking of the same painting I saw when I visited Münter, lo, those many years ago." They began walking around the gallery looking at the artist's other paintings.

Megan's attention was caught by a facsimile of Münter's handwriting penned in 1957 concerning her relationship to the little town of Murnau. She translated for Rick.

"'But never did I have such an abundance of views as here in Murnau between the lake and the Hochgebirge, between Hügelland and Moos.'"

"And she lived here all her life, then? I never did follow up on her personal life. Just loved her paintings."

Megan whistled softly, shaking her head.

"It's complicated, Rick. I did not teach our class about this aspect of her life. Didn't want to take the focus off her art. She and Kandinsky, who was eleven years older, were together twelve years—first she was his student in Munich in nineteen-two, then his partner. They became engaged. This in spite of the fact that he was already married to his cousin, Anna Chemyakin."

"*What!*"

"Yeah, I know. Shocking. Kandinsky did finally divorce Anna in nineteen-eleven—a bit late, I'd say. Anyhow, he and Gabriele traveled around Europe and North Africa for four years, then settled in Murnau in *her* house which she bought because *he* loved it. That's when they began to host other Blue Rider artists and where the famous Blue Rider *Almanac* was conceived."

"Oh, I remember that. You showed us pages from it in class. Full of folk art the Blue Rider artists found inspiring. So how long did they stay in the Yellow House then?"

"Only until World War I broke out in July of nineteen-fourteen. Because he was Russian, Kandinsky had to flee Germany. So, he moved to Switzerland at the beginning of August that same year. And Münter, who referred to herself as 'Frau Münter-Kandinsky' by then, went with him. She considered him her civil husband. But things didn't go well in their new environment and in November he left for Moscow and she went to neutral Sweden, waiting for him to join her there.

"But he procrastinated. Over the next three years his letters got shorter and fewer in between. He was indifferent to her cries of loneliness. Then early in nineteen-seventeen, the news filtered in: he had just married. In his own words later, he had fallen in love with the sound of a young woman's *voice* on the telephone."

"You are kidding."

"No, I am not. She was Nina Andreevskaya, daughter of a general, and they married in February of that year. Wanna know how old Nina was?" Megan looked demandingly at Rick. He took the bait willingly.

"How old?"

"*Seventeen.*"

"Yikes! And how old was Kandinsky then?"

"A few months shy of fifty."

"So, he was thirty-plus years older than she was. Did the marriage last?"

"Yes, it did, actually. Right up to Kandinsky's death in Paris in nineteen-forty-four. And Nina lived almost forty years more, handling his legacy and living the high life. Mostly in Paris, surrounded by a group of sycophantic young gigolos. She was addicted to high fashion and loved owning and showing off expensive jewelry, especially large diamonds."

"Hey, wait a minute, Megan. I think I remember something about Kandinsky's widow being robbed and murdered in the bathroom of her Swiss chalet. Am I right?"

"Yes. That was Nina. She was strangled to death. Terrible. At her mountain lodge in a glitzy ski resort called Gstaad. The killer was after her jewelry collection—all of it was taken. And the murderer was never identified. It remained an unsolved crime."

"Were any of her Kandinskys taken?"

"It is *said* not. She didn't have many left by then. Most of the paintings had either been sold or given to museums like the Centre Georges Pompidou in Paris and the Lenbach in Munich. But it is known that she held a few back and the rumor is that, right after they got married, she persuaded Kandinsky, who was not much into portraiture by then, to paint her image, not just once but several times. These paintings, except for one, have totally disappeared, as I found out when tracing Kandinsky's later works. Nevertheless, I ran into a lot of gossip about their supposed existence. An unscrupulous Swiss art dealer seems to have been involved at one point. And Nina obliquely mentioned them herself in a not-to-be trusted memoir she published about Kandinsky and herself."

"So, to leave Nina and get back to our beloved Gabriele, when did she return to Murnau? It must have been so very hard for her."

"Oh, it took quite a while. She was very, very bitter. Not until the early thirties did she return. But there is a happy ending. She found a kind and intelligent companion—a Berlin art historian and critic named Johannes Eichner—and although Gabriele remained single, they lived out their lives together in the Murnau house. When we go over to the church and visit her grave, you'll see his headstone next to hers."

"So, you didn't meet him when you visited her?"

"Unh-uh, he died a few years before she did."

"Hmm. Considering the way Kandinsky treated Münter, I'm not sure I'll ever look at another Kandinsky the same way again," Rick mused as they climbed the museum stairs.

"Oh, try not to let that diminish your appreciation of his wonderful work," Megan counseled. "It's hard sometimes, but it's important to separate what you know from what you see. Same thing applies in music: some composers of heavenly music have been real scoundrels."

The friends fell silent as they walked around the rooms in which Münter was displayed. The one devoted to her graphic art also had a few local nineteenth-century works and a media alcove which Megan took advantage of, happy to sit for a few minutes.

. "Are you ready for lunch?" Rick asked after returning from looking at the art on the lower floors.

"Absolutely. Why don't we look for a place out by the lake? That could be fun. And we'd be lunching by Gabriele's beloved Staffelsee with its seven little islands." Suddenly a frown wrinkled Megan's brow and she was staring off into space.

"What's up?" Rick asked.

"I'm just thinking. You know, I told you that I could see part of what had to be a Münter self-portrait on the wall when I peeked through the window of the Yellow House."

"Right?"

"Well, now, how come a Münter artwork was there if the house is now in private hands and nothing further was acquired by the Schlossmuseum after the transfer?"

As Megan's imagination ran rampant, dramatic conspiracy theories were voiced over lunch at the Café Münter am Staffelsee. Somehow, Megan was determined to get to the bottom of what she now enthusiastically referred to as the "Münter Mystery."

After lunch, the pair returned to town and took a last walk around. Several of the street vistas that Kandinsky, Münter, and their guests had painted were still recognizable.

"See that pink house and the green one next to it on the left, and the yellow house facing us on the right with a green balcony on its third floor?" asked Megan as they came to a stop.

"Ah-ha. Very colorful."

"Well the exact same houses are in an early Murnau street view painted by Kandinsky that's in the Dallas Museum of Art. All kinds of marvelous brush dashes and dabs."

"Lucky Dallas. I'm beginning to like Kandinsky again."

"Of course you should like Kandinsky! I'm sorry I ever told you about his private life and what a jerk he was toward Münter."

"Okay, I'll try to separate the personal from the product in the future."

"But that too could be wrong, Rick. Think how knowing about van Gogh makes us understand the intensity of his art. Or knowing the facts of Egon Schiele's personal life explains his angstful self-portraits."

"What would you say in the case of Münter then? To know or not to know?"

"I'd say that her personal history did not measurably impact her art. She stopped working for some ten years, but when she began again her motifs were stable and positive. And she buried *her* feelings about Kandinsky's betrayal to the extent that, as I think I've told you, she valiantly hid the many dozens and dozens of works he'd left behind in Murnau from not one, but three searches by the Nazis. It would have meant prison or death for her if they'd been found."

"You didn't tell me there had been actual searches of her house! Good grief! Where did she hide the works exactly? You just said cellar."

"Yes, in the cellar behind a cleverly contrived second, fake wall. You have to remember that although *he* was out of her life forever, she always treasured Kandinsky's *work*. And then when she turned eighty she gave that tremendous gift to the Lenbach Museum—not only one hundred and twenty of his early paintings but dozens of his sketchbooks, letters, and several thousand pertinent photographs."

"*Thousands* of photographs?"

"Yes. Some seven thousand it was, if I remember correctly. She'd been an avid photographer ever since her young days in Texas documenting everything with her Eastman Kodak camera. Remember? I've described to you how when I visited her, she thought the camera was still in the house somewhere."

"I remember everything you say about Münter. Listen, dear Megan, I really want to visit her grave. Shall we check out of the hotel and drive over to see it now before we leave Murnau?" Rick asked.

"Of course. And from there we'll drive on to Ludwig's Lake Starnberg castle. After that it's only about thirty minutes to Munich, and we want to get there in plenty of time to find that apartment the Lenbach is housing us in. It would be good to have a little bit of time before our six o'clock dinner with Katrina Keller."

Some twenty minutes later they were staring down at the gravestones of Münter and Eichner, just to the left of Murnau's church. It was on a hill and looked across town to the hill opposite. Just as Megan had said, they could clearly see the Yellow House and Rick delighted in using the telescopic lens of his Leica. Unlike Megan, he was not one for cellphone photos.

***

Schloss Berg was on the east side of Lake Starnberg south of Munich and it only took forty minutes to reach it. When they pulled up, Rick was disappointed. Once again, a Schloss that didn't look like a castle or a palace. Only a large three-story building with high-pitched roof and small dormer windows. No crenellations, no towers. Just a large manor house.

"It really did look like a castle in Ludwig's day," Megan assured him. "In fact, to the four corner towers already there he added a fifth. And in homage of his beloved Wagner, guess what he called the tower?"

"Tristan?"

"You're incredibly close. Isolde. But the castle and its towers were badly damaged in World War II and, as you can see, it was restored in much simpler fashion."

"Okay, so let's see if we can figure out the path through the woods Ludwig took down to the lake where he drowned."

They did not have to search for long. A sign pointed the way and when upon arriving at the lake shore they saw a large cross in the water at the shallow spot where the bodies of Ludwig and his so-called keeper, Dr. von Gudden, were found floating. A little memorial chapel stood opposite the cross.

"Is it true that Ludwig had been declared insane by the time he was brought to Schloss Berg?" asked Rick.

"I don't think they used that *word*. He was pronounced medically incapable of ruling, forcefully deposed, and brought to the isolation of the castle in the middle of the night."

Megan and Rick went over the various explanations of Ludwig and von Gudden's death.

"The bothersome thing for me is that no water was found in Ludwig's lungs," Rick mused. "And Doctor von Gudden's body presented blows to the neck and head. Some people think that's pretty strong evidence that Ludwig killed him, then committed suicide."

"Or, since he was a strong swimmer, Ludwig might have begun swimming across the lake to escape his keepers at the castle, and had a heart attack."

"Then, again, why was no water found in his lungs?" Rick insisted. "And why was his body found *with* that of von Gudden's in waist-deep water near the shore?"

"Someday what really happened will be explained. Who knows whether it was murder or suicide. It seems so believable, considering Ludwig's shock at being spirited out of Munich at four in the morning and conveyed to his own Berg castle, a prisoner. It's all very sad."

They stood looking at the simple cross in silence for a few minutes.

"Well," said Rick finally, glancing at his watch that showed the time to be three-thirty, "what do you say we cheer ourselves up by continuing on to Munich? After all, we have a full agenda of things to do there before you speak on Monday, and it's already Friday."

28

HIS TRAIN FROM MONACO to Nice was delayed for an hour and a half as police searched it, responding to what turned out to be a bogus terrorist threat. Impatient Baron Heinrich von Frauenberg was furious. He would miss his flight to Munich and the chance to confront the man who had temporarily taken over his Paleo residence at such a meager price. He had hoped to catch him around dinner time, but now the next available flight would not arrive in Munich until eleven in the evening.

Oh, well, Heinrich comforted himself, perhaps it was better for him to deal with the Russian in the morning when he would be fresher. Idly, he wondered if the name Rasputin could have any link with the self-proclaimed Russian faith healer who exerted such influence over the last Czar of the Russian Empire and his German wife Alexandra. He had mesmerized the reclusive Romanov family with his calm, authoritarian prayers at the bedside of their little son Alexei, who suffered from hemophilia. Miraculously pulling the boy back from death, the monk seemed to have used only the force of his magnetic personality to heal the heir to the throne. Later theories held that he had simply stopped allowing his patient to take the blood-thinning precursor to aspirin—salicylic acid buffered with sodium. A man of immense physical strength as well as overwhelming presence, Rasputin's hold on the imperial family came to a gruesome end in 1916 when a band of jealous nobles, using first poison, then clubs, and finally revolvers, attacked him, then threw him into the freezing Neva River. Autopsy reports indicated that he was still breathing when he hit the water. Perhaps this new Rasputin would come to an equally bad end.

Heinrich's new flight to Munich was not due to leave for another four hours, so he lingered over dinner at one of the more discreet airport restaurants. The head waiter frowned at him as he entered in his black long-sleeve coveralls. Over several glasses of Vicomte Single Malt whisky, Heinrich rehearsed exactly what he would say to Rasputin concerning his demand for additional payment for use of his Paleo. It was only fair, after all.

29

FOUR LARGE VANS from four nearby German towns were parked in place near the Propylaea end of the Königsplatz in Munich. Posters for the event had not yet been unloaded. It was only five o'clock. The protestors were guided by their local host, Walter Krankenhauer, to the far side of the huge square. They stopped in front of what was now a school for music and the performing arts, but which in Nazi times had been the *Führerbau* in which the 1938 Munich Agreement was signed annexing the German-speaking part of Czechoslovakia designated as the Sudetenland.

"And this great square was just grass until Hitler times. Only then was the stone paving laid out. That's how Mussolini saw it when he joined Hitler to greet thousands of parade marchers." Krankenhauer was in his element.

The visitors were fascinated and, seeing the sincere interest, he directed their attention to low platforms that once supported two small edifices in imitation Greek style built as Honor Temples for the remains of sixteen martyrs killed in the failed Munich Beer Hall Putsch of 1923. Hitler himself was wounded and given a twenty-four-day trial which brought him precious publicity and imprisonment at Landsberg Prison, where he wrote *Mein Kampf*. The visitors nodded knowingly.

"Unfortunately," Krankenhauer concluded his narrative, "the American occupation army demolished our two Honor Temples in nineteen-forty-seven."

Seeing the look of indignation on the faces of his listeners, he attempted to lift their spirits.

"But one of the great events that took place in this square was the bonfire burning of un-German books in nineteen-thirty-three by the German Student Union. It was accompanied by music, songs, speeches, incantations, and fire oaths. An awesome spectacle."

One of the group, an eager young boy with shaved head, naïvely asked what books were "un-German." Krankenhauer answered with enthusiasm.

"Books written by pacifists, liberals, socialists, communists, religious, and Jewish authors, that's who!"

Coincidentally, the identical question had just been asked on the opposite side of the Königsplatz. Megan and Rick had checked into their Munich residence at the corner of Brienner Strasse and Richard-Wagner-Strasse and were marking time until their six o'clock dinner with Katrina Keller of the Lenbach Museum. With forty-five minutes to spare, they stood at the Propylaea end of the square, near the museum, admiring the placement of the Glyptothek, with its marvelous collection of Greek and Roman sculpture, and its sister building opposite housing the national collection of antiquities. Recalling that Nazi book burnings had occurred in the front of these two buildings, Rick turned to Megan, who was taking photos with her Google Glass, and inquired who some of the persecuted authors were.

This was a question Megan was able to answer, as she had taught about that dismal chapter in history.

"Well, for starters, the man who wrote *Bambi*, Felix Salten."

"What could possibly have been wrong with *Bambi*?"

"Nothing. It was because Salten was Jewish."

"Oh, I didn't realize that."

"Freud's works were set on fire, of course, but also Jewish authors of the past, such as Heinrich Heine, whose nostalgic poems had been set to music by

Schubert and Schumann and Brahms. The interesting thing is that a line from one of Heine's plays concerning the burning of the Quran foretold what could happen. It goes like this and I'll say it in German first: '*Das war ein Vorspiel nur, dort wo man Bücher verbrennt, verbrennt man auch am Ende Menschen.*' It means: 'That was only a prelude, there, where they burn books, they will ultimately burn men.'"

"Makes one shiver, so prescient."

"And it wasn't just authors, of course. Remember the Degenerate Art Exhibition Joseph Goebbels staged for Hitler that I showed in class? It featured works by Blue Rider members. And remember the parallel exhibition that year of nineteen-thirty-seven called the Great German Art Exhibition?"

"Yes, and I certainly do recall the riveting photos you showed of Hitler attending the Degenerate one and that the paintings there were purposely poorly hung along with sarcastic placards commenting on them."

"Right. And you know what? Once after I taught that class, emphasizing Hitler's persecution of the Jews, a student came to me during my office hour afterward and asked: 'Professor Crespi, what is a refugee?'"

"I'm not totally surprised," Rick said sadly.

Megan's attention was redirected to the Glyptothek. Its exterior lights had just flipped on and the silhouettes of a large, tight-knit throng of people heading in the direction of the Propylaea stood out against them. Rick followed Megan's gaze.

"Wonder where they're all going?" he mused.

The answer was not long in coming. After swarming over to four vans parked alongside the Luisenstrasse, the throng regrouped at exactly five-thirty in front of the famous gateway where it gave onto the Königsplatz. Only now they were holding up posters and wearing armbands with swastikas. They began to chant in unison. Passing pedestrians and tourists stopped to watch, many of them holding up their cellphones to record the event taking place in front of the Propylaea.

"What are they yelling?" Rick asked.

"They're shouting 'Only German art for German museums.' Over and over." Megan and Rick began following the crowd.

"Oh, wow, look, on some of the posters they've got Kandinsky's name partially blotted out by huge Xs." Rick began walking more quickly.

"And see over there!" Megan exclaimed, trying to match her friend's pace.

"Some of the banners have reproductions of an abstract Kandinsky painting. It's the same image on each banner."

"Maybe those neo-Nazi types think people nowadays have no idea who Kandinsky was," Rick offered.

"Perhaps that's why they have two sets of posters then? One with his name Xed out and the other with a reproduction of his work?"

"This is getting scary! We're witnessing a neo-Nazi anti-foreign artists protest and Kandinsky is the example they've chosen." Rick was fascinated. He took out his Leica and began photographing the bizarre scene.

Megan, for once, did not take photographs. She was too taken by the way in which the Königsplatz was rapidly filling up with curious onlookers. What seemed like a frenzied few seconds was actually becoming twenty minutes. Two press vans arrived and photographers were eagerly capturing the scene. Entranced, the growing crowd followed the protestors as they suddenly wheeled about and began to march through the Propylaea, waving their banners and shouting their slogan: *Nur deutsche Kunst in Deutschen Museen!* They were not marching into the square. They were *leaving* it. Taking a sharp right onto the Luisenstrasse. Where were they going? Megan realized what was happening.

They were marching to the Lenbach House Museum.

As though hypnotized, Megan and Rick followed the marchers as they swarmed past a multistoried fountain and came to a halt in front of the U-shaped, saffron-colored original villa part of the museum. The chanting continued ever more loudly. Time sped by as hysteria began building to the breaking point. Lights went on inside the museum.

The front doors of the villa opened. A man and a woman stepped out and raised their hands attempting to quiet the unruly crowd.

"Oh, my god, that's *Katrina!*" Megan gripped Rick's arm.

The man began to shout at the crowd.

"Listen to me! I am Doktor Max Mürrisch, director of this museum. You are trespassing. Leave immediately."

"You show *Danish* art!" a man's voice cried out right behind where Megan and Rick were standing at the back of the crowd. The protestors roared their anger. Then the museum woman appealed to them.

"Please! Please! We are famous around the world for our *German* art. We have Lenbach, we have the Blue Rider..."

"You have *Kandinsky!*" The man in back of them yelled again. Megan turned and gave him an angry look. A heavyset man in jeans and a hoodie, he exuded authority and seemed to be the leader of the mob, exhorting them onward, admonishing stragglers.

The next thing that happened was dumbfounding. On command, half of the demonstrators turned toward the other half holding the Kandinsky images and, producing propane vapor torches inconspicuously strapped to their poster sticks, set the Kandinsky images on fire.

The conflagration was instant. Flames shot up some ten feet, erupting raggedly along the line of protestors. Hysterical onlookers tried to escape the conflagration in front of the museum only to be blocked by the curious crowd surging toward them. More press arrived on the scene. Live videos were being simulcast on German TV and amateur streaming lit up YouTube.

Someone threw a brick at the villa doors. The director ducked just in time and ran back into the museum. Other bricks followed. Katrina stood her ground, begging the rowdy crowd to calm down. The sound of sirens grew louder. Within minutes armed police were on the scene, routing the now fleeing demonstrators. Krankenhauer stood his ground for a final few seconds and hurled a brick at the museum woman. It hit its mark. Just in front of him, as he pivoted and sought to disappear in the crowd, Krankenhauer heard a woman shout something in American-sounding English to her companion whom she called "Rick," whereupon they both began running in the opposite direction of the bolting crowd.

"*We've got to get to Katrina, Rick!*"

Megan broke into a gallop toward the villa and through the disintegrating line of flaming poster holders. Rick followed close behind. They reached Katrina who was writhing in pain. She looked at them blankly without recognition. Quickly Rick examined her. There was a small bruise on the side of her head where she had fallen to the ground. Her upper body presented no injuries and the same was true for her lower body and legs. But blood was oozing from one of her shoes. When Rick started gently to remove it, Katrina began screaming uncontrollably.

"We need to get her out of here and to a hospital, Megan. She may have a concussion. And her right foot. The brick's cracked it open and broken at least one metatarsal bone, maybe several. I'm going to apply pressure and you hand me those splintered bits of poster stick there. I need to make a splint while you go get an ambulance."

The crowd had thinned somewhat, as had the press presence, and police were questioning groups of bystanders. Impatient at the thought of waiting to talk to a policeman, Megan looked up Munich emergency numbers on her iPhone and immediately found the one for "*Rettungsdienst*"—Rescue Service. She dialed 098-19222 and a terse female voice demanded "Crisis?"

"I have a woman here who might have a concussion and whose foot has been broken in a protest demonstration at the Lenbach Museum."

"Broken foot? We don't send ambulances out for a broken foot."

"*What?*"

"We don't send out our ambulances for a broken foot."

"Well, *damn you!*" Megan heard herself shouting into the phone.

"And can you tell me what you saw, *gnädige Frau*?" A policeman was addressing her.

Megan wheeled to face him, her anger still at full throttle and after a clipped report she asked if it were customary in Germany to turn down an ambulance request for a woman who had a head wound and her foot broken by a terrorist.

"Depends if she can walk on it or not, I'd suppose."

"I give up." Megan sighed and made her way back to Rick and Katrina as fast as she could. It was already a few minutes to seven and beginning to get dark. Her friend was lucid now and when she saw Megan, her face brightened in recognition.

"I think our dinner date is off, Megan," she said, smiling wryly.

"And I think we're driving you to an emergency care center to get you treated properly," Megan replied.

Rick had done an impressive job of staunching the bleeding and fashioning the stick pieces into a temporary splint which he had bound with his necktie. But it was important to have the woman treated at a clinic as quickly as possible.

"I've introduced myself to Katrina, and she knew you'd be right back," Rick said.

"Yes. I wanted to get ambulance help from the police, but they're too busy, so I found the number and called an ambulance myself but they refused to come for 'just' a broken foot and a possible concussion."

"Look, ladies, you stay here and I'll get the car and drive up as close to you as I possibly can. And in the meantime, Katrina, do not put any weight on that foot."

"You couldn't *pay* me to."

Rick stood up and pushed his way through several noisy knots of people, making his way back to the apartment building where the car was parked. Within minutes he was able to make his way back along the Luisenstrasse until he came abreast of the Lenbach villa. Daringly, he parallel parked between two police cars. Wooden barriers had been set up alongside them on the sidewalk. In another minute, he was carrying Katrina in his arms toward the car. He and Megan solicitously positioned her in the front passenger seat and they were off before the police took notice. A minute later Katrina slumped in her seat; she had passed out from the shock to her system.

"Probably better that way," said Rick.

"Okay," Megan was reading her iPhone map, "we head south toward the Frauenkirche and a privately-owned walk-in—ha!—is just nearby on the Marienplatz, let's see, ah huh, number eighteen. Called UHMD—for *Unfall-Hilfe MD*. The Marienplatz is where the huge town hall is. We can't miss it."

After a delay caused by some street repair work, they drove into the enormous square and pulled up in front of a very discreet UHMD. Katrina woke up when the car came to a stop and with the aid of a concerned paramedic, Rick carried her into the establishment while Megan took the car and began searching for a parking place. She had to settle for a side street. When she returned to the UHMD waiting room Katrina was still being attended to. Rick looked at Megan and smiled.

"Good news. Katrina does not have a concussion. They stuck her through the CT scanner and everything is okay. They just came out to tell me the good news."

"Oh, thank heaven for that. I really was scared for her."

Fifteen minutes later the physician on call appeared and waved them both into the room where Katrina was being cared for. Her third and fourth metatarsal bones had indeed been broken, just as Rick had suspected. And she was wearing a cast that came up to just below her knee, completely covering her ankle and foot. There was an opening for her toes. As Rick had done earlier, the UHMD doctor commanded her not to put any weight on her foot.

"Not even to drive?" Katrina was extremely concerned.

"*Especially* not to drive," both physicians in the room said simultaneously, one in German, the other in English.

"You won't be able to bend your right ankle anyway," Rick explained, "so you couldn't drive even if you wanted to. You'll just have to use an Uber to get to and from work."

Katrina was given a pair of crutches and instructed how to use them while Megan hurried back to bring the car around. Rick helped Katrina ease slowly down onto the back seat and Megan laid the crutches on the car floor beside her.

"Now we'll drive you home, dear. Do you have food enough?" Megan was concerned about her friend because she knew she was a single mother and had a young son. Katrina had periodically emailed her photographs of the boy. He must be four or five by now.

"Yes, there is plenty of food at my place and thank you both so much. For everything. Fortunately, Herbert is out of the city for the weekend with his nanny."

"Oh, so you'll be alone in your apartment then? Katrina, I don't think you should be all by yourself tonight." Megan looked at Rick, who was driving. He seemed to guess her thoughts and nodded.

"Listen, dear. I could stay with you at your place tonight. Or if you prefer, you could stay with us at the museum apartment you so kindly reserved for us while we're here. It's just a block from the Lenbach, after all."

"The Lenbach! *Um Himmels willen! Great god in heaven!* I've forgotten my appointment there this evening! What time is it? The man will think I've stood him up."

"It's fifteen minutes after eight. What man?"

"Igor Rasputin. You don't know him, Megan. He's from Ukraine. Odessa. He owns some magnificent Kandinsky works and has founded a 'Russian Patriots' museum there. Has already built up a core collection based on Kandinsky and Münter. Works unknown in the West."

"Interesting. No, I don't know his name."

"Oh, dear, I have no idea how to contact the man. He will be waiting for me at the museum. I was supposed to let him in to the museum after you, Rick and I had had dinner. He was coming at eight in order to take state-of-the art photographs of our Kandinskys to reproduce for his museum in exchange for loaning his Kandinskys to us for a show."

"You're in no state to handle that now, Katrina."

"You're right. But I've got to call the night guard Niki Wächter immediately and tell him to admit a Herr Rasputin who will be waiting at the villa door. Wächter can supervise the photographing just as well as I could."

"Good idea."

Despite her discomfort Katrina was able to draw her cellphone out of her jacket pocket and dial the museum guard's number. When the night watchman answered she told him exactly what to do with her eight o'clock visitor.

"Ah, I feel better now. That poor man! He might have waited for me in vain."

30

RASPUTIN WAS INDEED APPROACHING the door of the Lenbach House Museum. Two hours earlier he had been at Paleo tending to last minute details with his men when the sound of shouting outside one street over became so loud that they all hurried over to Luisenstrasse to see what was going on. What they beheld was both irritating and full of possibilities.

A mob of neo-Nazis holding signs demanding "Only German Art in German Museums" was advancing on the Lenbach House Museum. The sign bearers were followed by a curious crowd that grew larger every second, especially after the trouble makers set fire to their posters, some of which had the image of a Kandinsky artwork on them. Fascinated, Rasputin and his men watched as police and press arrived. The demonstrators surged toward the old villa part of the museum and yelled accusations as two museum staffers—a man and a woman—tried to calm them. Rasputin recognized the woman immediately. It was Katrina Keller, due to provide him entrance to the museum in another two hours.

God damn it! Was the mission imperiled? Would there be police swarming outside the museum for the next unknown number of hours? Rasputin glanced at his men who were looking at him questioningly. After a moment, he made a decision.

"Okay, let's go back and proceed as planned. Only we will advance the time of operations. We shall start *now*."

It was a daring idea. They would use the demonstration as cover for any noise the operation might make. All museum personnel were engaged with the crowds. Especially as the ruckus had just turned nasty. Bricks were being hurled and Rasputin saw one of them hit the Keller woman. She fell to the ground. That was inconvenient. She might or might not be incapacitated. She might or might not meet him at eight as they had agreed. He would return to the museum at the appointed time just in case.

Meanwhile, returning to Paleo was the right thing to do. The basement gallery with Kandinsky's paintings would be deserted now. Any possible noise from the long awaited final breakthrough into the museum cellar storeroom would be unheard. Paleo's six-foot-high by-four-foot-wide tunnel stretched for thirteen feet through clay-like soil underneath the Richard-Wagner-Strasse. It had taken Alyk two weeks to dig and sleeve it using a one-man pneumatic auger with cutting rotative head. Now his work would finally pay off. Tonight was the night.

31

FROM HER VANTAGE POINT just beyond the new wing of the Lenbach House Museum, Raisa Sokolova observed not only the noisy demonstration going on, but also the man she had had under surveillance ever since he left the Mandarin Oriental Hotel earlier that afternoon. He was standing with three men, all keenly watching the protest march on the museum. From their posters and their chants, the noisy rabble was obviously a neo-Nazi incited event. Raisa saw Katrina Keller appear in front of the museum villa door, trying to quiet the raging mob. She saw her collapse when a lobbed brick hit her. And she saw Rasputin turn and say something to his men. She followed them as they walked swiftly back to the Richard-Wagner-Strasse and disappeared inside the same building she had followed Rasputin to previously. Something was definitely up. Resolving to remain on the job as long as necessary, she looked around for a spot where she could be comfortable yet out of sight. The museum's loading dock almost opposite was perfect. Its short entry drive was steep and would give her cover as well as an ideal vantage point. Reassuringly, she gripped the small pocket pistol she always had with her. A 7.65mm Beretta, the weapon had a stout recoil spring to keep the action pushed forward and its barrel used a pivot pin that, when the latch was depressed, popped up. With the breech open and the barrel tipped up, she could load, unload, and check to see if she had a loaded chamber with a flick of the lever.

Almost two hours had passed when Raisa, never leaving her observation post, spied Rasputin reemerging from the building and walking at a very fast clip toward the front of the Lenbach museum, where both crowds and police had finally dispersed. She followed the man and was surprised to see him knock at the villa door. She was even more surprised when she saw him admitted. Glancing at her watch she noted it was eight o'clock. What would anybody be doing knocking on the door of the closed museum at that time of night? And how was it that someone immediately let him inside?

32

MEGAN KNEW IT WAS THE BETTER THING TO DO. Of course Katrina wanted to be in her own home and of course she wanted to call her son's nanny and hear that all was well. So Rick, who was driving, listened to her carefully enunciated instructions as how best to get to Osterwaldstrasse 89 in Schwabing and they were off.

"Thank goodness I have a ground-floor apartment," Katrina breathed.

"You are in luck there. Are you sure you don't want us to stop and get you a few groceries?"

"You're too kind, Megan, but I really do have everything I need at home."

"All right, just remember though, if you change your mind, you are more than welcome to stay with us at the museum apartment and then you'd be only one block from work."

"Right now, all I want to do is sleep. But, Megan, I *will* take you up on your offer to stay overnight with me if you really mean it. I didn't realize how awkward it was going to be with this cast, and now I have to admit that I'm afraid of falling."

"Of course I'll stay with you tonight," Megan said, looking at Rick for approval. He nodded in vigorous agreement. They drove on to Schwabing in silence. All of a sudden Megan realized she would be without what she called the "senior" pills she had to take every night.

"Do you think it's going to be serious if I miss taking my senior pills for just one night? They're back at our apartment," she whispered to Rick. He was aware of the serious medical circumstance that necessitated the medications she took every night. A medical condition Megan had told only a few intimates about.

"I wouldn't worry about it this one time. You'll likely not even feel a nudge of withdrawal, but just be sure to take them again tomorrow morning *and* evening."

"Oh, you can be sure I will."

"You're a very conscientious patient."

When they pulled up in front of Katrina's building it was clear that Megan was doing the right thing to stay overnight with her. Once they got her out of the car, taking care that she put no weight on her right foot, she complained of dizziness and blurred vision.

"Both can be side effects of the Vicodin they gave you at the urgent care place. Not to worry. It's better that you're not in pain now," Rick assured her.

"Worry? Ha, ha, no, of course I'm not to worry." Katrina was becoming light-headed.

They steered her to the front door and watched her awkwardly unlock it and then the door to her apartment.

"Oh, it's good to be home. Now where is my bedroom?"

"Let's go down this hall," Megan said, making sure her friend was using the crutches correctly and keeping the weight off her foot. They got to a bedroom full of toys and Megan encouraged her dazed friend to continue down the hall to the next bedroom. It was larger with a double bed and women's garments were on a clotheshorse. Obviously, Katrina's room.

"Do you need to go to the toilet before we get you to bed?"

"Yes. I guess you'll have to help me?"

"Of course."

They moved slowly toward the bathroom on the far side of the bedroom.

"Here, let me hold your crutches while you face me and put your hands on my shoulders. Then I'll lower you to the seat."

Katrina did as Megan directed. When she finished they reversed the procedure and Megan guided her to the bed.

"Let me help get you out of your clothes and then you just lie down and go to sleep. That's what you need."

"Oh, yes, I do so want to sleep now."

"If you need to go to the bathroom again, call out and I'll hear you. Don't try to get out of the bed until I can get to you and hand you your crutches. Here, I'm laying them right beside you on this." Megan took a chair and placed it next to the bed.

"Right. I'll call you." Katrina's eyes closed and she fell asleep immediately.

Megan drew a quilt over her and went into the living room. She saw a large leather couch and headed straight for it. She would sleep in her clothes tonight.

33

AT FIVE MINUTES TO EIGHT Rasputin, a small black carrying case in his left hand, had emerged from the Richard-Wagner-Strasse building and walked back to the Lenbach House Museum. The crowd had dispersed. As agreed with Katrina Keller, he went to the museum's villa door on the off chance that she had recovered from the brick attack and was actually waiting for him.

He stooped to pick up one of the stray bricks that had fallen around the doorstep, then knocked loudly on the door. Almost at once it was opened a crack and a man's voice asked if he were Herr Rasputin. Upon affirmation, a uniformed man opened the door wide, beckoning the visitor inside.

"Frau Doktor Keller sends her apologies that she cannot be here in person and she has instructed me to take you to the Kandinsky gallery where I am to supervise..."

The guard's sentence was never completed. Rasputin raised his brick and hit the man hard on the side of his skull. The man dropped to the ground, mouth open, eyes staring, and blood gushing from his head. His attacker squatted by the body and calmly felt for a pulse. There was none. Good. Emergency part of The Plan taken care of. Now to enable the others to join him in the Kandinsky gallery.

Knowing the exact location, Rasputin bolted down the main staircase to the basement and entered the Kandinsky gallery. He strode straight to the inconspicuous storage closet at the opposite end and placed his carrying case beside it. Opening his wallet, he took out a credit card and slipped it between the closet door and the knob, fiddling with it until the card popped the lock. The next ten minutes were spent removing the contents and shelves of the small room. Out of his carrying case Rasputin withdrew a Bosch 18V cordless hand drill powered by a lithium battery and went to work on the inner wall opposite the closet door. Another minute and Alyk's face was smiling at him through the first hole drilled in the wall. Eight minutes later, a six-by-four-foot opening admitted both Alyk and Tigr.

While Rasputin stood guard, his two men took down all the Kandinsky paintings—eleven of them. Small photographic markers were affixed to the wall where the individual works had hung. As soon as a painting was removed from the wall, Tigr carried it over to the cleared-out storage closet and passed it through the fresh opening in the closet's back wall. Waiting for it on the other side of the tunnel was Dzhim. Now they had close to an extra two hours, having begun at a little after six rather than at eight o'clock as originally planned. The men did not feel rushed and they worked smoothly together. Transfer of the Kandinsky paintings to the two Paleo workshops did not take as long as they had originally anticipated.

Then the intricate labor began in earnest. It commenced by photographing each artwork under bright box lights with Tigr's three-dimensional scanning application. It replicated, with forty million color points a shot, Kandinsky's gestural and tactual touch.

Unconventionally, however, the large texturized duplications also included the front sides of the artworks' frames, and Tigr's sizeable format 3D printer encompassed and reproduced them as well. The large gossamer overlay sheets were then developed one by one in the giant four-and-a-half by four-and-a-half-foot vat Alyk had provided.

Once developed, the wet images were transferred and affixed with hairdryer heat to the old canvasses acquired by Alyk at antique shops. Their surfaces had been scraped and newly framed with wood having the exact dimensions, if not always the same grain, of the original frames—something Alyk had photographed and precisely calculated during his visit to the Lenbach museum. A tourist with a purpose. The new images reproduced not only the artwork but the surrounding original frame face.

The result in each case was a visually indistinguishable clone of the original painting.

By three-fifteen in the morning each of the eleven original Kandinskys had been replicated. "In duplicate," as Dzhim had insisted, taking no chances. The men were almost an hour ahead of schedule. Alyk returned to the basement tunnel entrance and awaited Tigr, who, one by one, brought down the clones Dzhim was hand-drying upstairs. Affixed to their substitute frames, the sides of which had been colored to match the originals, they looked exactly like the original artworks. Each time he received a new picture, Alyk deftly carried it through the tunnel and into the Lenbach's basement showroom, hanging it precisely where the original had been. By four in the morning the gallery looked exactly as it had at six o'clock the evening before. Dzhim, Tigr, and Alyk all joined Rasputin in the great rectangular room and gazed around in admiration. Alyk took down the two sensors that had guided his tunnel excavation. Then while Rasputin remained in the gallery, his three men re-entered the tunnel and plastered over their side of the storage closet. Rasputin daubed plaster on the closet wall from his side and fastidiously replaced the shelves in front of it. He then returned to their places the paint cans and cleaning equipment kept in the storeroom.

Their work almost completed, Alyk returned with Tigr and Dzhim to the Richard-Wagner-Strasse building and up to the ground-floor vestibule where Dzhim had already neatly positioned the eleven Kandinskys against the walls. They began encasing the paintings in bubble wrap. The straightforward task was completed in record time. With great care the trio placed the artworks close to the front door. From there they would be loaded into the moving van scheduled to arrive at five o'clock.

Before rejoining his men, Rasputin had an additional bit of business to conclude in the museum. He walked back upstairs to the main entry of the villa and looked down at the floor and the night watchman he had dispatched a few hours earlier. Then opening the front door a crack and checking for any passersby, he dragged the corpse partially outside and laid the bloodied brick next to its head. Leaving the villa door slightly ajar and blocked by one of the dead man's feet, he walked briskly past the museum's copper-faced addition and back to the Richard-Wagner-Strasse building. It was almost five o'clock. A moving van would be there any minute. The Plan had worked. Brilliantly.

34

THE PIERCING SOUND of a high-pitched scream woke Megan from a troubled sleep at six-thirty in the morning. Jumping up from her couch in the living room, she rushed into her friend's bedroom. Forgetting her right foot was in a cast, Katrina had gotten up to go to the toilet and stepped with her full weight on the broken foot. She was rocking back and forth in pain and gasping.

"Katrina! Why didn't you call me?" Megan was aghast and frustrated. The crutches she had carefully laid on a chair by the bed were on the floor. The chair was on its side.

"I'm sorry, Megan, it was just such a natural thing to do. I didn't think about my foot at all," Katrina blurted out, looking chagrined.

"What time is it?"

In one vigorous motion, Megan down-wristed her Apple Watch.

"Six-thirty and forty-one seconds," it announced.

"We might as well get up," said Katrina, still rocking in pain.

"I'm for that. Let me make breakfast. Remember we didn't have dinner last night."

"*Du lieber Gott*! You're so right. Help me get to the bathroom and then the kitchen and I'll make us coffee."

Megan picked up Katrina's crutches, handed them to her, and after the bathroom stop they carefully made their way to the living room and the small kitchen beyond. It opened onto a cozy dining nook that opened onto the living room. A box of Schoko Muesli stood on the kitchen counter, and several ripe bananas hung from a stand nearby. Just right for the sort of breakfast Megan liked best. Any other fruit around? Looking inside the fridge she gave an exclamation of joy. Katrina was well stocked with blueberries and strawberries, as well as yogurt and milk. Perfect. Her ideal breakfast components right there for the mixing.

"You're the first person I know who likes adding yogurt to cereal," Katrina said with approval as they sipped their coffee.

"Maybe it's a German thing. I was introduced to doing so by a physician friend in Hamburg, Toennies Maack. It was also he who taught me not to pronounce 'stil', as in 'Jugendstil', with a Germanic 'sh' sound, since 'stil' comes from the Latin." Megan smiled, proud of this bit of arcane knowledge.

"He was correct. Even down south here in Munich we know to pronounce it that way. It's just laziness on most people's part. Speaking of which, I can't wait to show you some of the charming Art nouveau-like works by Kandinsky we have on exhibit now. We don't usually hang them, but now that the abstract, Paris-period Kandinskys are in the basement, there's room for them."

Nourishment was making them feel better and Katrina poured a second cup of hot coffee for her guest and herself.

"Now Megan, won't you please, please tell me what the theme of your lecture for us on Monday is going to be? Your title 'Double Kandinsky' is so intriguing. I presume it's connected with your catalogue raisonné of his later works. But what does it mean?"

"Ah, that will have to remain a mystery until I give the speech. But I can promise you this. You are going to like it."

"Oh, but we *always* like your lectures, Megan. You're so cruel not to explain the title," Katrina pretended to pout.

"I'm actually dying to tell you, but we'll both just have to wait."

"Grr." Katrina made an angry face.

"Will you want to go to the museum today?" Megan asked.

"Oh, yes. I need to see what damage may have been done to the exterior by the protestors. And I have an Everest of work to get through in my office. As long as I'm sitting down I'm sure everything will be all right."

"Do you think the police made any arrests? Those contemptible brick throwers. Hey, let's turn on the TV and see how the demonstration was covered."

"Oh, we should have thought of that right away," Katrina said. She started to stand up, then felt her cast encumbrance and wisely reached for her crutches.

"Is your TV in the living room? Let me turn it on."

"Yes, it's in the bookcase facing the couch, only you can't see it until that cabinet door in the middle is slid back."

Megan walked over to the unit, pushed the sliding door of the cabinet back, turned the television on, and quickly found a news channel. The fifteen-minute commercial break was just finishing.

"Oh, good, we'll get the whole news cycle," Katrina said, hopping on her crutches toward the living room couch. She was becoming more adept at them by the minute. Megan sat down beside her.

The first news item was about a passenger plane crash with no survivors off the coast of Greece, but the very next event covered was what the anchorwoman called "a murderous neo-Nazi night at the Lenbach."

"*Murder?*" Katrina cried out loud.

Film footage showed demonstrators tangling with police, posters ablaze, and bricks being thrown. It appeared that none of the protestors had gotten inside the museum, but the night guard who had opened the villa door to see what was happening had been hit and killed by a brick.

"Oh, my god, that has to be Niki Wächter!" Katrina said in agitation. She began to tear up as the coverage continued.

A man had been arrested in regard to the crime, one Walter Krankenhauer, known to have neo-Nazi ties. The protesters' demand was that only German art be shown in German museums. Their particular animosity was directed at the twentieth-century Russian artist Wassily Kandinsky and the many works by him in the Lenbach House Museum. The television image switched to a shot of Dr. Max Mürrisch, director of the museum, serenely assuring his interviewer that there had been no interior access or damage. The Kandinskys were safe and sound.

"Oh, I've got to phone Max immediately," Katrina exclaimed. "Even *he* might be wondering if I'm all right."

Both women chortled when the televised Mürrisch continued speaking.

"I addressed the crowd myself, trying to calm them."

"Did that help?" the interviewer asked.

"I believe it did. Afterward, I reentered the museum and exited by way of the back entrance."

"Why, that *coward!*" Katrina exploded.

"Yeah. That means he has no idea you've been hurt. Or even interest.

After all, you two were out there together trying to quiet down the crowd. You'd think he would at least make sure you were okay."

"That's par for the course. He has absolutely no interest in his staff. He's a loner and he's arrogant. Just last week one of the guards quit because Max didn't like the way he was standing and read him the riot act in front of astonished museum visitors."

"And you work alongside this man? Poor you."

"Well, so far he hasn't focused on me. He's more interested in procuring additional funds from the city for his ambitious exhibition ideas."

They focused on the television news again. It seemed that Munich was not the only city in which anti-Kandinsky protests had been held. Synchronized marches had occurred at exactly six o'clock the evening before in Hamburg, Berlin, Düsseldorf, Dresden, and Stuttgart as well.

Megan's Apple Watch discreetly signaled that it was time to stand up and move around. She did so and at the same time noticed it was almost ten o'clock.

"Let me give Rick a call and see when he might be ready to drive out here and pick us up."

"That's fine, but remember I need time to shower and get ready. And in my case, it's going to take longer than usual." Katrina looked down at her leg and made a wry face.

"Hmm, maybe I can't take a shower. I guess I shouldn't get the cast wet," she said ruefully.

"Right. But if you have some plastic sacks and rubber bands handy, we can make your cast waterproof."

"Oh, wonderful. I do have both."

"Do you think you'll be all right getting into the shower yourself or do you want me to help?"

"I can manage, I think. I'll call if I need you. And by the way, you don't have to wait for me to finish before you freshen up. My son's bathroom also has a shower."

"All right, then. But be careful!"

"That's a given."

Forty-five minutes later both women were dressed and feeling renewed, even if Megan's clothes were the same ones she had worn the day before. She banished regrets that her morning exercises would not be taking place and turned her thoughts to the present.

"Now I'll call Rick." Megan proudly showed Katrina how she could make a call on her Apple Watch, as long as her iPhone was nearby.

"That's amazing!" A few seconds later Katrina commented quietly how good the amplification was when Rick picked up. His voice sounded chipper.

"I was wondering when I was going to hear from you ladies. I didn't want to bother you in case you were still sleeping"

"No, no, we've had breakfast, showered, and are dressed and ready to take on the day."

"I'll come get you right away, then. Should take me only ten minutes now that I know the way."

"Perfect. We'll be outside in front of Katrina's building."

Katrina waved Megan over to the bookshelves after the call finished. She wanted to show her the latest museum catalogue. It documented a Franz Marc exhibition the Lenbach had staged recently. As they sat down to page through it together, Katrina's landline phone rang. It was within reach and she answered immediately.

"Hallo?"

The expression on her face changed from one of inquiry to one of disbelief.

"*Where* have you looked, Diliana?"

The answer was inaudible to Megan but she could sense the sudden tension.

"*When* did this happen?"

The answer seemed to galvanize Katrina.

"Call the police *right now*! I'll be there as soon as I can."

Katrina slammed the receiver down.

"What's happened?" Megan asked in alarm.

"*My son is missing!*"

35

UNSEEN, PUZZLED WITNESS to Rasputin's entry into, then quixotic departure from, the Lenbach some nine hours later, a sleepy but persevering Raisa Sokolova had followed her quarry back to the Richard-Wagner-Strasse and watched him reenter the building at number 33. It was five in the morning. Why had he not returned to his hotel for the night? Why had he spent hours in the museum, and whose uniformed body had the man dragged out of the museum? *What the hell was going on?*

Returning to her previous vantage spot in the museum's sloping loading dock, she realized how hungry and tired she was. She had relieved herself twice in the bushes across the Luisenstrasse from the museum, but had not had the forethought to supply herself with anything to eat. Damn it, who would have thought the Ukrainian would stay so long in the museum?

The street was deserted and just as Raisa's head was beginning to nod in preamble to snoozing, the sound of a slow-moving, very large vehicle caught her attention. At the end of the street was a creamy white *Cargo Logistik* moving van, its logo painted in large blue letters over what looked like a yellow exclamation mark. Raisa dashed out of the loading dock and ran across the street. She stood out of sight within the door frame of a building with a good view of the dock.

So, this was it. There *was* going to be a pickup at the Lenbach. Boris was correct to be concerned that Rasputin had made a deal with the museum. This was why Rasputin had spent so long in the Lenbach.

But the van did not enter the museum dock. Instead it was moving steadily down her side of the street. It came to a stop at number 33. What?

A uniformed man on the passenger side of the van stepped out onto the sidewalk, walked up to the front door, and rang the bell. Almost immediately the door opened and four men appeared. They seemed to be in consultation and one of them ran to the front of the van and began gesturing to the driver to pull up farther so that the rear of the vehicle was parallel with the entry door of the building. This done, the driver of the van got out and joined his mate, walking to the back of their van and opening the rear doors. Then they all went inside the building.

Raisa took advantage of their temporary disappearance to photograph the license plate on the back of the van, then she scurried across the street and back down into the loading dock. The museum obviously was not part of whatever was taking place. Unless it stored items in this building just behind it? Not likely. Raisa's view of the white van was unobstructed and she switched her cellphone from photo to video. Whatever was going on, she would have footage of it to send Boris.

She did not have to wait very long to find out what was going on. Rasputin himself held open the front door of the building while five men emerged. The two men wearing uniforms were obviously with the van. The other three were carrying a large, flat object measuring over four-by-four-foot square and encased in bubble wrap. The van men climbed up into the back of their vehicle and expertly received and loaded the item handed up to them.

After putting a wedge into the open front door, Rasputin joined what became a slow but steady human conveyer belt for the next hour. The carefully wrapped flat objects were obviously paintings and, with a final count of eleven, Raisa calculated, could mean only one thing. They had to be the same eleven paintings she had recently noted hanging in the Lenbach's basement gallery. *The Kandinskys!*

36

A QUITE INEBRIATED Heinrich von Frauenberg arrived at the Munich airport late that Friday night. After a brief visit to his favorite brothel he took a taxi to the juncture of Richard-Wagner-Strasse and Briennerstrasse. From there he walked to the street behind his building, Augusten-Strasse, and, slipping through several back courtyards, arrived at the rear of his building. It was a secret route he used to take as a teenager to avoid his father's scolding for staying out too late. Entering Paleo from the basement cellar he slipped quietly up the building's back stairs to the attic and passed out on a heap of blankets.

He awoke early the next morning. Far too early. It was only five-thirty. In a zombie state, he staggered through the attic door that led to Paleo's long roof balcony. He had always loved the view of central Munich stretching out before him in all directions. From where he stood, he looked right down on the red roofs of the old villa part of the Lenbach Museum, and from there, on the far side of Luisenstrasse, the giant Propylaea—magnificent entrance to the Königsplatz. Bending over the balcony railing to look down at his own street, he was astonished by what he saw. A large moving van marked *Cargo Logistik* was parked right at *his* Paleo's front entrance and several men were loading it with bubble-wrapped items from the house.

How *dare* they? Outraged, he watched for several more minutes. The man Rasputin was among the thieves. What nerve! So that's why he wanted sole temporary possession of Paleo. To steal its furnishings and paintings. That stupid Russian must think the old artworks were far more valuable than they were worth.

Should he put a stop to it? Heinrich turned, then hesitated. Perhaps not. Far better that the burglary play itself out so charges against the man could be enhanced from attempted burglary to burglary. Or? An even better idea. Not having Rasputin in prison left him ripe for blackmail. Now there was something that could be exploited for years. Or could it? If the haughty foreigner did not live in Germany, as apparently he did not, how could he ever find him? No, he must think of something else. But what?

Staring back down at the continuing scene he noticed another witness to the event. It was a woman with short brown hair, dressed in dark blue slacks and matching jacket. A Lenbach Museum guard perhaps? Almost out of sight, she was standing at the bottom of the museum's inclined loading dock and it was clear that she was following every movement of the men across the street. In fact, she was holding up her cellphone, obviously recording the scene. But if she were a museum guard why hadn't she called the police?

What the hell. *He* would call the police. He picked up his cellphone, dialed 110, and from his roof balcony perch reported a possible crime scene in progress. When the police arrived he now knew exactly what he was going to do. Re-entering the building, he slipped soundlessly down the back stairs of Paleo to the ground floor. Odd. Nothing from the household seemed to be missing. Furniture and paintings all still in place and intact. Concealing himself inside a butler's pantry, he waited expectantly for the sound of sirens. This was going to be a lark.

Rasputin's plan to load all eleven artworks was progressing nicely toward its goal to be finished by six-thirty. If this kept up they would finish well within the hoped-for time limit. Rasputin wanted the van to be out and on the road by six-thirty. Before local traffic tied up the streets. And especially before anyone from the Lenbach showed up for work.

All six men stopped dead in their tracks at the sudden two-note blast of sirens approaching. Moments later two green-and-white BMW cruisers with flashing lights pulled up, one at either end of the van, effectively blocking it. Police sprang out from both cars and surrounded Rasputin and his men with guns drawn.

"What's going on?" one of the officers demanded, looking from the men to the van and back. "We have reports of a burglary at this address."

Before Rasputin could answer, a tall young man dressed in black coveralls emerged from the front door of the building. Reassuringly, he faced the police and held his hands up for calm.

"Hold on, officers, hold on. I am Baron Heinrich von Frauenberg, and this is my residence, my *building*. I assure you there is nothing untoward going on. Here is my driver's license."

The officer closest to him took it, examined it closely, and passed it on to his chief.

"How do we know you own this building?" the chief asked suspiciously.

"Take a look at the cement scroll above my front door. See? The letters spell out the name Frauenberg."

It was true. The man's carved surname appeared on the front of the building.

Heinrich turned and gestured to Rasputin, who had been frozen to the spot.

"This man is my agent and my friend. He is in charge of transporting some of my family things from here to my villa in Monaco. Everything is totally all right. There is no need for concern."

"Well, if you say so. But I must ask you to state, sign, and swear to an affidavit as to what you've told us. Here. My officer will write it out for you."

Heinrich turned to Rasputin who was staring at him, too dazed to speak.

"So sorry this happened, my friend. Let me sign this affidavit thing and then your men can get on with the loading of my things."

A few minutes later the police, satisfied that no crime had been committed, began slowly returning to their patrol cars.

"And, oh, Rasputin, I'd like to talk to you inside the house, please," Heinrich said, facing the startled man and gesturing toward the front door.

Like a faithful hound, Rasputin silently followed his "friend" inside the building where Heinrich put his hands on his hips and faced the bewildered man.

"Listen here, Rasputin. I don't give a damn what you are doing out there or in here. Obviously, it's not my household things you are moving. You don't need to tell me what you're up to. I am not interested."

Rasputin shifted his weight from one leg to the other.

"What you do need to do," Heinrich continued slowly, enunciating each syllable, "*and I mean immediately, is pay me another million euros for my silence.*"

37

"BUT WHAT DID YOUR NANNY SAY about your boy, Katrina? How could he have wandered away like that?"

The two women were in Katrina's Schwabing living room and still looking at each other in disbelief.

"Diliana said he was especially cheerful and in good spirits this morning while she was preparing breakfast. She could hear him singing and playing the harmonium in the other room. She didn't pay much attention when the sounds stopped and when breakfast was ready she called him to the table. But he didn't come, he..." Katrina's voice broke as tears flooded her eyes.

"Go on," Megan said gently.

"He didn't answer her calls. When Diliana went to get him, the living room was empty. She kept calling his name and went through the entire house, upstairs, the attic, even the basement, but there was no sign of him. Then she searched for him outside, of course, but he didn't answer her calls. She looked up and down the garden and grounds but there was absolutely no sign of him. Oh, Megan, do you think Herbert might have been kidnapped?"

"Of course not, Katrina. Of course not. It has to be a case of his simply wandering off beyond the property. How close is your country house to other houses?"

"Perhaps a five-minute walk."

"And Diliana will have called the police by now."

"Yes. Yes. But I have to get there *now*. I can't wait just hoping they have found him. And even if they do, I still want to be with him, hold him."

"Of course, I understand, Katrina," Megan said soothingly.

"With this damn broken foot, I can't drive. I guess I'll call an Uber."

"Absolutely not! Rick and I will drive you. We'd be only too happy to. You know my lecture isn't until Monday evening."

Katrina was strangely silent for a minute. She seemed to be mulling something over. Then she spoke.

"If you wouldn't mind driving me to Murnau. That's where my country retreat is."

"How wonderful. We were just there on account of Gabriele Münter, of course, and we couldn't get enough of it. Why, we'd love to return. Rick ought to be here soon. Shall we pack a few items and go outside and wait for him?"

"I don't need to take anything; I have everything there."

"Good. So, let's lock up and go outside and wait for Rick." Megan was thinking glumly that she would be wearing the same clothes again today. Then she chided herself for not giving her whole attention to the urgency of a missing child.

They exited the house just as Rick drove up. Unaware of the tense situation, he was smiling broadly and waving Megan's cosmetic bag that contained her senior pills.

"Oh, thank goodness! Rick. How *clever* of you to remember."

"That's not all I remembered. Look on the back seat. You'll see another pair of your slacks and a matching shirt. Plus, socks and undies."

"You are a saint! But let's get on the road. We don't have time for me to change now."

Rick looked puzzled.

Once they were seated in the car Megan explained that Katrina's son was missing. They needed to drive directly to Murnau.

"We'll get there as quickly as is safe to drive," he said reassuringly.

Once again Megan and Rick were off to Murnau.

38

RAISA HAD WITNESSED and documented on her cellphone the whole baffling operation as it unfolded at Richard-Wagner-Strasse 33. It was obviously a heist of some sort, directed by Rasputin. Six men were involved, four coming from the building, and two in charge of the moving van. Hoping to sabotage the activity, Raisa had called the police and reported a burglary in progress. They showed up so fast that she wondered if a neighbor might not also have called in the suspicious activity taking place at five in the morning. Surprisingly, the officers left after only twenty minutes or so. A seventh man had emerged from the building and talked earnestly with the police captain. At one point, they both looked up at the building's façade for some reason. Apparently satisfied with whatever had been discussed, the officer called off his men. What could the seventh man have said?

After the van drove off—an event fully documented on her cellphone—Raisa left her post, found an open convenience store, and bought a cold can of Spezi, a banana, and crackers, consuming them on the spot. She was ravenous and this at least gave her the energy to get back to her hotel.

Once in her room, she stretched out on her bed, and turned on the television set opposite her. Good god! The Lenbach Museum director was on the news being interviewed about the anti-Kandinsky demonstration of last night. When asked if any of the Kandinsky paintings in the museum had been damaged, the director assured the interviewer that all of them were safe. Nothing had been touched inside the museum. Nothing was missing. Raisa was completely mystified. How could that be?

Time to report to Boris. It was a little after eight in Moscow. He would have had his morning coffee and be in a receptive mood.

"Ah, Raisa. I've been looking forward to your next report." The man sounded almost genial.

"Some amazing things have happened, Boris, since we last talked. I'll try to summarize. At six o'clock last evening from my post across the street opposite the Richard-Wagner-Strasse building Rasputin has been visiting so mysteriously—told you he had a key to the place—I suddenly heard the sounds of a tremendous ruckus coming from one street over. There were loud shouts and jeers and soon the sound of police sirens. Rasputin and three of his agents exited their building and hurried over to Luisenstrasse to see what was going on. After about ten minutes they all walked back to number thirty-three and disappeared inside."

"What was the protest about?"

"Oh, interestingly, it was about the presence of non-German art in the Lenbach House Museum. The crowd was carrying signs that read 'Only German Art in German Museums,' and there were other signs with facsimiles of one of the Lenbach's abstract Kandinsky paintings. I saw the protesters, at a given signal, set the placards on fire. It was quite a spectacle. The police had to break it up."

"Fascinating. So no Kandinskys welcome in Germany! Well, Germany's loss. Let's see. How can we manipulate this? Perhaps Rasputin worked up some neo-Nazis and paid them to demonstrate. We could denounce him to the police."

"Wait. There's more."

"More?"

"A lot more. The associate director Katrina Keller, who was outside the museum appealing to the crowd to stop, was struck to the ground by a brick. Don't know what happened to her. Almost immediately after that Rasputin and his men returned to their building, so I had to follow them back. And now listen to this! Some two hours later, a few minutes before eight and after the police had dispersed the crowd, Rasputin re-exited the Richard-Wagner-Strasse building and walked quickly back over to the villa door of the Lenbach. He went right up to it, knocked, and within seconds the door opened and he was admitted!"

"*What?*"

"Yes. He was instantly allowed inside, even though the museum was closed."

"That's it! That's it! Haven't I told you all along that Rasputin has a deal with the Lenbach to buy some of their Kandinskys. 'Deaccession,' the museum would call it."

"There is still more to tell you, Boris."

"Go ahead. I am listening." He was hanging on his agent's every word.

"I stayed watching the front door of the Lenbach villa straight through the night, from six o'clock until the early hours of this morning. Without food.

I hope you understand my charge for all this nighttime surveillance is going to be high, Boris, high."

"Yes, yes. You've earned it. It will be waiting for you when you come back to Moscow. Did Rasputin ever come out?"

"Yes. And it's really lucky that I remained. Not only did he come out—this was at a little before five this morning—he dragged something out with him. It was the uniformed body of a guard, motionless, obviously dead. Then Rasputin wedged the door open with one of the dead man's legs and laid a brick next to his head. Made it look as if one of the demonstrators had killed him."

"Ah, clever."

"Yes, ingenious. Then he hurried back to Richard-Wagner-Strasse thirty-three. I followed him at a distance and slipped back into my post at the bottom of the museum's loading dock across the street."

"And this was at five in the *morning*?"

"Yes, and I'm not finished yet, Boris. There's more and it's absolutely incredible. Pour yourself another cup of coffee."

"Actually, I just took a swig of vodka."

"All right. At exactly five o'clock this morning a moving van pulled up right in front of number thirty-three and the two men with it were immediately admitted into the Rasputin building. And..."

"*A moving van?*"

"That's what I said, Boris. A moving van. You'd be proud of me. I ran across the street and photographed the van's license plate. Also took a shot of the side of the van. It's one of *Cargo Logistik's* vans. So we'll be able to trace it. And I got back to my hiding place just in time."

"Good thinking, Raisa. Good thinking."

"But now listen to this. A few minutes after the van pulled up to the building and a man from the van went inside, *four* men came out the front door, Rasputin holding it open, another leading the way, and two of them carrying a very large flat object in the shape of a square. It was sheathed in bubble wrap. The two men connected with the van climbed inside it and slowly maneuvered the object up and into the vehicle. And as soon as their article had been received, the men, including Rasputin, hurried back into the building and then reemerged with another flat, bubble-wrapped object. Nine of the objects were square, two of them were smaller by about thirty centimeters and rectangular in shape. *Obviously, they were paintings.*"

"What are you telling me?"

"I'm telling you the six men were loading paintings. In two sizes. Eleven of them! I counted them. *That is the exact number of Kandinsky works on canvas I counted in the Lenbach basement gallery just a few days ago. Eleven.*"

Raisa could hear Boris take a quick sip of his bracer. His voice quavered when he spoke.

"And this transfer of eleven paintings happened at the building *opposite* the Lenbach and not at the Lenbach loading dock itself?"

"Correct. But here's the stunner, Boris. I just watched this morning's news before calling you. The Lenbach Museum director was being interviewed about the anti-Kandinsky demonstration last night. When asked if protestors had gotten inside the museum and defaced the Kandinskys, he declared, adamantly, that no damage whatsoever had been done to them. *And no Kandinsky works were missing.*"

"None were missing? I can't comprehend this. So, who could the eleven paintings be by?"

"I haven't told you the end of the story yet. Are you prepared?"

"As much as I can be." Boris was by now almost whining.

"While the robbery was going on, and knowing the eleven paintings had to be by Kandinsky, I decided to call the police and report that a robbery was taking place. They arrived in no time and began questioning the men. Suddenly yet another man, quite young, came running out of the building holding his hands up and yelling at the police. There was a conference and he suddenly wheeled around and pointed up at the building. Everyone looked up to wherever he was pointing. I couldn't hear what he was telling them but whatever it was, the police finally drove off with no arrests made. Rasputin went inside with the young man while the others finished loading up."

"And the moving van got away with its load?" Boris was speaking in almost a whisper now.

"Yes, but as I said, we will be able to trace it since we know what company it belongs to and we have the license plate number. I'll send you the pictures and video immediately."

"It *has* to be a deal between Rasputin and the Lenbach. There can be no other explanation," Boris said furiously.

"I think so too. Why, for example, was he given entry into the museum at eight o'clock in the evening right after an anti-Kandinsky protest had been broken up? And why did he remain in the museum during the night and much of the early morning? And what about the dead museum guard? Is it possible that he tried to stop the burglary in progress? Or since he was at the villa door, perhaps he was trying to prevent anyone from coming inside—or exiting. There are a thousand questions."

"Rasputin is an outright *criminal*, Raisa. You've done superb work. My men will track that damn van and we will find out its contents and destination, come hell or high water."

39

LASZLO TOGARASSY, owner of Munich's new *Blaue Reiter* gallery, had been glued to the morning news. A neo-Nazi protest had been staged against the Lenbach House Museum because of the fact that it housed a "foreign" artist like Wassily Kandinsky. A guard was dead and an arrest of the protest leader had been made. Thankfully, the museum's Kandinskys were intact.

"But could we be next?" Iris Togarassy expressed out loud what her husband was thinking. She continued, touching his arm with concern.

"The fact that our new show is Kandinsky. Surely those neo-Nazis know about us."

"We'll just have to see, darling. I am certainly not going to close the show or take the paintings down."

"But perhaps you should take down *your* paintings?"

40

"Megan? Katrina? How about allowing me to be the chauffeur, while you both get comfortable in the back," Rick had offered, realizing the two friends needed to talk. Commuter traffic was already beginning to clog the city roads and he was eager to get onto Autobahn 95 toward Murnau.

After the women were seated in the back, Katrina quietly began to enunciate her worst fears while Megan pressed her hand reassuringly.

"How could my five-year-old little Herbert have just disappeared? Diliana said almost no time had passed between when he stopped playing the harmonium and when she called him to breakfast. He couldn't have gotten that far away on his own. I'm going to call Diliana again and see if she's heard anything from the police."

Katrina's call was a disappointment. There still was no trace of Herbert.

"But why on earth would anyone want to *kidnap* him?" Megan looked at her friend.

"I think I know why," Katrina said with obvious reluctance.

Megan waited for her to continue, but instead Katrina sat in silence, staring straight ahead. She decided to take another line of thought.

"Listen, Katrina, we ought to go straight to the police station when we reach Murnau."

"Yes, yes. I was thinking exactly the same. Best to do so."

They rode in silence for some time. Then all of a sudden Katrina turned her whole body to Megan and, looking her in the eye, began speaking. Her voice quavered.

"Listen. There's something I have to tell you. But you and Rick must promise, *promise* to keep what I tell you in total confidence."

"Yes, of course," Megan answered and Rick nodded vigorous assent.

"I think perhaps I know why Herbert has been kidnapped. The Münter House in Murnau. It belongs to me."

"*You own Gabriele Münter's house?*" Megan was flabbergasted.

"Yes, I am her grand-niece. My mother fought for years to have the Bavarian State cede the house to her after Münter died because *her* mother— Gabriele's sister Emmy—was never repaid the sizeable amount of money she lent Ella to help buy the house. I continued the fight. For years. Eight months ago, I won the case and immediately closed the house down. There were just too many valuable artworks inside it. And too many curious tourists. Just last year one of the reverse-glass paintings mysteriously disappeared. You might have seen that in the press."

Megan fought to cover her surprise and disappointment. So that was why she and Rick had been unable to get inside the house. She decided to be frank.

"First of all, Katrina, I think it's fascinating, marvelous that you are the grand-niece of Gabriele Münter. You never told me. I'm just a little bit hurt, to be truthful."

"I am sorry, Megan. I haven't wanted it to be known, you see. Only a very few people are aware of the fact."

"Of course it must be so gratifying for you that you now own the Münter House."

Megan paused.

"But at the same time, I have to say it's a tremendous shame that lovers of her work can no longer visit where she created them and kept them."

"Oh, but that's not so, Megan. They will be able to visit the house eventually. But first I must find the funds to afford guards." Katrina's answer was earnest and immediate.

"That's a relief to hear. Perhaps you could initiate something like an international 'Friends of Gabriele' online and attract donations that way."

"I think that is a good suggestion, Megan."

"But secondly, what I don't understand, is why you think Herbert's being missing has anything to do with the *house*."

"I can't explain it. I just have a feeling, that's all. Acquiring the house is the only change that's happened in my life of late."

"And when I described to you the meeting I had with Gabriele back in nineteen-sixty-two, you never said a word about being her grand-niece." Megan couldn't help feeling slightly hurt.

"I wanted to, believe me, but my lawyer had insisted I tell no one. That was when he was representing me in the restitution effort."

They were silent for a while. Finally, the first sign for Murnau appeared.

"When we get there can you direct us to the police station, Katrina?" Rick glanced back at her briefly.

"Right. It's very near the hospital on Schererweg. Just keep going straight when we enter the town proper and I'll tell you when to turn right. And then we'll be at the top of Schererweg. I don't know which side of the street the police station is on. I just know it's near the hospital." They made their way into the small town and following Katrina's directions soon found the police station on their left.

Despite her cast and crutches, Katrina was the first to reach the building. She spotted a uniformed officer emerging from her office.

"*Do you have a lost child here? A little boy?*"

"Oh, yes we certainly do. Are you his *mother*?"

Katrina could only nod her head vigorously. Tears were streaming down her cheeks.

"We've been trying to find you, but all your child could tell us was his first name and that you were at 'the museum.' Ah, here he is!"

"*Mutti! Mutti!*" Little Herbert had pushed open the office door and was running toward his mother.

"Oh, Herbert, darling! Where have you been? Why did you leave Diliana?"

"To see the horsies. Horsies!"

"Your nanny called us again about thirty minutes ago," said the policewoman. "Told us that she had called you and you were on your way here from Munich. We went out to your house and began our own search. On a larger radius. And we found him on the far side of a neighboring hill, in a stable looking at the horses in their stalls. The owners weren't at home and your nanny had left the house to look for him again, so we brought the little boy here. We'd begun calling various museums in Munich but had very little to go on."

"Thank god you found him."

Suddenly Herbert began clapping his hands repetitively and smacking his lips over and over again.

"Is he hungry?" asked Megan solicitously.

"No, no. It will pass. He's having one of his fits. I'm used to it."

Herbert soon became quiet and looked around in confusion. His repetitive movements had stopped. Slowly his blank stare cleared and again he said *Mutti* to his mother, looking at her questioningly. Showering the boy with endearments, Katrina began hugging and rocking him. She thanked the policewoman effusively.

Rick, who had been observing the scene intently, whispered to Megan that the boy seemed to have a form of epilepsy.

"Wouldn't he be having seizures then?" she whispered back.

"Not necessarily. That would be the grand mal form of epilepsy. This presents possibly as a partial onset seizure."

"A partial onset seizure," Megan repeated slowly. "Sounds terrible!"

"Children often grow out of it on their own. But that could be why he looks so baffled right now."

After a few more minutes during which Katrina continued to reassure and hug her child, Rick went over and asked quietly if she had the child's medication with her. Katrina looked startled.

"Oh, my god! Diliana gives it to him right after breakfast. And he was missing *before* breakfast. We've got to get to the house right away!"

41

RASPUTIN'S EARLY MORNING encounter with the impudent baron boy had unnerved him. Fortunately, his men were outside finishing up the loading of the moving van and no one had heard the outrageous demand von Frauenberg had made. A million more euros for his silence! The leering leech next to him would not move until he called in the transfer of funds from his bank to the brat's Monte Carlo local Crédit Suisse bank in Monte Carlo.

And yet there was something he could do about it. It would only take twenty-four hours.

42

ENERGIZED BY HER REPORT to Boris Zima and despite her lack of sleep, Raisa was one of the first visitors to enter the Lenbach House Museum when it reopened to the public after the police finished their examination that morning. She hurried to the basement gallery, half expecting to see a sign saying that it was closed to viewers. But there was nothing irregular. When she entered the Kandinsky gallery everything looked exactly the same as it had two days ago. Nothing was out of place. No changes had been made. Methodically,

Raisa counted the paintings on the wall. Eleven. Coinciding with the first time she had reckoned them. She stubbornly counted them once again. Eleven.

How could this be? With her own eyes, she had witnessed eleven paintings being loaded into a moving van just opposite the museum loading dock. True, they were coming from the number 33 address opposite and not the museum itself. But how to explain the *identical* number of objects? And the fact that Rasputin himself was in the museum for some nine hours?

Exasperated and exhausted, Raisa left the museum and returned to her modest hotel near Rasputin's Mandarin Oriental. She had set things in motion with her fanatical employer as far as tracking the mysterious moving van was concerned and now she was going to indulge in some desperately needed sleep.

43

FOLLOWING KATRINA'S DIRECTIONS, Rick drove west up the slope just beyond the Münter house, turned, and came to a stop at the front gate. Megan did not mention her previous visit to the the house and the glimpse through the window she had already had of the inside.

Hearing the car drive up, a worried-looking Diliana appeared at the door as Katrina was unlocking the gate. Little Herbert, now completely recovered from what his mother had described as a "fit," ran toward his nanny and hugged her excitedly.

"I saw horsies, Dili, I saw horsies!"

"Yes, but you should have *told* me what you wanted to do. Oh, thank god you've found him, Frau Keller, thank god."

"The police discovered him in a horse stable owned by the people two hills over. They weren't at home, so no one knew about Herbert's wandering so far away."

Katrina turned to her companions and made introductions. A sudden thought caused Diliana to cut them short.

"Good lord! He hasn't had his medication. Come with me *immediately*, young man."

Following painfully but quickly in their wake with her crutches, Katrina managed the two steps and caught up with her friends inside. She came to a stop in front of Münter's self-portrait, a glimpse of which Megan had gotten during her previous, unmentioned visit to the house. Rick was riveted. The colorful oil was a life-size bust portrait with just the tip of the artist's palette showing. Her brown hair came down to just below her ears and her head was tilted, a thoughtful expression on her face. The picture was nicely mounted with a gold inner band and a thick black outer frame.

"I think I'm falling in love," Rick said, smiling with pleasure at his hostess. Megan was studying the staircase banister and panel which Kandinsky had decorated so long ago.

"Come into the living room, do come," invited Katrina.

They entered, and Herbert, his pill downed, ran ahead of them, a toy locomotive clasped to his chest. Megan had remembered correctly. A traditional Bavarian wood stove stood to the left, and next to it against the wall was the sofa she had once sat upon. On the walls were small paintings by both Münter and Kandinsky, some of them reverse-glass works with images of saints. The patterned yellow wallpaper on which they hung reflected the gold of their halos. A dark wood-paneled dining nook took up one corner and exactly matched, to Rick's pleasure, the 1912 painting Münter had made of it showing Kandinsky animatedly conversing with a fellow artist, Erma Bossi. A couple of folk art statuettes lined the top of the panel and above them were some nine reverse-glass paintings by Kandinsky.

Across the far part of the room a red-draped casement window gave access to the view of Murnau which Münter and her lover had painted so many times. Rick walked over and took in the familiar view with its pitch-roofed castle on the left and the church with its onion-shaped bell tower on the right. Such a typical sight in Bavaria. Rick thought of one painting in particular by Kandinsky in which a golden yellow had been assigned to both white buildings. The luminosity of the low Alpine surrounding always brightened the artist's palette.

"It was not possible to reconstruct the adjacent music room in which Kandinsky's harmonium was, but at least the instrument is still here." Katrina's voice interrupted Rick's musings.

"*Mutti*! Shall I play for your guests?" Herbert looked up from the train track he was assembling on the living room floor.

"Oh, yes, let's hear Herbert play the harmonium," Megan urged. "*Kandinsky's* harmonium," she added with reverence.

The boy boosted himself up onto a low hassock in front of the instrument and sounded a minor chord with his left hand. Megan was intrigued. Then she was surprised as the boy's right hand initiated a sad, soaring melody accompanied by ever changing three-finger chords. Impressive for a boy of five.

"So, he plays by ear, does he?" Megan asked his mother who was hovering proudly over her son.

"He also reads notes, but he prefers playing by ear. Composes new melodies all the time."

"You must be very proud of him."

He may well also have the savant syndrome, Rick thought to himself, wondering if the boy could be autistic rather than epileptic, as he had first thought. He did not want to bring it up with Katrina, but a look at the boy's pills would probably produce the answer. Because the boy looked a bit plump for his age, it was possible he was on a selective serotonin reuptake inhibitor like sertraline or citalopram. But if his initial diagnosis of epilepsy was correct, then he would be on valium or one of the newer extended-release drugs like Oxtellar. Perhaps he would have a chance to find out if their tour of the house included the kitchen where presumably the pills were kept.

"Play some Bach for my friends, *Liebchen*," Katrina was saying.

Instantly Herbert changed from a dreamy, stooping posture to an erect, alert one as, faultlessly, he executed a performance of Bach's virtuosic Fugue No. 3 in C sharp major from *The Well-Tempered Clavier*, Book 1, pumping the two foot treads seamlessly. His new audience was stunned. Yes, definitely a savant, Rick decided.

After enthusiastic praise from his mother's guests, the boy, looking pleased but overwhelmed, returned to his locomotive and train cars on the floor.

Megan took out her iPhone, selected the Amcrest app, and brought up a live view of Button lapping up his dinner.

"Herbert, this is my doggie back in Texas. See? He's eating dinner right this very moment."

"Oh, *Mutti*, I want one!"

"Someday perhaps, darling, if you are very, very good and don't wander off again." She hurriedly changed the subject.

"There's one thing I want you to do and remember to do from now on, Herbert."

"What *Mutti*, what?"

"If you ever, ever find yourself alone and away from home again, I want you to tell anybody you see what your *Mutti's* name is and where she is. All right? Just say '*Katrina Keller, Lenbachhaus. München. Katrina Keller, Lenbachhaus.München.*' Let me hear you say that."

Looking very serious, Herbert complied. He repeated the words several times.

"Excellent, my little treasure, excellent."

Katrina turned her attention back to her guests.

"Our kitchen has the same wonderful view across the valley as the living room does," she said, beckoning them to follow her across the hall. Diliana stepped out of their way as they entered and Rick took a quick glance at a prescription bottle on the table where two empty cereal bowls still stood. The label said Oxtellar XR, a new once-a-day, extended release medication for partial onset seizures. So, I was right the first time, Rick concluded. A bit young to be giving them to him. But if it's controlling actual seizures and not having side effects, then I suppose her physician knows best. Hmm. Wonder how Katrina affords it though. It's extremely expensive.

"Who painted this delightful blue sideboard?" Megan's question interrupted Rick's thoughts.

"It's most likely by Kandinsky. The snaking lines and little dots are on furniture he painted upstairs. The dark blue skirting board is original, as is the light blue wallpaper in here. So is the red terrazzo floor."

"It must have covered all of the ground floor then," said Megan, "because Münter's nineteen-twelve painting of Kandinsky talking with Bossi in the dining nook also shows the floor as red."

"You are so right," Katrina smiled in approval. "Yes, all this was refurbished to look as it had looked in pre-World War I times when the Bavarian State restored the house in nineteen-ninety-nine."

"Oh, so you were not the one who restored it?"

"Good heavens no. I could never afford such a thing. It's all I can do to maintain the house as it is now."

Megan looked out the window. It did indeed have the same vista as the living room. She remembered a wonderful view of the house from the back Münter had painted showing a woman in red at the room's open window.

"Now, obviously I'm not going to be climbing any unnecessary stairs with this frightful cast on," Katrina said, smiling at her guests, "but don't let that stop you from taking a look around. You can see the studio and two loaded palettes; the more brightly colored one with a slight arc is Kandinsky's, the paler one that can fold shut is Münter's."

"Is that where they slept?" Megan asked. She had certainly not been shown this part of the house by Münter.

"Right. You'll see the original bedrooms with their decorated washstands and, in Gabriele's room, her painted bed frame. Kandinsky's topcoat and hat are laid out on the bed in his room. *We* don't sleep up there, of course; we sleep down here in the back room next to the kitchen. And Diliana sleeps up in the attic. A cozy arrangement for all when we come up here weekends."

Megan and Rick were delighted to be invited to inspect the second floor. They climbed up the winding wooden staircase and took their time admiring the sparsely furnished rooms, the walls of which were hung with reverse-glass and oil paintings by both artists. Münter had painted the headboard and footboard of her narrow bed and a traditional folk art-decorated wardrobe stood next to it. Kandinsky's bed did indeed have his black hat and topcoat on it and the room contained a desk and bookcase that had been painted a bright orange by the artist. A small portrait of the house graced one side of the four-shelf bookcase. Megan pointed to it.

"See what I mean, Rick, about how, if you look at it from the garden side, the house seems as if it has three full stories in addition to the attic?"

"I do, I do."

They walked into the studio, which they both knew from Münter's 1909 portrayal that included a humorous glimpse of Kandinsky in the connecting room reading a book in bed. A white washstand and a supply of metal water pitchers stood to the right of the studio's blue draped window. On the left a three-drawer white washstand decorated by Kandinsky showed the miniscule figures of himself on a galloping horse urging Münter to follow him on her lagging horse.

"Perhaps this was symbolic: his command to her to follow him in the bolder painting he was creating?" Rick asked.

"I like that. Although he did encourage her to go her own way." They were both squatting to examine the amusing little frieze on the middle drawer.

"Yikes! I can't get up. You've got to help me Rick. I keep forgetting I can't do this anymore."

Gratefully, Megan took Rick's proffered hands and he pulled his former professor to her feet. She walked over to look at the two palettes laid out on top of a small chest of drawers which was decorated in traditional folk art style. Four slim paint brushes lay by Münter's palette and a cluster of some fifteen or so brushes stood in a small glass jar by Kandinsky's. Megan glanced at the small black-framed painting above them. It depicted a pink street leading the eye into the canvas past a couple of houses. Flame-like trees were indicated in yellow brushstrokes. Megan studied the picture intently, then backed away and took not only a Google Glass of it but an iPhone shot as well.

"Should you be doing that without asking Katrina first?" Rick asked timidly.

"Can't help it. Documentation."

"We'd better go back downstairs. She will begin wondering what we're doing up here," Rick said, watching nervously as Megan continued to "document" the rooms and their contents. They turned back into the hall and walked toward the inviting glass-paneled door that opened onto the front balcony. Megan looked through one of the panes at their parked car, then carefully climbed back down the Kandinsky staircase.

"This is all so truly wonderful, Katrina," Megan said with sincerity. But she did not hold back in her next sentence.

"And the extraordinary restoration makes it all the more important that you open the house to the public."

"You must understand, Megan. It *is* my intention to do so. Absolutely. I just have to figure out how to pay for it. And now with Herbert's..." Her voice trailed off.

Megan quickly changed the subject. Looking at the wall opposite them, she commented on Münter's cheery 1910 painting of Kandinsky, dressed in a blue country jacket, seated at the dining nook behind a large white pot with handle and spout, blue cream pitcher, and brown sugar bowl. A green and red rooster's head pot holder and a basket with three oranges completed the inviting arrangement. Megan pointed to the painting.

"Do you think that's a coffee pot or a tea pot, Katrina?" She knew the answer but affected ignorance.

"Oh, tea, definitely tea. Kandinsky was a great drinker of tea and Münter became so."

"It's interesting that, so long after their breakup, she kept this particular portrait of him on her wall. In fact, I remember admiring it when I visited her so many years ago."

"Well, it represented the most intense, most exciting time of her life after all. A time when she was in close contact with leading members of the Blue Rider movement. Party to their innovations and aims."

"Even though she did manage to alienate the wives of both Marc and Macke. If those two artists hadn't been killed in World War I, it is doubtful she would have kept up with them," Megan added.

"Yes, she was pretty much of a loner until Johannes Eichner came into her life and brightened it."

Megan stood up and walked over to the painting.

"It *is* a copy, isn't it?"

"Oh, yes, and a good one, too, don't you think? The original is now in Jerusalem's Israel Museum." Katrina did not know she had just passed Megan's veracity test.

Rick, realizing that Katrina needed to rest after the emotional turmoil of the morning, made a suggestion.

"Look, Katrina. I know you don't have supplies here to feed lunch to two extra people. So why don't Megan and I go into town for lunch and you take a rest and eat something here when you're hungry. Is there anything we can bring you from town?"

"Yes, that is very thoughtful of you, dear Rick. I am suddenly feeling quite tired. Thank you."

Megan was angry with herself that she had not realized how exhausted Katrina must be. She tried to make up for it. Quietly she conferred for a moment with Rick, who began nodding his head vigorously. Smiling broadly, Megan turned to Katrina.

"Do you think you will be in good enough shape to return to work Monday?"

"I certainly plan to be."

"Well, then, here's what we propose. We want to be out of your hair but available for the return trip to Munich and your apartment. So, since Rick is eager to see Ludwig's castle at Herrenchiemsee, why don't we leave you here with Herbert and Diliana until late tomorrow afternoon and we'll all go back together?"

"Oh, that sounds lovely—so much fun for you two. Have you been to that lake before, Megan?"

"Once, but it was years and years ago. So, it will be a nice adventure for both of us."

Hugs were exchanged all around—plenty for Herbert too—and the two Americans were soon happily off in hot pursuit of their colorful friend, King Ludwig II of Bavaria.

44

UNDER NO CIRCUMSTANCES was Rasputin going to be out another million euros to that goddamn brat of a baron standing next to him. Yes, he would make the call to his bank to transfer funds to the Crédit Suisse Bank branch in Monte Carlo and to the account number the man had scribbled onto the piece of paper he was waving in his face. But he would be using the code established long ago with his banking agent in Geneva. A code that, regardless of what he was told, the agent would wait twenty-four hours before execution of the order. That would give Rasputin time to deal permanently with the smug young man standing in front of him who had had the nerve to blackmail *him*. Under the watchful eyes of his antagonist he dialed the bank and placed the order. It would expire in twenty-four hours.

45

IRIS AND LASZLO TOGARASSY need not have worried about neo-Nazi backlash at their Blue Rider Gallery. Saturday, the day after the violent demonstration at the Lenbach House Museum, turned out to be their best business day since opening the exhibition. It was as if people wanted to show their respect for Kandinsky by showing up at the gallery and its *Hommage à Kandinsky* exhibit. Sales were brisk and a number of people actually bought some of the paintings on view in the gallery's inner room, which had been opened once visitors began showing up.

Both Togarassys were regaled with enthusiastic endorsements by visitors affirming the importance of the Russian artist for twentieth-century art. They praised not only the originality of his expressive Blue Rider period in Munich, but also the extraordinary pictorial vocabulary of his later Bauhaus period in Weimar and Dessau, when his non-objective canvases of 1922 to 1933 inspired new directions of Gestalt psychology in art. Gallery copies of Kandinsky's Bauhaus book *Point and Line to Plane* sold out, as did reprints of his earlier famous essay *On the Spiritual in Art*. Also bought up quickly was a new paperback edition of the original *Blue Rider Almanac*, first published in 1912 in co-editorship with Franz Marc. For his essay, "Spiritual Treasures," the genial animal painter's illustrations included Chinese paintings, German woodcuts, Picasso works, and children's drawings.

A tall, blond music student was devastated when the last copy of the *Almanac* was sold just before he could get his hands on it.

"Oh, I so want to have, in the original facsimile, what the composer Arnold Schönberg wrote for that publication!"

"And what was that?" Iris asked, not being thoroughly acquainted with the contents of a book that contained fourteen major essays and almost 150 illustrations featuring art and folk art from around the world.

"He called it 'The Relationship to the Text,'" answered the student, "but in addition, the *Almanac* contains a facsimile of his song 'Herzgewächse' and facsimiles of songs by Anton Webern and Alban Berg as well. Oh, I'm really very, very disappointed you're out of copies."

"If the crowds are as large next week as they are today we'll be ordering more, so do try to come back," Iris assured him.

As Laszlo passed by his wife on his way to the inner room with a client, he whispered to her. "At this rate, I may have to spend all day Sunday painting."

Iris smiled at him encouragingly.

Hommage à Kandinsky was a huge success.

46

IT WAS SATURDAY AFTERNOON and Chief Detective Dieter Löser, a robust young man, clean-shaven except for dramatic long sideburns, sat across the interrogation table from one of the men his officers had arrested the night before. A self-proclaimed neo-Nazi, the heavyset man was being held on charges of incitement to riot, breaking fire regulations, and aggravated murder in the death of one Niki Wächter, night watchman at the Lenbach House Museum. The detective was eager to get on with the questioning as he had promised his wife, Penelope, an overnight trip to their lake house.

"And how far would you say you were from the entrance to the original villa part of the museum, Herr Krankenhauer?"

"I can tell you that I was at the back of the crowd, urging my people on in what was a perfectly legal demonstration, as you ought to know," Krankenhauer answered evenly.

The detective considered the man's arrogant answer and haughty demeanor. Could that be influencing his opinion of the man's truthfulness? Krankenhauer's condescending attitude was irritating him. And the other arrestees had uniformly identified him as their leader. Löser leaned forward and looked the man in the eyes.

"And what did you do when your people started throwing bricks at the museum?"

"They were not my people. That's not what we were there for. We had assembled for a peaceful protest of the outrageous fact that works by foreigners flood our German museums."

"And do you see setting dozens of posters ablaze in a crowd as being a 'peaceful protest'"?

"The brief burst of small flames hurt absolutely no one. They were under control at all times."

"Just like the bricks? Like the one that killed a night watchman?"

"I tell you none of my people were involved in that."

"And how would you know if you were at the back of the crowd?"

"This is becoming outrageous. For god's sake, there were a lot of other people standing around watching. Curiosity seekers, tourists, people from the neighborhood. It's entirely possible that one of them used our protest as a cover."

"As a cover? What do you mean? A cover for what?"

"I'm thinking someone wanted to get inside the museum. After all, the dead guard was found at the entry door, wasn't he?"

"So, someone who wanted to get inside the museum just happened to be there when your demonstration took place?"

Krankenhauer shrugged his shoulders. Silence ensued. Löser decided to change his line of questioning.

"And where do you think the bricks came from? We found absolutely no damage to the brick paving by the museum. Not a single brick had been pulled up. Someone in your group must have brought them with him."

Krankenhauer was tired. The incessant questioning was irritating him. All of a sudden, he remembered seeing two foreigners, most likely Americans, rush toward the female museum official who had been felled by his brick. He proceeded to utilize that observation.

"No one from my group had bricks or any other projectiles with them. But I can tell you who did. Just as I was calling off our demonstration, complying with police orders, mind you, I noticed two people in front of me in the crowd and they each had a brick. As I passed by, one of them hurled a brick at a woman who had come out of the museum and was trying to quiet the crowd. The brick knocked her to the ground. That is what I witnessed."

"Really? Can you give me a description of the two people you saw?"

"One was a man, of about middle age, tall, with black-rimmed glasses and graying hair. The other was a woman. She was short and definitely much older than the man. Although her hair wasn't white. It was brown, but you could just tell it was dyed and that she was older, maybe even twenty years older. His mother, most likely. And she was wearing one of those Google Glass devices."

"And they both had bricks?"

"They both had bricks."

"Anything else?"

"She called him 'Rick,' and they were probably American. At least he was."

47

RAISA FELT RESTED after a long sleep back at her hotel. She woke up a little after one in the afternoon, and food, not Kandinsky or Boris Zima, was on her mind.

She was doubly irritated then when her cellphone rang just one minute after warm Knoephia soup had been placed on the table in front of her at the hotel restaurant. It was Boris.

"Yes?"

"Raisa. Now *I* have news for you."

"And what is that?" Her potato dumpling soup was not going to stay hot very long.

"I have intervened with the *Cargo Logistik* van."

"How do you mean 'intervened'?"

"Just outside Bratislava. And I even got it pulled to the side of the road by the local police."

"Goodness. How did you do that?"

"I simply called the main police office, pretending to be the distressed van driver, and reported that I had been robbed of my van. Said two men had stolen it."

"That's quite a ruse."

"It worked. The van now has a new itinerary and a new driver and mate." The excitement in Boris's announcement was almost palpable.

"How so?" Raisa questioned.

"The original driver and his helper were encouraged to abandon their task. In fact, they are no longer in a position to inconvenience us."

"You mean they were *killed*?"

"Let us say they were permanently persuaded."

Raisa could only think what might happen to *her* should Boris be disappointed in her work. If she should become an "inconvenience." Her pocket Beretta was her only protection. She quickly took a spoonful of her soup.

"And the police officer who stopped the van?"

"Let us say he is no longer active."

Raisa put down her soup spoon. She was beginning to feel nauseated.

"And I have fascinating news as to the original destination of the van and its occupants," Boris continued.

"And that is?"

"Odessa."

"My god! So, it *was* Rasputin after all.

"Yes. That freaking god-damned crook!"

"And the paintings *are* the Kandinskys then—all eleven of them?"

"My crew only took the wrapping off three of them. But they e-mailed me photos of the paintings and they are definitely by Kandinsky. I enjoined them not to unwrap any more. Take a look at your cellphone in a few minutes. I wanted to tell you the good news in person, but now I'll send you the actual photos. Just wait till you see them!"

"That's amazing, Boris, amazing." Raisa had regained her composure.

"Well, it was *your* perseverance that made this possible and *your* clever idea to photograph the van."

After a few more minutes they hung up and Raisa returned to her now room-temperature soup. Heisting the heist was a tremendous accomplishment. Her bill to the gluttonous Muscovite would be tremendous as well.

48

HEINRICH VON FRAUENBERG was immensely pleased with himself. By threatening to expose him as a thief, he had forced the wretched Ukrainian Rasputin to wire his Monaco bank another million euros. A million euros! He strode out of Paleo, over to the nearby taxi stand on Luisenstrasse, took the first one in line, a cream-colored Audi, and instructed the driver to take him to the airport. He wanted to get back to Monte Carlo and his beloved yacht as soon as possible. No need to alert the crew of his arrival; he would just appear.

He did not notice the taxi that was following. Nor, once inside, that a heavyset man was standing in line very close behind him at the Air France ticket counter. Close enough to hear what his destination was. After Heinrich moved away the man repeated the destination to the agent, paying in cash rather than by credit card. Once aboard the hour-and-a-half flight to Nice, the man adroitly took a seat across the aisle from his target, unfolded a newspaper and spent the trip apparently absorbed in it. One of the articles he actually read happened to be about Grace Kelly, the American actress who married Prince Rainier of Monaco in 1956, and the fatal car accident that somersaulted her and her daughter over a cliff in 1982. Only the daughter survived and all Monaco mourned the death of their beloved and beautiful Princess. The paper was still shielding the man's face as Heinrich exited the plane. An identical procedure took place after Heinrich purchased a train ticket. The man behind him in line bought a ticket to the same destination.

When the young baron emerged from the Monte Carlo train station and trotted down the steep incline to Port Hercule he was not alone. His stalker was a safe distance behind and, stopping abreast of the Casino La Rascasse at the foot of the pier opposite, watched him walk to a luxurious three-story yacht docked at the far end. He boarded it. That was all Alyksandr Miesel needed to know. He would not have to use his pistol; he would use the yacht.

It was five o'clock in the afternoon. Turning toward the casino, he pulled out his cellphone and called his employer.

Rasputin answered curtly after the first ring.

"What news?"

"He's moored in Port Hercule and, fortunately, at the very end of the dock."

"Do it tonight then."

"All right. It will have to be late though. Do you still want me to call?"

"If you are successful, yes. It is not about the lateness that I am concerned, it is about the success of your mission. If you miss him on the yacht, get him at his bank on Monday morning. You've got the details. And remember, I'm paying you ten thousand euros for your success." Rasputin had decided to take no chances with his twenty-four-hour hold on money orders. After all, it was theoretically possible that his surly blackmailer might reach a Monaco bank Monday morning just before the hold expired.

Miesel grabbed a taxi and had the driver drop him off at a motorcycle shop he had located on Google. He surveyed the models and paid two-hundred-and-sixty euros for a used motorcycle with side and top cases, then rode to a large hardware store nearby. They carried exactly what he was looking for. He invested in the equipment, once again paying in cash, and loaded the cycle cases. He stopped at a service station for gas. Now he would return to the dock and wait for nightfall. The casino portico, with all its comings and goings, would make an ideal waiting spot and he and his bike would be relatively inconspicuous. With time on his hands he also stopped at a nearby pizzeria.

Heinrich was furious. His remaining two crew members had given themselves the day off and perhaps the night as well it would seem, for they were nowhere to be found. Typical. They had done this before once. And the yacht's inside lights were blazing. He reset the timers to go on at eight and off at two in the morning, his usual bedtime. Suddenly realizing he had not eaten for hours, Heinrich hurriedly left the yacht, loped down the pier, and headed north into town toward his favorite restaurant. Glittering gathering spot for film stars and high-stake gamblers, it was located in the sumptuous belle époque Hotel de Paris, a half-hour's walk away.

The young baron remained long after he consumed his food, planning what he would do with the new euro infusion into his bank account. Damn! He wouldn't be able to touch the funds until Monday. But he planned to be inside the bank the moment it opened that morning.

His reverie was broken by hearing his name quietly uttered. Approaching him, her face wreathed in smiles, was a glamorous female escort he had hired a number of times. She was in the company of an elderly man who was intent on reaching a table across the room.

"Off duty at eight," she whispered to Heinrich as she passed him. "How about some fun tonight?"

"Deal. I'll wait here." A smile crossed Heinrich's face. From now on he would be able to afford such indulgence whenever and wherever he wished. He ordered a brandy and settled down for some solitaire on his cellphone. He would not be alone long.

49

MEGAN WAS DRIVING THIS TIME. She knew the route as she had driven it once before. The sun was out and after a long, relaxed lunch in town, she and Rick were both in chipper spirits, glad to be off and by themselves for a while. Rick was on his Blackberry finalizing their reservation for a suite with a panoramic lake view at the Yachthotel Chiemsee in the small town of Prien.

"And now we have about a one-and-a-half hour-drive east to Chiemsee and our luxury hotel," Rick said, stretching his long body and studying the paper map Megan had brought along. He noticed something southeast of their destination.

"Hey! How'd you like to make a side trip and take in Hitler's Eagle's Nest?" Rick was a World War II buff and his eye had caught the name Berchtesgaden on the map near Salzburg.

"Looks as if it's only two hours from Murnau on the map."

"Hmm. Tempting, but I don't think so. It's almost as far as Salzburg and a dip below that."

"Oh, yes, I do see what you mean on the map. But aren't you tempted?"

"Only on your behalf, honey. I was there years ago and I must say once is enough. There's really not all that much to see. Really."

"What *did* you see?"

"Well, first you have to take a bumpy bus up the winding forest road of the Kehlstein mountainside, which takes you to the brick chalet on top that served as Hitler's so-called teahouse for visiting higher ups. It's a really narrow road and studded with lots of short tunnels. From the top, where the buses park, you can see both Austria and Germany—something that of course appealed to Hitler, the Austrian *Führer* of Germany. The chalet was built for him as a fiftieth-birthday surprise by Martin Bormann, you know."

"Yes. I've seen stock footage of the Führer receiving visiting dignitaries. Also of Eva Braun prancing happily about. Poor woman!"

"So, when you do get to the top you first have to walk through a long brick tunnel, then wait in line to enter an elevator up to the actual house. And *that's* what stands out in my memory. The elevator. It's lined with a copper-colored mirror—the four walls, elevator door, and ceiling too. You stand there, glancing at your own reflection, and then it dawns on you that Adolf Hitler has been reflected on the very same wall where you now are! Imagine!"

"Yikes! That gives me the creeps."

"That's exactly what I felt. It was a preternatural experience and I've never, ever forgotten it."

"Okay, I guess I can live without seeing Eagle's Nest. This trip at least."

"Good, and we can get to Chiemsee that much earlier. We're about to join highway eight and that'll take us straight to Prien and our hotel. We can rest a bit, look around town, and find a restaurant right on the lake for this evening."

"I'll find the restaurant right now." Rick turned his cellphone back on and began a search. He did not have to search very long.

"Aha! I've found one you are going to love. It's in a feminist location."

"Huh?"

"I'm telling you, Frau Doktor Crespi, it's in a feminist location." He teased Megan.

"Come on. What are you talking about?"

Rick grinned widely, then disabused his friend.

"It's on the Fraueninsel, right in the lake. You should have guessed what I was talking about."

"Oh, boy, you really got me this time," Megan conceded. "I have always liked it that the Chiemsee has two main islands, the Herreninsel—men's island—where Ludwig's castle is, and the smaller, of course, Fraueninsel—women's island. So, what's the restaurant? It could be fun taking a ferry out to the island. Should be a beautiful night for it."

"It's called Hotel-Restaurant Inselwirt, and has good reviews. One says it was 'the most wonderful meal I think I have ever had.' What does 'wirt' mean; I know 'Insel' means island, but what does 'wirt' mean?"

"It means 'host.' Good thing for a hotel and a restaurant to be. Okay, let's do that this evening and have our own five-course meal."

"Wonder if we should make reservations?"

"Yes. Let's call and make it for eight o'clock. Good idea." In a playful mood Megan affected what she thought of as a Scottish accent with matching vocabulary.

"Aye, sure an' we do not want to feel rushed, me dearrr boy, an' do ye not know I be welcoming a wee lie-down in the bye and bye."

The drive to Prien and its great alpine lake, the largest in Bavaria, would take only an hour and a half but it was already almost four o'clock. Megan decided to pass the time by asking her physician pal to talk about his profession and how he felt about it now, some twenty-five years into it. She was surprised by his outburst.

"Don't get me wrong, I love my profession and the good it can do, but anyone who thinks doctors make lots of money has it all wrong. On the whole, unless we have millionaire parents, we begin our careers dirt poor. After four years of med school, at about forty-four thousand dollars a year, coming to a total of one-hundred-and-seventy-six thousand dollars, let's say, and then six years of specialty training with yearly salaries in the thirty-thousand dollar range, well, we're up to our hips, not knees, in debt because of accruing interest payments on the huge amount we owe. On top of that many of us don't have regular working hours, as you well know."

Megan digested the information slowly, admitting she had not thought of Rick's profession from that point of view.

"That's why, about fifteen years ago, I decided to found a stock market investment group for me and some of my fellow physicians. The idea took fire and we've done quite well—debts finally paid off, and a steady drizzle of extra income."

"What a terrific idea! How clever of you, Rick."

"Not so much cleverness as downright necessity."

"Well, whatever the motivation, I'm proud of you. And your two boys will be well taken care of." Immediately, Megan wished she had not mentioned Rick's boys, as they were now without a mother. A painful silence ensued while they both concentrated on the mountain scenery with its remarkable healing powers.

50

THE VODKA TYCOON OF MOSCOW had dispatched his number one agent, Ivan Ivanov, to handle the waylaying of the *Cargo Logistik* van. The two unwitting vehicle drivers had selected a southern route for the tedious thousand-mile trek to Odessa, one that would take them from Bavaria through Austria, Slovakia, Hungary, Romania, and Moldova. But they were barely past Bratislava when a Slovakian police car, having received reports that the van had been stolen, pulled them off the highway.

As the two men calmly showed the van's paperwork to the officer who had commanded them to step down from their cab, a silver gray Porsche station wagon pulled up beside them honking urgently. A blonde woman in the front passenger seat rolled down her window. Smiling at the three curious men who had turned to look at her, she abruptly raised a compact Beretta 93R machine gun from her lap and burst fired a round at them. She did not need to fire another. Three corpses lay bleeding by the side of the highway.

Seconds later two men in the back seat of the station wagon jumped out and without a sound set to work. With practiced speed, they placed the three bodies inside the police vehicle and drove it into the nearby forest. After they had run back and climbed into the van's cab, they waited, with motor running, for the station wagon in front of them to pull out onto the highway. Some nine miles later the two-vehicle caravan turned into a deserted rest stop and came to a halt at the far end. The station wagon parked on the highway side parallel to the rear end of the van, blocking the view of any passing motorists. The Porsche driver, Ivan Ivanov, a lean, red-headed man in his forties, and his wife and partner in crime, Natasha, exited the car and walked to the back of the van. Its rear door was already raised and the two men were in the process of unloading one of the large bubble-wrapped items within.

"I think two more unwraps will suffice," Ivanov directed, helping the woman strip back bubble wrap and revealing the four-by-four-foot oil painting within. He stood back and aimed his cellphone at the canvas, taking one full picture and one detail of the signature. The same procedure took place with two more of the Kandinsky works. Then the paintings were carefully rewrapped and reloaded into the moving van.

From the back of the station wagon the men then removed two five-gallon paint canisters with hoses attached to them. They were capped with eighteen-inch spray wands. The men aimed them at the truck's sides and within minutes the *Cargo Logistik* logo had been obliterated by dark blue paint on both sides of the van. The cab and rear door of the van were also given a dark blue covering. Finally, Russian license plates replaced the original German ones.

"Now here is your itinerary," Ivanov said to the new drivers of the van, spreading out a large paper map in front of them. The two men were from Moscow's poorest and most crime-ridden district, Kapotnya, some twelve miles southeast of the city center, and they were not familiar with the city's cultural landmarks.

"You drive directly north through Slovakia, and Czechia past Brno, enter Poland—note there's some construction on the highway here—and head to Warsaw. Spend tonight somewhere on the loop outside Warsaw. Then tomorrow, Sunday, get an early start, drive northeast through Belarus via highway ninety-nine here—there are several tolls—and you should arrive at Moscow around ten or eleven in the evening, depending on traffic. Remember you'll be crossing a time zone and it will be an hour later there. Above all do not speed. We don't want you stopped for a traffic ticket. You will call me once you reach the outskirts of Moscow and have found a place to overnight. At that point, I will give you your destination specifics. And I shall then alert my patron to be ready for your arrival at ten Monday morning. He doesn't want you to unload at night. Payment will be made upon delivery."

Ivanov looked at the two expendable drivers and smiled.

51

AWAKENING FROM A FIVE-HOUR NAP, Igor Rasputin found his wrath waning. That upstart Paleo owner who had had the colossal nerve to threaten him with blackmail was about to be neutralized by his trusted aide Alyksandr Miesel. He had paid off the discreet boys from Amiinyi handsomely, and they would be on their way back to their beloved island after spending a few more days at Paleo enjoying Munich. Rasputin himself had returned to his hotel for some much-needed sleep. He would return to Odessa the next morning, Sunday. After all, it was going to take a good two days for the cargo van holding his newly acquired artworks to make the trip from Munich to Odessa. And there was one more thing he wanted to do in the Bavarian capital. He had seen an article in the local paper lauding the choice of a new gallery to host an exhibition intriguingly entitled *Hommage à Kandinsky*. This he had to see.

Thus, refreshed from his nap and comfortably full from a late lunch at his Mandarin Oriental hotel, he hailed a taxi and directed its pleasant female driver to take him to Hohenzollerngasse 36, the Schwabing location of the *Der Blaue Reiter* Gallery.

It was the gallery owner himself, Laszlo Togarassy, who greeted Rasputin along with two other people at the door.

"Welcome, welcome. I am sorry, but just now the gallery is so full that under fire laws I am not allowed to admit any further visitors until a few people have left. Please bear with me."

Seeing the glut of people inside, Rasputin contented himself with looking at the extraordinary Kandinsky featured in the gallery's main window. Rectangular in shape, it was a riotous hymn to the three primary colors and their luminous secondary color blends of pink, crimson, lavender, orange, and green. They shaped themselves into two rows of village house facades, a fence, windblown trees, waving fields, and distant mountains. Muscular dabbing brush strokes animated and dispersed the cascading colors and yet were sporadically kept under control by black outlines. A surprising burst of black dominated the upper left center of the painting. Was it a very large tree, Rasputin wondered, staring at the swaying outlines extending far above the house roofs? Individual dabs of green across the black mass supported such a reading. And yet the tree itself seemed to be abruptly cut off at the picture's center by a row of crimson, red, purple, blue, and yellow houses and distant yellow-green fields. Could this be two separate pictures conjoined?

"You can come in now if you'd care to."

The man's voice jolted Rasputin, so deeply engaged had he been in the seductive painting. It was the gallery owner again.

"But tell me," Rasputin heard himself asking the smiling man, "is this Kandinsky in your window a complete picture or two paintings of the same period joined together?"

"Ah ha," a pleased Lazlo Togarassy answered. "I see you know your

Kandinskys. You are at the same time correct *and* wrong. It is one and the same canvas, which I can prove to you when we go inside and you see the canvas back, but it was painted upon by two different artists, close friends, in fact lovers."

"I understand. You must be speaking of Gabriele Münter, since the ensemble is so unmistakably Blue Rider in style."

"Exactly. This is why I have put the unusual artwork in my window. It symbolizes in actuality the closeness of approach of two of the Blue Rider artists."

"Is it for sale?" Rasputin asked eagerly, somewhat surprised by his own rush of enthusiasm.

"I am sorry. This one painting is not for sale. I consider it the lodestone of the exhibition. May I introduce myself? I am Lazlo Togarassy, owner of the gallery."

"And I am a Blue Rider fan, Boris Zima from Moscow." Rasputin was delighted with himself for thinking of taking on the identity of his greatest rival.

"Goodness! I have certainly heard of your famed collection. What an honor to have you here. Please, do come inside and see what we have in store for you. I promise not to disturb you until you have finished examining the works. But I do hope you will seek me out afterward."

Rasputin did indeed reengage with the jovial, proud gallery owner after he had closely examined all the works in the exhibition, rather a feat in itself as the place was so crowded.

"I congratulate you on assembling such a fine representation of Kandinsky works from all major periods. That there could still be this many not in museums or private collections is indeed a surprise. And I see the labels are almost all pinned now with small 'sold' flags. This is truly extraordinary. How long has your show been open?"

"Only a week. Attendance had been quite good but today, after the terrible anti-Kandinsky demonstration at the Lenbach House Museum of last night, the gallery has been literally mobbed. People were lined up outside before I even opened up. And yes, almost everything has been sold. It is truly amazing."

Lazlo was also relieved. After leaving the man from Moscow to look at the exhibition further, he headed into the back showroom, hastily ushered admiring onlookers out, closed and locked the door.

52

"LOOK AT THAT STREET SIGN, Rick, our Yachthotel is on an ob-noxious street," Megan said as they turned off Seestrasse and approached their hotel on Prien's shore.

"Ha! I see what you mean. 'Harrasser Street.' Well, there is an extra 'r' in the word at least."

A smiling porter appeared as they drove up to the entrance of the large, five-story hotel. He carried their bags through the cheerful lobby to a very long registration desk made of knotty pinewood and fronting the cove outside where numerous yachts were docked. Deep blue water beckoned the visitors.

"You have the top floor suite as requested but," the clerk stole a glance at Megan, "I must tell you that there is a circular staircase up to the attic bedroom and..."

"Thank you for your concern, but that will not be a problem for me," Megan interrupted, somewhat miffed. "Or were you concerned about my son here, perhaps?"

Rick grinned. He had often heard Megan's introduction of him as her son to strangers. And now that they were sharing a suite it seemed rather handy.

"I think I can contend with the situation," he reassured the solicitous clerk.

With the porter leading the way, they took the elevator to the fifth floor and entered a charming white-walled sitting room trimmed in light-colored pinewood with rustic wicker couch and chairs grouped around a glass coffee table. The room had the same cheerful blue carpeting used in the lobby and sported the same narrow conjoined wooden rafters above. And it was true: a narrow, wooden circular staircase took up one fifth of the room. Megan could hardly wait to climb up it and see what the panoramic view was like from there.

As soon as Rick had tipped the porter and they were alone, both mounted the stairs and were soon exclaiming at the charming attic room, the walls of which were the same light knotty pinewood as the reception desk downstairs.

Two double beds were against the wall. There was only one thing wrong. The panorama Megan had expected to view could only be seen by raising the slanting clerestory windows with their attached poles. She would have to stand on tiptoe. Nevertheless, the spectacular bathroom made up for the disappointment. In addition to an oval shaped, all-glass shower compartment, a cedar wood sauna beckoned.

Megan was in ecstasy. She so loved saunas that she had installed two of them, a free-standing one in the backyard of her Dallas home and another in the indoor poolroom of her Bonham lake house.

"Oh, boy! You can bet I'll avail myself of this before we leave the lake. I could skip my morning exercise and take the sauna instead."

"So, you like saunas. I don't. You can have it all to yourself."

"I was planning to, Rick."

"Just pulling your leg."

"I hope so."

"Hey! Wanna take a look at the yacht harbor out front before we swim to our Fraueninsel restaurant?"

"Good idea."

A few minutes later, after learning from the reception desk that island ferries picked up passengers every half-hour at the hotel waterfront, they were outside and down by the water, admiring the sparkling nautical display along four extended piers. Some twenty yachts of various shapes and sizes were docked and the predominant wrap color was blue.

"Absolutely charming," breathed Megan.

"Let's go sit over there and enjoy the show." Rick pointed to a group of inviting armchairs with blue cushions under a large blue canopy.

Avoiding a group of rather noisy people already seated, they headed for two isolated chairs under the far corner of the awning and settled down to observe the lively, ever-changing scene.

Children were running and playing on the hotel lawn and their merry shouts filled the air. Megan had forgotten to take off her Google Glass and so she took a few shots of them.

After some ten minutes of silent enjoyment she nudged her fellow spectator.

"You know what, Rick? I was thinking. The last time I got to enjoy a sauna in Europe was in Finland when I stayed with the descendants of the twentieth-century painter Akseli Gallen-Kallela at his famous home in Tarvaspää."

"Was that when you were engaged with hunting down a lost work by Gustav Klimt?"

"Well, that was another time. This time I was in Helsinki on Helene Schjerfbeck business—setting up an exhibition of her works—and afterward I skedaddled up to Tarvaspää to visit the Gallen-Kallela family as well. And by the way, Rick, the stress is on the first syllable of 'Helsinki,' not the second, as you pronounced it. The first syllable is stressed when pronouncing almost all Finnish words. Same is true of Czech words. As with the painter Oskar Kokoschka, whose father was a Czech goldsmith."

"Correction noted. Who the HE-ck is HE-lene SCHJERF-beck?" Rick had been the object of his friend's eruptive corrections more than once and took them in stride.

"She was a Finnish contemporary of Gallen-Kallela and painted portraits and landscapes that evolved from keen realism to, you could say, stringent reductivism. She led a very confined life dominated by a disapproving mother. Quite the opposite of Gallen-Kallela who, because of his pungent illustrations of Finland's national epic, was active on the international scene. He even visited Taos, New Mexico when he was in America. Wanted to see native Indian art."

"I don't remember your ever teaching us about them."

"Too many fascinating artists; too little time," Megan sighed. "But I did get to write about them in a chapter on Scandinavian art for a book called *World Impressionism* a couple of decades ago."

"It's a pity you couldn't have included a lecture on them in one of your courses, though."

"I guess the criterion has to be whether or not the artist was truly first-rate for starters, and if she/he contributed to the history of art and human history, meaning changing perceptions, originality, psychological content, social impact, and so forth."

"So, Kandinsky had it and your two Finnish exponents didn't?"

"Well, that's rather stringent, but yes. After all, as early as nineteen-thirteen Kandinsky helped point the way to abstraction. Ultimately, he used color as his *subject matter*, versus using it to define objects. And remember, he possessed synesthesia. Music conjured certain colors for him. He called what he did in his later Bauhaus years 'non-objective' art; whereas we call it abstract.

Just as Arnold Schönberg himself never used the word 'atonal" for his subsequent twelve-tone serialism. It's no coincidence, after all, that Wassily invited Arnold to contribute to the *Blue Rider Almanac*."

"Uh huh. And I remember you taught us about the contemporary Russian Suprematist artist Kasimir Malevich and his approach to geometric abstract art via Picasso's Cubism and Italian Futurism. Loved the large black square paintings you showed by him, and, of course, I often visit the tilted white square on white at New York's Museum of Modern Art."

"Oh yes, suddenly abstraction was *the* way to go. Think of Mondrian in Holland, for example. His was geometric whereas you could characterize Kandinsky's art as lyrical abstraction."

"I certainly agree with that. Even at his most geometric, he's always poetic."

Their lively art conversation was interrupted by the long hoot of a horn. The island ferry was approaching. Grabbing her trusty cloth shoulder bag, Megan followed Rick to the dock and after a small group of cheerful passengers descended, they hurried onboard and got a good spot at the front railing of the ship, where they would be able to see the car-free Fraueninsel, much smaller than the Herreninsel, which they would be visiting the next morning.

Rick began reading about the Fraueninsel on his cellphone and suddenly gasped at a photograph.

"Guess who's immortalized there, Megan?"

"Nuns?" She was referring to the island's Benedictine convent.

"That too. But no. There's a cenotaph to General Alfred Jodl. He was one of the ten World War II Nazi criminals condemned to execution by hanging at Nuremberg. Look, here's a photograph of the family grave. See, his name, writ large, is at the bottom of the large cross." Rick's fascination with World War II was aroused.

"But he's not actually buried there then if it's a cenotaph," asserted Megan.

"No. He's not buried anywhere. He and the other nine war criminals were cremated, along with Hermann Göring, and their ashes were scattered in Munich's Isar River."

"I guess the authorities wanted to be sure their gravesites would not become magnets for extremist organizations."

"Most likely. By the way, Jodl was wounded in the famous plot to assassinate Hitler at the Wolf's Lair in nineteen-forty-four. Suffered a head concussion from the explosion."

"So, he was a member of Hitler's inner, inner circle. Wow." Megan was intensely interested in the history of both world wars. So many of the artists about whom she taught had been affected by them.

Rick was the first to catch sight of the small island and he pointed it out to his friend who was surprised to find it on her left-hand rather than right-hand side. The larger island was closer and on their right. It was seven-thirty in the evening and there was still plenty of summer sunlight. The ferry stopped briefly at Ludwig's Herreninsel before docking at its sister island some fifteen minutes later.

The walk to the Benedictine complex was short and the island's cemetery with its Jodl cenotaph was near and the gravestone was easily recognizable.

"Just look at that!" Megan was pointing to a fresh wreath of flowers laid at the foot of the cross.

"Surely looks as if some neo-Nazi group found it," Rick said, shaking his head.

"I hope they aren't anywhere near us."

"Oh, I doubt there's a local branch here on an island of just three-hundred permanent inhabitants. I just read that statistic online."

"Maybe it's time to go to dinner."

"Yes, can you hear my borborygmus? Rick looked serious.

"Your *what*?"

"My stomach growling."

"Show off!" Actually, Megan liked learning about anything medical and often had to stop herself from asking her good-natured friend too many questions.

The Inselwirt Hotel Restaurant was even more charming than anticipated, with white walls and several wood-framed bay windows looking out at the boats docked a few feet away. They were led to a table that gave onto the nautical view and next to an animated German couple who were eating and drinking with gusto. They appeared to be in their late thirties. The woman had short brown hair with bangs covering her eyebrows and the man displayed somewhat exaggerated sideburns. He stopped talking and glanced sideways at them as they discussed various items on the menu, looking keenly at Megan when she ordered a grilled chicken dish known as Hendl.

"I've had delicious Hendl in Austria," smiled Rick.

"Yes, I can believe that. It's both an Austrian and a Bavarian specialty." Megan continued to study the menu. Then she smiled and pointed to an item on the last page.

"Look, Rick, did you see this? They serve 'Kloster Liqueur' produced by the nuns." Neither Rick nor Megan noticed that the man next to them had abruptly twisted around to look squarely at them at the mention of Rick's name.

"We certainly must have that after dinner in their honor."

Their meal proved to be delectable and they did indeed order the liqueur Megan had spotted on the menu. When it was served, complete with a choice of miniscule vanilla and chocolate cookies, Megan bent her face low over the ensemble and stared at it.

"What on earth are you doing?"

"What does it look as though I'm doing? Taking a Google Glass of it, Rick. I want to remember this..."

"*Please stand up. You are both wanted for questioning in the murder of a museum guard in Munich.*"

Chief Detective Dieter Löser had recognized the couple next to him and his wife. They were the two Americans described by neo-Nazi suspect Walter Krankenhauer. The man had just been referred to as "Rick" and the older woman wore a Google Glass.

A perfect match.

53

HEINRICH HAD BEEN CAJOLED into staying the night with Lady Rosa, as the young prostitute called herself. She would stop charging him if he would stay after they had played his sex games and give her some business advice. She had saved enough money, she told him, to buy independence from her pimp and wanted to relocate far from the man's reach, but still stay in Monte Carlo. They had discussed various possible neighborhoods but in the end Heinrich felt he had to warn Rosa that no area in the city would be safe from a pimp who would certainly track down one of his errant cash cows and probably kill her on the spot.

"That's just the way it is," he consoled her when she burst into tears. They made love again, this time out of tenderness, and the night extended into the wee morning hours.

54

PONDERING HER FUTURE with Boris Zima, now that, thanks to her, the Kandinsky heist had been redirected to Moscow, Raisa began to take serious stock of her situation.

She could not stop thinking about Boris's casual acknowledgement that the drivers of the waylaid cargo van had been murdered. To say nothing of the police officer who had pulled them over. The same thing, she reasoned, could happen to her should she somehow also become an "inconvenience."

Certainly Boris would ungrudgingly pay the high charge her services as his personal secretary and now foreign agent mandated. There was no question about that. And he had actually complimented her on her work. But she had to take into account that, with the exception of the new team of drivers, she was the only person who knew about the hijacking and the new delivery destination as well as the original destination. This put her in possession of highly sensitive information that might eventually place her in danger. Boris, after all, was fanatical about his Kandinsky collection. One that few people had ever been granted the honor of viewing in toto. Raisa herself had never been invited to see the many Kandinsky paintings hidden away in his reputed fortress-like dacha just beyond the Moscow Novodevichy Convent.

Boris was also a mercurial man. Witness the sudden withdrawal of his offer to donate to Rasputin's crazy Patriots Museum project in Odessa. She had to write him the bad news. Now Boris considered the man his rival, and he had proven how prepared he was to defend his territory, his collection. In fact, to add to it. Certainly, Rasputin would eventually figure out who was responsible for the cargo van's disappearance with eleven Kandinskys.

A plan began to formulate in Raisa's mind. Not so much a betrayal as an insurance policy. Time would tell whether she would have to initiate it, but in the meantime, she would be on her guard.

55

RETURNING FROM HIS INTERESTING VISIT to the *Hommage à Kandinsky* show, Igor Rasputin picked up a copy of the *Süddeutsche Zeitung* in the lobby of his hotel before dinner that evening. Back in his luxurious suite, he watched the news on television. It was still obsessed with the riotous events at the Lenbach.

Turning off the TV, he settled down to read the popular Bavarian newspaper. Most items repeated what had just been covered on the newscast, including more reporting on the dramatic Kandinsky protest and "subsequent" death of the museum's night watchman, but one seemingly unrelated item caught his eye. It mentioned that a Hamburg-based *Cargo Logistik* van had vanished after picking up a shipment in Munich. Company officials were mystified as no road trouble had been reported. Police in Slovakia had, however, received reports of a stolen *Cargo Logistik* van and one of their officers had reported chasing it down near Bratislava. No more had been heard from the officer and it was not known whether he had confronted the vehicle's driver. A search was now on for both policeman and van.

Rasputin's jaw dropped and he could feel his pulse racing. What in god's name? A *Cargo Logistik* van reported stolen? One that had loaded in Munich? And last seen in Slovakia? That could only mean one thing. It was *his* chartered van. With all his Kandinsky paintings inside. Damn!

If this were true, and it must be, who could have intercepted the van?

Rasputin's pulse rate increased dangerously. A blue vein stood out in his forehead. He felt the urge to vomit. Who had waylaid his van? He knew immediately.

That goddamn Boris Zima.

56

MEGAN AND RICK were nonplussed. To be told as they sat in their cozy Fraueninsel restaurant that they were wanted for questioning concerning a murder!

"Who are you?" Rick finally asked, twisting toward the man who had been sitting at the table next to them, and defiantly continuing to sit.

"I am Chief Detective Dieter Löser of the Munich Police Department," the grimly serious man with long sideburns said, flashing identification papers at Rick. His wife, still seated at their table, looked as surprised as Megan and Rick.

"Now look here, Officer Löser," Megan said, indignation reddening her cheeks, "we are not criminals. There is no need to treat us as such. I am a retired professor and my friend here is a distinguished physician." The restaurant's other diners and staff had fallen silent as all stared at the unusual scene.

"I'm sure there has been some mistake," Rick said, taking over. "Why don't you allow us to pay our bill here and we will gladly follow you outside and answer any questions you have."

Löser seemed slightly mollified. He signaled a nearby waiter and told him to bring the checks for both tables. After both parties had paid, they walked to the restaurant exit and stood facing each other outdoors near the hotel dock.

"Answer this single question," Löser commanded. "Were you in Munich at the Lenbach House Museum protest last evening?"

"Yes," Rick and Megan said at the same time.

"You do not deny this?"

"No." Rick spoke for them both.

"And did you have bricks with you?"

"*Bricks*?" Megan almost shouted in disbelief.

"Yes, bricks. The museum's night watchman was killed with a brick thrown from the rioting crowd. And we have a witness who says one of you threw it."

"That's simply outrageous." Megan was furious. Rick laughed in disbelief.

"We will discuss this on the mainland. There is no more to be said now." Löser raised his cellphone and called the Prien Police Station.

In silence, the four walked to the approaching ferry and returned to the mainland where two waiting police cars conveyed them to Prien's main police station. Rick and Megan were escorted to separate rooms and relieved of their cellphones.

Löser interviewed Megan first.

"Why are you in Germany?"

"For pleasure and for business. I am showing my dear friend, Dr. Rick Bodewell, Bavaria and the King Ludwig castles and I am giving two lectures, one at the Lenbach, Monday evening, and the other at Schloss Berg on Wednesday evening. That is why we were on the fringes of the surprise protest march. We were to have dinner that evening with the Lenbach's associate director, Frau Doktor Katrina Keller. She can confirm this herself if you will telephone her."

"I shall, in time. But I want to hear your account of things. What can you tell me about the demonstration?"

"We were in the Königsplatz whiling away the time until our dinner appointment at six and all of a sudden we saw a group of demonstrators with banners march from the square toward the museum. So, we followed them. First there were just shouts at the director who was trying to quiet the crowd. A man behind us seemed to be the leader because he was hurling accusations at the director, things like 'You have Danish art' and 'You have Kandinsky.'"

"Did you see what he looked like?"

"I did because I shot him a dirty look. He was a big, burly man, dressed in blue jeans and a hoodie."

Löser realized the retired professor's description fit Walter Krankenhauer. But they might have been in it together. After all, the neo-Nazi had specifically identified the couple he now had in custody. They could have turned on each other.

"What happened next?"

"Oh, it was terrible! A brick was hurled from behind us and it hit our friend Doktor Keller. Landed on her foot. She fell to the ground striking her head. We broke through the crowd and ran to her. The brick's force had broken her foot. Doktor Bodewell immediately administered first aid and then he ran through the crowd to get our car so we could drive her to an emergency clinic. We couldn't get an ambulance to come to her."

"And which clinic was this?"

"The one in the Marienplatz. Very efficient. They made sure she didn't have a concussion and they fitted her with a cast and crutches. Then we drove Katrina home and I stayed with her overnight."

"And what time did you get to the clinic?"

"A little after seven."

"All right, Professor Crespi. You will remain here now while I question your travel companion."

"May I have my cellphone back? I'd like to call Katrina Keller."

"Absolutely not. I shall be the one who telephones Katrina Keller."

Löser left the room, closing the door firmly behind him, and walked down the hall to a room right off the front desk where a baffled Rick was waiting to be interviewed.

"Doktor Bodewell, I need to hear your account of what happened last night at the Lenbach and why you were there in the first place."

The physician's story exactly matched the professor's description of events. And he added one piece of information she had not mentioned. Megan Crespi was an internationally respected authority on Wassily Kandinsky. She would be the last person to protest the Lenbach's holdings of the Russian artist.

Löser was now convinced that his two American detainees had no connection with the death of the night guard. As if in confirmation of his conclusion, a notification came in on his Messenger app from the Munich coroner's office stating that autopsy evidence pointed to the time of death as eight o'clock or later on the night of the riot. This was, to say the least, an interesting turn of events. Walter Krankenhauer was in police custody at that hour and, according to their accounts, his two Prien detainees were with Katrina Keller. Now all that needed to be done was to confirm their stories. He placed a call to the museum woman, identified himself without mentioning her two friends were with him, and asked her to describe the events of the night before. Her story agreed in every detail with the couple's narration.

"Has something come up?" Katrina asked him. "Do the police know who killed Niki?"

Löser replied that the case was still under investigation and that was why he had called her. He would contact her again when they arrested the culprit. As of now there were no leads.

A few minutes after his call to Keller, Löser reunited the Americans, told them he had talked to their colleague, and they had been cleared of any suspicion. They were free to leave. He gave them both his card, should anything occur to either one that might shed light on the death of the museum guard. And at his behest one of the local police officers drove the pair back to their hotel. Löser then called Munich and told his colleague, almost reluctantly, to release the neo-Nazi detainee on bail. Although he would still have to answer to charges of breaking fire regulations and incitement to riot, he had been cleared of suspicion in the death of the night watchman.

***

Exhausted from the evening's unexpected events, Megan clattered up the circular staircase in their suite and went straight to bed. Rick turned in early as well and chortled in agreement with his friend's goodnight remark.

"Well, I guess we've had our excitement now for the trip!"

57

ROCKING GENTLY BACK AND FORTH on his motorcycle seat at his Casino La Rascasse post, Alyksandr Miesel glanced again at his watch and yawned. It was one in the morning and the ostentatious luxury yacht at the end of the pier still glowed with interior lights. What the hell time did that spoiled son of a bitch go to bed, anyway?

Caressingly, he again ran his fingers over the items in the bike's side cases.

58

"I WILL BE STAYING ON A FEW MORE DAYS," Rasputin was telling his housekeeper in Odessa on the phone. It was early Sunday morning and there was no need for him to fly back to meet a *Cargo Logistik* van that was not going to appear. He could probably do more in Munich at the moment than back home.

"You will be notified before my arrival," he concluded, hanging up.

His next call was to Pavel Meninkov, an Odessa private detective he had employed once to investigate one of his cargo line office managers who he suspected was siphoning off funds from the firm's monthly payroll. His suspicions had proven to be correct and the cashier landed in jail for a suitable number of years. The detective was also fluent in several languages, speaking faultless Slovac, Czech, Romanian, and German. Yes, Pavel was the right man. And he had his home number. He dialed it.

"Meninkov here."

"Pavel, it's Igor Rasputin. I have a pressing job for you. I hope you are free and able to travel immediately."

"For you, sir, I am always available. What are the details and where would you require me to go?"

"Slovakia. To the police station in Bratislava. I need you to represent yourself as an agent of the German moving van company *Cargo Logistik*. You will be trying to trace one of its vehicles that apparently 'disappeared' near Bratislava on its way from Munich to Odessa. It contains priceless paintings I bought in Munich from a private collector who does not want his identity to be known. Hence the matter must be handled with extreme confidentiality as far as the local police are concerned. Refer to the van's contents only as artworks. The contracted destination was Odessa, but I am ninety-nine percent certain that the van is now headed for Moscow. By the fastest route, I would predict. I need you to get on that too, as fast as possible. Do you think you can handle all this?"

"I have contacts in all the countries the vehicle would have to pass through to reach Moscow: Slovakia, Hungary, Romania, Moldova, and, of course, Russia. I'll alert them immediately. Did you by any chance make note of the license plate?"

"Actually, my agent in Munich took pictures of it as well as the van, so I can get the images to you immediately."

"Perfect. I will send the pictures and instructions to my agents and I shall leave for Bratislava within the hour."

"Fine. There is one other thing."

"Yes?"

"The two van drivers helped load the paintings—eleven of them. So they are aware of what the cargo is. One scenario is that they themselves have stolen the contents, hoping to sell them on the black market."

"But that would take a certain degree of sophistication, would it not?"

"Right, I agree. But even the most remote of possibilities has to be considered."

"When we find the drivers and their *Cargo Logistik* vehicle we will be able to determine that."

"The main thing is to prevent that van from reaching Moscow. I hope you understand."

"At any length?"

"At *any* length."

59

THE "MÉDITATION" from Jules Massenet's *Thaïs* sounded on Megan's iPhone at seven in the morning. Who could be calling so early on a Sunday morning?

"Hello?" she answered drowsily.

"Megan. It's Katrina. Just wanted to know how your excursion to the Chiemsee is going."

"Oh, um, very well." Abruptly Megan sat up, realizing she had something important to add.

"That is if you don't count being detained by the police!"

"Oh?"

"Yes. While we were calmly eating dinner at a nice Fraueninsel restaurant last night, a man at the table next to us suddenly stood up, flashed his badge at Rick, and said we would have to go with him to the Prien police office to be interrogated concerning the murder of a night guard at your museum."

"Oh, poor Niki. Was this man a policeman?"

"Yes. Well, a police detective. He wanted to know if we had been at the anti-Kandinsky protest the night before and if so what our exact actions were. He seemed very suspicious until—and we were questioned separately—he found that Rick's and my accounts jibed in every aspect. He also said that he would call you. Did he?"

"He certainly did. That's actually why I called you. It sounded as if he were interrogating me. Wanted to know the exact times of things, like when you ran up to help after the brick hit me, and what emergency clinic you'd driven me to. But after I'd told him everything I knew, he seemed satisfied. Did he not tell you?"

"Not specifically. He just said we were cleared of suspicion, gave us his card in case we thought of anything more to tell him, and had an officer drive us to our hotel."

"What an unsettling experience. Well, that's why I called you so early. Wanted to catch you before you'd taken off for the day."

"I'm glad you did," said Megan. "Do you think it could have been one of the protesters who killed Niki?"

"Probably, but it's hard to believe it was done on purpose. Apparently, Niki opened the villa door again to see what was going on. I think it's more likely that it must have been a stray brick that hit him. The way it did me. But in his case, it turned out to be lethal. I'm so upset about this. He left behind three children, you know."

"At least the police are actively looking for the person responsible for his death. This detective Dieter Löser seems to be very tenacious and I don't think he's going to be dropping the investigation any time soon."

"Hope you're right. Well, everything is okay here. Herbert is now asking hourly when we will get a Maltese. You really started something there, Megan. When do you think you'll be back in Murnau?"

"Oh, probably around six-thirty or seven if that's not too late for you."

"That's fine. That way we can get back to Munich by eight and have dinner there. Diliana has already taken the train back after I gave her the day off. So where are you going this morning?"

"Herreninsel. We're going to say hi to Ludwig."

"Okay. Enjoy it and we'll see you soon. And by the way, I'm awfully glad you are not under arrest. It would be an embarrassment for our museum if we had to announce that due to our distinguished speaker's detainment by the police, the evening lecture was cancelled."

60

WELL, IT WAS ABOUT TIME! The lights had finally gone off inside von Frauenberg's yacht. It was a little past two in the morning when a sleepy and irritable Alyksandr Miesel again checked his watch. There was still activity at Casino La Rascasse, which stayed open until 4:30 am, seven days a week. Just the kind of casual cover Alyk welcomed.

Parking his motorcycle near the pier, he opened up the vehicle's back case and pulled out the ten-pound propane tank he had bought hours earlier. He slid it into the backpack he had stored in the left-side case and put the pack with tank on his back. From the right side case he withdrew and assembled the long hose and metal lead of the vapor torch. Attaching it to the tank on his back, he tried out the squeeze valve. Extremely responsive. He was ready.

Soundlessly Alyk walked his cycle down the wharf to the luxury yacht. There were no lights on. All was totally dark. His target should be asleep by now. After turning his cycle around for a quick escape, Alyk pointed the cast iron head of his torch directly at the lowest deck of the craft and squeezed the trigger. The shooting flames fanned out swiftly, bathing the vessel in an ascending orange vapor and the sound of popping wood filled the air. Time to get out, before flames reached the yacht's fuel tank.

Noise from the casino covered the sound of Alyk's cycle as he roared up the pier at breakneck speed.

The explosion that occurred a few minutes later, however, was heard all over the harbor.

61

RAISA HAD DECIDED TO INITIATE the bold plan that had been building in her mind. But she needed to check whether Rasputin was still at his Munich hotel. In all likelihood, he had already returned to Odessa after seeing his cargo van off yesterday morning. But there was a chance he had delayed his departure from Munich, just to catch up on sleep, if nothing else. God knows she had needed to.

It was early Sunday morning. A good time to approach his hotel's front desk and find out. She walked the two blocks from her modest hotel lodgings to Rasputin's dazzling Mandarin Oriental and a cheerful receptionist informed her that Herr Rasputin had postponed his departure date.

This was very good news. Raisa chose a discreet corner in one of the several hotel lobbies, one with a view of the elevator bank, ordered iced tea, and then telephoned the hotel, asking to be connected to Herr Rasputin. He answered almost immediately. Raisa spoke in Russian.

"You do not know me, but I know that earlier last week you had dinner at the Tantris Restaurant with the Lenbach House Museum's associate director, Katrina Keller."

There was silence on the other end of the line. Finally, a guarded voice answered.

"So?"

"I have reason to believe she is an agent of Boris Zima." Raisa heard what she expected. A loud gasp.

"What do you mean? *Who are you?*"

"I am an admirer of our magnificent Russian artist Wassily Kandinsky, and I am sitting downstairs in one of the lobbies of your hotel."

"I see. You have my attention. Will you come up to my suite or shall I come down to you?"

"A neutral setting is desirable."

"All right. I will come down. Which lobby are you in?"

"The green one facing the elevators." Raisa's voice had an assured, commanding timbre.

"Give me a chance to get dressed."

Eight minutes later, a grim Igor Rasputin emerged from the elevator and almost ran into the black-haired woman who had spoken to him on the phone.

She was slim and tall, fifty perhaps, and seemed totally in possession of herself.

"Let us go over there," Raisa pointed to the corner couch she had staked out. Her iced tea was on the table in front of it, claiming the space. Rasputin was the first to speak.

"All right. Who are you and how is it that you believe what you have told me is true?"

"I am Svetlana Chernykh and I am taking a great chance to tell you how it is I know what I know." She fell silent.

"If you want my discretion you have it."

"I would need more than that. I would require your oath to keep what I tell you between us."

Rasputin was impressed by the urgency and authority in the woman's low voice.

"I do not like this, but you have my word, my oath."

"I am Boris Zima's private secretary." Rasputin looked pale, staring at her, waiting for her to say more.

"As such, I am privy to his business dealings and the details of his extraordinary art collection. I know from having overheard two of his telephone conversations that he hired an agent to monitor your activities while in Munich."

"How would he know that I am in Munich?"

"He keeps track of all your trips outside Ukraine. Also of all visitors to you in Odessa."

"Does he know *why* I am in Munich?"

"He does."

"And do you know why Katrina Keller would be secretly working for him?"

"Money."

"For money?"

"Yes. She has a young son with costly medical problems."

There was a pithy pause as Raisa took a sip of her iced tea. Finally Rasputin spoke.

"Shall I take it that you are aware of a certain recent consignment of mine?"

"That it has been hijacked, yes."

"*You say it was hijacked*?" Rasputin's worst fear that his *Cargo Logistik* van had been waylaid was now confirmed. He would call Pavel Meininkov immediately so they could update their actions. Try to prevent the van from reaching Moscow.

"Yes. Your van was hijacked outside Bratislava."

Zima's secretary certainly knew what she was talking about. But why would she be telling him? Betraying her employer and coming to him?

"Why are you giving me this information?"

"Because I want protection. Protection from Boris Zima."

"You need protection? From your own employer?"

"Yes. Because I have knowledge of a number of his, shall we say, unusual recent dealings concerning the enlargement of his Kandinsky collection in Moscow. Now I am afraid that my usefulness is coming to an end. In other words, I fear for my life." Again, Raisa was telling more truths than lies. Being an "inconvenience"—Zima's word—was not something she wanted to be regarded as by him.

"I see. I see. And how do you think I could help you?"

"One thing is certain. I will not be returning to Moscow. Instead, I should like to resettle within the ambit of your powerful reach. I am willing to live here in Munich or in Odessa. Perhaps I could even be of some use to you."

Rasputin was struck by the idea. As a person who was familiar with Zima's ways and desires, this Russian with a Moscow accent could be extremely useful. He looked at the woman long and thoughtfully, calculating how much he could trust her.

Raisa calmly returned Rasputin's stare. But her heart rate was up. Would the ploy work?

"Svetlana Chernykh, I have one question for you. Would you be willing to work for me in the same manner and concerning the same sort of undertakings as you have for Zima?"

"I would."

"Then let us drink to new beginnings." The man from Odessa caught the attention of a waiter and ordered two Chudnoff vodkas—one of the best vodkas native to Ukraine.

As Rasputin gave his order, Raisa relaxed ever so slightly. Playing the double agent card could be her ace in the Russians' competitive game for the winning Kandinsky hand.

62

WHAT COULD BE A BETTER COMBINATION? Sunday morning *and* a sauna? After her early morning conversation with Katrina about Detective Löser's inquisitive call and her own experience at the police station, Megan had given herself permission to skip her usual exercises and instead treat herself to a long sauna session. She had turned it on the moment she got up from bed and now it was hot and ready for her. How she loved the steam that exuded every time she refreshed the heating element with water provided in a little alder wood bucket with its matching wooden dipper. The soap supplied had a birch scent and the long-handled back brush was firm yet gentle. A broad scrub cloth with loop handles had just the right rough texture and Megan pulled it back and forth not only on her back but also on her legs and feet. Ah, what luxury. She felt enormously refreshed as she dressed for the day.

Rick too was all the better for his run along the lake shore and they enjoyed a relaxed, hearty breakfast together.

"So, tell me a bit about what we have in store at Ludwig's castle," he demanded. "And why it's called 'Herrenchiemsee castle' and not 'Herreninsel castle.'"

"Yes, it does get a little confusing. The complex of buildings relating to Ludwig on Herreninsel in the Chiemsee is called Herrenchiemsee. Clear?" Megan was grinning.

"Clear as Chiem."

"Good way to put it. You know, we can't just drop in on Ludwig's castle when we feel like doing so. It can only be visited as part of the guided tours that begin at the ferry stop. And no photos are allowed. Unfortunately for me, it's about a fifteen-minute walk through the island's forest before we even catch sight of the castle."

"We'll walk very slowly then."

"No, we won't walk at all. I'll treat you to one of the horse-drawn carriages lined up at the island's dock."

"Okay. Sounds nice and regal."

"The carriage takes us as far as a long, manicured, rectangular park and then we'll still have to walk past lots of fountains and statues before we get to the castle. It's actually much more a palace than a defense castle, since Ludwig built it as a faithful replica of Louis the Fourteenth's palace at Versailles."

"Oh, good. We don't have to go to France to experience Versailles then," Rick winked at Megan.

"Well, that's certainly one way to look at it. Of course, this version has nineteenth-century improvements: Louis didn't have indoor toilets or central heating. Ludwig did. And we'll see a marvelous Hall of Mirrors—purposefully outdoing the original at Versailles as far as gold and porcelain and paneling and chandeliers and candles are concerned. It runs the length of the building with views of the grounds and fountains."

"I can't wait to see it. Are you ready, Megan?"

"Just let me finish taking my senior pills." She began gulping down the last of her vitamins, fish oil, and prescription tablets.

"Good lord, Megan. How many things are you taking?"

"Well, aside from my multivitamin and calcium citrate, I take fish oil, vitamin K, and vitamin B twelve. Plus cranberry for you know what and this PreserVision soft gel twice a day for the macular degeneration that's beginning in my left eye."

"Yes. Good product. Contains A, C, D, and E vitamins, as well as zinc, copper, lutein, zeaxanthin, and..."

"Stop! How do you know all that?"

"Because I take them too. But you know, Megan, you don't really need to take all those other supplemental vitamins."

"Perhaps not, but I just feel better doing so. Have for years, decades. And anyhow, every few years we're told that so and so is ineffective, then a reversal comes telling us it's super effective. And just look at coffee! Now they're saying that the more you drink the longer you'll live, whereas a few years ago they were advising us to limit our coffee drinking to one cup."

"It's all a case of how much you like bright yellow urine."

"Oh, stop it!"

"Shall we get going? It's almost noon already." Rick could see he was not going to change Megan's superfluous vitamin habit. And he knew she truly needed her daily doses of desvenlafaxine, olanzapine, and lamotrigine for her bipolar disorder. Never mind that they might lead to weight gain. Years ago,

Megan, who had always been so cheerful and upbeat as a teacher, had confided in him that after the descent of a sudden, deep depression from nowhere and haunted by suicidal thoughts she could not throw off, she had sought the help of a competent psychiatrist who had been able to stabilize her with the three bipolar drugs she now faithfully took. The process of finding the right balance had taken almost two years. It was like trying to turn an ocean liner around, her physician explained helpfully. But now she was back to her usual sunny, confident self. And she was religious about taking her pills.

They walked down to the hotel pier and boarded a sleek white-and-tan ferry that went first to Fraueninsel and then to the Herrenchiemsee island. Boarding with them was a man in blue jeans and with a hoodie covering most of his face, even though the weather was hot and humid. He went straight to the back of the ferry where Megan and Rick had stationed themselves and stood at the railing staring down at the trailing water.

"Hey, Rick. Look over there! Isn't that fat fellow with the hoodie the same man who was shouting insults at the Lenbach director Friday night?" Rick studied the man Megan had indicated.

"I think you're right. Looks like the same man."

"Wonder what he's doing out here?"

"Well, if he gets off at Fraueninsel we'll know. Remember the Alfred Jodl cenotaph we found there and how I doubted that the island contained any local neo-Nazis?"

"Of course I remember. So perhaps the cenotaph is a discreet meeting point for Bavarian members of the party."

"Interesting idea."

Megan's theory was confirmed when the ferry docked briefly at Fraueninsel. Herr Hoodie, as she now referred to him, was the first person off and seemed to know exactly where he was going as he walked briskly away from the pier and in the direction of the island cemetery they had visited just yesterday.

"Do you still have the card of that Detective Löser who questioned us last night, Rick?"

"Yeah. It's in my wallet."

"Well, we might want to tell him we've seen the man who was behind us at the anti-Kandinsky demonstration. Perhaps he had something to do with the night watchman's murder."

"Okay." Rick opened his wallet, pulled out the detective's card, and handed it to Megan.

"Here, *you* call him."

Megan did so and even though it was a Sunday, Dieter Löser answered almost immediately. He listened to Megan's message and thanked her, remarking that the man, one Walter Krankenhauer, was well-known to the force and had in fact been arrested as the demonstration broke up. He had been interrogated but, due to the time factor between his being in custody and the death of the night watchman, they had had to release him. Löser did not mention that Krankenhauer had tried to implicate his caller and her companion. Instead, he wound up the conversation by urging Megan to keep his card.

"What a good citizen you are," Rick said after the phone call was concluded.

"At least if there's a riotous neo-Nazi demonstration on the Fraueninsel, police will have a suspect."

"Sometimes I think you should have been a detective rather than an art historian."

"The two are rather parallel. We do engage in a lot of investigation in my discipline, after all. There's provenance to determine, authenticity, date, condition, and if figural, identification of the persons portrayed."

The ferry was nearing Herrenchiemsee and they lined up at the gangway. It was just as Megan had described, with horse-drawn carriages awaiting those who preferred to ride to the castle. They took advantage of the bumpy conveyance that slowly wound its way through a lush forest leaving them at its furthest perimeter. Rick was not disappointed by the panorama of Ludwig's three-story palace and its long, rectangular gardens. He whistled in appreciation as they walked toward it past two great spurting fountains and twisting marble statues. Once at the grand entrance they joined an English-speaking tour and were told immediately that no video or photography was allowed. As if to emphasize the injunction, one of the younger tour guides hung behind the group as they moved into the ornate vestibule, keeping an eye on stragglers. Megan was one of those and her Google Glass was inconspicuously at work.

The Hall of Mirrors—one third larger than the Versailles original—had all its many candelabra lit and was indeed dazzling. As for the other equally ornate rooms, only twenty of the seventy originally planned had been completed. The highlight for Rick was the lavish dining room with its single great chandelier, completed for the king even though he only managed to spend ten days at the castle before his mysterious death. And because the moody ruler of Bavaria always took his meals in solitude, he had had a dining table built that could hoist his meals up from the kitchen below. "The magic table," their tour guide called it. Rick stared up at the enormous central chandelier made of Meissen porcelain and was told it was the largest in the world.

"No wonder Ludwig went bankrupt," he whispered to Megan.

"You bet. It was his wild spending as well as erratic behavior that finally contributed to his abduction and confinement at Castle Berg. And you know what happened there."

"Ha! Except that no one knows for sure what *really* happened on that night. I still think Ludwig killed his keeper, then himself."

"So do I."

Time passed quickly. They visited what had once been a monastery but was now a gallery full of not very interesting art. By the time they found a horse and buggy to take them back to the ferry dock it was close to five in the afternoon.

"We've missed lunch, but I guess we'd better pick up our bags at the hotel if we want to make it back to Katrina's by six-thirty." Rick looked inquiringly at Megan. She nodded in agreement, then reached into her sling purse.

"Here, have one of my Butterfinger bars. I always carry some for emergencies." Rick accepted gratefully. He had not eaten one in years.

The friends were soon on the road back to Murnau. Rick drove this time while Megan began fine-tuning her laptop's PowerPoint images for the lecture she was to give the next evening at the Lenbach.

Even though the morning had started off with Katrina's call relating her conversation with Detective Löser, after sauna and palace, it had been a perfect day. And, thank goodness, with no unscheduled excitement. Well, maybe for a moment when they spotted the loudmouthed man who had been behind them at the anti-Kandinsky demonstration on their Chiemsee ferry. Why on earth was he going to little Fraueninsel?

63

HIS UNSCHEDULED MEETING with Boris Zima's former secretary concluded, Rasputin was on the phone with the agent he had sent to Bratislava.

"Pavel, I have just had reliable confirmation that my van was hijacked. I think it is still important, however, that you check with the local police as an investigator from *Cargo Logistik*, just in case they have any up-to-date info. By now they might have a sighting or an actual arrest. We have to stay on top of their information."

"Right. Incidentally, you've reached me as my plane sits on the tarmac waiting to take off for Bratislava. I'll call you as soon as I've pried out what the police there know."

"We've got to find out how close to Russia the van is."

"Right. Some associates of mine are already fanning out east along the major highways searching for the van. And one of them just confirmed to me that a *Cargo Logistik* van was clocked at one-eighteen in the afternoon yesterday paying the toll on that three-mile strip of highway that enters Slovakia from Austria. So that's something."

"Good. Good. Yes, that's something."

"Especially since the van will have the dated toll decal on its front window now."

"Ah! In case there are several *Logistik* vans in the country, you'll be able to identify mine."

"Exactly."

64

"*WHAT THE HELL HAS HAPPENED?*"

Heinrich had walked back across town from his extended evening with Lady Rosa. It was close to six in the morning and the streets around Casino La Rascasse were entirely blocked off by yellow police barriers. Fire trucks were parked at the base of the casino pier and police were swarming over the area.

"Please tell me what's going on here," Heinrich addressed a gawking woman standing next to him at the iron barrier.

"There was a huge fire that broke out on the pier during the middle of the night. It spread from boat to boat, and only the ones nearest the casino were saved."

Heinrich turned pale.

"Only the yachts closest to the casino were not burnt?"

"Yes. See where that firetruck is? Those five boats near it are the only ones left."

At this, Heinrich bolted across the barrier and ran toward the pier. A policeman yelled at him just as he came abreast of the firetruck.

"Hey you! Go back, go back!"

"I've got to see what condition my yacht is in."

"Hold it right there. Nobody gets on that pier. Or what's left of it."

"But my yacht, my yacht!"

"If it's not one of these five boats here, then you don't have a yacht."

"Good god! I can't believe it."

The policeman took pity on the distressed young man.

"Where was your yacht docked?"

"At the very end of the pier on the left side."

"That's where the fire began. And apparently no crew members were on board to quench the flames. Sorry. I'll have to take a statement from you. We are of course trying to determine the exact cause of this massive conflagration, but from what we have ascertained so far it seems to have started at the end of the pier."

After he had told the officer everything he knew, Heinrich turned away, his eyes staring sightlessly. He had just lost everything he loved. And where in god's name was the crew? If those two slackers had been on board when they were supposed to be, they could have spotted the fire and at least attempted to put it out. God damn them, sneaking away from his yacht! They had done this once before when he was away in Munich and returned without notifying them in advance of his arrival. He thought they had learned their lesson.

All at once he realized he had no place to go and only the clothes on his back. He might actually have to get a hotel room in his own port city. What irony. But then a thought lifted his spirits. Tomorrow, Monday, he would be at his bank the moment it opened to claim the one million euros Rasputin had transferred to his account. He could make a new beginning.

65

ALYK WAS STILL IN MONTE CARLO that Sunday morning. Despite his employer's admonition to do so, he had decided not to call Rasputin at two in the morning to report his success. Instead he had gone to a cheap hotel by the railroad station to catch up on much-needed sleep. By nine o'clock he had consumed breakfast and a barista coffee upstairs at a McDonald's on Boulevard Louis XI with a choice view of the harbor. Back on his motorcycle he decided to take a look at how much damage his torching the baron boy and his yacht had done. Police barricades were all over the place and as he pulled up to a stop in front of one of them he could see the scope of damage to the pier and docked vessels.

"Were there any fatalities?" he asked a policeman in sham concern.

"No, we were lucky there, as far as we know. Nobody was on board their boat when the fire broke out."

"What shape are the boats in?"

"A few were okay, but most of the boats were damaged."

"Even that big super yacht at the end of the pier?"

"Especially that one. Seems that's where the explosion happened and the fire started."

"And you say everyone survived the fire?"

"We think so, but it's an ongoing investigation. The fellow who owned that super yacht was especially upset. I would be too, if I owned a half-million-euro yacht like that."

Revving his bike, Alyk turned away. His pulse was racing faster than the motor and he felt short of breath. Thank god, he had not yet called Rasputin to report his success. But how to find his quarry in Monte Carlo? He smiled in relief as he remembered something. The insolent, high-living punk would be showing up tomorrow morning at Monte Carlo's Crédit Suisse to collect the one million euros Rasputin had been blackmailed into wiring him.

He would be there too.

66

IT WAS AN OVERWHELMING NUMBER. Rasputin's agent Pavel Meninkov could not believe the figures. There were thirty-two *Cargo Logistik* vans with Russian destinations, some twenty-four of them already in Russia. He had learned this from the home office in Hamburg, by pretending to be a Slovakian government official. And an officer to whom he presented himself early Sunday morning as a *Cargo Logistik* representative at Bratislava's main police station corroborated it.

"Each day we receive an accounting of how many border toll decals are issued to vehicles with foreign license plates. In addition to five-hundred-and-eighty-six automobiles, forty-one vans entered of which twenty-three were registered as belonging to your company."

"And their destinations?"

"No. We are not a *communist* country. We do not inquire as to destinations. Many of them are, after all, making deliveries in Slovakia."

Pavel had thanked the officer and was about to leave when a policeman ran past him into the building shouting at his fellow officers.

"They've found him! They've found Stanislav!"

"Where, where?" Officers gathered around the excited man.

"His squad car was parked hidden in the bushes on a turnout fronting the D4/R7 bypass. A hunter discovered it. Stanislav had been shot dead. And two other men were in the car, also shot to death. They have to be the drivers of the stolen van he was tracking because the last thing we heard from Stanislav was that he had found the van and was in the process of pulling it over. And so far there are no clues as to who did this."

"That's terrible! So Stanislav actually found the stolen van. But if he had to shoot its drivers then who shot him?"

"We'll just have to wait for the autopsies and identification of the bullets.

Whether they're all of the same caliber. Nothing of help was found in the car."

"I want an immediate alert out to all squad cars," ordered the chief of police who had joined his officers. "Tell them to be on the lookout for a stolen *Cargo Logistik* van last seen above Bratislava and probably heading east. The drivers are armed and dangerous. Probably already responsible for three deaths, including one of our own."

***

Pavel had heard enough. The hijack had been a deadly one. Three lives! The murderers were driving the van at that very moment. And now the Slovakian police would be his rivals in tracking down the van. Hell! There was the possibility they might find it before he or his agents in the field did.

The single advantage he had over the police was that he alone knew the van's destination: the Boris Zima estate in Moscow, just beyond the city's famous Novodevichy Convent. Rasputin had told him the collector's house was a pseudo dacha of castle-like size, with high walls all around the property. One side was contiguous with the convent's circular fortification wall. Another side shared one of the adjacent Novodevichy Cemetery walls. Let his agents continue to sweep major highways of Slovakia, Hungary, Romania, and especially Russia's direct neighbor, Moldova, for the cargo vehicle. But should they miss tracking it down, he would now head straight for Moscow to concentrate on the city streets circling the Novodevichy convent boundaries and leading to the Zima estate just beyond.

Another thought then occurred to him. The hijackers had the balls to kill anyone in the way of their plans, even a policeman. They could also be cunning enough to load the van's contents into another type of cargo vehicle. What if he and his agents were going after *Cargo Logistik* vans in vain? It might not be too late for him to intercept a large van from any commercial company spotted near the Novodevichy Convent or Cemetery. Or even no company at all. Just one van capable of holding eleven large paintings plus their crates or bulk wrapping.

He called his agents with terse new instructions concerning what to be on the lookout for, then drove on through the day and deep into the early morning hours in his stalwart Lada Granta sedan. Exhausted but energized, he arrived in Moscow at five-thirty Monday morning. Pray he was not too late.

67

THE SUNDAY TRAFFIC had been light and the two Americans arrived in Murnau a full hour earlier than they had planned. Katrina and Herbert were in the back garden and waved enthusiastically as the Opel passed them on its way to the front door.

Herbert ran to them when they entered the house. He was very excited.

"I can play a Bach *organ* fugue! It's in G minor. I learned it while you were gone. I can't play the notes in the bass clef, but I can hum it. May I play it for you?"

Megan and Rick beamed at him and nodded yes at the same time. The boy ran over to the harmonium, scrambled onto the hassock, and began to play the composer's organ Fugue in G minor. He played it perfectly, but Megan noticed what sounded like a faint vibration throughout the piece. It was present with every note of the fugue, but especially when Herbert's left hand took up the fugue's tenor entrance of the subject. Megan wondered whether anyone else heard it and looked around questioningly. But Katrina and Rick were intent on the boy's faultless rendition of what in the organ world was known as the "Little G minor." They all applauded enthusiastically when Herbert concluded, vigorously pumping the two foot pedals, and sustaining at length the glorious G *major* concluding chord.

But again, Megan was troubled by what seemed to be a low vibration while the magisterial chord was held. It was not the pure reed sound a harmonium of this type would emit. Actually, the sound was more like a rattle. But a rattle of what?

After the boy had been heartily praised, Megan quietly moved the hassock out of the way with her foot so she could stand facing the harmonium, her hands poised over the keys. She pushed one of the pedals vigorously up and down with her right foot, and now they could all hear the sound she had heard.

"Oh, I suppose we need to put some oil on those old foot lifts," Katrina said.

"I'm not sure that's it. The sound is more like a rattle than a squeak.

When's the last time you had this harmonium pulled out away from the wall?"

"Well, years ago, when the house was refurbished in the late nineties. Remember, I told you we couldn't reconstruct the music room where it first was. So, the harmonium had to be moved and installed where it is now. That would be the last time it was moved. I certainly haven't moved it. Why do you ask?"

Megan's curiosity was piqued. Without stopping to ask Katrina's permission she stepped to one end of the harmonium and pulled it slowly toward her and away from the wall. She bent over and tried to see behind the instrument.

"Katrina, I want to look at the back of this thing. Would you or Rick mind pulling the harmonium away from the wall on your side, please?"

Katrina was closer than Rick, so she pulled her end of the old instrument out from the wall. There was nothing unusual to be seen. The large backboard covered the cabinet's width and height and was screwed into place.

"Could I have a screwdriver?" Megan was unstoppable in her determination to find out what could be making the rattling noise. She herself did not quite understand why she was so eager. She just knew she had to find out.

"Here, I'll do it," offered Rick when Katrina returned with a screwdriver. It took longer than any of them expected, but finally Rick lifted the board away from the back of the harmonium.

"Well, here's the rattling culprit!" Megan exclaimed. They were looking at the back of an unframed two-by-two-foot canvas.

"I can't believe this! Turn it around. Let's see." Katrina urged tensely. Rick carefully rotated the canvas while the remnants of a large cloth fell off from the top. The cloth had rotted, but the canvas surface was in relatively good condition and the subject matter was immediately recognizable.

It was a bust portrait of Münter signed and dated by Kandinsky.

"*Heiliger Strohsack!*" Katrina gasped, her mouth open in disbelief.

"What a marvelous portrait," Rick said, backing off to see it better. He knew every portrait and photograph that had ever been made of his favorite painter. But he had never seen this.

Megan bent down to study the signature and date. There was more than that on the canvas.

"Ah, Kandinsky's not only signed and dated the portrait—nineteen-hundred-and-ten—but he's also written this below his signature: '*Murnau, unser Paradis auf ewig*.' Murnau, our paradise forever."

"Boy, oh boy, did he ever break his word on that!" Megan's voice was thick with sarcasm.

Katrina nodded her head in vigorous agreement.

"No wonder she felt he had wrecked their relationship and her life," a sympathetic Rick added.

"The likeness is just beautiful," Katrina said, stepping back from the image. Her great-aunt's face looked directly out at the beholder and her auburn hair was swept up in a bun. Her lips were slightly parted and a happy smile illuminated her features. She wore a thin black band around her neck. The center of the band supported a single large pearl. When Katrina's eyes took that in, she gasped again.

"But I *have* that necklace! My aunt gave it to my mother and after she died I found it among her things. Always thought it was remarkable in its simplicity. I can show it to you when we get back to my apartment."

The mesmerizing portrait continued to hold their undivided attention.

"This discovery is really quite remarkable," Megan announced reverently, as she recovered from the excitement of finding an unknown Kandinsky. "As far as I can recall, the oeuvre catalogue of his early Blue Rider works doesn't include this painting. It is not known. I've never seen a reproduction of it. Have you, Katrina?"

"Definitely not."

"I guess the question has to be *when* Münter relegated this artwork to the back of the harmonium," Rick speculated.

"Yes," agreed Megan. "Did she do it right after Kandinsky left her for good and married Nina in nineteen-seventeen, or did she hide it from the Nazis during World War II? Either way, what a clever hiding place she thought of. It could have remained here for decades more if the cloth cover hadn't disintegrated causing the canvas's wooden stretcher strips to absorb and transmit vibrations from the reed."

"Wait a minute. Reed?" Rick was puzzled.

"Sounds strange, I know. But this harmonium follows the standard practice of forcing air, by pumping the pedals—the bellows, you could say— through a vibrating piece of thin metal in a frame behind the keys and casing. The metal piece is called a reed."

"And that's why you heard what you thought was a rattling?"

"Exactly." Megan beamed at Katrina.

"Well, dear, what do you think you will do with your new Kandinsky? Keep it for yourself, sell it, give it to the Schloss museum here or to the Lenbach?"

Katrina was silent for a long minute, her face a study. To sell the Kandinsky would solve the problem of unknown years of expensive medication for Herbert. But Rick had held out hope to her in that regard. The boy had a good chance of simply outgrowing his epilepsy. New thinking in the field recommended tapering the afflicted child off medication gradually. That was heartening. Unaware that her friends were staring at her, Katrina continued to consider all options. Then at last she spoke, slowly and with emotion.

"The portrait is too valuable to keep in my Munich apartment or here. I would not think of selling it. No. I will give it to the Lenbach."

"Brava!" cried Megan.

Rick walked over and gave Katrina a long hug.

"I think you've made the right decision to share this intimate, important portrait with the world. And more people will see it at the Lenbach—*your* museum—than they would here in Murnau.

"We must celebrate this miracle!" Katrina exclaimed. "Would you rather eat a celebratory dinner here in Murnau or back in Munich?" Katrina looked expectantly at them.

Before Megan or Rick could answer, Herbert shouted.

"Here, here! At the castle!"

"You can eat at the castle?" Rick sounded intrigued.

"Oh, yes. It houses a great restaurant, the Schlossvogel. Their Wienerschnitzel is super, and we could sit outdoors. There's a great view."

"Then let's do that," Megan decided for the group.

No one was disappointed in the food and the weather was ideal for dining outside, although the slatted wooden chairs could have been more comfortable, especially for poor Katrina in her foot cast.

"A toast to Münter *and* to Kandinsky," Rick proposed. They clinked their glasses and continued with their feast. After dessert, they lingered over espressos while Herbert amused himself drawing with crayons on the notepad his mother had thoughtfully provided.

"Megan, won't you tell us now what the enigmatic title of your lecture for us tomorrow means? 'Double Kandinsky?'" Katrina was vigorously stirring her espresso.

"I would if I could, but the element of surprise would be missing." Suppressed delight made Megan's eyes sparkle.

Katrina looked at Rick.

"Do *you* know what the title means?"

"I wish I did, Katrina. She hasn't even let me see the *images* for her speech, much less explained the quixotic title. Maybe it just means she's giving the lecture twice?" He chuckled with merriment.

"Well, that I am," confirmed Megan. "You know I'll be repeating it at Schloss Berg on Wednesday."

"And you can bet I'll be there to hear your lecture again. Or, rather, I'll send my Doppelgänger Katrina Keller to take in the lecture."

Happy grins were exchanged all around and little Herbert, sensing the good cheer, began hugging himself and laughing.

"Oh, you've got to let me photograph Herbert. He's so darling like that," said Megan, quickly producing her iPhone and taking a shot before Herbert's self-hug ended.

Rick smiled to himself. How many times had he seen Megan suddenly take a photo of whatever person or scene she found worthy of immortalization?

"And tell us what you would say if you get lost again, Herbert," his mother commanded.

"*Katrina Keller. Lenbachhaus. München. Katrina Keller. Lenbachhaus. München,*" the boy answered proudly.

By eight-thirty they were on their way to Munich. The conversation took an interesting turn when Rick asked Katrina who the main Russian collectors of Kandinsky were.

"Well, there are two of them. One lives in Odessa and the other lives in Moscow. I've met them both and they couldn't be more different. I've mentioned the Odessa one to you, Igor Rasputin. Remember? The night I was hit with the brick I missed a dinner date with him. Although he lives in Ukraine, he is a passionate Russian nationalist. He's a member of the SRRV—*Make Russia Russia Again*—movement and he's devoted his life to assembling Kandinskys of all periods for a specialized museum he's building in Odessa. I think it's going to be called the Patriots Museum or something like that. I had dinner with him, at his invitation, just a few evenings ago when he was in town. He showed me a photograph of what will be the heart of the museum's collection: two Kandinskys in one. Hard to describe, but you could say it was two canvases in one. The lower, object-filled half looks like the Blue Rider period—there's even a white swan—while the upper half has swirling color globes against an immense black background, probably from his Bauhaus period. What a masterpiece! I'd give anything to have it in the Lenbach collection."

"So, is that why he met with you? To make you jealous?" Rick was curious. "No, no. The purpose of the meeting was to propose an exhibition of his Kandinskys at the Lenbach. I suppose to give his collection more international repute, give it a certain cachet. I found it a most attractive idea."

"And I'd guess his offer was based on a trade—the Lenbach Kandinskys in an Odessa show?"

"No. Strangely enough, he himself brought up the impossibility of an exchange exhibition, knowing that our late Paris-period Kandinskys had been traveling for two years due to the construction of our new wing. I have yet to find the time to get those artworks into my lab for condition evaluation. After their return, our brilliant new director had those eleven Paris works relocated from their hallowed space on the third floor to the basement gallery." Katrina's sarcastic tone was not lost on her friends.

"It's hard to believe Rasputin didn't want something in return."

"No. All he asked was the favor of being allowed to bring in his camera team some evening after museum hours to take high-quality photographs for permanent display in his own museum. Rounding out Kandinsky's career, you know."

"And did he?"

"Actually no. Unfortunately, he and his crew were scheduled to do so on the very evening the anti-Kandinsky demonstration happened. And I haven't heard from him since. I'd agreed to meet him at eight o'clock. Remember? That's when I called Niki Wächter on the way from the emergency clinic to my house and told him to admit Rasputin. That was the last time I heard Niki's voice, poor man."

Rick changed the subject.

"And who is the other major Russian collector of Kandinsky?"

"His name is Boris Zima, and considering that "zima" means cold or unpleasant in Russian, his surname is appropriate. I met him only once, at a Kandinsky exhibition in Moscow where he lives in what I am told is an immense dacha and which shares a wall with the famous Novodevichy Cemetery. I've not seen his Blue Rider collection; only heard it's stunning.

The talk moved on to the Munich police search for the night guard's murderer and they arrived at Katrina's building a few minutes before ten.

"Will you be all right alone with just Herbert this evening, do you think?" Megan was prepared to spend another night with her if necessary.

"Yes, yes, it will be okay because Diliana is going to stay nights now while I'm incapacitated."

"Excellent. Then we'll will see you tomorrow evening at the museum for my lecture."

"Wonderful. We're so looking forward to it, Megan. It would be good if you could come a half hour early, say six-thirty, for a run-through with our technician."

"Absolutely. Was just going to ask you if I could. I'm still fiddling with the PowerPoint so it would be good to have a complete tryout before the speech. I'll bring a thumb drive of the images for your technician to use because occasionally I've experienced problems showing Mac-engendered lecture images on European projectors."

"Megan can never stop 'improving' her images." Rick looked at the woman who had used slides when he studied with her. He knew how intriguing she now found it to be able to enhance her image layouts. No more slides on a white background for her. And how convenient to be traveling with a flash drive rather than with two carousels of slides. Yes, his old teacher had entered the twenty-first century with gusto.

He found a parking place right by the entrance of the building where they were being put up by the Lenbach in a very comfortable, modern apartment.

"What would you like to do tomorrow other than glance over your evening lecture," Rick asked.

"Take it a little bit easy in the morning, then go tour Schwabing and see where Kandinsky and Münter hung out. We could have lunch there and then pay a surprise visit to The Blue Rider Gallery. If it's open on Mondays. Or maybe we should go there first. It's high time we find out what Iris Togarassy's husband is up to with his *Hommage à Kandinsky* exhibition.

68

THE SIMULTANEOUS BLOWOUT of two tires just outside Minsk was totally unexpected and cost Ivan Ivanov's two drivers, Dimitri and Anatoly, some four-and-a-half frustrating hours on the Belarus highway before they could continue to Russia. Thank god for cellphones. They had contacted a truck tire supply store in Minsk and after an excruciating delay the damaged tires were replaced. Payment was another thing, however. Neither man had enough cash on him to cover the tires, delivery, and installation. Nor did either one of them possess a credit card. There was only one thing to do, and they had done it before in similar situations. Dimitri engaged the agent in conversation while Anatoly stepped casually to the man's right. Suddenly he knocked the agent to the ground with a powerful punch to the side of his head. For good measure, Anatoly hit him again on the right temple. Hoisting the unconscious man back up into his truck, the two men positioned his head and shoulders over the steering wheel to look as if he had fallen asleep.

As a precaution, Dimitri suggested they reinstall the German license plates on the van, since they had had to give the number of their Russian plates to the tire company when they called for help. That way, should they be stopped by the police, the license plates would not match the information given by the company when it reported their mechanic had not returned.

"Hell," mused Anatoly out loud, "maybe we should spray paint the van again as well? We've got two canisters of black in the back, you know."

"Yeah, that's not a bad idea. Great camouflage. Throw anybody searching for us completely off the track."

At the next highway turnout Dimitri and Anatoly quickly carried out their self-assigned task. The van that had once been creamy white, then dark blue, was now black.

All this delay meant they would not reach Moscow until well after two in the morning. What to tell their chief? He was already back in Moscow and was expecting a call from them around ten o'clock that evening announcing that they were on the outskirts of the city. It was already a few minutes past ten and they were still at Minsk.

Anatoly took the leap. He called Ivanov and gave him the news.

"I don't give a damn how late you get to Moscow. That's your problem.

What I do care about is that you are both ready to enter my client's premises at precisely six tomorrow morning. That means you be there early. At least fifteen minutes early. You got it?"

"Yes, sir! Can you give us the location now?"

"Yes, now I will give it to you. You'll be taking the southwest route into the city, so get onto the third ring road, and proceed to Novodevichy Cemetery. It will be on your right, across from the stadium, and south of, but adjoining Novodevichy Convent..."

"Novodevichy Cemetery? Stadium? Convent?" The man from the slums of Kapotnya was suddenly overwhelmed by the flood of unfamiliar information.

"But of course you know Novodevichy Cemetery, you fool! Some of our country's greatest citizens are buried there—Chekhov, Gogol, Gromiko, Yeltsin, Elizaveta Glinka, just recently after that terrible plane crash off the Black Sea, Shostakovich, Prokofiev, Rostropovich..." Ivanov's voice trailed off. What was the point of talking culture to these two uncouths? Back to business.

"Park as close to the cemetery gates as you can, and on the same side of the street as the cemetery, that's the east side, and I'll drive up in the Porsche at exactly five minutes to six. Then you will follow me to my client's gated grounds next to the cemetery and we will continue to the annex at the back of his mansion. I expect you to be punctual to the minute."

"Yes, sir! To the minute."

69

"IF YOU GET to the Novodevichya Embankment and the Moskva River, you've gone too far," Rasputin had told his Ukrainian countryman when giving him directions to Boris Zima's Moscow home. Now, at five-thirty in the morning, with no sleep to speak of, Pavel Meninkov was driving by the former Lenin Stadium, recently renovated and renamed Luzhniki Stadium. It was on his left and just beyond on the right a glimpse could be had of the wall and entry gates of Novodevichy Cemetery. Zima's residence lay just sixty feet beyond and on the same side of the street.

Pavel spotted the ornate cemetery gates, drove past them and brought his white Lada Granta sedan to a halt just in front of Zima's recessed double gates, blocking any entry or exit. This time he would not only be looking for a *Cargo Logistik* van, he would be on the watch for any vehicle of any color and with any license plate. Any vehicle that was large enough to contain eleven paintings.

70

BORIS ZIMA HAD AWAKENED at four that Monday morning. His excitement over the delivery of Rasputin's stolen art was palpable as he gasped for air and felt his racing pulse. He had instructed Ivanov to be in front of his house gates at exactly at six o'clock. He was to confirm his presence by cell-phone. Then Zima would push the button that opened the gates electronically and admit both Ivanov and the expendable drivers of the cargo van.

Two hours to wait. He was about to become owner of eleven of the most important works Kandinksy had ever painted. True, he would not be able to share his collection with anyone. But fine. That perfectly fit his solitary life. He had neither wife nor children nor living relatives. But he had innumerable comrades—his growing trove of Blue Rider artists. What better friends could one find than his silent companions?

71

ANYBODY STROLLING PAST Moscow's Novodevichy Cemetery toward the Moskva River a little before six that Monday morning might have noticed a bizarre ballet, one might say, of vehicles.

First on the scene was a white Lada Granta sedan. The driver, a male, slowly passed the cemetery entry gates, then backed up and parked in front of them. After a few minutes, he started up the car again and slowly drove some sixty feet farther down, toward the Novodevichya Embankment. He came to a stop alongside an almost invisible wrought-iron gateway set back from the street. With the engine still running, the man exited his car and popped its hood. He disconnected the battery cable and the engine died immediately. Leaving the hood up, the man got back into his car and in another minute, was glued to his cellphone.

Second on the scene was a large black moving van with German license plates and two men in its cab. It parked right in front of the cemetery gates. The engine was left running and the men remained in their cab, staring around in all directions.

At five minutes to six a third vehicle appeared—a silver gray Porsche station wagon driven by a red-haired man probably in his forties. In the front passenger seat sat a blonde woman, most likely also in her forties. The station wagon cruised slowly past the parked van and pulled over to the curb just in front of it. The driver made a brief cellphone call, then honked his horn lightly once, and pulled out into the street again. Immediately the van pulled away from the curb and followed the Porsche. Some fifty-five feet farther along, the two-vehicle caravan slowed to a crawl and then stopped abreast a white Lada Granta sedan, its hood up and parked directly in front of a recessed wrought-iron dual swing gate.

It was then that the driver of the Porsche wagon sprang out of his vehicle and ran over to the sedan. He was gesticulating wildly. The sedan driver appeared to be just as animated. The yelling back and forth continued for some minutes until the sedan occupant brandished a pistol. The Porsche driver jumped back and ran over to the waiting cargo van. He issued a command to the vehicle's driver, then jumped into his wagon and pulled out onto the empty street again, backing up until he was some twenty feet behind the cargo van. The van then backed up a car's length and parallel parked at the curb just behind the sedan, pulling up so close that its front fender actually touched the rear fender of the car in front.

Then a strange scene occurred to which no one was witness except the actors themselves. At a hand signal from the man in the Porsche, the driver of the black cargo van began pushing the white sedan steadily forward. The sedan's hood was still up, totally blocking the view of the man in the driver's seat. Rapidly increasing its speed, the van suddenly stopped. Its impetus and release shoved the sedan off the road, across the Novodevichya Embankment, and into the Moskva River. Car and driver sank immediately, disappearing permanently from view.

The bizarre ballet was over and the black swan had triumphed.

72

THE DOORS TO THE MONTE CARLO BRANCH of Crédit Suisse opened at eight Monday morning and Heinrich was the first to walk through its doors. Eagerly, he strode up to the nearest cashier's window and asked for the sum in cash that had been wired to his account two days earlier, Saturday.

A frown crossed the cashier's face. No new deposits were recorded in the specified account.

"How much was the sum in question, sir?"

"You can't miss it. One million euros." The cashier's eyebrows rose and she reentered the account number. Only a paltry sum was in the account. Less than one hundred euros.

"I'm sorry, sir, there is no record of a recent deposit."

"But this is impossible. I was present when the sum was transferred by a colleague in Munich very early Saturday morning."

The cashier shrugged her shoulders and repeated what she had said. Heinrich began shouting hysterically.

"This is unacceptable! You are making a mistake. Let me speak to your bank officer. He will clear this up."

The "he" turned out to be a she and a further search was made of the claimant's account with the same negative results.

"But it was a simple transfer," Heinrich whined, "by another one of your own clients. He made it at six-thirty Saturday morning. I was standing next to him when he did it."

In an offer to help the distressed client, the cooperative officer asked for details of the transaction and the name of the person who had initiated it. She then made a search of Crédit Suisse international and came across the name Igor Rasputin.

"We register an Igor Rasputin in Ukraine. Could that be the man you are talking about?"

"Yes, yes, that's the man. And I tell you I was standing as close to him as I am to you when he made the call from Munich to his Crédit Suisse bank."

The bank officer was scanning Rasputin's account data. She frowned as she came to one item, then spoke gently, trying to soften the blow.

"Sir, I think I've found the explanation as to why no funds have been deposited to your account."

"Yes, yes? What?"

"There is a directive on Monsieur Rasputin's account which stipulates that after a twenty-four-hour waiting period, if the bank has not heard from him directly, any withdrawals or transfers of money he may have made are not to be executed."

"*What?*"

"Yes, sir. You say the transfer command was made at six-thirty Saturday morning. It is now eight-twenty Monday morning. The intervening twenty-four hours' waiting time specified has expired with no direct word from the transferer, and therefore Monsieur Rasputin's standing order has been carried out. The transfer has been automatically cancelled."

His face ashen, Heinrich staggered out of the bank and sank down at a nearby café one street over.

***

Forty minutes later, at exactly nine o'clock, Alyksandr Miesel stood in front of the Monte Carlo branch of Crédit Suisse, waiting for the doors to open. They did, and several clients came out. Alyk gasped.

Unlike Munich, the branch here had opened at eight o'clock, not nine.

73

"HE PROBABLY DOESN'T even know I was hurt in the fracas, Diliana."

It was early Monday morning and Katrina was waiting for the Uber she had called to drive her to the Lenbach. She had again managed to take a shower in her short cast, but knew she was not supposed to drive her own car to work. Diliana had remarked that Herr Doktor Mürrisch should have sent a car for her.

"Oh, I'm sure he doesn't have any idea I was hurt. I meant to call him after Megan and Rick brought me home from the emergency room, but too much was going on, especially when I got your call that Herbert was missing." Katrina pulled the boy over to her and pretended to spank him.

"Still, I think he should have had the courtesy to check on you. Didn't you say he went back inside the museum when people began throwing bricks?"

"Yes, that he did."

"So, your boss is a big coward. That's what I say. A coward."

"I suppose you could add that to the list of what his staff calls him, me included."

The first thing Katrina did after the Uber deposited her at the villa entrance was to go down to the basement gallery and look at the Kandinsky paintings. Yes, she had heard Mürrisch say on television that no harm had come to the Kandinskys, but she wanted to check for herself. Slowly. Leaning on her crutches she moved from one familiar painting to the next. Everything was in order. She need not have worried. But after the venomous anti-Kandinsky demonstration Friday evening, she had to admit she had been haunted by the thought of damage to the precious works.

And now it was time to inform her uninterested boss that she was still alive after the brick attack.

She found him in his office staring intensely at his laptop.

"Oh, hi, Katrina. Look here, I've videoed my television interview with the press about the Kandinsky demonstration and now I can look at it whenever I want to. I've already sent it out to a host of friends." His eyes fixated on the screen, he did not look up at his colleague.

"How nice." Katrina's sarcastic tone escaped Max's ears.

"Would you like to see it?" He pivoted the laptop and held it up facing her. It was then that he noticed the crutches and cast.

"*Ach*! What did you do to yourself?"

"It's not what I did to myself, Max, it's what the brick-throwing crowd did to me." She could not resist adding "After you left the scene."

"Well, it was the only wise thing to do, Katrina. You couldn't tell what that insane crowd was going to do next. You heard me try to quiet them down. And you heard the crazy accusations they yelled at me. The only thing to do was to turn my back on them and go inside. I'm surprised you didn't do so as well."

Not a word of commiseration, Katrina thought. I am in the palpitating presence of an egregious egotist. Rather, I should say he has a narcissistic personality disorder. Perhaps someday I'll have the courage to tell him that to his face.

"I did leave, but not until I was knocked down to the ground by a brick and was helped to an emergency clinic by two friends."

"Listen. I have an idea, Katrina. With all this Kandinsky publicity being kicked around, I think it might be clever for the museum to capitalize on it and have a small, but special Kandinsky show. You know, get those *Blue Rider Almanac* things down for a while and bring a few of the Paris-period abstracts upstairs to pair alongside some Bauhaus pictures and early Munich Blue Rider works. What do you think? I think we could even make some money on it by way of the gift shop as well as the regular ten-euro entrance fee."

"You asked my opinion, Max. It seems to me that if we featured Kandinsky right now, it might serve as a further boiling point for another demonstration."

"On the contrary. I don't think we'll be hearing from that motley crew again anytime soon. And I bet newspapers will fall all over themselves commenting on the bravery of the Lenbach to do such a thing. Yes, I think we will do it. Glad you agree with me. I'll leave the artwork choices to you."

Katrina sighed audibly, turned around on her crutches, and resolutely headed for her office. It seemed that hosting Megan's lecture this evening was the only satisfying part of her job.

74

"HEY, I JUST FOUND THEIR WEBSITE and they *are* open on Mondays. Closed only on Sundays."

Megan and Rick were sitting in the small kitchen of the apartment provided by the Lenbach and, exercises and breakfast over, Megan had opened up her MacBook Air and begun searching for The Blue Rider Gallery website. It was distinguished by blue-toned photographs of all major members of the movement, including women artists Gabriele Münter, Marianne von Werefkin, and Expressionist dancer Clotilde von Derp. The present show, *Hommage à Kandinsky*, was touted as being extended another month due to "unparalleled interest in this great artist."

"It opens at ten. Shall we go straight there and tour Schwabing afterward?"

"Fine with me," Rick murmured, absorbed in an article he had pulled up on his laptop about new developments in light-sheet microscopy of large clinical specimens with the same level of detail as traditional slide-based histopathology.

They took an Uber to the gallery, already full of excited visitors, and paused to admire the single large painting displayed in the front window. It was unframed.

"The right-hand side looks more like Münter than Kandinsky although certainly the left-hand side is by him," Rick said, puzzled.

"I've read about the existence of this joint work—and you're right, he painted the left half and she did the right half—but I've never seen it in person. The last I knew of it, a Japanese collector owned the painting. Wonder how Togarassy got hold of it."

"Or maybe made an exact replica of it?" Rick shared Megan's dim view of the gallery owner after their encounter at the Togarassy house with a "completed" Kandinsky, of which the original hung in its famous, unfinished state at the Lenbach Museum.

The pair made their way into the crowded interior and tried to look at the fifteen paintings on the wall, but it was hard to obtain a full view as so many people stood in front of each work, pointing and talking excitedly. Most of the paintings had red bows on the frame bottoms, signifying they had been sold. The majority of the works were abstract, only a few were from Kandinsky's earlier Murnau/Blue Rider period. Megan looked around the room, then nudged Rick.

"Look over there at the entrance to a back gallery. That older woman. It's Iris Togarassy."

The woman with bangs and gray hair hanging down at shoulder length, was in animated conversation with two teenagers, one of whom was holding up a modern reprint of the *Blue Rider Almanac*. Iris, gesticulating dramatically, seemed to be explaining the bright colored image of a reverse glass painting to them. As Megan and Rick watched, a tall, black-haired man in his seventies emerged from the inner room, putting his right hand on Iris's shoulder and pushing her lightly against the far doorframe and out of his way.

"And that has to be Laszlo Togarassy." Rick said before Megan could.

"Let's go over to Iris and say hello and see if hubby joins us or maybe she calls him over, okay?"

Rick nodded and they made their way through the room to Iris. Her face lit up when she saw them and she quite forgot the teenagers she had been instructing.

"Oh, how wonderful. You've come to see our show. Let me get Laszlo over here. You're here. I'm so happy!"

The elderly beatnik, which was the only way Megan could describe her, pushed through the crowd and a few minutes later reappeared, beaming, her arm linked through her husband's.

"Here are the two Americans I've been telling you about. Doktor Bodewell, who repaired my dislocated shoulder so brilliantly, and Professor Crespi, the Kandinsky expert."

"Ah, yes. Thank you so much Herr Doktor for helping my wife, and you, Frau Professor, I am overwhelmed by the opportunity to meet you in person and here at my gallery—my dream of a lifetime come true. Such an honor to have you and your distinguished colleague here."

Megan found it difficult to respond in kind, as, based on the evidence in his own home, the man appeared to be a knowledgeable forger of Kandinsky. She affected a small smile of forbearance.

"There are too many people here right now for me to give you a personal tour of the fifteen Kandinskys I have gathered together from various private collections, but let me take you into the back gallery which is less crowded and show you my personal homage to the painter."

Somewhat surprised by the offer, they followed Laszlo into the smaller room, passing the two teenagers who were still engaged in leafing through the *Almanac*.

What they saw was jaw dropping. Famous Kandinsky works from both great periods, Blue Rider and Bauhaus. And all of them in respected museums across Europe and America. How could this be?

Laszlo smiled broadly, correctly reading the stunned expression on the faces of his two visitors from America.

"I see you are surprised. Yes, these are all world-renowned Kandinskys. But they are all copies. *My* copies in fact. You will note that on the lower right of each and every canvas is inscribed in miniscule but readable capital letters '*HOMMAGE À KANDINSKY*' and then below, in miniscule script, my own signature." Laszlo took a picture off the wall and held it up to them for close inspection.

"Oh!" Megan and Rick gasped simultaneously. What a relief. Laszlo Togarassy did not have criminal intentions. He was a dedicated painter. And a good one. Megan was the first to speak.

"And the *Mounted Warrior* we saw in your home—it was 'completed' by you then?"

"Indeed, it was. To celebrate Iris's and my fiftieth wedding anniversary. I am so familiar with this marvelous artist's brushwork and way of pictorial thinking, that I was bold enough to create my vision of what the picture would have looked like, had he completed it. And, of course, in this particular case, I have noted down on the back of the canvas that the original, unfinished picture can be seen in the Lenbach-Haus Museum. Otherwise, just the usual '*Hommage à Kandinsky*' and my signature on the front."

Megan was relieved to hear this bit of information, as her Google Glass photograph of the work was taken from too far away to ascertain anything about any signature.

"Isn't my husband amazing?" Iris Togarassy's voice boomed in her ear. She had joined them and was looking adoringly at the man she had married so long ago.

"Yes, he does amaze me, that's for sure," Megan was able to say sincerely.

"And of course, I do not make replicas in the same size as the original. That would be deceptive. They are all smaller than the originals, usually by thirty centimeters, so there can be no mistaking them for actual Kandinskys, if you follow me."

"Yes," said Rick turning to Megan, who, he knew, was helpless with math. "That's smaller by a good twelve inches—a visible difference."

"Have you been to the Lenbach Museum gift shop recently? They carry copies of my completed *Mounted Warrior* image. They tell me the sales are good."

"As they seem to be here," Megan said, pointing to the room from which they had just come.

"Ah, yes. It took me a good twenty-five years to assemble those fifteen works. Got almost all of them from either foreign auctions or descendants of private collectors who simply were not interested in art; including one family in Japan that owned a Paris-period work. Of course, they knew their painting's approximate value, but they were willing to sell it to me for less just to be rid of it. Imagine! Wanting to be rid of a Kandinsky!"

Megan was beginning to like the enthusiastic, dedicated man in front of her. He must be younger than she by only five years or so and his energy was contagious. Glancing at Rick she could see he had melted a bit as well.

"If you noticed in the front room, it has already been sold. I place a red ribbon at the bottom of any artwork that has been bought."

Rick spoke up. "Yes, we did notice and with a bit of awe, at least on my part. Who could have thought that there would be so many Kandinsky lovers right here in Munich with the wherewithal to purchase such valuable artworks?"

"Only two persons were from Munich actually. The rest came from across Europe and just day before yesterday, from a museum in America: the Dallas Museum of Art."

"Goodness! That's where I live," Megan said with excitement. "And we do already have a gorgeous Kandinsky—a street view of the Burggrabenstrasse in Murnau from nineteen-eight, plus a small number of early as well as late graphics. Which painting did the museum buy?

"Let me show you."

Laszlo led the way through the onlookers to the far side of the front room and proudly pointed to a large1923 abstract painting titled *Composition with Chessboard*. Megan realized it was a large oil version of one of the artist's nine graphic works already in the museum's collection. A colored print entitled *Orange—Composition with Chessboard*.

No wonder the director wanted to acquire it. The vertical composition constituted an aerial toss of floating geometric forms against a white background—colored circles, black squares, rectangles, runs of connected triangles and semi-circles in red, black, green, and yellow, with a black-and-white-checkered "chessboard" square on the upper left of the composition. Many readings could be given to the varying shapes from a large, spread-winged bird in flight to a balding human head to a set of floating paint brushes. The largest shape, the underpinning of the composition, was rendered in muted orange.

"What do you see as the message he wanted to convey?" Laszlo asked Megan.

"Perhaps it is a message about shifting balances. In this case the balance of unequal values and how harmony can issue from their ever-changing spatial relationships. Certainly, the three free-floating black squares that have 'escaped' the chessboard argue against preordained, rigid, unchanging configuration."

The three Kandinsky lovers studied the abstract work in collegial silence. Finally, Laszlo broke the silence.

"You have heard of the horrible demonstration against the Kandinsky holdings in the Lenbach Museum of course?"

"Goodness, yes," Megan replied. "We were unwilling prisoners in the middle of the marchers, as a matter of fact. We saw the museum's associate director get hit by one of the bricks that was thrown."

"Oh, no. Not Katrina!"

"Yes. You know her then."

"I constantly go to her for advice. She is so generous with her time. And such an authority on the Blue Rider artists. Do you know how she is now?"

"Much better, although she's still in a lower leg cast and on crutches. We were with her over the weekend at Murnau and drove back last night. Her mood was good."

"Well, I must give her a call later today. As you can see, one of the unexpected results of that shameful anti-Kandinsky demonstration was to rocket visitors my way. Except for our opening night, the gallery has never had so many visitors. And some of them have bought my replicas. Even more have purchased copies of the new edition of the *Almanac*.

"Yes," affirmed Rick, "we were charmed to see two teenagers looking at one with Iris."

"Iris tells me you will be giving a lecture on Kandinsky at the Lenbach this evening. We will certainly be there. So looking forward to it."

Just then a man asked Laszlo if he were the gallery director and could he answer some questions he had about one of the paintings on display. Excusing himself, Laszlo tended to the potential customer while Megan and Rick waved goodbye at Iris and made their way to the door. Once outside, they began to laugh at their mistaken judgment of Herr Togarassy. And then it was off to partake of the bohemian life and food of Kandinsky and Münter's beloved Schwabing.

75

AND IT'S ALL *HIS* FAULT. That damn Russian crook who had cheated him out of one million euros.

Cashless young Heinrich sat in a café near the Monte Carlo branch of Crédit Suisse and simmered. He had just been through one of the most humiliating experiences of his life. Turned down by not only a cashier but by a bank manager for funds that should have been his. Funds that should have been transferred to his account. He had actually been in Rasputin's presence when the man picked up the phone and issued instructions to transfer one million euros to his account. How could *anybody* have known that there was a twenty-four-hour cancellation order on such transactions in Rasputin's account?

The Russian was a thief of the lowest order. From the attic window of his own house in Munich, Heinrich had witnessed the man and his servile workers steadily transferring large flat objects to a cargo van parked in front of Paleo. The items looked as if they could be paintings. A dozen of them, likely. But from where? Nothing in Paleo had been touched. Obviously, they had been assembled and stored there. In *his* Paleo! No doubt they were stolen items. The obvious candidate was the museum right across the street. But despite a wild protest there the night before which had been picked up on television, and despite the moving van episode the following morning, there had been nothing in the papers or on television about any theft at the Lenbach. Or at any other museum in Munich. Well, even so, the fact of Rasputin's having rented and filled a moving van should interest the police. And Heinrich could claim that valuable items had been taken from his Paleo.

Now his mind was no longer simmering, it was erupting with volcanic intensity. What he wanted to do was get the Russian in trouble with the police. Bring him down. He would tell the police, if they remembered a previous visit to him at Paleo concerning a reported burglary, that Rasputin had held his mother—bless her—as hostage at an undisclosed site. That he had threatened to kill her if her son alerted the police. To destroy his yacht if he went to the police. Yes, in fact it had to be Rasputin who was responsible for the loss of his precious yacht. Hoping he was sleeping in it at the time of the fire. God, he almost was!

Heinrich would have his revenge.

76

EVERY INSTINCT TOLD RASPUTIN it was that damn Muscovite collector Boris Zima who had hijacked his *Cargo Logistik* van. And now Zima's former secretary had confirmed it. The woman told him she feared for her life. Could he believe her? *Should* he believe her? She might be extremely useful if, god forbid, Pavel Meninkov were unable to prevent the van's delivery of *his* Kandinskys to Zima. He should be receiving news in that regard any hour now.

His thoughts turned acrimoniously to the Lenbach Museum's associate director, Katrina Keller. Zima had gotten to her! He believed Svetlana Chernykh on that score. His genial dinner conversation with Keller, during which she agreed to letting the Kandinskys be photographed, must have been immediately reported by her to Zima. That is how his rival knew he and his photo crew were going to be admitted to the museum by Keller last Friday evening. God knows what would have happened had she not been knocked down by that lucky brick throw! She probably would have secretly alerted the police, then denounced him and his crew as having criminal intent after they entered the museum. Yes, that was the likely scenario.

And Keller's initial report must have been the cue for Zima's activating a local agent to maintain a 24-hour vigil over the museum's loading dock. That agent would have spotted the arrival of his *Cargo Logistik* van and the subsequent loading of the van with his eleven Kandinsky paintings. And approximately six hours later that van was hijacked by Zima. Oh, yes. That was what happened. Exactly what happened.

And it was all Katrina Keller's fault.

Rasputin smiled a bitter smile. He had a mission for his new turncoat agent, Svetlana Chernykh.

77

"WHAT TYPE OF FOOD do you feel in the mood for?" Rick looked at Megan and smiled. They were standing in front of Schwabing's Saint Ursula church and had just compared it with Kandinsky's painting, thanks to the image Megan had pulled up on her iPhone.

"Italian. Always Italian. And I remember a very good restaurant near here called Garbo. It's cozy and they use a wood-fired oven for their pizzas. Thin crusts. Yum."

"Why's it called Garbo?"

"No idea. Maybe the owner just thought it would bring glamour to the restaurant."

"I just want to be alone," Rick quoted the actress's legendary line from the film *Grand Hotel*.

They continued their discussion of Greta Garbo over what proved to be a truly delicious four-cheese pizza.

"Did you know that she collected art and that she acquired at least one Kandinsky painting?" Megan looked at Rick with a professorial expression that echoed the question.

"Of course not. How do you know that?"

"From the catalogue raisonné of his early works. You can learn all sorts of neat things from the provenance of an artwork."

"Well, here's one thing I know without the help of an oeuvre catalogue," Rick said in self-defense. "Did you know that Edward G. Robinson had a rich collection of French art, mostly Impressionist, but also including a Géricault, a Delacroix, two Gauguins, a Matisse, a Chagall, and a Picasso?"

"I did know he was one of the first Hollywood actors to collect art, but I did not know he had anything other than Impressionist works. Thanks for broadening my education, Rick." Megan was sincere. She loved acquiring new information, being corrected in other languages, and was always grateful for grammatical help, especially in thorny German.

"And you might be amused to know, Rick, that film director Billy Wilder, who built up a terrific collection of art, including four watercolors by Schiele, occasionally included one of his paintings in his films."

The banter continued through lunch and by the time they finished it was almost three in the afternoon. Rick looked at Megan, assessing her with his physician's eye.

"I think we should go back to the apartment so you can get a nap in before we leave for your techie run-through at the museum tonight."

"Yikes. I didn't realize it was so late. Yes, good idea. I am more tired than I realized. Let's do go back. And if there's time before the lecture, I'd like to take a quick look at the Paris Kandinskys in the basement gallery."

78

STILL RECOVERING FROM SHOCK at the café near Crédit Suisse's Monte Carlo branch bank after his disastrous experience there, Heinrich suddenly realized something. He did not have the funds to take a flight back to Munich where he planned to denounce duplicitous Rasputin to the police. His credit cards were maxed out and he barely had enough euros in his wallet to buy a train ticket. Now he would have to travel via Marseille to get up to Germany. Damn! If he caught the eleven-twenty-three, which he could just barely make, he would not reach Munich until six the next morning, and even that, only with two station changes. Almost eighteen wasted hours. Double damn!

He could only hope that shithead Russian was still using Paleo when he got there.

79

RASPUTIN'S WATCH showed it was already past noon. Why hadn't he heard again from Pavel? According to their last conversation, his detective was about to drive on from Slovakia to Moscow and keep tabs on all vehicles approaching Zima's place. Earlier, Pavel had voiced to him his thought that the original *Cargo Logistik* van might have been replaced by the hijackers with another vehicle. And then there was that abortive call a little before six this morning. A call that had awakened Rasputin and then gone dead right after he answered. The caller ID gave the name Pavel Meninkov, but when Rasputin called him back there was no answer. He had tried calling several times during the morning, and simply could not understand his agent's frustrating silence.

God forbid his eleven Kandinskys were in the possession of Boris Zima!

80

IN HER CROWDED OFFICE at the Lenbach, Katrina was attempting to get through some of the stacks of paperwork on her desk before going on to the Everest of e-mails awaiting attention. Her dual roles as associate director and restorer meant she was greatly in demand. So absorbed was she in her work that she did not notice the silent entry of her boss.

"Oh, by the way, Katrina, I forgot to tell you something," said Max Mürrisch.

Katrina almost jumped out of her seat at the sound of his grating voice. "Yes?"

"I won't be able to attend tonight's lecture by your professor friend, um, what's her name, Martha Crispy."

"It's Megan Crespi," Katrina answered with barely concealed contempt. She was so angry she decided to pry.

"That is a real pity. Has something come up?"

"Yeah, sort of. Old girlfriend who can't swim has to be let down gently I'm not taking her to the Bahamas with me tomorrow. New girlfriend who can scuba dive going with me."

"I see." This sorry excuse for a man could never let anybody down gently, Katrina heard herself railing against him.

"Just report whether there's good attendance, if you would. And if the gift shop made a good profit." Mürrisch turned on his heel and left.

Wordlessly Katrina stared at the disappearing figure of the director of Munich's august Lenbach Museum. Perhaps he would drown in the Bahamas.

81

ELATION WAS NOT THE WORD for it. Boris Zima was experiencing ecstasy. With one bold action, he had become the possessor of some of Kandinsky's most interesting non-objective works. He owed this new status to the greed of his rival Igor Rasputin. What an idiot. How could he place stolen Kandinskys in his intended Patriots Museum and have it open to the public? There were, after all, international laws concerning stolen masterpieces. Now if he had wanted them for his personal, totally private delectation, that would be a wholly different matter. This is where they differed. Rasputin wanted public acclaim; he treasured his privacy.

But there was one person with whom he could share his joy. Someone who would understand the magnitude of his accomplishment. And that person was Raisa Sokolova. She was still in Munich at her request, ready to relay to him any information she might pick up at a much-touted public lecture on his artist at the Lenbach by an American art historian. The speech was titled

"Double Kandinsky." Now what in blazes did that mean? Perhaps it was an exposé of counterfeiters of the artist. Famous forgeries. Or could it concern the one Kandinsky in Rasputin's known collection that he himself coveted: the one called *Swan Lake*. It was indeed a double Kandinsky in a sense, since the lower part was in the Blue Rider style of recognizable surround—even a lake and a swan—while the upper part radiated the swirling planets characteristic of the artist's later years. Well, he would know soon enough. The lecture was this evening, and Raisa would be calling him right afterward.

In the meantime, under the watchful eyes of reliable Ivanov and his wife, Natasha, the two van drivers had finished their unloading and were stripping the works of their wrappings.

Soon they would be finished, soon they would hang the works, and soon their usefulness would come to an end.

82

WHILE HE ANXIOUSLY WAITED to hear from Pavel on any action at Boris Zima's estate, and from Alyksandr concerning Heinrich von Frauenberg's demise, Rasputin had to admit that his extended stay in Munich had proven to be advantageous. Not only was the wretched Muscovite's female defector now in his employ, he had decided they would both attend a Kandinsky-related event at the Lenbach Museum that evening. He wanted Chernykh to have a look at Katrina Keller, the woman who had betrayed him, and concerning whom he had an assignment. And it could prove humorous to hear what an art historian from Texas could possibly have to say about Russia's greatest artist. A Russia he hoped would soon again include his beloved Ukraine.

83

"I THOUGHT IT WOULD BE BETTER to let you sleep," Rick was saying to Megan who had just woken up much later than she had planned. It was almost six-thirty, the time set to meet with the Lenbach technician. Now she would not be able to take a look at the abstract Kandinskys in the basement gallery before the lecture. Well, thank goodness the museum was only a few steps away.

"You were right about my needing a longer nap," she admitted. "Do you know Eleanor Roosevelt's three travel rules that got her through all the hundreds of cross-country appearances she made on behalf of her husband?"

"Nope. What are they?"

"Never stand if you can sit, never sit if you can lie down, and never pass by a restroom without going in."

"Love them!"

Within seconds Megan had gotten into what she called her "perpetual lecture outfit." It consisted of black slacks, black socks, and black shoes, and a long-sleeved red blouse. Over it she wore a beautiful, slenderizing black vest with embroidered red trim that she had acquired in Alaska years earlier. With the vest on she did not have to wear a bra. She had always wondered why women wore the uncomfortable things anyhow. Well, truth be told, she did know the answer to that, but style had never been her thing. And after a successful bout with breast cancer she especially appreciated the comfort of not wearing a bra. She became known for her great variety of vests, even in the hottest of circumstances, and when she was given a roast upon her retirement, one male student presented a "fashion show" of Crespi vests to hysterical audience appreciation.

This is what Rick, aware of Megan's chapter with cancer, was remembering when Megan reappeared from the bathroom fully dressed and looking refreshed.

Tucking the lecture's thumb drive images into her vest pocket, Megan smiled at her patient travel companion and indicated she was ready to go.

Still and all, it was a pity she couldn't glance at those eleven Kandinskys before her talk.

84

THE LENBACH MUSEUM'S technical support man, Heinrich Wölfflin, was most professional and the run-through of Megan's PowerPoint imagery went without a hitch. She had asked Rick to stay out of the auditorium while she worked with Heinrich, as she wanted her speech to be a surprise to him as well. Rick had good-naturedly agreed and went off to see the basement gallery Kandinskys as much as on Megan's behalf as his own.

It was indeed remarkable to see the energetic abstract works painted, as the introductory didactic explained, during the artist's post-Bauhaus period and in his final city of residence, Paris, where he lived from 1934 until his death from cerebrovascular disease in Neuilly-sur-Seine ten years later. The gallery layout was perfect for display of the eleven canvases: three large ones on three of the rectangular room's walls, and two smaller ones on either side of the entry door. The Paris works, although abstract, were certainly different from the private "thought forms" of ascending and descending circles, lines, squares, and triangles of the artist's Bauhaus period. These canvasses supported checkerboard grids at times and at other times seemed to be growing grounds for amoeba-like squiggling forms against monochromatic backgrounds. At other times, crisply articulated forms reminiscent of primitive art appeared at the core of individual canvases.

Rick could easily lose himself in any one of the beckoning, mesmerizing paintings. And so he did, for about twenty minutes. Then he became conscious of the time and realized he should get moving if he wanted a choice seat for viewing Megan's images. Six minutes to go. He took a last appreciative look around and trotted up the stairs to the museum auditorium.

It was already filled almost to capacity. People were beginning to line the walls and the only seat that would be free was Megan's in the front row, where she was sitting now with Katrina, waiting to be introduced by her. Two people, a woman and a man, had temporarily left their front row seats and were standing in front of Megan and Katrina, the man leaning over and talking earnestly. Rick approached and was introduced to Igor Rasputin, visiting Munich from the Ukraine. The woman stepped away, apparently too shy to be introduced to the group.

"You remember the Kandinsky painting *Swan Lake* I've told you about, don't you, Rick?" Megan looked excited.

"I certainly do. The one that looks Blue Riderish below and Bauhauslike above."

"Well, Herr Rasputin here is the fortunate owner of that, what one could call a 'double' Kandinsky artwork, and it is to be the centerpiece of a new museum that he will open in Odessa soon."

"How wonderful!" Rick beamed at the unsmiling, serious man.

The phrase "'double' Kandinsky artwork" had not been missed by Katrina, who concluded with satisfaction that she now understood Megan's lecture title. The talk would be about Rasputin's *Swan Lake*. How fortunate that the Ukrainian was still in Munich. He had not been particularly gracious when he and his female companion approached her just now. She apologized to him about having missed their eight o'clock meeting at the Lenbach the night of the protest demonstration.

"As you can see, one of the bricks hurled by the crowd hit me on the foot."

Rasputin affected a look of concern. Raisa, now standing farther back and out of Katrina's direct line of sight, stared expressionlessly at the woman she had denounced to Rasputin as being in cahoots with his arch rival Zima. She raised her eyes in time to see two men slip into the back of the auditorium. They looked familiar. Where had she seen them before?

And then it was time for the lecture to begin. Associate Director Katrina Keller walked to the podium, smiled at the audience, and introduced with gusto her distinguished speaker from America, renowned Kandinsky scholar, Professor Doktor Megan Crespi.

Megan rose to acknowledge the applause and walked to the podium. Out of the corner of her eye she saw Rick adroitly slip into her seat. Good for him, she thought. Smiling at Katrina she acknowledged her and her importance for the Lenbach Museum, then launched into her lecture.

The first two images showed a vivid Blue Rider Kandinsky on the left, one with figures, houses, and trees all economically suggested with vibrant, boomeranging strokes of the brush. On the right was a 1926 Bauhaus canvas titled *Several Circles* and enveloped in stratospheric black with swirling circles of different colors and sizes inhabiting its boundless depth. Endless repositioning, ever new biomorphic constellations. The contrast between the two artworks was arresting. Megan let the juxtaposition sink in for a few seconds, then spoke.

"Double Kandinsky. These two paintings say it all, don't they?"

The audience murmured agreement. Megan swiftly bundled up her lecture notes, picked up her iPhone, stepped to the audience side of the podium, and smiled.

"So, thank you very much for coming this evening..." Gasps of disbelief, then mirthful laughter took hold of the audience. Megan stepped back to the podium. She and the audience were one.

This had always been the atmosphere in which Megan functioned best and now she began her lecture in earnest. She brought up her second pair of images: on the left, a photograph of the young Kandinsky, on the right, one of Claude Monet's series of paintings of haystacks at Giverny. She quoted Kandinsky's words about his first encounter in Moscow with the Impressionist's motif in which the representational was subsumed by the gossamer detainment of shifting colors. Hue as motif.

"What suddenly became clear to me was the unsuspected power of the palette, which I had not understood before and which surpassed my wildest dreams."

Megan emphasized how it was not until the age of thirty that Kandinsky left the law profession his family had pressured him to enter and abruptly moved to Munich to study art. She reminded her listeners of another early, key experience in Kandinsky's life—a performance at the Bolshoi Theater in Moscow—that confirmed the synesthesia he had experienced but had had no words for since childhood. The images on the screen changed to a photograph of Richard Wagner and the first three bars of the Prelude to the composer's opera *Lohengrin*. Using her Apple Watch, Megan activated the iPhone on the podium and Wagner's mesmerizing music commenced. For Kandinsky, the prolonged chords triggered a synesthesia which he described: "I saw all my colors in spirit, before my eyes."

For the next forty minutes Megan traced the power of the artist's changing palette and the "sound" of his colors throughout his long career. A continuous career during which, because of "inner necessity," he strove for the form of content as he attempted to capture soul-scapes. To Kandinsky, as he wrote, "color is the keyboard, the eyes are the harmonies, and the soul is the piano with many strings." It was natural for him to use musical references since he had learned to play both cello and piano as a boy.

To the fascination of the audience, Megan read aloud Kandinsky's vibrant description of Moscow, after he was forced to return there because of the outbreak of war in 1914.

> The sun melts all of Moscow into one spot which, like a mad tuba, vibrates the spirit—the entire soul. It is the last note of a symphony which brings every color to highest life, which lets all Moscow ring like the triple forte of a giant orchestra and forces it to join in. Pink, lavender, yellow, white, blue, pistachio green, crimson red houses, churches, each in a separate song, singing with one thousand voices.

Megan mentioned that despite their beautiful symphonies of colors, fifty-seven of the artist's abstract works were confiscated by the Nazis for the 1937 Degenerate Art Exhibition. She concluded by circling in upon the contrasting themes of Kandinsky's two key periods: representational suggestion followed by abstract acrobatics of revolving form and color. Slowly, she enunciated the key to understanding the recurring suggestive shapes in Blue Rider canvasses. The recurrent motifs they represented were waves, a risen soul, boat, horse and rider, towers, cannons, lovers, troika, and ghosts. The audience responded with audible "ohs" and "ahs" as, what had seemed like merely strange shapes before, now revealed their thematic identity. Then Megan leapt to the meaning of her lecture's title.

"We've seen that Kandinsky's long career has bestowed upon us, his admirers, a double gift, a double Kandinsky."

The audience nodded in agreement.

"But what if I were to tell you..."

Two new slides appeared: an image of the Lenbach Museum on the left and opposite it, a photograph of the downstairs gallery where the abstract Kandinskys were on display.

"...to tell you that in the basement gallery of this very museum we have the phenomenon of double Kandinsky?"

The audience, including Katrina Keller, looked totally mystified.

"*To tell you that underneath the painted surface of each of the eleven Paris period abstract Kandinskys downstairs in this museum there exists a representational Kandinsky from the Blue Rider days.*"

The audience gasped its surprise. Katrina Keller's mouth fell open.

"Here is something that was emailed to me just days before I arrived here in Germany. It was sent by the granddaughter of Alexina Duchamp, the French artist's second wife. She had discovered it among her deceased mother's papers, and knowing my oeuvre catalogue work on Kandinsky, she forwarded it to me."

A single new image now occupied the screen. It was a letter written in French by Kandinsky to his neighbor and fellow artist, Marcel Duchamp. The concise handwriting was unmistakably Kandinsky's and the date 12 July 1939 headed the script. The artist referred to the somewhat cramped quarters of the secluded apartment Duchamp had found for him and Nina in the quiet Parisian suburb of Neuilly-sur-Seine, where Duchamp lived. The Russian artist, then seventy-two, went on to state that his three daily activities were walking, reading, and painting in his living room. Then followed the astonishing sentence that provided the key to the existence of "double" Kandinskys:

> Without space for new canvases, I have taken to painting interleafs over old ones on hand here that were done in Munich decades ago. On top of the thick interleafs I have now created eleven new and related works—a cycle of sorts. I do not feel a sense of loss for the old works since Fräulein Münter has irrevocably retained so many of my Murnau Blue Rider things; paintings that, I hope, will eventually go to museums. I have asked Nina to give this newly framed series to the Lenbachhaus Museum in Munich after my death.

As Megan translated into German from the French, sounds of astonishment were heard throughout the auditorium. She concluded as Katrina nodded vigorously in affirmation.

"And now you know what the title of my speech stands for and how lucky the Lenbach Museum is to own eleven unique examples of what we can truly call 'Double Kandinsky.' Dr. Keller, I hope you can forgive me for keeping this a secret from you until now."

Despite her cumbersome cast, Katrina jumped up, tears of joy running down her cheeks, and blew Megan a kiss as the audience began to clap with a fervor befitting the extraordinary occasion. Megan beckoned her to the podium and stood aside, smiling. Katrina strove to find the appropriate words. Finally, she spoke.

"Professor Doktor Crespi has just made today the happiest day of my professional life."

The audience began clapping again with no hint of abatement. Finally Katrina held up her hands for silence.

"It is now my hope that by the time she speaks again on 'Double Kandinsky' at Schloss Berg Wednesday evening, Doktor Crespi will have additional images to show you. Ones that should confirm without a doubt Kandinsky's statement of having painted eleven new pictures over eleven old ones. The Lenbach did indeed receive the Kandinsky gift in nineteen-fifty-two. During the twelve years of my tenure here it has been one of my greatest desires to have time to examine with UV light, infrared reflectography, microscopic and macroscopic images our eleven abstract Kandinksys. The occasion just never really presented itself, and for the past two years the paintings have been out on loan to other museums while our modern addition was being built." Katrina paused for effect, then continued.

"But now, as of just a few weeks ago, we possess the newest state-of-the-art technology and we will be able to examine the paintings using our new macro scanning X-ray fluorescence analyzer. We refer to it as XRF. It is one of only four in Germany. The results should be instantaneous and give us insight into Kandinsky's working methods as well. So, I hope to see some of you Wednesday evening at Schloss Berg, where Professor Crespi will be able to share the result of our findings."

After a new round of applause died, Megan was mobbed by excited Kandinsky fans. Laszlo and Iris Togarassy were among the first to congratulate her while Rick, still in his front row seat, smiled benignly at them.

At the back of the auditorium the two men who had slipped in just before the lecture began, were still standing in their places against the wall. They seemed to be in a state of shock. Finally, the "hermit of Amiinyi" turned to his younger companion.

"Oh my god! This puts a completely different light on everything, Tigr."

"Does it ever, Dzhim. We better get back to Paleo. Heaps of work to do before morning if you want to do what I think you do."

Without speaking to the lecturer, they walked quickly out of the museum.

***

Two other members of the audience did not linger to chat with the lecturer. Igor Rasputin and Raisa Sokolova—known to him as Svetlana Chernykh—had already inconspicuously left the museum.

85

THE ARDUOUS UNPACKING of eleven Kandinsky paintings had been completed a little after twelve noon under the watchful eyes of Boris Zima and his agents Natasha and Ivan Ivanov. It was Natasha, with her fine sense of interior design, who suggested the specific placement of the new artworks on the walls of Zima's enormous annex, where his Blue Rider paintings had been on private exhibit for so many years. Zima had had his art repositioned in anticipation of the delivery and an entire wall was available for arranging the new arrivals.

Even so, they would have to be partially stacked and while Natasha was supervising the carpentry involved, Zima signaled Ivanov to walk with him through the corridor to the main house. He spoke in a low voice.

"As soon as those two men have completed the hanging, it will be time to depopulate my annex. Have you determined your course of action?"

"Indeed, sir. I have two loaded hypodermic needles right here," Ivan gently patted his shirt pocket."

"You're going to tranquilize them first? What are you using?"

"M-ninety-nine; Etorphine. The dose takes an elephant down in minutes; a man in seconds. I'll be injecting them with a large dose in the carotid artery."

"But they'll only be knocked out for a few hours. You are going to *permanently* dispense with them, as agreed, are you not?"

"But of course. After I carry them back to the truck and load them in the rear I shall tie off their heads in plastic sacks. Suffocation will occur while they are still unconscious. It's the humane thing to do."

"Excellent. And you will dispose of their bodies where?"

"I'll be driving them and the van to their own Kapotnya neighborhood— apparent victims of gang war. Natasha will follow close behind and pick me up in the Porsche."

The two men returned to the annex. The picture hanging was completed. Ivan nodded at Natasha and she linked her arm through Dimitri's arm, chatting and laughing loudly, directing his attention upward to one of the paintings above his ladder.

As Dimitri gazed in the direction Natasha was pointing, Ivan walked quickly over to Anatoly, who was folding up his ladder, and stabbed him in the neck with the first of his hypodermic needles. Within seconds after Anatoly crumpled to the floor Ivan had reached Dimitri's side and administered the contents of his second needle.

Contemplating the pictorial arrangement on the wall above the two motionless men on the marble annex floor, Boris Zima turned to Natasha.

"Your installation is stunning, my dear, absolutely stunning."

86

"I DO NOT BELIEVE that American professor's outrageous claims." Rasputin was almost shouting at Raisa, the woman he knew as Svetlana Chernykh. They had come to a halt outside the Lenbach Museum's new addition.

"You realize that if this is true," he whined, "and Boris Zima has successfully stolen my Kandinskys, he will have not one but *two* series of paintings."

"We don't know whether the heist was successful, remember that," Raisa said soothingly. She had not yet checked in with Zima and was glad she had not, as she now had fabulous news for him. Providing the hijack delivery had been successful.

Rasputin's only answer was a frown that brought his bushy eyebrows down over his eyes. He glanced at his cellphone. Still no call from Pavel. What the devil was the man thinking? Why hadn't he tried to get back in touch since that first aborted attempt? And why did the man not pick up when he had repeatedly called him back? Surely the *Cargo Logistik* van had reached Moscow by now.

"Svetlana, your former employer would certainly be at his home waiting for the Kandinskys he stole from me, would he not?"

"Definitely."

"I do not comprehend why I have heard nothing from the agent I sent to find and trail my hijacked van to his home."

"Oh? You have an agent on the job?"

"Of course. Well, never mind that. The situation will resolve itself soon enough. In the meantime, Svetlana, I have a local assignment for you."

Rasputin had not forgotten that the Lenbach's associate director had betrayed him to Zima.

87

"MIGHT I ASK A SPECIAL FAVOR OF YOU," Megan said to Katrina after the last audience members had left the auditorium.

"Name it. After this evening's spectacular news, you deserve any favor I can do for you."

"Well, Rick got to see them before my lecture, but I still haven't had a chance to renew my acquaintance with the basement Kandinskys. It's been several years since I saw them last and that was in their old location upstairs. Might you let me just run down and look at them now, even though the museum is about to close?"

"Of course, Megan! What a small favor. You've earned a private audience with them. Let me just notify our night guard that we'll be downstairs."

Rick was smiling at Megan's enthusiasm. You'd think she'd be tired after her lecture and then conversing with all the people waiting in line to talk to her. He realized she was on a healthy adrenaline high. This was what kept her so young. Excitement and pleasure in her work. It was something he too experienced in his medical practice.

"I'll join you down there," Katrina said to them as she went off in search of the guard.

Megan did ask Rick to take the elevator down. Her body had suddenly given notice that she had been on her feet for the past hour-and-a- half and the long flight of stairs held no appeal for her.

"You know, Rick, recently when I watch films on TV and there's a scene in which someone sprints down or up a stairway without holding on to the rail,

I find myself watching in envious admiration. Never had that reaction before. Never even *noticed*."

"Not to worry. You're simply at an age when it's better to be careful than fleet."

The elevator doors opened onto the basement floor and eleven glowing Kandinskys greeted them. Quietly, in rapt attention, Megan proceeded from one work to the next. Katrina joined them. Together, rarely speaking, they made the rounds of the gallery together, ending up with the two smaller artworks on either side of the entry door.

Megan pointed to the one on the left.

"This one is very similar to the nineteen-forty painting at the Pompidou Center that Kandinsky titled *Bleu de Ciel*. Do you recall it, Katrina?"

"I do indeed. Your point is well taken. This one has the same population of evolving embryos floating in a light blue sky. The reds here really stand out in contrast."

"I find it odd that whoever framed it chose a light yellowish wood," Megan said, moving closer to the painting.

"It does seem to distract from the painting itself," admitted Katrina. "But that's the way it came from Nina, I'm told, already framed. The wood might be maple."

"Hmm. Yes, but maple tends to get yellower and darker. I think the wood is more likely to be black locust, which would explain the pale yellowish brown as it aged," Megan said, slipping a credit card size magnifying card out of her wallet. She held it up to the frame.

"There's something strange about this. Katrina, I'm going to do something no museum visitor should do." She touched the frame lightly. Then gasped in disbelief.

"This is no frame. It's *canvas*, not wood!"

Mystified, Katrina also touched the frame.

"My god, you're right. It's canvas. How could this be?"

"Might Kandinsky have painted the frame as an extension of his picture? Or have stretched his canvas over the frame?" Rick asked, fascinated by the excitement this discovery had ignited in his two friends.

"No, he never did that." Katrina was becoming defensive.

"I don't understand," said Megan softly. "Shall we check the other frames?"

"*Ja.* But better let me do it so you don't get into any conservationist trouble." Katrina went around the room gingerly touching each of the other ten frames on the front and on the sides. Facing her friends, she held her hands up to signify her confusion.

"This is incomprehensible. In every case the canvas extends completely over the frame. Only the frame sides, and I presume the backs, are wooden. And the wood is not consistent. Some of the frames seem to be dense hardwoods, like ash and oak; others look like soft hardwood, like mahogany or Dutch elm. And the wooden sides do not feel the same to the touch as do the 'wood' front edgings. They have a completely different texture. All of them!"

"Oh, boy, there is definitely something wrong here. With the fronts of the frames feeling like canvas, yet looking like wood," Megan said in agreement.

It was getting late and they were all tired.

"Tomorrow," Katrina announced with an air of finality and reassurance, "I promise you, we will take *all* the paintings down and examine them scrupulously, front, sides, and back. And we will subject them to our new XRF to get a better idea of why the frames seem incongruous. But, more importantly, our new macro scanning process will give us an accurate digital reconstruction of the images. And we'll be able to determine the paint colors that Kandinsky's letter to Duchamp states are underneath his interleafs separating the old from the new. Thank goodness, he painted thick interleafs. Who knows, we might even be able to *separate* the two paintings and have actual 'double Kandinskys.'"

"Hooray! Tomorrow we'll know all," Megan said enthusiastically. She dared not say what she was really thinking.

*The Kandinskys could be forg*eries.

88

RAISA WAS NOT AT ALL SURPRISED by Rasputin's "local" assignment. She knew how bitter her new employer was concerning his "betrayal" by the Lenbach's Katrina Keller. The betrayal Raisa had fabricated in order to gain his trust. Having manipulated the Ukrainian into asking what Boris Zima had contemplated having her do, she was more than ready to carry out her assignment tomorrow morning. This could put her in good standing with both employers.

But right now, after she and Rasputin had gone their separate ways, Raisa glanced at her watch and saw that it was almost ten o'clock. Only an hour later in Moscow. She would check in with Boris. Hear how the Kandinsky delivery went. She dialed Zima's private landline number.

"Ah, Raisa, I am in heaven. I have spent the last eleven hours absorbing eleven masterpieces. The Kandinskys have been hung and they are spellbinding."

"Wonderful, Boris, wonderful. And did everything go smoothly with the delivery?" Raisa was dying to know whether or not Rasputin's agent had been able to trace the van. Any contretemps, any face-off perhaps?

"Oh, they were about fifteen minutes late, that's all. Ivanov said there was a small matter he had had to take care of before they arrived, but certainly everything went smoothly after that. And the two van drivers are out of the picture, ha, ha, if you catch my meaning."

Raisa knew only too well what Boris meant. She hastened to tell him the extraordinary news that made her so indispensable to the quirky tycoon.

"Boris. Do you remember I said I'd like to stay over here in Munich to attend a Kandinsky lecture scheduled at the Lenbach Museum for earlier this evening?"

"Oh, yes. How did that go? No, wait a minute. Are you telling me that the idiot museum still doesn't realize its Kandinskys have been stolen?"

"Don't you remember, Boris, I told you that its director had been interviewed on TV Saturday morning after the anti-Kandinsky demonstration and he said all was well, no damage, no thefts? And how I visited the museum later that morning and that the basement Kandinsky paintings were still on display, just as they had been a few days earlier? Don't you remember?"

"Oh, yes, now I do. It slipped my mind. Too much going on here what with the installation of my new acquisitions and everything. So how do you explain it? Especially since I now have those paintings right here in Moscow."

Raisa had given what was indeed a mystery quite a bit of serious thought after her visit to the museum's basement gallery Saturday where all was as it had been before on her previous visit.

"The only explanation I can think of, Boris, is that Rasputin must have substituted excellent copies of the originals. Forgeries so good that, once reassured the paintings were still in the gallery, no museum official bothered to scrutinize the artworks further."

"Ah ha. That makes sense. I have to admit that was rather clever of Rasputin. I should have thought of such a scheme myself."

"Looks as if he did your work for you."

"Ha! In several ways. So. You were starting to tell me about the lecture this evening. What was the strange title concerning doubles all about?"

Raisa cleared her throat and spoke in a commanding tone.

"Prepare to be amazed, Boris. *You are not the possessor of eleven Kandinskys; you are the possessor of twenty-two Kandinskys.*"

"Good god, woman, what are you talking about?"

"I mean that the lecture title 'Double Kandinsky' referred to the fact that underneath your eleven paintings from the late Paris period, there are eleven works from the early Munich Blue Rider period."

"*What?*"

"It's true. Kandinsky mentioned the fact that he had painted over eleven old Munich canvases in a letter he wrote to Marcel Duchamp in nineteen-thirty-nine. The letter was just discovered. Crespi showed it as part of her lecture. And there is no doubt that it is in Kandinsky's handwriting. Yes, Boris, in one fell swoop you have twenty-two Kandinskys, not eleven."

"This is impossible to believe. But I so want to believe it. Raisa, you have been indispensable to me and now you bring me this fabulous news. What can I do for you in return?"

Raisa wanted to say: swear never to consider me expendable, but held her tongue. Instead she turned to a practical matter

"Never mind about that, Boris. You know I wish only the best for you. The thing to do now is to contact a conservator you can trust there in Moscow and have the works scrutinized by the most advanced means available to ascertain for certain what's beneath the top layer of paint."

"Yes, yes. Right, right. And what are the most advanced means?"

"As far as I can understand, it's a form of imaging that doesn't use film that has to be developed, but instead X-rays of some sort. Apparently, the new process can yield images and color almost instantly."

"So I would be able to look *underneath* the top painting and see what's below?"

"All I can tell you is that the Lenbach associate director told the audience at the end of the lecture that her museum now has the newest 'XRF,' whatever that means, and that they will 'macro-scan' examine the Kandinsky works tomorrow. She promised they would have some of the resulting images available for the repeat of the lecture at Schloss Berg Wednesday evening. Of course, I shall remain here and attend that lecture."

"Schloss Berg? I know of it. *Give me the exact time and details and I will be there as well.*"

89

BACK AT PALEO, Tigr and Dzhim worked in concert, slowly pushing and pulling the tightly crammed framed canvases from out behind their large upholstered bed heads. Dzhim had spirited the eleven original Kandinskys up to the bedroom while Tigr was feeding Alyk the clones one by one through the tunnel. As Alyk hung the new artworks in the Lenbach gallery under the watchful eyes of Rasputin, Dzhim and Tigr quickly substituted a second set of framed clones for the original Kandinskys and stacked them for packing on the ground floor.

It was the second set of clones that had been bubble-wrapped and loaded into the Cargo Logistik van. From the very moment they had accepted Rasputin's commission, the boys from Amiinyi had brazenly plotted to steal the original Kandinskys. They would offer to sell them to Russia's wealthy Kandinsky collector, Boris Zima. Rasputin's payment for their work had been a welcome shot in the arm, but it was not enough to sustain them for long or to pay Dzhim's mounting medical expenses.

And now, in light of what they had just learned at the Crespi lecture, they immediately decided upon an even bolder plan of action. One much easier to carry out geographically.

They would demand ransom from the city of Munich itself.

90

THE TRAIN RIDE with its two station changes had seemed endless, but Heinrich finally reached Munich at six o' clock on Tuesday morning. Lacking cash for a taxi he had to walk from the Hauptbahnhof to Paleo. Under ordinary circumstances he would have done that anyway, walking due north through the nearby Königsplatz, but this time he was impatient to get to his house. Perhaps Rasputin was still using Paleo and he could catch him in his sleep.

This time he did not have to enter his own property through the back cellar. This time he entered as he had every right to, through the front door. Stepping into the vestibule, he closed and locked the massive door without making a sound. It was six- twenty and there was not a sound or light anywhere in the building. Heinrich walked through the great salon and the adjoining small salon, through a butler's pantry and into the great kitchen. Perhaps there was something edible around. He suddenly felt hungry. It would be good to have something in his stomach before he searched the second story bedrooms for a sleeping Rasputin.

But now he heard footsteps. Someone was clattering down the main stairway. Soundlessly, Heinrich strode back through the rooms to the vestibule and faced the stairs. The overhead lights had been switched on and two men were running toward him. He had seen them before.

"Who the hell are you and what are you doing in here at this hour?" Tigr, in front of Dzhim, was the first to reach Heinrich. He had a pair of fire tongs in his hand and was holding them up threateningly.

"*Who am I*? I am the owner of this building, that's who I am. Paleo's owner. And I know who you are. You were loading a moving van here a few days ago when the police arrived answering a burglary report. I know because I made that call. I saw what you and your friends were doing at five in the morning in front of my house. So, what the hell are *you* doing here?"

The men stared at each other in a silent standoff. No more words were exchanged.

The scraping sound of a key turning a lock diverted their attention.

Paleo's front door swung open. A bald, heavy-set man stood assessing the scene confronting him for a moment. Then he reached inside his jacket and produced a Glock 39 pistol from his shoulder holster. Pointing it directly at Heinrich, he shot him twice at two yards, once in the throat and once in the chest. The young baron fell gasping to the floor.

His assailant was Alyksandr Miesel.

91

KATRINA WAS ALREADY UP and dressed at six that morning. She could hardly wait to get back to the museum and begin examining the basement gallery Kandinskys. Her experience as chief conservator was about to pay off she hoped. She rushed through breakfast and little Herbert accompanied her to the Uber she had called for a seven o'clock pickup. As it drove off she waved through the rear window at her precious boy and a smiling Diliana, who had joined him at the front door.

She let herself into the museum at the villa door, balancing on her crutches as she turned the several locks. Then it was up to her office and the usual bedlam there. Reluctantly she turned on her computer, not really wanting to see the number of e-mails awaiting her, but conscientiously checking just in case something really important had come in overnight.

Thank goodness. Nothing vital. The only e-mail she was tempted to open was one from her vacationing director. The subject line read prosaically "Having wonderful time." There was no text message. Just a close-up photo of director Max and his new girlfriend, both with scuba masks and in minimal swim suits.

I really ought to rain on his paradise and let him know about the unexpected state of the Kandinskys downstairs, she thought. But then she realized he wouldn't really care that much and it might in fact serve as an excuse for him to take all Kandinsky artworks off permanent exhibit altogether.

Instead, she took the elevator down to the conservation lab with its lead shield walls. She would have to wait for the associate conservator, Paul Ritter, to arrive, as he was the only person who had experience with the XRF yet. But he had already raved to her about the instrument's ability to determine the chemistries of painted linen canvas samples fed to it.

Impatient to get started at least, Katrina drafted the help of a guard who had just entered the room to check on who could be there at such an early hour.

"*Ach*, Reinhold, good you're here. I need your help in the Kandinsky gallery."

"Only too happy to oblige, Frau Doktor," the guard said, smiling at the museum's favorite staff member. He accompanied her as she moved down the hall to the gallery on her crutches.

"We need to bring this painting to the lab," Katrina pointed to the picture left of the entry door. Reinhold was a tall, muscular man and took the painting down easily from the wall. He carried it back to the lab, slowing his pace to match that of the Frau Doktor, and at her direction placed the framed artwork face down on a large table next to the wall-mounted macro-scanning X-ray fluorescence instrument that could be extended over the table.

"Now, if you don't mind, I'll ask you to return to the gallery and bring the painting to the right of the entrance door back here as well."

"Piece of cake," Reinhold said as he left the lab. Katrina smiled at the once overly popular cliché she had not heard for a while. She opened the set of instructions that had come with the miraculous new machine and sat down to study how to achieve an accurate digital reconstruction of the color pigments and image underneath the blue-backgrounded Kandinsky in front of her. The booklet lauded the system's ability to macro scan large area surfaces with high definition. The technique involved combining the scanned data to present a false color image based on elemental distribution so that not only could one get an image of what was underneath, but one could get elemental information to more accurately predict the colors and paints. Hmm. Not sure I understand this. And a warning about radiation. Best to wait for Paul.

Turning toward the painting on the table, she picked up an LED lighted magnifier and began studying the canvas back and frame. Interesting. The canvas was indeed at least eighty years old, if not older. The frame back appeared stressed and worn and was a dark yellow in color. This suggested that the frame could be older than the painting.

Katrina got Reinhold to turn the picture over and commenced

examination of the four wooden sides of the picture's frame. Now here was confirmation of the discovery Megan had made last night. The dark yellow of the hardwood sides was duplicated on the edges of the canvas front, so that it appeared to be a wooden frame front with color matching the sides of the frame. But the tactile sensation of the frame front was that of tightly woven threads of duck canvas. A true trompe l'oeil. And an inappropriate one, since Katrina knew Kandinsky was not interested in painting such three-dimensional objects.

After Reinhold brought in the second painting and substituted it for the first, Katrina made the same careful examination of back, sides, and front, and came up with the same result. Another trompe l'oeil. The texture of wood visually, but the touch of cotton duck canvas. What in the world was going on?

On the dot of eight, reliable Paul Ritter, entered the lab. He was a small man with white hair and clipped white moustache. His colleague greeted him with enthusiasm and described what she had ascertained so far. Paul was more than intrigued.

"Let's put this painting to the test," he said, pulling the XRF over the painting and lowering it to within a hand's length of the painting.

"Now watch this." Within minutes Paul had scanned the surface of the painting including the apparent outer frame. On their computer screen the macro XRF showed a false color image based on elemental distribution below the canvas surface. It also showed the staples and stretcher behind and a small tear in the bottom right quadrant.

"Is this what you wanted to see?" Paul asked.

Katrina blinked. The image underneath Kandinsky's painting was hardly what she expected. It showed in meticulous detail a farmer urging a team of oxen on in a furrowed field. In the back was a woman hanging laundry outside a small farmhouse. Typical Bavarian kitsch of a century ago. Certainly not a Blue Rider motif. And nothing in common with the Russian painter's Murnau scenes.

"No, it certainly is not. I was expecting to see an early Kandinsky painting."

"Odd. The under motif is definitely an oil painting. What the screen shows us is that the image on top is not oil. It is, rather, some form of a photographic print overlaid on the original farm scene painting."

"What? Are you saying that..."

"Yes! This top surface is not a Kandinsky oil. This is an exact photographic Chroma replica, both in texture and topography, of the Kandinsky painting known to us."

"In other words, a *clone*," Katrina said in a low voice when she recovered from shock.

"Yes. A clone."

During the next two hours all eleven of the Paris-period Kandinskys owned by the Lenbach Museum were examined. The result was always the same.

The paintings were all clones.

92

TWO PUNCTUATING VOLLEYS that sounded like gunshots at Richard-Wagner-Strasse 33 early Tuesday morning had been reported by the concierge next door to the police. Chief Detective Dieter Löser was on duty and he noticed that the same address was mentioned in two complaints received by the department just last Saturday and, like this one, quite early in the morning. In that case two police cars had been dispatched but after a number of people had been interviewed, no evidence of criminal activity had been determined. Looking at the file more closely, Löser saw that a *Cargo Logistik* moving van had been involved and this rang a bell. He remembered a report concerning one of the company's vans in Serbia en route from Munich to Ukraine. Its drivers, both with German ID papers, and a Slovakian policeman had been found murdered. There was no sign of the van. An update revealed that a vehicle with the *Cargo Logistik* van's German license plates had been discovered in Moscow's crime-infested Kapotnya district. Two unidentified bodies, probably gang members, had been found inside the van. Nothing else, no cargo.

So, the van sighted at Richard-Wagner-Strasse 33 had been waylaid in Serbia, leaving three bodies in its wake, and had ended up in Moscow, with two corpses inside. Five deaths. Obviously international trafficking, but of what?

Drugs, most probably. It might be a good idea to obtain a warrant and conduct a search of the Richard-Wagner-Strasse building.

One thing Löser did not have to pursue any longer was the interesting report the American professor Megan Crespi had given him about sighting neo-Nazi Walter Krankenhauer exiting a Herrenchiemsee ferry at Fraueninsel, home of a cenotaph to Nazi Alfred Jodl. He had dispatched an officer to investigate and it turned out Krankenhauer's mother lived on the island. End of story. Nevertheless, it would not hurt to keep tabs on the man and his activities in Munich.

93

"BUT WHY DID YOU KILL HIM?" Dzhim was staring at the body still bleeding on the floor.

"Rasputin's orders. The scum was blackmailing him for one million euros after he witnessed our loading the Kandinsky paintings Saturday morning. He realized something big was going on and that's why he stopped the police from interfering. Thought he could cash in. When I came back to the house from the van they were just standing there. Rasputin looked absolutely white and the young whippersnapper was laughing at him. On Rasputin's orders I pursued the man to Monte Carlo and thought I had him on his yacht there. But he eluded me. Wasn't on board when I torched it in the early morning. God knows where he was at that hour. And then yesterday morning I missed him at the Crédit Suisse where he was to pick up Rasputin's wired funds. Then I realized he might try to get back to his Munich house so I flew back last night and came over here early thinking I would lie in wait for him. Obviously, he got here ahead of me."

"But what are we going to do with the body? We can't leave it here." Tigr looked around nervously.

"No problem. We can open up the tunnel, drag him inside, and close it up again. But I'll need your help. Both of you." Alyk looked commandingly at the two hesitant islanders.

An hour later the gruesome transfer had been completed.

94

AFTER A TRIP TO THE GROCERY STORE for breakfast supplies, Megan and Rick had agreed to go their separate ways for the morning. They would hook up again for lunch at the Lenbach Museum's Café Ella where Katrina would find them and report on any double Kandinsky findings. Rick had an appointment with an old colleague at the renowned Ludwig-Maximilians University Clinic in its downtown facility. They wanted to compare notes on the latest treatment of patients with advanced-stage ovarian cancer. One of Rick's favorite professors in college, Eleanor Tufts, had died of the disease and he had a vested interest in the subject.

Megan's morning goal was a visit to Munich's *Ostfriedhof* where she wanted to photograph the gravestone of the distinguished neuroanatomist and psychiatrist Bernhard von Gudden, the man who had mysteriously died with King Ludwig. While reading online about her recently diagnosed dry macular degeneration, she had come across something called the "commissure of Gudden" in regard to fibers of the optic tract, and wondered if it could possibly be the same Gudden associated with King Ludwig. It was. Hence she was doubly intrigued.

She was aware of the cemetery's dark past during the Nazi period when its crematorium was used to dispose of some four thousand concentration camp prisoners from Dachau, Auschwitz, and Buchenwald. She did not find any memorial plaque acknowledging this, but she did locate the tall Gudden tombstone almost immediately. It was crowded with Guddens—full names, birth and death dates, as well as professions. The Gudden women were identified simply as "widows." Megan took a photo of all the names on the headstone for possible use in some future lecture. Then she took a close-up of just Bernhard von Gudden's name and identification. She was disappointed no mention was made of the Ludwig/Gudden death/murder, but the inscription was already long enough. It read: "*Kgl. Obermedizinalrat u. Prof. d. Universität, Direktor d.*

Oberbäyer.Kreisirrenanstalt München geb. 7. Juni 1824 gest. 13. Juni 1886." This translated roughly to: "Royal Chief Medical Counselor & University Professor, Director of the Upper Bavarian Regional Insane Asylum Munich born 7 June 1824 died 13 June 1886."

By the time she got back to the city center and the Lenbach's Ella Café, Megan's mood was somewhat glum; "cemeterial," as she told Rick, who showed up a few minutes later. He, on the other hand, was quite cheerful after a reunion with his fellow physician, Kurt Heilung. They had discussed a dramatic new treatment for ovarian cancer that shrank tumors. It was a drug known as ONX-0801 and it appeared to mimic folic acid in attacking ovarian cancer cells. Rick's excitement was infectious and Megan's doldrums quickly evaporated.

As they were finishing their delicious *Apfelstrudel*, Katrina joined them at the corner table they had requisitioned. The expression on her face was anything but happy.

"Megan. Rick. I have absolutely dreadful news to give you."

The two Americans looked concerned.

"Our XRF findings for each of the eleven Kandinskys have revealed something unthinkable." Katrina looked on the verge of tears.

"What? What? Do tell us." Megan pressed her friend's hand.

"I'll have to ask you both for your total confidentiality. As of yet, I am delaying informing our director."

Rick and Megan were quick to affirm Katrina's request.

"What we discovered to our absolute shock and disbelief is that all eleven of the Paris-period Kandinskys that came to us from Nina Kandinsky are *clones* of the originals. Clever photographic, texturized exact replicas. Indistinguishable to the naked eye. All of them."

"How terrible! So that explains why, when I touched the front of one of their frames, I experienced the feeling of canvas, not wood," Megan said.

"Exactly. The photographic overlay extended to the front edges of the frames, taking on their appearance and their color, if not their feel."

"Do you think Nina knew this?" asked Rick.

"No, I don't believe the paintings were clones when they came to us in the early nineteen fifties. The museum did do a pretty thorough examination of the works at that time and there was nothing unusual reported."

"So the 'cloning' must have occurred more recently then," said Megan. "But when? How?"

Katrina shrugged her shoulders in silence. Her face was a study of dejection.

"Do you think the anti-Kandinsky protest of Friday evening could have anything to do with this?" Rick was thinking of the murdered night guard.

"You mean, do I think the substitution—and that's what it has to have been—occurred during the demonstration?"

"It's something to consider," Katrina allowed.

"Yes," Megan joined in, "perhaps thieves entered somehow, killed the guard, and made the switch during all the pandemonium outside."

"Oh, my god!" Katrina gasped. "Remember after we got that foot cast on me and you were driving me home, how I suddenly recalled that I had an eight o'clock appointment that evening at the museum with the Ukrainian collector Igor Rasputin? I had agreed to admit him and his photography team to the museum so they could make state-of-the-art photographs of the basement Kandinskys. It could have happened then. Except that I didn't let them in. Niki Wächter did, and he was murdered for his effort."

"And he was found just outside the villa door, wasn't he?"

"Yes, that's right. But how could thieves have carried eleven paintings out of the museum without anyone's noticing?"

"Maybe they masqueraded as police?" Rick was trying hard to figure out the complicated logistics involved.

"How do you mean?" Katrina asked, intrigued by the idea.

"Well, perhaps they were in street clothes when they were admitted to the museum, but after substituting their clone Kandinskys, they switched to police uniforms and carried the real Kandinskys out."

"No," Megan objected, "they would have had to be carrying their clone paintings into the museum plus a change of clothes, plus all their photographic equipment. Not possible." Katrina nodded agreement.

"It's one hell of a conundrum."

95

IGOR RASPUTIN WAS IN A STATE TO BE TIED. His agent Pavel Meninkov, supposedly in Moscow, seemed to have disappeared off the face of the earth and he was going to have to admit to the fact, unconfirmed as it might be, that Boris Zima was now in possession of the eleven Kandinskys that were rightfully his. Furthermore, Alyksandr Miesel had not reported in yet concerning the assignment he had been given on Saturday to put that blackmailing owner of Paleo out of commission. Permanently.

And he would still welcome proof that his new agent, once in Zima's employ, Svetlana Chernykh, was entirely in his camp.

Just as he was pondering these irritating aspects of the waylaid Kandinskys' transfer to their rightful home in Odessa, his cellphone rang. It was Alyksandr.

"Why the devil haven't I heard from you?" Rasputin asked angrily.

"Sorry, sir. But I was not able to carry out your orders until just now. I followed von Frauenberg to Monte Carlo but my maneuver to catch him on his yacht failed and I did not learn so until Sunday."

"You *failed*? But didn't you intercept him at the bank yesterday morning then?"

"Um, there was an issue with the bank, sir. He arrived with two girl-friends and there was no chance to get him alone," Alyk lied gracefully, without hesitation.

"So *when* exactly did you put him out of commission?"

"An hour ago, sir. Right here in his own building. Dzhim and Tigr helped me dispose of the body."

"Don't leave. I'm coming right over."

96

LOOKS AS IF they're headed for the Englischer Garten again, Raisa conjectured, giving the Beretta in her belt a quick feel. She was following Keller's boy and his nanny after they left their apartment on Osterwaldstrasse in Schwabing for their afternoon outing. From her rented Volkswagen parked a few doors down on the opposite side of the street, she had kept close watch on the bugged apartment for about an hour.

Sure enough, the two entered the great expanse of green, one of the largest parks in Europe, and began walking in the direction of Monopteros, a small circular open colonnade with Ionic columns and rounded roof. From it one could see the tops of famous buildings around the city, and the temple was a favorite backdrop for tourist selfies. When the pair got within sight of the edifice, the little boy broke loose and began to run toward it, laughing and shouting that he would hide and his nanny should try to find him.

Perfect. Keeping out of sight, with the thick bushes and trees slightly below the Monopteros as cover, Raisa sped ahead of the boy and reached the back of the temple well before he got there. An elderly couple were photographing each other a few feet from her. All Raisa needed to do was wait. She did not have to wait very long. Laughing in glee, the little boy almost ran into Raisa, who scooped him up in her arms, scolding him loudly and covering his mouth. The elderly couple nodded knowingly, then turned back to taking pictures.

Holding the boy tight to her chest, Raisa pressed a chloroform-soaked sponge over his face and made a beeline down the hill from the back of the temple just as his nanny arrived at the building's front. It took the boy about twenty seconds to pass out.

"Herbert! Herbert!" Frantically Diliana ran around the building. She saw an older man and woman photographing each other and yelled at them.

"Did you see a little boy? A little boy just now?"

"Yes, yes, we did," said the woman. "Don't worry. His mother picked him up and he's just fine."

"His *mother*? Impossible. Where are they?" Diliana was screaming now.

"They went back down to the trees. Over there," the man pointed as he spoke.

Diliana began running in the direction the man had indicated, shouting the boy's name hysterically as she ran down the hill.

Still tightly pressing the now unconscious boy against her chest, Raisa left the park and ran the few blocks back to her car on Osterwaldstrasse. Thrusting him into the back, she slid in beside him and cut a piece of duct tape, removed the chloroform sponge from under his nose, and sealed the boy's slobbering mouth shut. She drove off just as Diliana was frantically running back to the apartment to call Katrina Keller.

Rasputin's assignment had been fulfilled.

97

"I TELL YOU HE'S COMING *HERE*!" Anxiously, Alyk looked from Dzhim to Tigr.

"Why?" Tigr was thinking of the eleven Kandinsky paintings upstairs in the bedroom. They were no longer concealed from sight but lined up against the wall in order to breathe.

"What do you think he wants?" Dzhim gave a quick side glance at Tigr. They shared the same apprehension.

"I think he's angry about how long it took me to get rid of the baron boy."

"Do you think he'll mind that we're still here?" Tigr was becoming anxious. What if Rasputin were to go upstairs?

"Nah. He said you two could stay till the end of the month if you wanted. I think he's upset that I had to dispose of the little shit here in Munich and not in Monte Carlo."

A suspenseful twenty minutes went by during which no one said anything. Standing in the entry hall, they all heard the key turning in the front door lock. Rasputin stepped inside, locking the door behind him. He nodded curtly to the islanders, then turned to face Alyk.

"You were an idiot to kill von Frauenberg in his own house. This could be traced back to me after our contretemps with the police here."

"I am so sorry. But it came down to that when he escaped me twice in Monte Carlo. It's just lucky I got here in time. He could have called the police and ratted on you, on us, I mean."

"Take me to the tunnel. I want to see how you masked the entry into the house."

"Of course, sir. I think you'll approve of our work." Alyk led the way to the basement stairs. Behind them Dzhim mouthed something to Tigr. He caught on immediately, turned back and ran silently up the stairs to their bedroom where he ripped the blankets off their beds and draped them over the row of paintings. Silently rejoining the men who had now assembled in the basement, he was able to send Dzhim an unseen affirmative nod.

"When the plaster has dried," Alyk was telling Rasputin, "no one will be able to tell the difference between the wall and the tunnel entrance."

"Not unless it's examined closely, and that's exactly what I'm concerned about. What if the police were to come searching for the missing owner of the building?"

Rasputin walked over to the drying plaster. He knocked on the wall next to it with his fist, producing a muffled sound, then he knocked on the plaster. A telltale echo sounded immediately.

"Oh, that's just great." No one could miss the angry sarcasm in Rasputin's voice.

"And what's that stench? By god, you can *smell* the rotting corpse from here!"

"We'll take care of it, sir. We'll open up the tunnel again and fill it with enough stuff to deaden the hollow sound. And we'll wrap the body so it doesn't stink."

"You didn't even do that? Listen, Alyk, if you think I'm going to pay you for all your blunders, you've got another think coming. The body was supposed to be disposed of in Monte Carlo, not Munich. And certainly not in the man's own house! You are all a bunch of idiots."

Rasputin looked furiously at the three inepts he had hired.

"You have forty-eight hours. I'll be back day after tomorrow to see how you've handled this mess. And if there's even the slightest trace of what's happened here, *I* will be the one to call the police."

98

MEGAN, RICK, AND KATRINA were still sitting at the corner table in Café Ella discussing the conservator's dismal findings.

"I know you want this to remain confidential, Katrina, but wouldn't it be a good idea to bring the police in?" Megan asked.

"That's all I've been thinking about while we've been talking. But the publicity! And first I really have to inform Max. Such a pity to interrupt his vacation in the Bahamas." It was the first time Katrina had smiled since joining them. It was a rueful smile and soon left her face.

"Listen, dear. You and I both know a Munich detective connected with the police force who might be able to help discreetly."

"Help with what?" Katrina said bitterly. "Is he also a conservator? Does he have experience with XRF?"

"No, of course not. And I don't mean that. I mean help with finding out when and how the substitutions were made. And who did it. I think Rick's suggestion that the whole thing could be connected to the night of those anti-Kandinsky demonstrations is highly likely."

Katrina looked doubtful.

"Look," Megan persisted, reaching into her wallet. "I still have his card." She read aloud from it.

"Chief Detective Dieter Löser, Munich Police. And there's his phone number and his e-mail address. Actually, I've already called him once about a sighting Rick and I had over the weekend of that dreadful neo-Nazi man who seemed to be leading the protest at the museum." Katrina took the card and looked at it.

"Oh, yes. He's the man who telephoned me the night you two were taken into custody."

"Well, we weren't actually arrested. We were detained for questioning," Rick clarified.

"All right. I'll think about it." Katrina reluctantly put the card in the pocket of her lab smock.

"But right now, for the next hour or so, I need to get some distance, Megan." A thought struck her and she made a wry face. "And what do you think we should do about the images I so foolishly promised the audience last night that we would be adding to your lecture at Schloss Berg?"

"Oh, boy, I hadn't thought that far ahead," Megan conceded.

"You could say the tests were still ongoing?" Rick volunteered.

"Yes, and after summarizing Kandinsky's career, I could change the end of my lecture a bit to address previous underpaintings that have been discovered in recent famous cases, say like the unfinished Rembrandt self-portrait that was found underneath his *Old Man with a Beard* painting."

"Right." Katrina looked somewhat encouraged. "I was in Grenoble when that artwork was first scanned using a dual energy X-ray imaging technique that showed the painting below the interleaf. And then the Lenbach sent me to New York's Brookhaven National Laboratory when the final results were announced. There, they had used the new macro-scanning X-ray fluorescence spectrometry..."

"Wait, wait, you're losing me," Megan interrupted whereas Rick was nodding in comprehension. "I know you told the audience about it after my lecture, and that the Lenbach has one of only four in Germany, but I didn't really understand what you were saying."

"It's a newly developed fluorescence microprobe system that enables large area surfaces to be scanned with high definition," Katrina patiently re-explained to Megan.

"Okay, now I follow your meaning, if not your vocabulary. I think that's the system they used in cases involving Goya, and Degas, and van Gogh, and even Picasso, right?"

"Yes. Picasso's early painting, *The Blue Room*, showing a woman bathing, has been scanned to reveal a hidden portrait underneath of a man with a beard resting his head on his right hand and dressed in jacket and bow tie. It's truly amazing what we can do now in the lab." Katrina's enthusiasm had replaced her previous dejection.

"Okay, so at the end of my lecture at Schloss Berg, after I've discussed some of those paintings, I could then show Kandinsky's letter to Duchamp, refer to the true meaning of my 'double Kandinsky' title, and then simply state that examination of the eleven Kandinskys is going to take more than a day. So, the audience should 'stay tuned.' What do you think?"

"Not bad. I suppose the Bavarian Kandinsky Society members won't be too disappointed that way."

Katrina's cellphone rang. Reluctantly, she pulled it out of the pocket of her lab smock. She looked down at the ID and answered immediately, a worried look on her face. Her eyebrows shot up.

"Where are you, Diliana? When did this happen?"

Her friends watched in suspense as, open-mouthed, Katrina listened intently to what the nanny was saying.

"Englischer Garten. All right. Stay there just in case. No, I'll call them." Katrina was trembling and her eyes were filled with tears.

"What on earth is it, honey?" Megan asked.
"It's Herbert. He's missing."

99

RAISA TURNED FREQUENTLY to check the back seat of her car and make sure the Keller boy was still unconscious. She was heading east now toward the Prinzregentenplatz and, just beyond it, Versaillerstrasse where the red brick St. Gabriel cloister was located. It was there that the sisters of Our Lady of the Love of the Good Shepherd had recently revived the age-old custom of receiving abandoned children through an outsized flap in the front door without their mothers' fear of identification. As in olden times, the nuns had an enormous letter box set in their front door. On the other side was a large wooden baby crib with an extra thick mattress and a number of pillows. A big bell was attached to the door flap to alert the sisters of a new arrival. Also on the door was a fingerprint pad so that a mother could leave proof of her identity, should she change her mind about abandoning her child. If she had not reclaimed her baby within eight weeks, it would be offered up for adoption.

Raisa spotted the cloister's red brick bell tower and in another few minutes she had pulled up to the front delivery door. Quickly she carried the unconscious boy to the huge hinged flap, read the directive on the fingerprint pad, and crammed the child through the flap. She could hear him fall on the other side. At the same time the bell alarm attached to the flap began ringing. Hurriedly pressing the fingers of her right hand onto the reclamation pad so she could retrieve her "surrendered" child when the ransom payment came through, Raisa turned and raced to her car. Twenty seconds later she was on the way back to her hotel.

She had two telephone calls to make. First to Rasputin and then to Zima. Why shouldn't both bastards pay her for what had been a daring kidnapping in broad daylight?

100

"*CALL DETECTIVE LÖSER, call him right now,*" Megan urged as she put a protective arm around her distraught friend.

"I'm too upset even to manage a phone number," Katrina sobbed.

"Then let me call him for you." Megan took the card she had given her friend, tapped in the number on her iPhone keypad and set it on speaker. Her call was answered almost immediately by Löser.

"Professor Crespi?"

"Yes. Thank god you answered. I need to report a kidnapping. It's the little boy of my friend Katrina Keller, the woman you called as a character witness the night you detained us, remember?"

"Of course, I remember. Are you there with her right now?"

"Yes, but I think she's too upset to talk." She looked inquiringly at Katrina.

"No, no, Megan, it's okay, I think I can talk now. Let me speak to him," Katrina blurted tearfully, reaching for Megan's phone.

"Hallo, hallo?"

"Yes, Doktor Keller. It's Detective Dieter Löser. Your friend has told me there's just been a kidnapping. Am I correct that it's your child?"

"It's my son, Herbert. He's only five and he has a medical condition. A form of epilepsy." Katrina began to choke up again.

"Has he had his medication for the day?"

"Thank god for that. Yes, he takes it with breakfast."

"So there is time then on that score at least. Was he taken from your home?"

"No. He was in the Englischer Garten with his Slovakian nanny, Diliana. It was she who called me just now and told me he had disappeared. He had run ahead of her to the Monopteros, yelling for her to find him, and by the time Diliana got there he was gone. She asked a couple who were there on the acropolis if they had seen him and they told her that his *mother* had taken him. Carried him down the hill behind the Monopteros. Diliana ran in that direction calling his name over and over but he didn't answer and she couldn't find him anywhere."

"All right, so we have the location. Can you tell me what your son was wearing today?"

"Let me think. Diliana usually dresses him. I believe he had on short blue pants and a white shirt. Yes, I'm sure of it now. He waved me off to work this morning and I remember that's what he was wearing."

"Good. And what color are his eyes and hair?"

"Brown."

"Good. And how tall would you say he is?"

"Oh god, I don't know how describe that."

"Tell him he comes up to my waist, Katrina. Detective Löser has seen me, so he'll be able to get an idea."

"I heard that, Doktor Keller. Yes, that gives me a good idea. He's about one hundred centimeters tall."

"That's three-and-a-half-feet," Rick whispered to Megan.

"All right, Doktor Keller. If you will give me your best cellphone contact number and your e-mail address, I will get started on this immediately. Also, I'll need your home address and landline number if you have one."

Megan was motioning urgently to Katrina to hand her back the phone for a moment. She gladly complied.

"Detective Löser, it's Megan Crespi again. I have a photo of Herbert taken just a few days ago. Let me send it to your e-mail address right away, okay?"

"Excellent. I'll pass it on immediately to all officers in the kidnap and home area. And I'll be sending a team to fan out over the Englischer Garten the moment we hang up. I'll be going with them."

"Thank goodness! We'll get off the line so you can go to work."

"All right. I'll be in touch the minute we have anything to report. Do tell Doktor Keller that."

"Absolutely. Thank you, thank you." Megan hung up.

"You heard that, Katrina? He'll contact you the moment he finds out anything."

"Yes, yes. *Oh, thank goodness you took that photo of Herbert!*"

101

THE TRIO AT PALEO was still smarting from the unexpected visit by their former employer Rasputin and his arrogant command that they re-plaster the basement tunnel entrance and get rid of the stink of the rotting corpse inside.

"And he's not even going to pay me for putting down his blackmailer," complained Alyk.

"Hell. It cost me a lot of money to fly back and forth from the Nice-Côte d'Azur Airport and take local transportation for the eighteen kilometers to Monaco and Heinrich's Monte Carlo neighborhood. I had to buy expensive equipment there—even a motorbike. I did complete Rasputin's assignment, after all, even though it was here and not in Monte Carlo. And you boys helped me clean up the scene. He should be paying you something as well."

It was clear to the island boys that their old friend was bitter. Was he bitter enough for them to take him into their confidence?

"You know," Alyk continued his diatribe, "I feel like denouncing him to the police. *Let* them find the tunnel. *Let* them find the body. We could just clear out of here. You could get back to Amiinyi and I could just plain disappear for a while."

The Amiinyi couple glanced at each other but said nothing. Alyk's diatribe was not finished.

"And, you know what, boys? I wouldn't be surprised if he accuses *us* of having stolen those damn Kandinskys from the museum."

Dzhim looked at Tigr and nodded. It was time. Alyk had turned against Rasputin. Irrevocably.

102

SOME IMPULSE IMPELLED RAISA to enter the Lenbach Museum after she dropped off her Volkswagen at the nearby Hertz rental office. She herself was wondering why she was doing it. After all, she'd been in the museum three times in the last week. Once, before the basement Kandinskys had been removed, again, right after they had been taken—and yet, incomprehensibly, were still there—and last night for the Crespi lecture when the paintings were *still* on display.

Knowing her way around by now, Raisa took the elevator to the basement level. The doors slid open to show a makeshift sign on a stand in front of her. It read "KANDINSKY GALLERY TEMPORARILY CLOSED."

Raisa was taken by surprise, yet felt confirmed in her initial judgment that the eleven Kandinskys had indeed been stolen from the museum basement by Rasputin. I'm glad I returned once more, she congratulated herself. Suddenly feeling hunger pangs, she took the elevator back up to the ground floor and walked over to the museum's convenient Café Ella. It was deserted except for three people huddled over a table at the far corner of the café. Raisa glanced at them, then looked again at the redhead. It was Katrina Keller. And she was with Professor Crespi and her ubiquitous male friend. Keller was sobbing and Crespi was attempting to comfort her.

How timely. A mother's grief. So touching.

Raisa immediately turned around, exited the museum, and took a cab back to her hotel. She now had two triumphant phone calls to make. But first she would satisfy her hunger in the hotel restaurant.

She picked a table facing the windows and ordered her favorite Knoephia soup again, stressing that it be served hot. Minutes later, just as she was about to slurp her first spoonful of the steaming liquid, her cellphone rang.

Shit! She looked at the ID and her anger dissolved. This time, however, the caller came second. She blew lightly on the delicious brew and swallowed several sips before answering the call from Boris Zima.

"Hello, Boris. I have interesting news for you."

"Well, I have news for you too and it's bad, very bad."

"Oh? What?" Raisa slowly sipped another spoonful of soup as she waited for alarmist Boris's explanation.

"I took your advice and got the head conservator from the Tretyakov, Stanislav Volkov, to come to my gallery. He brought what he called a 'point and shoot' portable XRF analyzer with him and applied it to all eleven paintings. Took him no less than an hour." Boris' voice was quavering.

"Yes? And?"

"There are *no* early Kandinskys under the paintings. Only old flower still lifes and maudlin farm scenes."

"*What?*"

"Pictures dating back to the early nineteen-hundreds. Nothing to do with Kandinsky."

"But he *wrote* Marcel Duchamp that he overpainted his old Munich canvases. I've seen the letter."

"Forget that. There's more to tell you and it's even worse."

"Tell me."

"The Paris-period images on top, *they are not paintings.* They are applied photographs with correct colors and even the textures of pigment and brush stroke. 'Clones,' Volkov called them. 'Clever clones.'" Boris's voice was an octave higher now.

"You're telling me that those eleven artworks Rasputin stole from the Lenbach Museum are not even paintings?"

"Yes, that's what I'm telling you. I've been gypped!"

Raisa's soup was room temperature again, but this time she did not notice. Her agile mind was racing. What if the museum had known all along that something was not right with Nina Kandinsky's gift of eleven works by her husband? No, that doesn't make any sense. Certainly, the pictures would have been examined by conservators in the museum lab upon arrival. *But where there is a clone there has to be an original.* So where are the original eleven paintings? Germany? Russia? Ukraine? Or perhaps Switzerland? Raisa recalled hearing that years after Kandinsky's death, Nina was murdered for her jewelry at her Swiss chalet. What if the murderers had also taken whatever Kandinsky works were in the house as well? Might there have been eleven of them? And from the Paris period?

For the life of her, Raisa could not come up with any answers to the multiple questions now assailing her mind. Then a likelihood opened up before her. She suddenly remembered the blurb she had read under the museum directory photograph for Katrina Keller. The associate director of the Lenbach was also the museum's chief conservator. Perhaps, because of her son's medical expenses, *she* had created the forgeries. She had the means and, no doubt, the knowledge, or at least access to it. Keller could have created the clones at night, when the museum was closed. One at a time. She might well have paid off any night guard.

Yes! This was the explanation. Now all that was needed was to find out to whom Keller had sold the eleven original Kandinskys.

"Boris, you may have been gypped, as you say, but this also could mean that Igor Rasputin was tricked as well."

"What do you mean?"

"I mean it is possible that someone working at the Lenbach created the clones and sold off the originals on the black market."

"God, what a thought! But who?"

"Think about it, Boris. Who would have been in the best position to have forgeries made?"

"The new director?"

"The chief conservator. Katrina Keller."

"Ah, that damn collaborator of Rasputin's!"

"Right. Remember, I told you that she has an invalid son, hence large medical expenses."

"Oh, I remember. Epilepsy, wasn't it?"

"Yes, epilepsy."

"Well, we had better find a way to get to her."

"What would you say if I told you I have her in the palm of my hand?" Raisa knew she had done the right thing. And just in time too.

"How do you mean?"

"I have her boy."

"You *kidnapped* him?"

"Yes. Thought it might come in handy. I completed the mission earlier this afternoon." Raisa did not hear the exclamation of approval she had expected. Or the usual offer to pay her handsomely for her initiative. Instead, there was silence on the line. Then Boris spoke. His tone exuded displeasure.

"I am not sure that was a smart thing to do, Raisa. My god, the police will be all over her. And if we try to approach her she might just flip. Denounce us to the police."

"But it was you who encouraged me. I thought that was what you wanted." Raisa was devastated.

"We shall discuss this in person, Raisa. I'll see you at Schloss Berg tomorrow evening."

103

FIVE MEN WERE ON THE CASE. This was the son of the associate director of Munich's great Lenbach Museum. He must be found. With a recent photograph of the boy in hand, Detective Löser's men were searching the streets of Katrina Keller's neighborhood but so far to no avail. Simultaneously, other officers had gone over the Englischer Garten with a fine-tooth comb, questioning every person they came across. One key piece of evidence had come to light.

An elderly couple walking down from Monopteros had been questioned and shown the boy's photograph. They recognized him immediately, declaring they had seen him being lifted up by a dark-haired woman, probably in her forties. They presumed she was the boy's mother since he did not resist. She had dashed down the hill with the child in her arms. A few moments later another woman with long black hair came rushing up to them asking if they had seen a little boy. When they told her what they had witnessed the woman ran off in the direction they pointed. She was yelling the name "Herbert."

Detective Löser called the distraught mother with the news. They now knew the boy had been taken by a woman in her forties with dark hair. Did she have any idea who that could be?

"I don't know who that might be. But the other woman who was shouting Herbert's name was my boy's nanny. Diliana is her name. She's the one who called and told me that Herbert was missing."

"We need to interview her right away. She may have a fuller description of the woman who took your son."

"She must have returned to my apartment by now."

"I'll go there. Immediately."

"Oh, thank you. I'll get home as fast as I can." Katrina looked anxiously at Megan as she hung up.

"No need to ask," Megan assured her. "Rick's already running to get the car. We'll have you home in minutes."

The Kandinsky conundrum they had pondered earlier could not be further from their minds.

104

THE ELEGANT BUILDING behind the Lenbach Museum which had once belonged to Baron Heinrich von Frauenberg, was now witness to organized bedlam.

Working in concert, Alyk, Dzhim, and Tigr were drilling through the dried plaster and panel they had so recently installed to wall up the entrance to Paleo's basement tunnel. As the plaster shards fell, a noticeable odor reached their nostrils—the metallic smell of dried blood. A lot of dried blood. Cramming some wrapping blankets under his arm, Alyk entered the tunnel and bent over to move the putrescent corpse he and the others had so recently shoved inside. It was not there! Instead a trail of dried blood led under the street and to the tunnel exit on the other side. Only there did a spooked Alyk finally see the body. Heinrich had not been dead when they sealed him in the tunnel. He had regained consciousness and tried to crawl forward. Well, this time he was really dead. Alyk kicked him, just to be sure. The stench was overwhelming. He dropped the blankets. He had to get out of there.

"Hey, what's going on?" Tigr shouted into the tunnel.

"Nothing. I'm coming." Alyk raced back and rejoined his friends. Never mind about trying to fill the tunnel with sound-reducing material. He simply could not go back in.

"We can plug it up now."

***

Dzhim and Tigr had watched as Alyk threw up. He sat on the floor hugging his knees against his chest while they re-plastered the wall. When the work was completed they went back upstairs followed by a silent Alyk. Suddenly he began raving.

"Rasputin! Rasputin got me into this nightmare situation. He had me do his dirty work for him. He had me kill. He promised me twenty-five-thousand euros for the job. Now I could kill *him*!"

The island boys exchanged glances and nodded. It was time to reveal the ransom scheme to their distressed friend.

"Come up with us to our rooms, Alyk," urged Dzhim. "We have something we want to share with you."

"Huh? Okay. Sure." A glum Alyk obediently followed his friends upstairs and into their suite. He entered the bedroom and stopped at the sight of blankets draped over what looked like a number of framed objects.

"We have the means here," Dzhim pointed dramatically to the blankets, "to bring you many times over the money Rasputin owes you." He nodded to Tigr. The younger man walked over to the blankets and in one dramatic move whipped them off

"*My god! It's the Kandinsky paintings!* But how can it be? I, you, Tigr, we all helped wrap and load them into Rasputin's van." Alyk was incredulous. Dzhim put a soothing hand on his shoulder.

"First, I must tell you that it has always been my policy to have a backup plan, whatever the task I take on. And that the cause I take on is a worthwhile cause. Secondly, in this case, Rasputin's planned Patriots Museum in Ukraine, I had heard via the grapevine that Russian President Yabeda Tupinsky suddenly withdrew his promised financial support for the project, even though he and Rasputin are both members of the *Make Russia Russia Again* movement. My suspicion is that incorporating Ukraine into Russia must have been moved to Tupinsky's back burner, what with all the present international tensions and crises."

Alyk was listening intently, his mouth slightly open, all the better to catch Dzhim's words.

"What this means," Dzhim continued, "although Rasputin won't admit it, is that his Patriots Museum may never get off the ground. Thirdly, I've learned that Russia's own major holder of Kandinsky works, Boris Zima of Moscow, has recently renewed his interest in expanding his collection and has cancelled a previous offer to give one of his pieces to Rasputin's Patriots Museum." Dzhim paused. This was a lot of data to load onto his friend, who was now rubbing his forehead trying to take it all in.

"Wait a minute," Alyk said. "Am I understanding correctly that we didn't load the real Kandinskys into that moving van Saturday morning?"

"Yes. The real ones, the originals, are right here in front of us."

"And these were supposed to go to Rasputin's Odessa museum which now, however, may not have the funds to finish construction, correct?"

"That's right. The two main supporters of Rasputin's museum have pulled out. Tupinsky and Zima."

"But when did you know this?"

"Right here in Munich, last Wednesday when just before we began our scanning, a reporter friend from Odessa emailed me the news. We immediately laid aside twenty-two frames from that huge batch of picture frames you had assembled in your workroom."

"And that's when you decided to create forgeries to ship to Rasputin?"

"I certainly wouldn't call them forgeries."

"Hey, they are genuine works of art in themselves," Tigr jumped in. "Topographical, texturized, exact color replicas. Looking at them through a magnifying glass, even touching the paintings renders the same result as would the originals under the same circumstances."

"Yes," Dzhim continued, "there was only one drawback with what we had to do in our backup plan. We needed to photograph the original Lenbach frame fronts along with the paintings, with the result that, although they look exactly like the original frames with their various colors and wood grains, their *feel* is the texturized touch of canvas, not of wood. But after all, museum visitors are forbidden to touch objects, aren't they?"

"You're right. Clever, clever." Alyk was beginning to appreciate the possibilities of the boys' backup plan.

"And since the replicas we hung in the museum give the impression that nothing has been altered, there was and is no reason for Lenbach conservators to examine them under spectroscope or the like. Not even a Kandinsky expert would notice anything just standing in front of one of them."

"So, after you heard from your Odessa contact, you decided to create *two* replica sets, one for Rasputin, who would probably never know the difference, and one for the museum. All this while *you* retained the originals we have right here in front of us."

Silence ensued as Alyk slowly walked from one painting to the next. After he had sized up all eleven of them he turned and offered his hands to the island boys.

"Brilliant. Ingenious and brilliant," he said. "So, what are you going to do next?"

"No, no, what are *we* going to do next, Alyk," Tigr hastened to make a point.

"I told you," Dzhim said earnestly, "that we have the means to bring you many times over the money Rasputin owes you. These paintings will bring us a fortune. And we will share it with you. Our friendship goes back many, many years, after all."

"Thank you. Thank you. Are you going to try to sell them to Zima then?"

"That was our original plan, but a far better idea has come up. One that involves no geographical relocation."

"What's that?" Alyk was enthralled.

"Think what the Lenbach would give to have the paintings back, undamaged, and within a few days. The city of Munich would pay a handsome ransom for their return. Think about it."

"Fabulous. No long-distance negotiations with Moscow. No dealings with a quirky art collector who could, after all, turn us down. No problems at border crossings."

Dzhim and Tigr smiled encouragingly at their friend.

"Now all we have to do is plan how to get our demand to the proper authorities without revealing our location," Dzhim said.

"Do you have any suggestions, Alyk?" Tigr laughed nervously.

"*Yes, actually, I do.*"

105

RAISA WAS STILL SMARTING from Zima's cool reception of her news that she had successfully kidnapped Katrina Keller's son. It was he, after all, who had toyed with the idea, encouraged her. "Long live epilepsy," he had even commented after she informed him of the boy's possible medical problem. So, no extra money waiting for her in Moscow. Cheapskate!

Never mind. Rasputin, who had specifically ordered the kidnapping, would receive the news with approval. And an additional benefit was that it would reinforce the man's confidence in her. The only factor not yet determined was payment. She was beginning to run out of funds, whereas it had been her plan to build up a nest egg with these two Munich jobs. Something she could retire on.

Right now, however, no more moping. It was time to report the success of her mission to her new boss. She dialed the private number Rasputin had given her and he answered after a few rings.

"Svetlana Chernykh?"

"Yes, sir. I am happy to report that your local assignment has been successfully completed and the person in question is in a safe house. The subject's mother is now aware of the fact and we need only make our demand."

"Oh, yes. All right. This should be useful. Let's see. First, I want the mother to know that betrayals invite paybacks. You might phrase it exactly that way in a message to her. Nothing specific. Just what I said. 'Betrayals invite paybacks.'"

"But wouldn't that be a giveaway as to who might have kidnapped her son, considering you had dinner with her to set up the photo shoot? And surely she's gone to the police by now."

"Oh, I will be in Odessa by the time you deliver the message. I'm taking a late-night flight back tomorrow after the Schloss Berg thing. I can't wait to find out what the Lenbach has *not* discovered under their putative Kandinskys. Ha! Should be quite a blast."

"So I will be *here* but you will be back in Ukraine?" Raisa was beginning to feel overwhelmed and insecure.

"Well, of course, what do you think, Chernykh? At the proper time, we will denounce Boris Zima as the man who stole the paintings. And that traitor, Katrina Keller, will be in anguish over the disappearance of her son and she will know why. Ha!"

"So, you're not thinking of demanding a ransom for the boy?"

"Oh, no. Don't think so. Too complicated. I just want her to dangle for a while. We'll release the kid eventually."

Raisa was not only increasingly uneasy, she was now also indignant. Rasputin was planning to be safely back in Odessa while she was taking all the chances in Munich. And how was she going to deliver a hate note to Keller? Why did *she* have to be the vulnerable instrument of Rasputin's vengeance?

"So, you are absolutely not interested in demanding money for the return of the child?"

"That's unimportant. I just want the mother to suffer for a few days."

"You may not care about a ransom, but *I* do!" After all, Boris Zima had previously heaped praise upon her and agreed to pay her big money, but he had yet to come through. And now Rasputin was asking her to take chances on his behalf. Raisa decided to take the leap.

"In fact, I expect to be reimbursed for expenses I've already accrued on your behalf. The car rental, for example." There was silence on the line. Then Rasputin spoke and it was not what his new agent wanted to hear.

"My practice is to pay for work completed, Svetlana Chernykh. After we let the boy go, and after we have revealed to the authorities that it is Zima who has the Kandinskys, we can talk about your remuneration."

Raisa experienced what seemed like a grenade exploding in her head. It cleared her mind. She would have vengeance, whatever it took.

And for starters, she would now neglect to inform Rasputin that his archrival would be attending the Schloss Berg Kandinsky lecture.

Let the cards play themselves out.

106

THE MOOD WAS GLOOMY and intense inside Katrina's apartment at Osterwaldstrasse 89. She had been driven there from the museum by Rick and Megan. Diliana was sobbing and mercilessly berating herself for having let Herbert disappear out of her sight, and his mother had to fight back her own tears. In the midst of all this Detective Löser arrived, accompanied by a female police officer.

"This is Officer Besorgt and she will be taking down your and your nanny's account of the events today that preceded the kidnapping of Herbert."

At the sound of her son's name Katrina lost her composure and began to sob.

"There, there, Frau Doktor," Officer Besorgt soothed, we will get to the bottom of this and your son will be safely returned to you. I know he needs medication once a day, and we can be thankful that he had it this morning."

"Thank heaven for that at least."

The officer began taking notes as she gently interviewed both women. Löser took the opportunity to look discreetly around the rooms of the apartment. Megan and Rick felt they were in the way, but on the other hand they wanted to be available for Katrina.

"We'll be outside in the car if you need us," Megan whispered in her friend's ear.

"Oh, there's no need of that. Please do whatever you planned to do today. You probably want to rework your PowerPoint for tomorrow evening's lecture."

"And that's the sort of thing I can easily do in the car. No, we'll be just outside. We insist." Rick nodded agreement and Megan patted her friend's shoulder reassuringly. Detective Löser said he would walk them to the car.

"Can you think of anyone who might hold a grudge against the Frau Doktor?" he asked once they were outdoors.

"Absolutely not," Megan answered, "but a disaster has hit the museum I think you should know about. I was in the act of attempting to persuade Katrina to notify you when she received her nanny's call that Herbert was missing. Given these new circumstances, however, I'll take it upon myself to inform you, but I beg you to keep it just between us for now."

"Of course, if you wish." Löser could sense Megan's agitation.

"All right. The museum owns eleven late Kandinsky paintings which are permanently on display in its basement gallery."

"Yes. Penelope and I have admired them."

"The problem is that at some point in the Lenbach's history, and we think it could be very recent, those eleven Kandinskys were somehow removed and eleven very clever clones were substituted."

"*What?*"

"Eleven exact replicas. They were detected only this very morning by Doktor Keller."

"But how could anyone pull off a major stunt like that without someone's knowing? The paintings are too large to be removed without detection."

"That is what we can't answer. The museum has state-of-the-art, continuous surveillance and alarms in place and of course it couldn't have happened during the day. I think it was something that had been planned for months and that whoever was behind it took advantage of last Friday's rowdy protest to make the switchover when all eyes were on the crowd."

"And that would have to be why the night guard was murdered. My god!"

"I do know one thing that might be useful. And I'm sure Katrina would tell you herself if she weren't so distracted by her son's disappearance.

"And what is that?"

"It's this. She had made an eight o'clock appointment for that very evening to meet and admit into the museum for a private photo shoot by his assistants, a famous Kandinsky collector visiting in town from Odessa. But we had to drive her to an emergency clinic at just that time for treatment of foot wounds she'd received during the riot."

Löser's eyes opened wide.

"You mean to tell me that people were going to be shown into the museum while an anti-Kandinsky demonstration was in process?"

"Well, Katrina couldn't possibly have known a protest was going to happen that evening."

Detective Löser did not give voice to his emerging thoughts. What if the woman were in cahoots with the Odessa visitor? A "*photo shoot*"? It could even be that her son was kidnapped to ensure her silence. Sure looked that way. That would explain why the guard was killed. Right now, however, it was important to keep everyone calm. He thanked Megan and promised to keep her confidence. For now. Returning to the house, he resolved to interrogate the Frau Doktor in a way that might elicit helpful details or even an outright confession. The museum switch and the child snatch had to be related in some way.

***

Once in the car, Megan pulled her laptop out of her shoulder bag and set to work. It would be good to concentrate on something other than Herbert's kidnapping.

"Wow. You are never without your iPhone or your Mac, are you, Megan?" Rick had noticed that his travel companion insisted on having her "vitals," as she called them, with her at all times. And yet she also carried paper maps of Germany around. She certainly had all bases covered.

While Megan began aggrandizing her lecture with images pulled from the Internet, Rick decided to do some online exploration of his own. Still fascinated by the mysterious deaths of mad King Ludwig of the Wittelsbach dynasty and his keeper von Gudden, he pulled out his own cyber connection to limitless world knowledge and began researching various URLs on his large screen Samsung Galaxy.

He came upon one very interesting blog by a lawyer, Ann Marie Ackermann, titled "Death of King Ludwig II of Bavaria: Was It Murder?" The author reviewed the official story of the king's taking an early evening walk on the Starnberg lakeshore in the company of his psychiatrist, von Gudden. When they did not return at 8 pm, a search party was sent. Around 11 pm a fisherman discovered the bodies of the king and the physician floating in shallow water. Curiously, the official autopsy found no water in the lungs of either the king *or* his doctor. But gasping drowning victims usually sink once their lungs fill up with water. For both bodies to be floating would mean that both men were the victims of "dry drowning," a rare phenomenon that occurs when the larynx goes into spasm and shuts off the airway, suffocating the person. Hence no water in the lungs. But a *double* dry drowning would be too rare a coincidence, as the occurrence rate of a dry drowning is only one or two percent of all recorded drownings, justly termed "wet drownings," as the lungs fill with water and the bodies sink.

Rick was fascinated. Especially when he read next that members of the Wittelsbach family later maintained that Ludwig had been *shot* and two bullet holes were apparent in his shirt, vest, jacket, and coat. The Countess Josephina Wrba-Kaunitz of the Wittelsbach Family was reported by two persons who visited her around 1957, to have dramatically announced that she would reveal to them the truth about how the king died. She showed them Ludwig's gray Loden coat. It had two bullet holes in the back. If true, why was this information suppressed? Unfortunately, the coat, along with the countess and her husband, were incinerated in a house fire in 1973. The countess's claim was nonetheless corroborated in a 1986 statement made by one Detlev Utermöhle, who had been present as a ten-year-old, that in addition to the two bullet holes found in Ludwig's coat, a third shot had killed von Gudden.

What a story of cover-up and deceit, Rick thought. If this were true, it could have been an assassin hired by the Bavarian ministers who had imprisoned Ludwig at Schloss Berg.

What else? Rick found a copy of the coroner's report. It was in German but a number of terms were Latin so that he comprehended most of it easily enough. It focused on measurements of the king's brain and skull. Laboriously, Rick translated one of the paragraphs:

The arachnoid on both convexities of the cerebrum was thickened and milky-looking. At one place, about the junction of the left first frontal and the ascending frontal, the arachnoid membranes had become thickened and raised by fibrous proliferation.

Then Rick came across several paragraphs that had been blotted out, with each one labeled "CENSORED." What was all that about? And why didn't the 1886 autopsy report concentrate on the condition of the body or report on any injuries? Rick looked over at Megan. She seemed to have come to a pause in her work so he asked if she would like to hear something really intriguing about Ludwig's death.

"Sure." Megan blinked her eyes in relief after constant staring at her computer screen.

"It seems that it is quite possible he was not a suicide and did not strangle von Gudden, but, rather, that they were both—hold on to your hat—*shot*. And that the whole thing was quashed in the coroner's report allowing what became the 'official' account to stick with the double drowning explanation."

Megan was totally intrigued.

"Golly, I wonder if I could include that in my lecture tomorrow, since we'll actually be at the scene of the crime. Whether it was Ludwig strangling Gudden, then 'dry' drowning himself and the already dead Gudden—another 'dry' drowning—or a case of both men being murdered by gunshots."

"Better stick to your announced topic—it's full enough as it is now, with your examples of 'double' Rembrandt, Degas, van Gogh, and Picasso." Rick smiled at Megan's enthusiasm. Her teaching had also included captivating things other than art history. He started to remind her of this when suddenly there was a pounding on the passenger side of the car. It was Diliana. Wide-eyed, she screamed:

"*Quick! The Frau Doktor wants you come to her! Something has happened!*"

107

THE AMIINYI BOYS LOOKED SURPRISED.

"I do have a suggestion," Alyk repeated. "About how we can secure the immediate attention of the museum. It will entail, however, the loss of one of these Kandinskys." He studied the paintings thoughtfully.

"This one," he said finally.

"Well, what's your idea?" Tigr asked. "Hurry up and tell us."

"Okay. We bubble wrap this one and place it inconspicuously in the museum's loading dock very early tomorrow morning while it's still dark. Then the minute the museum opens we call on a disposable cellphone and inform them of the item's presence. Inside the wrapping we put photographs of these other ten paintings, and a note saying something like this:

Want the other ten back? Leave one hundred million euros in cash inside a briefcase and place it securely upon the ledge of the only window in the old museum's fourth story attic by tonight at nine o'clock. If you comply, you will receive immediate word as to the location of the other ten paintings.

"What do you think?"

Both Dzhim and Tigr looked unconvinced.

"I understand the bait aspect of leaving one of the Kandinskys for the museum to have back, but how on earth are you going to retrieve a briefcase from the window of that one little box room atop the old villa part of the museum?" Dzhim was mystified.

"And the police will be out in force and will stop anyone who even approaches the museum," reasoned Tigr.

"Who said anything about anyone entering the grounds?" Alyk was enjoying the boys' bewilderment. He decided to enlighten them.

"Ever hear of a drone? That's how we're going to pick up the briefcase. From above, with a drone. We'll fly it over from the roof of this building, grab the briefcase from the sill of the open window, and steer the drone back here before the police can think twice."

"Have you ever *flown* a drone?" Dzhim asked sarcastically.

"I've been flying quadcopters since I was a kid. Haven't done it lately, but, like a bicycle, you never lose your muscle memory for the controls. I can still yaw and roll on a transmitter with the best of them. And I still have my old drone over at my place." Alyk spoke with authority and Dzhim and Tigr began to take his idea seriously.

"I would add just one sentence to the note inside the bubble wrap with the painting," Dzhim said.

"What's that?"

"If you do not comply exactly as specified the other ten paintings will be immediately destroyed."

"Brilliant! They won't dare not comply."

Tigr's enthusiasm was infectious. They got to work.

Thirty-three million-plus euros in cash per man was plenty of incentive.

108

"THEY'VE FOUND HERBERT!"

Megan and Rick had rushed back into the Keller apartment. They saw a jubilant Katrina and a busy Detective Löser giving terse commands on his cellphone.

"How? Where is he?" Megan cried. "This is wonderful."

"Someone from his office just called Detective Löser and reported that the abbess of a convent here in the city had filed a missing person's report. The convent takes in unwanted babies. But, they said, this was a four-or-five-year-old little boy, far older than the infants they were used to receiving. And can you imagine? Herbert had somehow been shoved through the large front door reception flap. He was unconscious when a nun found him and she noticed a smell like ether emanating from his mouth. When he came to, the nun said, he began calling for his mother. He kept repeating '*Katrina Keller. Lenbachhaus. München. Katrina Keller. Lenbachhaus.München.*' Just as I taught him."

"Oh, thank heaven!" Megan was overjoyed. It had already been such a hard day for Katrina.

"Officer Besorgt is on her way to pick him up right now," Detective Löser announced, putting away his cellphone.

"Tell me about this convent that accepts abandoned babies?" Rick asked.

"It's called the convent of Our Lady of the Love of the Good Shepherd and it's not far from the Prinzregentenstrasse," Katrina explained.

"Ah ha! Look what I've found," Löser suddenly exclaimed. He was examining the underside of the living room television set.

"You are being bugged." Using a handkerchief, he held up a very small rectangular black box with two short antenna wires hanging from it.

"See this? It's a voice activation micro listening device. That's how the kidnapper knew Diliana was taking Herbert out for a walk."

"You mean everything we've said at home has been heard by someone?"

"Heard *and* recorded. Using a handkerchief Löser slowly pulled a SIM card out of the little device.

"That's the end of that. We'll take it downtown and dust it for fingerprints."

"But why on earth would anybody want to bug me?" Katrina was totally baffled.

"It might have something to do with the property you own in Murnau, or to recent goings-on at the Lenbach," said Megan, attempting to speak in general terms and stealing a quick glance at Löser.

Reference to the museum sparked a sudden train of thought in the detective. That bigoted neo-Nazi Walter Krankenhauer had led the anti-Kandinsky protest at the Lenbach. True, he had to be released after questioning, but he was openly recalcitrant concerning his "nationalist" motivation for the anti-Kandinsky demonstration. The tail Löser had put on him after Professor Crespi's sighting of him at Fraueninsel, had reported that Krankenhauer returned to Munich. He was still under surveillance.

Löser kept coming back to the biggest conundrum of them all: how could eleven large Kandinsky paintings have been removed from a museum while simultaneously same-size, exact copies were installed in their place *without anyone's noticing?*

109

THE PILOT of Zima's private Cessna Citation M2 jet had been notified by his employer to have the plane ready for a flight from Moscow to Munich at noon the next day, Wednesday. At the moment, Boris was in his picture gallery trying to come to a decision about his eleven Kandinsky forgeries. Forgeries! The mere word disgusted and humiliated him. Had Rasputin done this to him on purpose? No, not possible. Raisa had been stalking the art addict from Odessa to keep him informed of the man's comings and goings in Munich and to ferret out why he was in the city. It was pure luck that she had been on the scene when Rasputin and his underlings loaded the van with paintings. Rasputin could not have known about her reports or that the van would be hijacked on its way to Odessa.

Ah! Wait a minute. Now he understood. That maniac Rasputin had obviously employed someone, perhaps one of the museum's own conservators, to make exact copies of the Kandinskys for his Patriots Museum. This explained everything. After all, the Lenbach Museum had not reported any theft. A theft like that would have been fodder for press and TV alike. And nothing further had occurred after incessant coverage of the protest demonstration of last Friday. No new breaking news. It would seem no Kandinskys had been stolen from the museum.

Boris looked at his new acquisitions with a different eye. They were not forgeries, they were *replicas*. That sounded better. That *was* better. He would keep the beautifully installed framed paintings. They were, after all, genuine works of art.

110

THERE WAS A WELCOME KNOCK at Katrina's apartment door.

"Herbert's here!" Katrina grabbed her crutches and hurried as fast as she could to open the door. A beaming Officer Besorgt stood on the threshold with the child's hand in hers.

"*Mutti, Mutti*," he exclaimed joyously as Katrina bent down to caress his face.

Everyone was smiling—Megan, Rick, Löser and Officer Besorgt.

"Where have you *been*, darling?" Katrina asked, leading him to the couch and sitting down.

"Many nice women wearing funny hats took care of me," proclaimed Herbert proudly.

"And before that?" The boy frowned.

"I walk with Diliana in the park."

"And?"

"I don't remember."

"You don't remember running up the acropolis to Monopteros?"

"I walk with Diliana. That's all."

Katrina turned to the others.

"Thank god he doesn't remember what happened," she murmured.

"That often happens in these cases," Löser said. Sometimes a person only remembers years later. Let's hope it's that way with your son."

Herbert pushed out of his mother's arms and ran to Megan and Rick.

"Are you going to take me on a car ride again?"

"Yes, of course, honey. But not today," answered Megan.

"Can I see your doggie on your phone again then?"

"I think it's family time now," Rick volunteered gently.

"Yes, we should let you be alone with your son now. You probably want to get him bathed and fed," Löser agreed.

"Thank you, yes. Oh, I'm so grateful. To all of you," Katrina's smile encompassed Officer Besorgt.

"Just one thing, Frau Doktor." Löser moved closer to her, then continued in a lower voice.

"It is extremely important that I meet with you at the museum as soon as it opens tomorrow morning. We have a number of items to go over and I want to be as helpful to you and the museum as I can."

"It would be a relief to talk to you, Detektiv Löser. There is a lot to tell you *and* I have something to show you."

"Excellent. Until ten o'clock tomorrow then."

111

IT WAS EIGHT THIRTY and the soft Bavarian sky was beginning to relinquish its daytime hues. Alyk had driven to his apartment and returned to Paleo with his drone. He would set it up and give it a trial run after nightfall and before the actual pickup mission Wednesday evening.

248

Dzhim and Tigr were consumed with curiosity. They had heard about quadcoptors and watched them in action photographing wild animals on television shows. But they had never seen a real one.

Alyk laid out the parts of the four-rotor drone mechanism on the table in his framing room, where a supply of antique frames was still stacked in a corner. He noticed the stack.

"So, you actually *stole* some of my frames without my noticing," he joshed the boys.

"It was for a good cause, don't forget that," Tigr replied good humoredly.

"If I'd have known how good the cause, I would probably have *given* them to you. Now look here. I'll show you the parts you have to have to fly and land a drone.

The boys crowded around the work table with its display of interesting objects.

Alyk lightly patted the open laptop on the table.

"This is my ground station. It receives what the drone camera sees and transmits to the ground. We don't want to make the drone too heavy, so I'm putting in a lightweight battery. And we'll use the most common frequency band, the 2.4GHz. With this one we don't have to have a license."

The boys nodded comprehendingly.

"My camera can pan and tilt and the real-time views are transmitted to the screen here," he continued proudly. "And if you wear this pair of video goggles, you will feel as if you are sitting in the drone itself. As if it is you who lowers the retractable long arm grabber for the briefcase."

"What happens if something goes wrong and you can't get the drone to return after it's completed its pickup?" Dzhim asked. After all, a briefcase filled with euros is hardly a feather load."

"I've got the likely weights calculated, not to worry. Plus, my drone has an autopilot so if there is a signal loss, it will fly back to me."

Dzhim and Tigr looked at the equipment with growing respect.

"It's dark enough now for a trial run," Alyk said, looking at the night sky. We can go up on the roof. Now, Tigr, would you like to try out the video FPV goggles?"

"You bet I would!"

112

RAISA HAD COME to a hard-won decision. She would reward *herself* since neither of her employers had. This was one thing the two men now had in common aside from their Kandinsky greed. Stinginess.

Zima hadn't always been so. In earlier jobs, he had paid her admittedly high bills without complaint and even complimented her on her work. But now, after her successful kidnapping of the Keller boy—something the Muscovite had *signaled* he wanted done—Zima showed no enthusiasm for using the high stakes card she had placed in his hand. And as for Rasputin, he seemed to have reneged on his assignment to grab the boy. He was more interested in psychologically torturing the mother than in demanding tangible ransom.

Her mind made up, Raisa left the hotel and walked to a convenience store that was still open at this late hour. Faking desperation, she told the night clerk that she had just been robbed of purse and cellphone, could she please make a call on the store phone?

"Sure. You poor thing. Here." He handed the landline phone to her and turned back to a line of waiting customers. Raisa dialed Katrina Keller's home number. Her call was answered after three rings.

"Hallo?" It was a woman's voice. Raisa hissed into the phone at her.

"If you want your son back alive, you will follow these instructions to the letter. Leave ten million euros in cash at..."

"Who is this? Are you the woman who stole my son? *May you burn in hell*!" Katrina banged the phone down.

Raisa heard the sound and was nonplussed. Did the woman not *care* about her invalid son? She handed the phone back to the clerk and walked back to her hotel in total dejection and hopelessness. What was worse, she now had no plan.

***

Katrina had hung up abruptly. Somehow, she had managed to tell that dreadful woman off. But now she was shaking all over. She needed to call Detective Löser immediately. Perhaps the police could trace the woman's call.

Where had she put the card Megan had given her? Shock was paralyzing her. She ran to her purse. The card was not there. Her lab smock! Yes, in all the turmoil she had absentmindedly worn it home. That's where it was. A minute later she was telling the detective what had just happened.

"And you did not tell her that Herbert is back with you?"

"I was so busy cursing her that I didn't get to that."

"This is good. The woman will think you don't have him and she will be stymied by your apparent lack of concern. At least temporarily. Now I want you to do something. Take a look at the display on your phone and hit 'last call.' Does it give you a number?"

"Yes, yes. I see it."

Katrina read it off and Löser told her he would trace it immediately and would get back to her.

Some twenty minutes later he called back.

"Dietrich Löser here. We traced the number and it belongs to a local convenience store, RB Markt. I've just come back from there. Seems a woman rushed in saying her cellphone and purse had just been stolen and could she call the police from their phone. The clerk gave it to her and got back to his customers. She didn't talk very long, handed back the phone, thanked him, and left the store."

"You have nothing then?"

"No, we do have something. A good description. See if you recognize her. She's fiftyish, has black hair, highly arched eyebrows, is tall and slender, and speaks in a low tone of voice."

Katrina thought as hard as she could. None of her acquaintances either in Munich or Murnau quite fit the description.

"I'm sorry," she finally said. "I just can't place anyone like that. Damn! I'm not helping you at all, am I?"

"Don't fret about it, Frau Doktor. We have good material to work with now."

"Oh, wait a minute! Wait a minute! I do remember a woman fitting that description now. She's not a friend or an acquaintance though, so that's why I didn't immediately recall her."

"Yes?"

"It was at Professor Crespi's lecture last evening in the Lenbach. Just before I went up to the podium to introduce her, a man with a woman companion came over to say something to me. I recognized him as we had had dinner together a few evenings earlier. The woman hung back so I did not learn her name. But she does match the description. She was quite striking-looking, rather reserved and distant, and her age, probably around fifty. I didn't hear her voice because she never said a word. She seemed aloof, hung back, and didn't join the conversation. But I noticed her once looking at me, quite intently."

"Ah, now we're getting somewhere. And who was the man?"

"A rather well-known Kandinsky collector from Odessa. He is planning to open a museum there based on his private collection of Blue Rider works, including Kandinsky. His name is Igor Rasputin. He's the man I arranged to meet the night of the demonstration at the Lenbach. I was going to let him and his team into the museum after hours to do state-of-the-art photography of the basement Kandinskys. But before that could take place, the riot broke out and I got hit by a brick, and had to be taken off for emergency treatment."

"And did this Rasputin fellow show up for your appointment, do you know?"

"I can't say. But as you know, our night guard, Niki Wächter, was found dead the next morning."

"I do indeed know. It was in regard to that murder that I called you for a character reference concerning Professor Crespi and Doktor Bodewell."

"Oh, yes. Sorry. I'm so muddled right now, what with that woman's call about Herbert and a ransom."

"Listen, Frau Doktor, this woman is going to wonder why you refused to pay to save your child. She's going to have to check to make sure he's still at the convent. That's when we get her. I'll alert the abbess and I have men out there right now watching the entrances. The woman won't get away if she goes back there."

"I hope not. I still can't understand why anyone would *want* to kidnap my son and ask a ransom. If they know us, they know that I'm not a wealthy person. That I could never pay a large ransom." Katrina's voice had become a quavering whimper and Löser did not want to press her further.

"Just know that we are at work on this night and day. And we'll meet and go over everything tomorrow at the museum, right?"

"Definitely. Thank you. Ten o'clock. Please come to the villa entrance. I have things to show you and tell you and just maybe they will shed light on what has happened tonight."

113

TIGR HAD FALLEN in love with drone flying. Under Alyk's guidance he had twice landed the quadcoptor on top of the Propylaea at their end of the Königsplatz. From the roof balcony of Paleo, they had a physical as well as video view of the monumental gateway. Alyk had also brought from his home two pairs of binoculars to watch the drone's flight. He and Dzhim were amused by Tigr's enthusiasm and they all enjoyed the night air and the 360-degree view of twinkling city lights from their high perch. So different from his and Dzhim's island home in the Black Sea.

Reluctantly, they trekked back downstairs to get some sleep. The bubble-wrapped Kandinsky, with the ten photographs and ransom note inside, was leaning against the vestibule wall ready for an early morning delivery to the museum loading dock across the street.

***

It seemed as if only an hour had passed when Alyk's jolting alarm went off at five am. He woke the other two men and just before sunrise they carted the precious package across the street and propped it deep down against the dock's sloping wall. Alyk telephoned the museum's general number, 23332000, and left a recorded message stating that an extremely valuable package awaited the museum director in the loading dock.

Then all they had to do was wait and watch. The view from Paleo's rooftop looked squarely down on the red roof of the historic yellow center of the Lenbach House Museum.

114

RAYS FROM THE EARLY MORNING SUN were already warming the rooftops of Munich when Megan and Rick woke up Wednesday. Rick went off on his forty-five-minute sprint around the neighborhood while Megan engaged in her complex exercise routine and got dressed. She was already sprinkling blueberries over the crisp contents of two cereal bowls when Rick returned. He made coffee while she hulled and cut up some strawberries, adding them to the bowls, then sliced a banana into the cereal mix. It was nine o'clock.

"Oh, nuts, we forgot to buy the yogurt," Megan complained as they sat down in the cheerful kitchen of the Lenbach apartment.

"Here, have some milk."

"Okay, but it's just not the same without yogurt." The two crunched away in companionable silence for a while. Rick refrained from saying that the kind of pasteurized, vanilla flavored, with added sugar yogurt she was fond of buying did not have the best health benefits that yogurt could supply. But there was no changing her morning routine or breakfast habits. He watched with amusement as she turned to her grand finale: one square of Lindt dark chocolate with sea salt. Every morning she tried to match or surpass her record of having broken and re-broken one small, inch-and-a-half square into twenty-six miniscule pieces. Her devouring of them began with the smallest pieces and slowly worked up to the larger ones, breaking them into two with her teeth, and ending with the largest piece which she methodically broke into four fragments. A little OCD there? Absolutely.

"So," Rick said, "are we still going to make a quick visit to the Nymphenburg Palace this morning as we'd planned, before we join Katrina at the museum?"

"Absolutely. We've been to the site where Ludwig died, so it's only right that we visit the place where he was born. And I want to show you the 'Gallery of Beauties' assembled by his grandfather Ludwig I. There are thirty-six of them and one was responsible for his having to abdicate the throne in eighteen-forty-eight."

"And you'd rather go out there than to the two Ludwigs's Residenz right here in town? Isn't it the palace of all the Wittelsbach monarchs?"

"Yes, that it is. But the best feature relating to our own mad Ludwig is something that had to be torn down just a few years after his death."

"What was that?"

"A winter garden. But not just any winter garden. It was a *Ludwig* winter garden with an ornamental lake, an artificially illuminated rainbow with periodic moonlight, an Indian royal tent, a Moorish kiosk, and a grotto."

"Sounds like Ludwig all right. So why was it dismantled?"

"Because Ludwig had it built on the *roof* of the Residenz's *Festsaalbau* and water began leaking from the fake lake down to the rooms below."

"Ouch! Well, at least Ludwig didn't live to see that fantasy destroyed. He really had a thing about lakes though, that's for sure."

They took a taxi out to the enormous Baroque palace with its great residential and ceremonial wings extending more than seven times the length of an American football field—a panoramic view if ever there was one.

"Do you remember that old movie from the 'sixties called *Last Year at Marienbad*?" Rick, the movie buff, asked Megan.

"I do."

"Okay, I bet you didn't know that it was mainly filmed right here at the Nymphenburg palace and park."

"No, I didn't realize that. Thanks."

They admired the park pavilions, fountains, and statuary, before entering the well-lit center building's great Stone Hall which rose to a height of three floors and was crowned by a lively ceiling fresco depicting the Greek sun god Helios in his chariot accompanied by other gods of antiquity.

Megan did not let Rick linger. She was eager to get to the *Schönheitengalerie*—the Gallery of Beauties—in the south pavilion. When they arrived, Rick understood why. There were the most beautiful women of early nineteenth-century Munich, ranging from the daughter of a shoemaker, to a beloved actress, to two of Ludwig I's mistresses. She paused before the latter two portraits.

"All right, Rick. Don't look at the labels. Which of these two women do you think was the cause of the king's abdication?"

The physician gamely studied the two portraits which were hung side by side as though looking at each other. Seemingly the same youthful age, perhaps just thirty years old, both were shown at waist-length in dark clothing; both were slim, had abundant ringlets of brown hair, and both had wide, dark eyebrows and large eyes. The woman on the left had an ample décolleté, revealing ivory-colored skin. By contrast, the lace-collared dress of the woman on the right covered her throat and, dramatically, she wore one large red flower in her hair which was framed by a short black veil in the back.

"Hmm, I can't decide. The woman on the right looks to me a bit feistier, more demanding. Perhaps she was the one?"

"Bravo! You chose correctly. She was a self-designated Spanish ballerina of indifferent talent, known by her stage name, Lola Montez. Actually, she was born in Ireland as Eliza Gilbert in eighteen-twenty-one and grew up in India. What shot her to fame was her erotic "Tarantula Dance" in which she wore no underclothing. She appeared all over Europe as well as Australia and America. One of her brief lovers while in Paris was Franz Liszt, and possibly Alexandre Dumas *père* as well. The affair with an aging Ludwig lasted much longer. He was besotted with her and she exerted enormous power over him, encouraging him to institute liberal reforms—something that did not sit well with his ministers. During the revolutions of eighteen-forty-eight she was driven from Bavaria by an angry mob, and she and the deposed king, who lived twenty more years, never saw each other again. But part of their letter correspondence still remains."

"What a woman! And in Victorian times, no less. What happened to her after the revolutions?"

"She went to California, England, and, as I said, Australia. But, she ended up in Brooklyn, working with 'fallen women.' She had lost her looks and was already showing the effects of tertiary syphilis. Just think! She was only thirty-nine when she died. Ludwig I outlived her by seven years. When I was living in New York and teaching at Columbia, I once drove out to Green-Wood Cemetery to find her tombstone. It refers to her not as Lola Montez, but as 'Mrs. Eliza Gilbert.'"

"Whew! What a story. Now tell me about this other woman here." Rick pointed to the portrait on their left.

"Okay, I know about her but don't recall her name, so let me read the identification."

Megan moved up closer to the painting and read the label beneath.

"Oh, yes. She was Marianna Marquesa Florenzi. Now I remember. She was born into the Italian nobility, and her liaison, well, better said, her friendship with Ludwig lasted over forty years. Although they only saw each other thirty documented times, he sought her advice, even in government matters, and much of *their* long letter exchange is preserved. I think something like three thousand from her and about one thousand, five-hundred of his replies. She outlived him by two years. When I first learned about her I thought I might research her and put her in one of my 'feminist' lectures because she was extremely well self-educated in philosophy and languages. She translated that polymath genius Gottfried Wilhelm Leibniz into Italian and helped spread knowledge of Immanuel Kant and Baruch Spinoza in Italy. I got excited about her when I learned that she was one of the first female students to study at the University of Perugia, because that's where my parents sent me when I was eighteen to learn Italian."

"I didn't know that about you."

"Sì, sì, my Italian father wanted me to learn 'grown-up' Italian and sent me to Perugia for a whole summer. The purest Italian is supposed to be spoken there. I think I disappointed him because I used my first month's pensione funds to buy a little motorbike—a Paperino—and a cello. I dropped out of classes and drove all over central Italy that summer."

"So, you never learned 'grown-up' Italian then?"

"Let's say that I'm best discussing art history and food in Italian, how's that?"

The portrait of Lola Montez called them back.

"You know," Megan mused, "I've thought for a long time that Lola was to Ludwig I what Wagner was to Ludwig II. An overwhelming inspiration and utter fixation."

"That's interesting, Megan. "Next time I listen to a Wagner opera, I'll try to listen to it through Ludwig's ears."

"Yes, do it! I did the same thing when I was writing my magnum opus on the changing image of Beethoven. A study in myth-making, I subtitled it. Turns out I was doing what the Germans call 'reception history,' but didn't know I was. So, for example, when I was writing about Berlioz, I listened to Beethoven with what I hoped was Berlioz's mindset. When I was writing about Brahms, ditto, and so on. Don't know if I was correct, but it was certainly intriguing."

"Well, now would you like to lead me to the room where our dear Ludwigchen was born?"

Megan's cheeks flushed slightly.

"Uh, Rick, I have to admit that I've never gone to it. These two femmes-fatales have pinned me to this room."

Rick chuckled and asked a guard how to find the Queen's bedroom where she gave birth to Ludwig II. It turned out to be quite nearby. They entered, looked around, and admired the old mahogany furniture. Not much else to see. Megan glanced at her watch. Plenty of time to do more things before they hooked up later that afternoon with Katrina at the museum.

"You know what I'd like to do next?" Rick asked Megan without giving her time to answer.

"I'd like to go back to The Blue Rider Gallery and talk to Laszlo Togarassy again. I just might buy one of his *Hommage à Kandinsky* paintings for myself."

"What fun! Let's do it." Megan was definitely game and she wouldn't mind seeing the double Blue Rider masterpiece in the gallery window again. She had her Google Glass on today and might be able to photograph it on the sly. Or perhaps, considering how genial the Togarassys had been, they might allow her to photograph it with her iPhone, in which case she could take some valuable details.

The two friends left the Castle of the Nymphs feeling uplifted and educated.

115

"FRAU DOKTOR KELLER, thank goodness you're here!" Greta Bachert, secretary to Max Mürrisch, greeted her breathlessly at the yellow villa door. It was a few minutes after eight and she had just picked up an urgent telephone message intended for the museum's director. But Mürrisch was away on vacation in the Bahamas. Keller would better know how to handle this strange message anyway.

"What is it?" Katrina had brought her boy with her to the museum. Until his kidnapper had been apprehended, she was not going to leave Herbert alone at home with just Diliana to cope.

"It's a man's voice telling us that a vital package is waiting for the museum out back in the loading dock."

"Let me hear," Katrina said, taking the phone receiver held out to her by the secretary. She listened intently then hung up.

"Will you let Herbert play in your office, please, Greta? I'll round up Reinhold. He'll have to bring the package in for us. I wonder how large it is?"

Herbert loved spending time in Greta's office because that was where a large model of the museum stood on a table. He liked looking through the rooms which could swing out to receive miniature reproductions of works being considered for a new exhibition's arrangement and display. And Greta was fond of the precocious boy who could be so silent and engaged for such long periods of time. He was no trouble at all.

"Ah, Paul!" Katrina turned toward her smiling fellow conservator who had just appeared at the office door. "Help me find Reinhold. There's a mystery package awaiting us in the loading dock, we've just been informed. And I have a strange feeling about it. Call it a premonition. Or just that I slept on the wrong side of my bed last night." Katrina was trying to downplay the sense of urgency she felt.

Reinhold, the good-natured burly guard was found and, at Katrina's pace, they took the elevator to the basement and proceeded to the loading dock. Reinhold pressed the button that raised the overhead doors from within. There, leaning against the ramp wall, and not visible at street level, was a bubble-wrapped flat item some ninety-by-ninety-centimeters in size. Reinhold brought it inside and, after closing the overhead doors, he began unwrapping the parcel under the bright lights of the room.

After the outer layer was removed, they came upon a large manila envelope affixed by duct-tape to the inner wrapping. Reinhold peeled the envelope off and handed it to Katrina. The first thing she drew out was a single page of paper, its text printed in 48-point italicized Arial black font. Katrina read it out loud:

Here's a cheer-up gift for the Lenbachhaus-Museum's careless misplacement of eleven Kandinsky paintings. Do you want the other ten back? Leave one hundred million euros in cash in a briefcase on the open window ledge of the old museum's fourth story attic room by tonight at nine o'clock. Do not inform the police. If you comply, you will receive immediate word as to the location of the other ten paintings. If you do not comply exactly as specified, or if any police are spotted on the museum grounds, the other ten Kandinsky paintings will be instantly destroyed. So sad for all.

The three museum staff members stared at each other in bewilderment. Certainly the message was comprehensible. But mystifying. The museum's "careless misplacement of eleven Kandinsky paintings"? Could this be a horrible joke played by one of their own staff?

Katrina reached back into the envelope and her fingers touched several small paper objects. She scooped them up and spread them out on a work table next to them.

They were individual photographs of the other ten Kandinskys.

"Great god! If we hadn't found proof before that our Kandinskys are clones, here it is in the flesh. Someone is bragging that they have our Kandinskys." Katrina was incensed.

"And the frames look to be the original frames as well, if I remember correctly," observed Paul Ritter, taking the photographs and examining them one by one. Reinhold looked from one to the other of his mystified colleagues.

"Rip that final layer off," Katrina commanded Reinhold, who was still holding the heavy flat object upright while straining to see the photos Ritter was sifting through.

Given the welcome go-ahead, he carefully pulled away the inner bubble wrap, thrusting it to the floor, and the object was revealed in all its glory. It was one of the two smaller Kandinsky paintings that had hung on either side of the gallery entrance door. And it and the frame were the real thing. Katrina touched the frame front. Yes, wood, real wood, not canvas. For the first time that morning she smiled.

"So what do we do now?" Paul asked anxiously. "We can't call the police."

"Miraculously, I have an inside contact. Detective Dieter Löser of the Munich police is coming here to confer with me at ten. He is extremely able and discreet. I'll call him immediately and ask if he can come right away. We don't want any uniformed police on the place, which is what might happen if I call the police department.

"Paul, would you kindly check the painting for any possible damage and then position it for an XRF macro scan. I want to see and photograph the image underneath."

"You've got it," answered the excited conservator.

Katrina made her painful way back to the director's outer office where Greta was sitting at her desk and Herbert was doing exactly what she imagined he would be doing: affixing small magnetic images of all the paintings owned by the Lenbach to the white walls of the museum model.

"Look, *Mutti*, look!" he cried when she entered the room. "I've just made an exhibition. Don't you like it?" Eleven miniature Paris-period Kandinskys had graduated from the basement gallery and greeted visitors when they entered the villa's main showroom.

How ironic, Katrina thought, as she patted her son's head and complimented him. But she had pressing work to do and needed to get to her office.

"I like your exhibition very much. Now see if you can make an exhibition of pictures with just animals in them, all right, darling?"

"Oh, yes, *Mutti*. What fun!"

Megan turned to Greta who was smiling at the boy.

"You don't mind if he stays with you here a while longer, do you?"

"Not at all, Frau Doktor. He can stay here all day as far as I'm concerned. He's a sweetheart."

Hurrying as fast as she could on crutches, Katrina entered her office, closed the door, and phoned Detective Löser. Fortunately, he answered her call right away. She could tell he was driving by his distracted tone. But when she told him what had just happened and that the museum was in "crisis mode," he was all ears, his tone terse.

"I'll be right there. Tell no one else."

"Are you in a squad car?" Katrina asked tremulously.

"No. You're right to ask. I'm in my own private automobile. I won't be making any waves when I arrive."

Katrina looked at the clock. It was eight-thirty. The museum did not open its doors until ten. That would give her time to show and tell Löser everything. She breathed a sigh of relief. Löser would know what to do. Should she really have to bring in the city of Munich? Admit a serious theft had occurred at one of its museums and that an outrageous ransom was being demanded?

Her landline phone rang. It was Max Mürrisch, calling from the Bahamas. Great timing.

"Hi, Katrina. Just calling to be sure everything's okay at the museum."

"Yes, Max. I would say everything is under control."

"Great! Just about to go scuba diving, but thought I'd check in."

"Enjoy your swim."

"I will. Ta ta." The director of the august Lenbach Museum hung up, reassured that all was well. Katrina exhaled a long sigh. What had happened could hardly be explained in a single phone call. She had made the right decision.

***

The debriefing, as Löser called it, took all of fifteen minutes. He had studied the ransom note carefully. The threat to destroy ten genuine Kandinsky paintings was horrifying. Katrina berated herself out loud for having agreed to a photo shoot with Rasputin. Of course that man from Odessa must have been involved. He could even have murdered poor Niki Wächter! And that unsmiling woman who was with him at Megan's lecture. She fit nicely Löser's description of the woman who called in the ransom threat to her from a local convenience store.

Then a cheering thought came to Katrina. An inspiration, really. She could at least confirm that early works from Kandinsky's Blue Rider period lay underneath the eleven Paris period works, just as the artist's letter to Marcel Duchamp had claimed. And she would so love to discover something positive on this most negative of all negative days. As quickly as possible, she pulled her crutches to her and stood up.

"Come downstairs with me, please, Herr Löser. I hope, I believe, in fact, that I may have something wondrous to show you."

His curiosity aroused, Löser followed the limping woman who was showing such courage to the elevator. His mind raced with possible scenarios as to how to handle the ransom threat.

116

"OH, PROFESSOR CRESPI, Doktor Bodewell, how marvelous to see you again!" Laszlo Togarassy smiled at the two Americans as they entered his gallery so unexpectedly. Iris Togarassy heard the excitement in her husband's raised voice and came out of the back room to join them.

"And what brings you here?" Laszlo asked, beaming at his new friends.

"It's because of me," Rick admitted. "I'd like to buy one of your Kandinsky creations. Haven't been able to get them out of my mind."

"I'm flattered, Herr Doktor. Flattered. Did you have a particular one in mind?"

"I don't suppose you've made a copy of the joint Kandinsky/Münter painting in the window, by any chance?"

"Alas, not yet. I just haven't had time, what with the show opening a few days ago and all. I only ferreted out that double masterpiece a month ago. It came from a Japanese art collector's heir, if you can imagine that."

"Do you think you might make one of your *hommage* replicas of it eventually?"

"Very likely, especially if you are in the market for one. But why don't you come to the back gallery where all my copies are. Perhaps you'll find another one that strikes you."

They all walked into the *hommage* gallery and Rick began closely to examine each work. He took his time, commenting on the colors and brushwork. Lacking the courage to ask permission should the answer be negative, Megan ambled back to the gallery show window to use her Google Glass to capture the painting on display. She paused before opening the front door, scrutinizing the edge of the unframed canvas.

From across the street someone else was also scrutinizing the Kandinksy/Münter work gracing the gallery's window. It was Walter Krankenhauer. He was sick to death of the continuing publicity the upstart new Munich gallery was enjoying with its Kandinsky show. Especially after the breakup of his protest demonstration *against* the artist at the Lenbach. Why didn't Munich's citizens understand or care about how German culture was being threatened?

He stood in an apartment house doorway facing the Blue Rider Gallery, calculating the flow of pedestrian and car traffic. In his pocket he had the means to provoke another anti-Kandinsky protest. True, a very small one, but, along with the printed cardboard message he intended to leave at the site, significant all the same. He chose his moment and began to run toward the gallery.

Just as Megan was turning to exit the gallery and photograph the double painting in the window, she saw a man in a hoodie sprinting straight at her. Her reflexes were twofold. She shrank back inside the open door while at the same time automatically activating her Google Glass. One second later an ignited smoke bomb whizzed past her head and into the gallery. Red smoke filled the air. The torch continued to burn for about thirty seconds.

"*What is it? What's happened?*" Rick and both Togarassys ran to Megan who was frozen in place. The front gallery was filled with swirling smoke and the stench of hydrogen sulfide infiltrated the shop. Megan found her voice.

"A man in a hoodie ran up with a smoke bomb and threw it right at the gallery. I was just starting to go out the front door when it happened."

Determined to catch the person who had done this, Laszlo dashed outside. Red smoke filled the gallery and the room gave off a stink like rotten eggs.

"Oh my god, the paintings could be ruined," Iris shouted, pulling the door shut in a panic.

"Do you have an oscillating electric fan?" Rick asked the frantic woman.

Iris nodded vigorously and ran to get it. Minutes later the fan was dispersing the smoke and the odor was beginning to fade.

"Just in time," Iris sighed in relief.

The gallery door opened again and Laszlo, his face covered with perspiration, entered.

"I ran in both directions, first that way, then this way, and shouted at people on the street. No one had seen anything. Not a thing! But this was on the ground by our door." He held up a piece of cardboard. The hand-printed message on it read: "*Only German Art for Germany.*"

"We have to call the police immediately," Iris declared. She was frightened, but even so, her flair for publicity kicked in. "And we'll call the press too."

While Laszlo was reporting the event to the police, Megan whispered to Rick.

"I think I know who that man was. We have seen him before. In back of us at the Lenbach protest, and on the ferry at Herrenchiemsee. Remember? I called Detective Löser about him."

"Yes, yes. You better call Löser again."

"You bet. *And* I have a photo of the smoke bomb thrower in the act."

"Not your Google Glass again!"

"Yes, thanks to wanting to photograph this," Megan turned and pointed to the beautiful double painting in the window.

117

"DO YOU THINK we should hide the Kandinskys again?" Dzhim put down his binoculars for a moment and looked at Tigr and Alyk. The men were sitting on folding chairs brought up from the basement to Paleo's attic balcony. Keeping watch over the Lenbach grounds was going to be a full-time job. If the police showed up they would have to call everything off and think of a new strategy. It was Dzhim's turn to study through his pair of binoculars the small, single-room attic story with one window over the villa entry door.

"Nah, I don't think we need to do that again. Better to have the paintings out ready to wrap and move," Alyk answered.

"See anything, Dzhim?"

"Just the usual tourists; one group of school children, another group of straggly adults being lectured to by a blonde guide outside by the fountain. She keeps pointing to the villa. Must be lecturing them on the architecture history. That's about it right now."

"Okay. But we need to have eyes on the ground and on the roof at all times."

"Anybody hungry yet?" Tigr had made sandwiches and brought them along with beer up to the roof.

"Not yet. Think I'm too nervous to eat," admitted Dzhim.

Alyk felt the same way, but he'd be damned if he would admit it. The waiting game had commenced.

118

"THIS is our XRF," Katrina was telling Detective Löser. They were downstairs in the lab and Paul Ritter was about to start a micro scan on the painting that had been left in the museum dock. Katrina had briefed the detective about Megan's discovery of the eleven Kandinsky clones in the museum and how XRF examination had confirmed they were clones. They had discussed their possible connection to the scary anti-Kandinsky demonstration of Friday. Now Katrina explained to the rapt detective what the XRF process could do for them.

"If this *is* the original Kandinsky, and the fact that the frame face is actual wood and not canvas makes me think it is, it will have the thick interleaf the artist referred to in his letter to Duchamp. If so, it will be possible to see the two images we hope are there. We'll obtain an accurate digital reconstruction of the image and pigments that are underneath the oil painting layer on top. Paul? Let's start the scan."

Löser stood watching the operation with fascination. Within minutes both conservators were exclaiming.

"We've got it! We've got it!" Katrina shouted. "There is an image underneath and we've reconstructed it. Looks like, yes, it *is* an image of the Yellow House at Murnau!"

"This means that the other ten Kandinskys must all also have images underneath the top ones." Paul was jubilant.

Löser smiled at the two conservators. They certainly deserved a break from the disasters that had afflicted their museum recently. Speaking of which....

"Frau Doktor, I'd like to take a look at the gallery where this and the other Kandinskys hung before they were stolen."

"Oh, yes, of course! I should have shown it to you right away."

"Paul will take you there and I'll catch up with you." Katrina swiveled around for her crutches.

The men led the way and waited for Katrina while Paul unlocked the doors. Once inside the deserted gallery—its white walls bereft of paintings—all three of them noticed a strange, unpleasant odor.

"Where's that coming from?" Löser asked, walking around the room. He stopped in front of the door to the gallery's utility closet.

"It's particularly strong here." He pointed to the door and turned its handle in vain. "Do you have a key?"

"Call Reinhold, Paul. He has the keys."

A few minutes later the smiling guard appeared, turned the bolt with his key, and opened the door to the storage closet. An ungodly stench permeated the room. Löser leapt forward.

"That's the stink of a rotting corpse. Quick, help me clear these shelves. There's something behind them."

The three men threw dozens of cans and tools off the shelves and onto the gallery floor. When the shelves were empty they saw fresh plaster on the wall opposite the door.

"We've got to break through," Löser commanded. "Plug in that small drill over there and start drilling. I'm calling for help." He took out his cellphone.

"Wait!" Katrina begged. "The ransom note specifically said that if any police are spotted on our museum grounds, the other ten Kandinsky paintings will be instantly destroyed." She looked at Löser beseechingly.

"You're right and I appreciate the situation," he answered. "Don't worry, I'll specify that a unit come in street clothes and form a tour group outside the museum. Do you have someone who could meet them and lead them inside?"

"Yes, yes. I'll alert her." Katrina called Greta and told her what to expect and what to do.

"I understand. And it's all right for me to leave Herbert at the moment. He's sound asleep on the couch."

***

The ruse worked. Within twenty minutes eight heavily armed policemen in street clothes were inside the basement gallery. The tedious removal of plaster had revealed a large tunnel and a ghoulish scene. A decomposing corpse lay face down on the ground, its arms stretched beyond its head toward them.

"All right men, let's move!" Löser led the way through the tunnel. It ran underneath the street behind and parallel to the museum and ended up in front of an exit sealed with fresh plaster.

"Bring up the drill," commanded the detective. A good ten minutes passed until finally an opening was cleared. Löser and his eight-man team entered a huge basement room that was almost completely filled with densely packed dirt that was stacked to the ceiling. Silently they swarmed upstairs. One room contained a pile of old frames and canvases. Racing silently up to the second story, they entered a large suite and came upon an strange spectacle. Ten large abstract paintings were lined up on the floor against the bedroom walls.

"*Good god, it's the Kandinskys!*" whispered Löser.

"Cover every room, every floor, the attic, even the roof." He led his men, cautioning them to move silently. There were five floors to clear. Some of the officers ran back down to the ground floor, searching every room. The same for the other floors. Nothing else out of the ordinary. In the attic they came upon a door leading to the roof balcony, Löser took the lead, his pistol drawn. He burst through the door.

The three surprised persons sitting in folding chairs leapt up but there was no place to go. Men in civilian clothes brandishing guns blocked the exit and instantly surrounded them.

"You're under arrest," Löser yelled. "Cuff them!" He called for a paddy wagon, then raced back down to the basement and through the tunnel. He burst into the gallery where the three museum people were waiting with bated breath. Katrina was standing, propped up on her crutches, barely able to bear the suspense.

"We've found the Kandinskys!"

119

THE CESSNA CITATION M2 JET LANDED without incident at the Munich International Airport at three in the afternoon. Boris Zima's limousine was waiting and forty-five minutes later it pulled up in front of Schwabing's newest gallery, The Blue Rider.

After dealing with two police officers who had come in response to their call, and after a thorough cleanup, the Togarassys had reopened the temporarily closed gallery. Two members of the press were among the people waiting to enter and Iris had led them into the back office where she briefed them on what had happened. She suggested a lead title or two for their stories and happily answered all their questions. One more anti-Kandinsky protest was fabulous publicity for The Blue Rider and she was making the most of it.

Greeting visitors at the front door, Laszlo noticed the limousine parked next to his gallery and the lone passenger who was exiting it. A thin, elderly man with thick white hair and a prominent nose, he exuded an air of authority.

"Are you the owner here?" Boris Zima looked from the front window display to Laszlo.

"I am. Do come inside."

"Is that Kandinsky in the window for sale?"

"I'm afraid that is the only work of art here that is not for sale."

"I am Boris Zima. Of Moscow. You are?"

"Laszlo Togarassy." The gallery owner stared at his questioner with surprise. Just a few days ago a man identifying himself as "Boris Zima from Moscow" had visited his shop. Surely there could not be two Boris Zimas from Moscow. Furthermore, each man had a different accent. But he held his peace and said nothing.

"Good," his interlocutor was saying. "Your reputation as a replicator of Kandinsky has reached my city. I have come here to see your work for myself and also to purchase some of the original Kandinskys you have on exhibition."

"Honored to meet you, sir. Do come inside and have a look."

Zima entered the gallery and slowly surveyed the room, his expression inscrutable. At last he turned to Laszlo, disappointment now written on his face.

"But I see by those ribbon markers that almost all your paintings have already been bought."

"True. Enthusiasm for Kandinksy is at a new high these days. All but two of ours have already been spoken for."

"But not yet paid for?"

"Well, not yet paid for in full. But down payments have been made."

"I desire all paintings in this room. I will pay you twice your price for each and you can return down payments to your customers."

"Impossible, sir. I cannot do that to my clients. It would not be honorable." Zima looked at the unblinking gallery owner and decided his refusal was immutable. Inconvenient, silly ethics.

"All right then, put sold markers on your remaining two genuine Kandinskys and let me see your replicas."

Laszlo led his eccentric visitor to the back gallery where twenty-four of his *Hommage* copies hung. They were all somewhat smaller or a bit larger than the originals, as stated on a placard by the door. Wanting no misunderstandings, Laszlo pointed out to Zima how, on the lower right of each canvas, capital letters spelled out "*HOMMAGE À KANDINSKY*" followed by his own cursive signature, "Laszlo Togarassy."

Zima took his time assessing the pictures. Then he turned to the baffled gallery owner.

"I will take them all. Give me a group price and I shall pay you in cash."
He pulled out a thick bundle of 500-euro banknotes and waved them in the
gallery owner's face.

"I want you to ship them all, including the two in your front gallery,
to my Moscow address. Here is the information you will need." Zima pulled
a card from the breast pocket of his jacket and handed it to Laszlo who was
trying to hide his stupefaction. This man had to be the real Boris Zima. Who
then was his impersonator?

Under the spell of the replicas stolen from Rasputin, Boris Zima was now
open to this new form of original art. Replicas. In one fell swoop he would be
able to add twenty-six Kandinskys to his extraordinary collection. It would be
the largest private collection of his fellow Russian's work in the world!

120

WHEN THEY GOT OFF THE U-BAHN at the Königsplatz station on
their way back to the Lenbach Museum, Megan and Rick paused to admire
the subway art. It was, actually, permanent art, provided by the city. The giant
representations spaced along the white walls of the subway and linked by a continuous red band, included images one could encounter in the two Königsplatz
museums as well as at the Lenbach. They ranged from ancient Greek vases to
Franz Marc's *Blue Horse*. A black-and-white historic photograph of the original
Lenbach villa was interlocked with the dramatically posed black-and-white
photograph Franz Lenbach used for the large oil portrait of himself with his
wife and their two small daughters that was reproduced in color next to it. All
four Lenbachs stared compellingly at emerging subway passengers. Rick and
Megan were only too happy to comply with the double invitation to visit the
eponymous museum.

As they reached Luisenstrasse, however, they saw something very wor-
risome. Three police cars were parked in front of the museum. They hurried
inside and asked for Katrina. She was in the lab, they were informed, and she

had left a message for them to join her there. When they entered the room the first person they saw was Detective Löser. He greeted them with a big smile on his face and pointed to Katrina, who was seated before a large-screen desktop computer. Her son stood grinning beside her, his arm around his mother's waist. She almost jumped to her feet when she saw them, completely forgetting crutches in her excitement.

"Megan! Rick! You aren't going to believe this. *The Kandinskys have been recovered! All of them!*"

The next quarter hour was spent with alternating narratives from Katrina and Löser. Every minute of the exciting events was recounted, from the loading-dock recovery of one of the eleven missing Kandinskys with its ransom note and photographs, to the literal unearthing of a corpse within an underground tunnel dug under the Richard-Wagner-Strasse from the back of the Kandinsky gallery's utility closet, the search of the residential building opposite where the tunnel ended, the discovery of the other ten Kandinskys in a bedroom, and the roof balcony arrest of the three criminals who had stolen the paintings. All within a block of the museum.

Detective Löser was included in the hugs of joy that followed. Paul Ritter brought in a bottle of champagne and Reinhold was right behind him waving six glasses in the air.

"*To Wassily Kandinsky!*" Katrina proposed after the glasses had been filled.

"*To Wassily Kandinsky!*" Five voices answered. Herbert echoed what the adults said, making six happy voices in all.

"And look here, Megan. Just look what I have for your lecture this evening." Katrina pointed to the screen before her. The American gasped. A row of the eleven recovered Kandinskys ran across the top of the screen. And there in a row beneath them were eleven images with recognizable Murnau motifs!

"You've done it, you've done it! You've solved the conundrum." Megan was jumping up and down with excitement.
"*Double Kandinsky, here we come!*"

121

AN ELATED MEGAN added the Murnau underpainting images to her "Double Kandinsky" lecture and transferred it to a new thumb drive. She, Rick, Katrina, and Herbert had, along with Detective Löser, whom they now all called Dieter, and his wife, Penelope, all walked over to the nearby Aposto München pizzeria on Luisenstrasse for dinner. Katrina had invited her fellow conservator, Paul Ritter, and Iris and Laszlo Togarassy to join them as well. It was to be a Kandinsky Pizza Celebraton Banquet before Megan's lecture at Schloss Berg that evening. Laszlo had insisted that he pay for everyone's meal.

Megan was in the middle of a bite of her delicious pizza Margherita when she realized Dieter had not responded to her phone message or acknowledged the photo she had sent him of Walter Krankenhauer running toward The Blue Rider Gallery, a sputtering smoke bomb in his hand. As she was sitting next to him, she turned and quietly asked him about it.

"Good lord, so much has happened, I forgot to tell you! My cellphone was off when you called—we were breaking into the tunnel—and yes, I did receive your photo. I am pleased to tell you that Herr Neo-Nazi Walter Krankenhauer is now in jail and he will remain there for quite some time. I'm so sorry you were caught in the middle of it, but your pictorial confirmation of the identity of the smoke bomber gave us all the evidence we needed to arrest him."

Noticing that Megan and Dieter were talking shop, Katrina directed a question to the detective as well.

"Tell us please, Dieter, did the three men you arrested carry out the Lenbach theft on their own initiative, or were they commissioned to do so?"

"It seems most likely they were acting for someone else, as only one of them actually lives here in Munich. The other two live on an island off the coast of Odessa." He gave Katrina a meaningful look.

"Oh, my god! Then that has to be Igor Rasputin from Odessa who was behind all this. I feel so totally stupid, being duped by him. Just imagine! I actually *arranged* for him and his men to be admitted to the museum that horrible evening of the anti-Kandinsky demonstration."

"Ah, but there is one other, very strong possibility," Dieter said. "A private collector in Moscow named Boris Zima. Seems he has been interested in expanding his collection of Kandinsky. What alerted me is the fact that I have reports on a *Cargo Logistic* van being loaded at Richard-Wagner-Strasse thirty-three last Saturday morning, then a *Cargo Logistic* van was hijacked the next day, and finally an empty *Cargo Logistic* van was found late Sunday evening with two murdered men inside in a crime-infested neighborhood of Moscow. And no cargo. So, strong evidence points to Boris Zima as well."

"*Um Gottes Willen!* Boris Zima. He is one of the two fanatic private collectors of Blue Rider artists," Katrina affirmed. "Remember, Megan? Rick? I told you about Moscow's Boris Zima."

"Did you say *Boris Zima*?" asked Laszlo from across the table. They nodded.

"Boy, oh boy, can I ever tell you something about him. Seems there are *two* of them. A couple of days ago a man visited my gallery, introducing himself as Boris Zima from Moscow. And just today another man who called himself Boris Zima came into the shop. He was literally oozing with euros and had a passion for Kandinsky such as I've never seen. Tried to bargain and buy *every one* of the Kandinskys in the front gallery, regardless of the fact that all but two of them were sold. So he bought the two remaining paintings still on sale and in addition *all* twenty-four of my *Hommage à Kandinsky* replicas! He gave me well over three hundred five-hundred euro notes as down payment for everything after asking for a 'group price,' and he left the Moscow shipping details and billing address with me. That's why I'm treating all of us to dinner tonight. Iris and I are now practically *millionaires!*"

Everyone at the table gasped.

"Well, congratulations, Laszlo," Dieter said calmly. "This new Boris must indeed be the real, billionaire Boris if he was casting paper euros around like that. But can you describe the two different men for me, please?"

"Well, both spoke German with a Russian accent. The man who came in on Monday was probably in his late fifties, had exceptionally square shoulders, and was bald."

Katrina nodded in recognition. That was surely Rasputin. Laszlo continued.

"The man today was older, had a very prominent nose and a full head of white hair. He was almost obnoxiously self-confident."

"Dieter, which of the two possibilities do you consider the more likely?" Rick was intrigued. The table fell silent, all eyes on the detective.

"Tell them your theory," Penelope urged.

"All right, this is my working hypothesis. I think Rasputin arranged to have the paintings stolen and was shipping them to Odessa when Zima somehow got wind of the theft, perhaps through an agent here in Munich, and had the *Cargo Logistik* van hijacked near Bratislava, and redirected to Moscow."

"But if all the original Kandinskys were found just across the street from our museum," Paul Ritter asked, "then what was being stolen?"

"You may find this preposterous, but I suspect there may have been *two* sets of clones. One set installed in the Lenbach here, and the other set destined for Odessa but sidetracked to Moscow." Dieter's audience was enthralled by the theory.

"So that makes two sets of 'victims' as well," Iris Togarassy suggested. "The Lenbach Museum staff and the Ukrainian-Russian duo."

"Agreed," Dieter responded. "The big question now is who made the clones? My men are obtaining confessions from the trio we arrested as we speak. When you look at their professions you will understand how likely it is that they are the forgers. The fellow from Munich is a civil engineer and woodworker, one of the men from the Odessa island is a computer genius, and the other man is a science photographer. Put two and two together and you get three cloners."

Everyone laughed. The case seemed practically solved. Katrina, however, was looking pensive. Then a self-confident, happy expression illuminated her features.

"Listen, everyone. I think I know who Zima's agent is. It's a woman. She was standing next to Rasputin just before your lecture, Megan. Remember? You were talking to him, and this very glum, black-haired woman with theatrical arched eyebrows was just standing there, shooting me looks. She is the same woman described to Dieter by a store clerk who let her use his phone to call me with a ransom demand."

Rick spoke up, to Dieter's surprise. "I wonder though if she could have been Rasputin's agent if she was with him, and not Zima's."

"Both are excellent candidates," Dieter agreed. "I've added this mystery woman to the bureau's list of suspects. We'll run her down, don't worry. We already lifted the kidnapper's fingerprint from the convent's reclamation pad. The ridge density, lack of Y chromosome presence, and double-sized X peak certainly indicate it was a woman. And we have men watching the convent, should she return for the child she thinks is still there. Good thinking, Katrina and Rick."

The two persons praised by the detective both blushed with pleasure. Dieter gave a last pronouncement before returning to his now-cold pizza.

"*We're talking about six proven or probable criminals now. We've arrested three and we'll get them all!*"

122

WHEN THE MERRY MEAL WAS FINISHED, it was still only a little after five o'clock. Plenty of time for all of them to make the thirty-minute drive via the A95 to the Starnbergersee for Megan's lecture at seven o'clock. Katrina and Herbert would ride with Rick and Megan. Everyone was in a festive mood.

Katrina especially. She had received a highly confidential phone call just before they left the museum, and its content was smoldering in her, ready to explode. Cautioned not to say anything until the press came out with it the next day, she nevertheless decided, once in the privacy of their car, to confide in her two cherished American friends.

"Megan? Rick? I have something fantastic to share with you, but the world is not to know until tomorrow's newspapers blare it. Not a soul at Schloss Berg this evening must know. All right? Do you promise?"

Utterly mystified, they both eagerly promised.

"And Rick, dear, keep your hands on the wheel, because I'm about to scream." Megan twisted around to gape at Katrina in the back seat.

"*Max Mürrisch has been fired!*"

They all screamed. "Why?"

"'Dereliction of duty.' The city of Munich was distressed that the director of the august Lenbach House Museum left on a vacation to the Bahamas so soon after the brutal murder of a museum night watchman."

"Serves him right. I'm sure most of the museum staff will be pleased," said Megan.

"I have another piece of news that won't be out until tomorrow's papers." Katrina was smiling from ear to ear.

"Tell us! Tell us!" Rick demanded.

"*I am to be the new director of the Lenbach.*"

Rick did almost drive off the road at the sound of Megan's happy shriek.

"Oh, Katrina, that's marvelous, marvelous," she cried.

"And that's only half of it. With the substantial raise in salary, I'll be able to open the Yellow House back up to the public."

"Fabulous," Rick declared, taking the word right out of Megan's mouth. "Well deserved, and I bet the staff is happy with the city fathers' choice," he added. They chatted about the change in Katrina's fortune until they caught their first sight of the blue Starnbergersee.

"Hey, Katrina and Rick, I bet you didn't know that T. S. Eliot mentions this lake in his long poem *The Waste Land.*" When both admitted their ignorance, Megan quoted the opening lines as best she could remember:

"April is the cruelest month, breeding
Lilacs out of the dead land, mixing Memory and desire, stirring
Dull roots with spring rain,
Winter kept us warm, covering
Earth in forgetful snow, feeding
A little life with dried tubers
Summer surprised us, coming over the Starnbergersee
With a shower of rain. . ."

"Sort of spooky, what does it all mean?" asked Katrina.

"Guess what? I don't really know," Megan admitted. "It's quite obscure, and you have to recognize the allusions to many different religions. It's in five parts, and the fourth section from which I quoted, a short one, is called 'Death by Water.'"

"Ah, so it's secretly about the deaths of Ludwig and von Gudden, with that mention of Lake Starnberg," joked Rick.

Once they reached the northern tip of the lake, the little village of Berg was just another ten minutes south.

"Here's a question for you, Megan. Did you know that Dietrich Fischer-Dieskau had a home in Berg?" Katrina quizzed.

"No, I didn't. How interesting."

"Yes, he died in his sleep there just ten days short of his eighty-seventh birthday."

"What a gift that baritone was to music. I treasure his early recording of Schubert's *Winterreise*. And I actually met his accompanist Jörg Demus once in Vienna."

While the two women chatted on enthusiastically about classical music, Rick glanced back at Herbert now and then. Interestingly, the child had shown no signs of seizures or unusual physical conduct since his return home. And he exhibited no memory of the kidnapping. Perhaps he, like so many other epileptic children before him, some seventy-five percent of them, would simply grow out of epilepsy if his meds were gradually decreased to the point of nothing. He had had a chance earlier to tell Katrina about this most recent medical finding.

"Now tell me, Katrina," Megan asked, leaving Schubert behind, "*where* exactly am I going to speak at Schloss Berg? I thought the manor house was in the possession of the latest Wittelsbach family member and closed to the public."

"That's true, no tourists are allowed. They are permitted in the park surrounding the Schloss, and one can even take the forest path down to the lake that Ludwig and von Gudden took that fateful night. But last year permission was granted to hire the great hall for lectures and musical performances. The Bavarian Kandinsky Society *and* the Munich Wagner Society have joined forces to rent the hall for tonight's lecture. And a very large screen plus projector are already in place. So, we're all set. You can even have a run-through if you like."

"Oh, I won't need that, thank you. Aside from sprinkling in under-paintings discovered in Rembrandt, Degas, van Gogh, and Picasso nothing much has changed in my lecture. Except the grand finale! What fun this is going to be."

"I think it's so nice that Dieter and Penelope Löser are coming to hear you," Katrina said.

"I'm honored. I know how busy he must be, especially with all that's happened just today."

"I was reading that there is one more Ludwig residence at, or rather, *in* the Starnbergersee," said Rick.

"Oh, yes," Katrina acknowledged, "you're talking about Rose Island, the *Roseninsel*. Ludwig took advantage of its seclusion to receive at his villa personages such as the Czarina Maria Alexandrovna and, of course, Richard Wagner. And his favorite cousin, Sisi, as she was called, soon to become Empress Elisabeth, wife of Austria's Kaiser Franz Josef. You know, her younger sister Sophie Charlotte was briefly engaged to mad Ludwig, but he kept postponing the wedding and finally called it off most abruptly."

"There's a great film, I think it's from the nineteen-seventies, by Visconti about Ludwig and Sisi meeting at *Roseninsel*. Romy Schneider played Sisi," recalled Megan with enthusiasm. "I can't remember who played Ludwig…"

"*Mutti*, can we go to *Roseninsel*?" begged Herbert, whose attention had been caught by the word "island."

"Another time, yes, for sure. But not tonight, dear."

"Have I told you, Katrina, that Megan and I have changed our minds about how Ludwig and von Gudden died?" Rick asked.

"Didn't Ludwig drown his physician and then commit suicide?"

"That's been the general theory," answered Rick. "The Wittelsbach family still refuses to allow an autopsy. Even though it's now possible to examine a corpse by giving it a computer tomography—a procedure that wouldn't touch the body, but it would show up any gunshot wounds. But now, my online searches have revealed, new evidence indicates they were both shot. In the back. And the sounds of shots were heard and reported by at least one fisherman. The double drowning interpretation was most probably a cover by Ludwig's ministers. Did you know that they had outfitted Schloss Berg with barred windows and doors with observation slits and no door handles?"

"Yes. Everything about Ludwig is fascinating," agreed Katrina. "For example, the Wagner Society has released more of the some six-hundred-letter exchanges between Ludwig and Wagner. They contain homoerotic phrases such as, from Wagner, 'I am in your angelic arms,' and from Ludwig, 'Stay, adored one for whom alone I live, with whom I die.' Of course, we know that Wagner encouraged Ludwig's idolization of him, and who knows…?"

Katrina looked at her son and lowered her voice. "He may even have allowed some non-genital physical contact. At any rate Wagner purposefully led him on so that he would continue to finance production of his operas."

"And I just read that Ludwig's war minister was forced to leave office because in his final years Ludwig recruited possible paramours from one of the minister's cavalry units, the Bavarian *Chevaux-légers*." said Rick.

"You mean he was *open* about being gay?" Megan was surprised. "I thought he tried all his life to suppress and hide those tendencies. Where did you come upon the specificity of what you've learned, Rick? The *Chevaux-légers*, I mean."

"Ha! I had plenty of time to research the latest Ludwig findings on my cellphone while we were sitting outside Katrina's house and you were working on your PowerPoint."

"I think you have a Ludwig fixation now, Rick."

"I agree! And Wagner now as well." They smiled affectionately at each other.

"Here we are at Berg!" Katrina called out. It was a very small town, a village really, with a minimum of hotels and restaurants. They passed right through and drove on to the Schloss gatehouse. A number of cars were already parked outside the gate and people were walking up to the rectangular, vine-covered manor house with its exaggeratedly high-pitched roof. Its lights were lit and sparkled invitingly.

Rick parked the car and the quartet began walking to the Schloss. Iris and Laszlo Togarassy and Dieter and Penelope Löser were just ahead of them and they hurried to catch up. Herbert immediately ran up to Penelope and gave her a hug.

"Well, aren't you the cutest little man," Penelope said, scooping him up in her arms and returning the hug. She continued to hold him as they walked toward the Schloss.

The hall was filled to overflow when they walked in, and the technician was already in place.

"Please show only the opening slide," Megan cautioned as she handed him her thumb drive. The images beamed up on the screen were the same she had showed at the Lenbach lecture on Monday—a comparison of two radically different Kandinsky paintings, the one on the left from The Blue Rider period, and the one on the right from the Bauhaus years.

Left and right also figured in the audience seating disposition with an aisle down the middle. Two attendees were unaware of each other's presence: Igor Rasputin, sitting on audience left, and Boris Zima, in an aisle seat on audience right.

One audience member was aware of both the Muscovite and the Odessan. She was Raisa Sokolova, alias Svetlana Chernykh.

Smiling at the eager audience, Katrina gave an enthusiastic introduction of Megan, ending with the promise that tonight something would be shown that had never been seen before. As one, the audience members leaned forward in anticipation.

Megan did not rush through the lecture. She again traced Kandinsky's extraordinary career, both as an artist and a thinker. Once more, and to the delight of the Wagner Society members, she discussed his synesthetic discovery upon hearing Wagner's *Lohengrin*. She traced the painter's career from Munich to Moscow to Weimar, then Dessau, and finally Paris. After a sprinkling of Rembrandt, Degas, van Gogh, and Picasso under-image discoveries, she read aloud the Russian's key letter to his fellow artist, Marcel Duchamp. A new image followed. It was a photograph of the XRF instrument in the Lenbach lab, the one Katrina had used to macro-scan through Kandinsky's heavy interleaf to the under layer and obtain digital reconstructions of the images beneath.

She paused, then showed the eleven astonishing results. The audience gasped. Megan had lined her images up just as Katrina had, with the eleven Paris-period overlays in a top row, and the clearly recognizable Blue Rider underlays in a matching row below. Here, then, were *eleven unknown works* by the artist, and here, then, the precious gift of a "Double Kandinsky."

There was no pause after Megan stopped speaking. Someone in the audience began clapping wildly at her last word and the sound was enthusiastically taken up by everyone in the room. Soon the audience rose to its feet, still applauding. It was then that Zima saw Rasputin across the room. At almost the same instant Rasputin spotted his arch rival. As if guided by an unseen puppeteer, the two men strode to the back of the hall and silently confronted one another. They glowered at each other with mutual hatred.

"Let us go outside. We have an account to settle," Zima hissed at Rasputin.

"You're goddamn right we do," Rasputin hissed back.

They stepped outside the building and walked quickly away from the exiting crowd, down the same forest path leading to the lake shore that King Ludwig and von Gudden had taken so many decades ago.

Following her two miserly employers from a safe distance was Raisa Sokolova. She felt nothing but hatred for both men now. They had cheated her, they had used her, they had driven her to kidnap a child for whom no ransom had been paid. Her life was a wreck. She would have revenge. Just as the men neared the lakeshore, Raisa drew her pistol from her waist and fired three shots. Two hit Rasputin in the back of his gray jacket, one hit Zima. Both men fell to the ground right at the water's edge of Lake Starnberg. Raisa knelt over their bodies, confirmed they were dead, and turned the pistol toward herself. She placed it against her heart. Only one bullet was needed.

***

Alerted by the sound of shots, Dieter Löser came running down to the lake shore. Others arrived, including Megan and Rick. They stood speechless, looking at the grisly scene before them. Three bleeding bodies lay prone on the ground. A woman and two men.

Katrina, with Herbert in tow, was the last to arrive.

"*Mutti*! *Mutti*! That's the lady who doesn't like me!" He pointed to the black-haired woman on the ground whose arched eyebrows were spattered with blood. A pistol lay beside her.

"Oh, no, darling, don't go there, don't look!" Katrina pulled her son back with one hand and turned him away from the lake. It was the mystery woman who had been so aloof at Megan's lecture. She told Dieter so in a whisper. He nodded affirmation, then slowly began turning over the bodies of the two men, searching for identification. Katrina watched in growing wonder. She recognized one of them.

"Dieter, I know who one of these men is! That one. It's *Igor Rasputin*."

"And the other one is Boris Zima," the detective said. "I've downloaded photos of all major Kandinsky collectors around the world and I'd recognize that face anywhere."

"So now we have all six of the Kandinsky theft players," he concluded. "Three of them alive, three of them dead."

"And the chronology," speculated Rick out loud, stepping closer to scrutinize the corpses, "is, first the two men are shot in the back—two shots for Rasputin, one for Zima—and then the killer, the woman, commits suicide."

"That looks to be the situation exactly, although we'll have to wait for the coroner's report, of course." Dieter responded.

Rick stepped even closer to the bodies on the ground, examined them thoughtfully, then turned to them all, an expression of wonderment on his face.

"*Think about it! What we have here is a re-enactment of the double murder of King Ludwig and Doctor von Gudden!*"

***

While the detective called for backup, Megan and Rick slowly walked Katrina and Herbert back toward Schloss Berg and the car. Most of the audience was gone now and only a few stragglers, curious about the gunshots, lingered. Herbert seemed to have taken the scene in stride after his initial excitement. Rick watched him closely and told Katrina he thought he would be all right. The child had no understanding, after all, of what had just happened. When he saw Penelope Löser, to whom he had formed such a spontaneous attachment, he ran to give her a hug.

"What a dramatic end your already dramatic lecture has had," Katrina said, turning to Megan.

"God, I think I've had enough drama to last me for a year," she replied, shaking her head.

"Ditto that," Rick chimed in.

After two police cars and three ambulances had come and gone, Dieter rejoined the waiting group. Leaving his professional self behind, he looked at them and grinned, showing a beautiful set of white teeth.

"What say, everybody, we clear our heads, leave all this behind us, drive back to Munich, and meet at the Hofbräuhaus?" His question was answered by hearty yeses.

"And mayn't I come as well?" asked Herbert.

"But of course, darling, you may come too."

Megan looked at the friends grouped around her, old and new: Rick, Katrina, Herbert, Iris, Laszlo, Dieter, and Penelope.

"Yes," she said, looking at all of them. "It's time to raise *ein Glas Bier* and celebrate the safe return of all eleven Kandinsky paintings."

They raised imaginary glasses.

Then Megan spoke again, looking directly at Katrina.

"And long live XRF technology. It has solved the Kandinsky conundrum, given the Lenbach Museum, and therefore the world, 'Double Kandinsky!'"

Readers Guide

1. After attending Wagner operas in Bayreuth, art history Professor Megan Crespi and her former student, surgical oncologist Dr. Rick Bodewell, are driving through southern Germany on their way to visit "mad" King Ludwig's castles. Suddenly an aggressive motorcyclist comes out of nowhere, forcing the car in front of them to veer into a ditch off the highway. The occupant of the other car is Iris Togarassy and she suffers a dislocated shoulder. Rick offers to reset it and they go to her nearby home. After the shoulder is successfully reset, Megan notices a painting on the living room wall that is at once familiar to her and not familiar. She studies it and realizes it is an exact copy of Wassily Kandinsky's unfinished *Mounted Warrior* in Munich's famous Lenbach House Museum. But this one is finished! What a conundrum.

2. Billionaire Igor Rasputin is furious. Russia's president Yabeda Tupinsky has withdrawn financial support for his dearest project, the structure already well under way. And the Kandinsky collector in Moscow, Boris Zima, has withdrawn his offer of a painting donation. Brooding, Rasputin suddenly knows what must be done. It necessitates initiating The Plan. What is Rasputin's project and does it have any nationalistic aspects? Do we know what The Plan is?

3. Katrina Keller, grand-niece of a famous great-aunt, has won her prolonged lawsuit against the Bavarian State for return of her great-aunt's house in Murnau. Her grandmother Emma had loaned half her inheritance for purchase of the Yellow House in 1909, but had never been paid back. Katrina's profession will keep her in Munich, but she will be making frequent visits with her little five-year-old son Herbert to the village on the Staffelsee. Do we have any idea who Katrina's famous great-aunt is? Where is Murnau?

4. Her damaged shoulder relocated, Iris talks with Megan and Rick over tea in her living room and tells them her husband Laszlo has just opened an art gallery in Munich's Schwabing district called The Blue Rider. They discuss a 1903 Kandinsky "finished" painting across the room from them on the wall. In pain from the car accident, Megan does not walk over to examine it closely. Instead a surreptitious photo taken with her Google Glass will have to suffice. When

Megan mentions that they plan to visit Murnau, they learn from Iris that the Münter House Museum is now privately owned and is no longer open to the public. We learn that as a young student from Texas, Megan had visited Münter and shown her photos of places the artist had been as a young girl. Some instinct prompts Megan not to mention to Iris that she had met Kandinsky's partner in person.

5. We learn about the ballerina Alexandra Danilova's 1997 bequest of a 1914 Kandinsky painting titled *Swan Lake* to one Igor Rasputin in Odessa. What had Kandinsky said when he gave Danilova the painting? Who is Marigold Lamb?

6. The neo-classical building at Richard-Wagner-Strasse 33, facing the back side of a glaring new copper tube-sheathed addition to Munich's famous Lenbach House Museum, had not changed since its construction in 1899. Neither had its ownership. High living young bachelor Heinrich von Frauenberg, last scion of one of Bavaria's most ancient noble families, had inherited the handsome edifice, "Paleo," but little else. What happens that saves him financially?

7. When the city of Munich appoints Dr. Max Mürrisch as new director of the Lenbach House Museum, conservator Katrina Keller, who had held the post ad interim, is deeply disappointed. What does Max do that angers Katrina? And who asks for a private consultation with her?

8. Back on the road to Füssen, Megan and Rick discuss the two castles, and the childhood of Ludwig. What are the details? And what does Megan pull up on her iPhone?

9. Dzhim Kabalovitschy, the "hermit of Amiinyi," the small island in the Black Sea near Odessa, is a computer wizard and lives with the younger Tigr Chastnyy, a famous science photographer. What is the technique they have developed that, in the right hands, would be a boon to museum conservators, but in the wrong hands, a danger? And why is Igor Rasputin visiting the two "island boys," as he calls them?

10. Megan and Rick visit the two Ludwig castles, Hohenschwangau and Neuschwanstein. How are they different from one another?

11. In Munich, Katrina has dinner with Igor Rasputin. He shows her a photograph of a Kandinsky work that will be the center of his museum, but a Kandinsky of two worlds. Describe the painting and explain why this is so.

12. The Amiinyi island couple have arrived in Munich and their friend Alyksandr Miesel is looking forward to showing them their spacious second-floor suite at Richard-Wagner-Strasse 33. Miesel's studio and living quarters are below on the ground floor. Both apartments have been provided by a mutual wealthy Ukranian friend, and both face the back of the new Lenbach House Museum addition. Can we guess who the Ukranian is?

13. In Moscow, vodka baron Boris Zima receives a progress call from his agent in Munich, Raisa Sokolov. She informs him that his rival collector, Igor Rasputin, is having dinner with the Lenbach House Museum's associate director Katrina Keller. Why does this worry Boris? And how does Raisa calm his fears?

14. Rick and Megan plan to visit Ludwig's Linderhof Palace and then go on to see Richard Strauss's villa. Where is the villa and what side trip do they plan to take as well? What hotel and in which town do they plan to stay that evening? Why does Rick jokingly but correctly diagnose his former professor as having a touch of Obsessive Compulsion Disorder?

15. Rasputin has a request of Katrina. He would like permission to photograph with new state-of-the-art techniques the abstract Kandinskys in the Lenbach Museum. She agrees and asks what evening, when the museum is closed, would he and his team like to come. What is Rasputin's answer?

16. Tigr and Dzhim have returned to Paleo after dinner with "Alyk" Miesel, who shows them the studio in which they set up their camera and photo-developing equipment. What are the items he has already installed for them? And what does he answer after being asked when certain paintings will be obtained?

17. Laszlo Togarassy is told by his wife Iris that the American professor she had met might come by to see his gallery. What is Laszlo's reaction?

18. Berlin-based *Germany for Germans* party boss Ottkar Hasstmann is in Munich visiting the Munich party boss, Walter Krankenhauer. What are they planning

and for which day? What relationship does their movement have with the events of Hitler's rise to power?

19. In Monte Carlo, young impulsive Baron Heinrich von Frauenberg has lost badly at five-card poker. He owes the casino 40,000 euros. What ingenious idea comes to him and why would he fly to Munich that very Friday?

20. Boris is sure Katrina Keller is in cahoots with his Moscow rival. Raisa tells him she followed Rasputin to a building facing the back side of the Lenbach and that he entered with his own key for a stay of only ten minutes. She informs Boris that she has bugged Katrina Keller's apartment, and that on weekends she has followed her and her child Herbert to the Englischer Garten. She observes something strange about the boy. Something that could put pressure on Keller should they need to kidnap him. What medical condition might he have? And what is Boris's reaction?

21. After overnighting in Murnau, Megan and Rick walk over to the Yellow House where Münter had lived. What shocks Megan about the grounds? What measures does she take and what does she see? At the Schlossmuseum, where Münter's works are displayed, they are told that no one knows the identity of the new owner of the Münter house. What kicks off Megan's conspiracy theories? What else do they visit later and what is their final destination?

22. From the Königsplatz in Munich, neo-Nazi Walter Krankenhauer leads a huge protest mob toward the Lenbach House Museum. Posters are set afire and bricks are thrown at the museum personnel. What is the demonstration about? Katrina tries to calm the crowd. A hurled brick hits her and Megan and Rick rush to her aid, driving her to a medical emergency clinic. What are her injuries and what does she suddenly remember that causes her to call the museum's night guard?

23. At Paleo, Rasputin and his men hear shouting one block away and run over to watch a demonstration in progress right in front of the Lenbach. Rasputin decides his long-planned operation should begin immediately. What comes into play now?

24. Raisa Sokolova has been trailing Rasputin and spies him and his men rushing to see the demonstration in front of the Lenbach. For whom does she work and what does she witness? Does she see Rasputin again that night?

25 With a brick, Rasputin kills the Lenbach night guard who opens the museum door to him. How does he link up with his three men in the basement Kandinsky gallery? What important things do they do next? Has Rasputin's Plan worked?

26. Megan and Katrina are watching TV coverage of "a murderous neo-Nazi night at the Lenbach" with the killing of a night watchman and arrest of neo-Nazi Walter Krankenhauer. The phone rings. It is Herbert's nanny. What dreadful news does she have to tell Katrina?

27. Raisa Sokolova stations herself overnight in bottom of the Lenbach Museum delivery dock to keep an eye on the comings and goings at Richard-Wagner-Strasse No. 33 opposite. At five in the morning she hears a large vehicle approaching. It is a white *Cargo Logistik* moving van and she witnesses the loading of eleven flat bubble-wrapped objects in the van. Some six men are involved. This could only mean one thing. What is it?

28. Having sneaked back to Paleo from Monaco, Heinrich von Frauenberg observes Rasputin and his men carry eleven large flat bubble-wrapped objects to a moving van. What does he do? And what does he tell Rasputin he must do?

29. Raisa reports to Boris Zima all the events: the anti-Kandinsky demonstration the night before, the loading of eleven paintings into a moving van early that morning, and a mystifying TV interview with the Lenbach director. What was so perplexing about the interview? What is Boris's reaction?

30. Rick drives Megan and an anxious Katrina to Murnau. On the way, she tells them her secret about the Gabriele Münter house. What is the secret and why does she think it could be the reason her missing son may have been kidnapped? Once at Murnau they head for the police station. What do they find there? Why is it crucial that Katrina's son have his morning medication?

31. At the Münter house in Murnau, Rick and Megan slowly tour all the rooms, admiring the art. By whom is the art? Realizing Katrina must be exhausted, they take their leave until late the next afternoon, Sunday. Where are they going?

32. Chief Detective Dieter Löser of the Munich police sits across the interrogation table from the man his officers had arrested the night before. A self-confessed

neo-Nazi, he is charged with breaking fire regulations and incitement to riot. What is his name and with what else is he charged? What does he tell the detective that incriminates Megan and Rick?

33. Raisa, at lunch after a long nap at her hotel, receives a call from Boris. He has "intervened" with the *Cargo Logistik* van: the driver and his partner are no longer an "inconvenience." What does he mean by this? Raisa wonders what might happen to her, should she also become inconvenient. Boris tells her about the van's most interesting new itinerary. For where is it bound?

34 After forcing Rasputin to wire his bank one million euros, Heinrich takes a flight back to Nice and a train to Monte Carlo where his yacht is docked. Who is following him and what measures does the man shadowing him take? Does Heinrich stay aboard his vessel?

35 The vodka tycoon from Moscow has dispatched his number one agent Ivan Ivanov to handle the waylaying of *Cargo Logistik's* van. Where and how is this achieved?

36 Rasputin visits the *Hommage à Kandinsky* exhibition at The Blue Rider Gallery and is much taken by the window display of a Kandinsky that appears to be two paintings linked together. How does he introduce himself to Lazlo Togarassy? What does Laszlo do?

37. Megan and Rick check into Prien's Yachthotel and later take a ferry to Fraueninsel for dinner. Whose cenotaph do they locate? When Megan addresses Rick by name and takes a Google Glass photograph of her dessert liquor what totally unexpected event occurs?

38. Katrina calls Megan early on Sunday morning to discuss their mutual experience with the Munich detective Dieter Löser. What are their experiences with him?

39. Alyk Miesel finally attends to his task at two in the morning. Why has he waited so long? What does he do next that causes him to speed off in the direction of the Monte-Carlo train station?

40. Raisa makes contact with Rasputin at his hotel, introducing herself as Zima's former secretary, "Svetlana Chernykh." What is her purpose for doing this?

41. Heinrich returns to the Casino La Rascasse dock around six Sunday morning only to discover police barricades around his pier. What has happened and what lifts his mood?

42. Consulting with the Bratislava police, Pavel Meninkov realizes the hijackers could be using a different van. The important thing is to get to Moscow ahead of them. He drives the nine hours to Moscow and arrives at 5:30 Monday morning. Perhaps he is not too late. Too late for what?

43. Megan and Rick return to Katrina's Murnau house early and Herbert plays a new piece he has learned for them: Bach's organ Fugue in G Minor. Throughout his performance Megan hears a strange vibration, or perhaps rattle. What extraordinary discovery do they make when they remove the back of the harmonium?

44. A double tire blowout above Minsk has caused Ivan Ivanov's men, Dimitri and Anatoly, to lose four and a half hours on the Belarus highway before they can continue on to Russia. What do they resort to and why do they then spray paint the van black and change its license plates back to the original German ones? Their meeting point is the Novodevichy Cemetery in Moscow. What time must they be there?

45. Around six Monday morning three vehicles appear by the Novodevichy Cemetery and enact a bizarre ballet involving a silver gray Porsche station wagon, a black *Cargo Logistik* cargo van, and a white Lada Granta sedan. What is enacted and how does the bizarre ballet end?

46. Heinrich is at the doors of the Monte Carlo branch of Crédit Suisse at eight o'clock on Monday morning to collect his one million euros. But the cashier, then the bank officer, decline payment. Why? On what basis? At exactly nine o'clock, Alyksandr Miesel stands in front of the same bank waiting for its doors to open. They do and several clients exit. Alyk gasps. What terrible mistake has he made?

47. Katrina, on crutches and in a cast, takes an Uber to work Monday morning and seeks out Max Mürrisch in his office. He is watching the video he made of his TV interview and does not notice her crutches. What does he propose to her? And why does she diagnose him as having a huge narcissistic personality disorder?

48. Monday morning Megan and Rick visit The Blue Rider gallery and meet its owner Laszlo Togarassy. How and why does their opinion of him change?

49. Rasputin is bitterly thinking about Katrina Keller's supposed betrayal of him to Zima. He has an assignment for his new agent, "Svetlana Chernykh." Who is she really? And what is the assignment?

50. In Moscow, Zima is in ecstasy at becoming the new owner of eleven artworks. By whom were they painted?

51. While awaiting news from Pavel concerning his stolen Kandinskys, Rasputin has to admit his extended Munch stay has been productive. Why? And who will he bring with him to a lecture by Megan Crespi on Kandinsky at the Lenbach Museum?

52. Rick admires the basement gallery Kandinskys while Megan runs through the images in her speech with the Lenbach technician. The auditorium is full and the audience eagerly follows Megan's lecture. The climax comes when she reveals the true and literal meaning of the title "Double Kandinsky." What is it? Excitement grips the audience and Katrina Keller promises a speedy follow-through with state-of-the-art XRF. What does this technique do?

53. After people have left the museum auditorium Megan asks Katrina if she could take a look at the basement Kandinskys. What strange thing is it, occurring with all eleven paintings, that captures Megan's attention?

54. Raisa conveys extraordinary news concerning Zima's eleven Kandinskys in Moscow and explains what the "Double Kandinsky" lecture given by Megan Crespi at the Lenbach Museum revealed. She advises him to secure a reliable conservator to examine the Kandinskys. What does Boris suddenly decide to do?

55. Back at Paleo, Tigr and Dzhim pull out the eleven objects hidden behind their bed headboards. What are these objects? And from whom will they demand a ransom for them?

56. Heinrich the cashless finally arrives in Munich and gets to Paleo by 6:20 Tuesday morning. Tigr and Dzhim hear him enter and confront him. What does Heinrich angrily tell them? And who suddenly ends the silent standoff? Is anyone killed?

57. Katrina and her conservator colleague Paul Ritter examine with an XRF scanner all eleven of the late Paris-period Kandinsky paintings. What surprising things do the scans show? What is the sad conclusion they now have to make about the paintings?

58. Alyk Miesel explains to the island boys why he has shot Heinrich. Why and on whose orders did he do so? What do they do with the body?

59. Megan visits the *Ostfriedhof* to find the grave of Dr. Bernhard von Gudden. With what two very different things is his name connected? When she joins Rick and Katrina at lunch, Katrina swears them to secrecy and tells them what the XRF scans have revealed. What is the mind-blowing discovery?

60. Raisa follows Diliana and Herbert to the Englischer Garten. To what particular spot do they go? What happens next? Do people notice?

61. Rasputin arrives at Paleo and bawls out the men, especially Alyk, for not having handled the Frauenberg murder and cover-up adequately. Why does Tigr sneak upstairs? Rasputin commands them to re-plaster the tunnel entrance. What else does he tell them to do? Will he pay them for the job?

62. Megan and Rick are still sitting with Katrina in the Café Ella when Katrina's cellphone rings. It is Diliana. What shocking news does she tell Katrina?

63. Raisa drives to the cloister of the sisters of Our Lady of the Love of the Good Shepherd. What age-old custom has the cloister revived and how does that suit Raisa's callous actions?

64. Megan urges Katrina to let her call Detective Löser immediately and report what has happened. They do so and Megan sends Löser a crucial photograph taken just a few days ago. What is it and what and how will it help?

65. Raisa returns to the Lenbach Museum and finds a sign saying KANDINSKY GALLERY TEMPORARILY CLOSED. Why is it closed to the public? She also spots Katrina Keller with Megan and Rick in the café. Keller is weeping. Why does this please Raisa? Back at her hotel she receives a call from Zima. He is devastated by what his Moscow conservator has discovered about his eleven new

Kandinsky paintings. What has he told Zima? To cheer him up Raisa tells him about what she has delivered to the cloister of the sisters of Our Lady of the Love of Our Good Shepherd. What is his surprise reaction? He'll discuss things with her tomorrow evening in person. Where will that meeting take place?

66. Alyk, Dzhim, and Tigr reopen the tunnel at Paleo. There is a terrible stench. Why? Alyk makes his way through the tunnel. What does he find? Back in the cellar room Alyk throws up. Why? The island boys decide to let him in on their secret. They show him the amazing items hidden in their bedroom upstairs and explain what was sent to Rasputin and what they had placed in the Lenbach Museum. They can now demand ransom from the City of Munich. Why? What is Alyk's reaction?

67. Still smarting from Zima's cool reception of her daring coup, Raisa now calls Rasputin. His reaction only embitters her more. Why?

68. Sitting outside in their car after driving Katrina home, Megan works on changes in her lecture for the next evening and Rick finds fascinating information online about the possible murder, rather than suicide of King Ludwig at the site where they will be tomorrow evening. Suddenly Diliana appears yelling that Katrina wants them. Something has happened! Can we guess what?

69. Alyk tells the Amiinyi island boys his daring plan. While it is still dark they will place one of their Kandinsky paintings bubble-wrapped along with a ransom note in the museum loading dock, then alert the museum when it opens. What is the ransom and where is it to be delivered? What unthinkable threat is made if the museum does not pay the ransom?

70. Raisa, furious that neither Rasputin nor Zima have paid her for her work, decides she will demand a ransom for Herbert Keller from his mother for herself. How does she go about this and what is the result?

71. On the roof balcony of Paleo, where they have a view not only of the Königsplatz and its Propylaea but also of the villa roof of the Lenbach, Alyk, Dzhim, and Tigr are testing out Alyk's plan. How will they obtain the ransom money without police intervention?

72. At eight Wednesday morning Katrina has brought Herbert with her to the museum and is greeted with the news that there is a strange recorded phone message for the director about a vital package in the loading dock. One of the museum guards brings it in and rips off the bubble wrap. What good and what bad items do they find inside? Katrina calls Detective Löser who comes over immediately and debriefs her. She blames herself for having allowed Rasputin and his team into the museum for a photo session. But she has one happy thought. She hopes she can show Löser something positive down in the lab. What could that be?

73. Megan and Rick revisit The Blue Rider gallery as Rick thinks he might like to buy one of the *Hommage* paintings. While he studies Laszlo's replicas, someone else is scrutinizing the outside of the gallery. The man in the hoodie makes his daring move. What does he do? How is it that Megan, by chance, is able to photograph the man in action with her Google Glass? She will email the photograph to Löser immediately. She knows who the man in the hoodie is. Do we?

74. Using their new XRF scanning technique, Katrina and her fellow conservator Paul Ritter examine the Kandinsky found in the museum's loading dock. What is the marvelous result? Löser asks to see the empty gallery where the stolen Kandinskys had hung and a terrible stench greets them when they enter. After emptying the storage closet they find fresh plaster covering what turns out to be a tunnel. What are the exciting events that follow and who is arrested?

75. Zima arrives in Munich and heads straight for The Blue Rider gallery where he astounds Laszlo by his impromptu action. What is it?

76. Early that Wednesday evening, before Megan's lecture at Schloss Berg, a celebration pizza dinner is held near the Lenbach with Dieter and Penelope Löser, Iris and Laszlo Togarassy, the two Lenbach museum conservators, and little Herbert. They are all on a first name basis now and take turns asking Dieter questions about the tunnel and what happened on the roof balcony of the building opposite the museum. What is Laszlo's surprising story of the "two Boris Zimas" about? Penelope urges Dieter to tell the group his theory concerning the Kandinsky conundrum. What is it? What does Katrina remember that helps to identify Raisa as an agent of Rasputin? What are Dieter's words at the end of dinner?

77. The final denouement. Rick is driving Megan, Katrina, and Herbert to the Starnbergersee and Schloss Berg where she is to give her lecture, amplified now, by the eleven images under Kandinsky's eleven Paris-period paintings. What are they? On the way, they discuss the latest evidence on the double death of King Ludwig and Gudden. What amazing succession of events does it reveal? After Megan's lecture and its enthusiastic reception, three members of the audience leave immediately. Who are they? They head down to the lake shore along the same forest path King Ludwig and Gudden had taken. As they reach the water's edge, three shots ring out, and then a fourth one. What has happened? And what amazing historical parallel does Rick point out as he and his companions stare at the bodies on the ground? Later that evening, back in Munich, it is time to raise a glass of beer to celebrate the return of the stolen Kandinskys and the solving of the Kandinsky conundrum. To what vital player in all this is the final toast dedicated?

www.ingramcontent.com/pod-product-compliance
Lightning Source LLC
Chambersburg PA
CBHW020434030726
47495CB00006B/1800